Dear Reader,

For more than three years, I lived in southern Ireland, and while there I learned that the Irish have a great devotion to preserving their heritage, which includes belief in the old religion and in honoring the feminine. Thus began my adventure into the Sacred Feminine Principle . . . months later I came to read about Mary Magdalene. What a shock to learn her history has been distorted throughout the ages.

I went to Ireland for a sabbatical, but I found myself on a quest; Mary Magdalene seemed to always be on the edge of my mind and I wondered when her truth would be told. When my agent called, asking how I felt about writing fantasy, I came up with the idea for this book. I wanted to write about the power of love over fear and I used the historical figure of Mary Magdalene to show that power.

Writing this was like writing my first book; I felt such freedom! *Shifting Love* was sold in 2002. Imagine my pleasure when *The DaVinci Code* was published in 2003. I was stunned and thrilled someone was correcting history. Mary Magdalene's time has come.

I am fortunate to be the launch author for Tor's new line of paranormal novels. This was my first venture into fantasy and I liked it so much that I'm now writing my second, based on two of the secondary characters in this book. Thank you for allowing me to rent space in your head for a short while. I never take that for granted, and I do hope you enjoy reading this book as m

D1041227

When Maggie was ten, she stared into the eyes of a raven and found herself at one with it, feeling the bones in her body shift, the pores on her skin open to accommodate shiny black feathers. She could feel the thrust of air under her beautiful wings, could see the earth from a dizzying height . . .

One night when she was twenty, she and her boyfriend were together on top of a granite mountain, staring up at the stars. He professed his love, and Maggie tried to let him down easy.

He threatened to throw himself off the side of the mountain. Who knew he would actually do it?

When she shifted into the form of a rabbit and ran away into the woods, answers came in the shape of a wolf—a wolf who shifted into a man named Marcus Bocelli. He become her mentor, and recruited her into the service of love and balance—and for fourteen years Maggie has served this secret society.

At thirty-four she has learned her lessons well. She knows the difference between romance and love, how difficult real love can be as her feelings for Marcus swing between irresistible attraction and frustrated annoyance. In truth, she knows it really doesn't matter how she feels since Marcus isn't a man to plan any kind of normal life.

And then she met Julian McDonald, and her entire world changed . . .

Shifting
Love

Constance
O'Day-Flannery

tor paranormal romance

A TOM DOHERTY ASSOCIATES BOOK
NEW YORK

SHIFTING LOVE

Copyright © 2005 by Constance O'Day-Flannery

Edited by Anna Genoese

A Tor Book
Published by Tom Doherty Associates, LLC
175 Fifth Avenue
New York, NY 10010

www.tor.com

Tor® is a registered trademark of Tom Doherty Associates, LLC.

ISBN-13: 978-0-7653-5888-2
ISBN-10: 0-7653-5888-3

First Edition: November 2004
Second Edition: December 2007

Printed in the United States of America

0 9 8 7 6 5 4 3 2 1

DEDICATION

*This one is for the two Dons
And their extraordinary wives,
Vickie and Lori*

ACKNOWLEDGMENTS

Pat Burke, who showed me great friendship and "the best time of my life" in Ferrypoint. You made Ireland a wondrous adventure.

Cristopher Sterling, who went through heaven and hell with me and whose heart remains golden.

Marie and Ray O'Shea, Jim and Jane Horner, Bruce and Gilly Bell, Mossy and Mary O'Mahony, Ithel and Mike from Blackwater, and all the girls at Murphy's Pharmacy. Thank you for the laughter, the music and, most especially, your friendship and support. Each hold a place in my heart.

Pat Trowbridge, whose wisdom and unswerving friendship have been a pillar of strength and provided a great source to look in the mirror and laugh at ourselves.

Colleen Bosler, whose patience is unlimited when it comes to friendship. Thank you for ours.

Richard Curtis, my agent, for first planting the idea of contemporary fantasy in my head and Anna Genoese, my editor, whose skill made it a better book.

Miko Miles, for handling computer glitches and being so generous with his time.

Kristen and Ryan Flannery, for never complaining, for always understanding having a writer for a mother, and for *being* who you are . . . truly wonderful adults I am blessed to have sent into the world on their own adventures.

PROLOGUE

Long ago
The trees thought they were really people
Long ago
The mountains thought they were really people
Long ago
the animals thought they were really people
Someday, they will say
Long ago
The humans thought they were really people.

—Johnny Moses, native American

Magdalene O'Shea had known ever since she was a young child that she wasn't like other little girls and, somehow, some instinct told her to keep this discovery to herself. While they were busy playing with dolls Maggie had been out in a field, fascinated with nature. When she sat in the high fragrant grass, she would stare down at the ground and see a different world, one that most adults missed. From that time on, she tread carefully upon the earth with innate respect. When she was ten she realized she could enter that mysterious natural world. The first time had been frightening, staring into the eyes of a raven and finding herself at one with it, feeling the bones in her body shift, the pores on her skin open to accommodate shiny black feathers. She had been terrified, thinking she might never return to human form. She didn't know how it happened, but she felt as if she had become the raven, could feel the thrust of air under her beautiful wings, could see the earth from a dizzying height, could even report back to her mother the conversation she'd had with a neighbor while Maggie, as the raven, perched on a fence not ten feet away. Of course her mother thought she had been hiding in the bushes and she was punished for eavesdropping. After that, Maggie knew she couldn't confide in anyone. Her secret life became filled with the loneliness of one who is different and feels apart from the rest of the world.

By fourteen, when her own nature rose high and wild within her, she yearned to express it and used her powers of shape shifting to spy on the boy she liked in school, learned what was in his heart and shaped herself and her interests to suit his. But she soon got bored as there was no challenge. By the time she was eighteen she was running wild, shifting into cats, rabbits, even a butterfly to spy on her teacher preparing her final term exam. She landed on the test paper, preening her gloriously colored wings for the teacher's admiration while memorizing the answers.

She read esoteric books, trying to find answers, but nothing could explain why she had this strange power. She got into college easily, though her actual knowledge of subjects was little and her attitude toward learning nonchalant. She had her own way to sail through life. When she needed extra spending money, she would shift into a fly or a spider and memorize the safe combination of the local bookie. Later that night she would return under the door the same way, resume her human form, take what she needed and put it into an envelope, shove it under the locked back door to an alley, and then shift into an insect to crawl out herself. She wasn't completely without heart, for she always shared with the street people on her way back to her dorm. And she only took money from people who preyed on the weaknesses of others. She was twenty when her life altered radically. She had used her powers to become exactly what James Michael Hennessy wanted in a girlfriend. James was a tortured soul, a poet at heart, but his family had him slated to take over the family rock quarry business.

One night she and James were together on top of a granite mountain, staring up at the stars, discussing what they wanted from life, and James professed his love. Maggie, who had no intention of anything more than a romance, tried to let him down easy, but James became distraught and threatened to throw himself off the side of the mountain. His sense of the dramatic had initially attracted her, but all she'd wanted then was to get away.

Who knew he would actually do it?

She'd been so startled that she had immediately shape shifted into a terrified rabbit and had run off into the woods. She ran and ran, searching for a burrow to hide in when, suddenly, without any warning, jaws were around her small neck and she was roughly dragged into an open space in the woods. She smelled the feral scent of the wolf and her own fear. She was going to die and she knew in her heart she deserved it.

Instead, incredibly, the wolf began to turn into a man who held her squirming body under his and demanded that she come forward and show herself. It took some time for Maggie to realize what was happening as she watched the ferocious wolf transform. Slowly she released her fear when she found herself staring into the eyes of a very handsome man with an expression she didn't dare challenge.

Into her life appeared Marcus Bocelli, shape shifter, teacher, guardian of the secrets. She was taken to his rustic home in the woods and it was there she learned who she was and how she had been misusing her powers. She was told she needed tutoring and she also needed to make reparation to balance out the damage she had done. A life had been shattered through her misuse of power and she would spend her own life in service to love until her debt is paid. Like her namesake, she was an intelligent woman who would administer to others.

Weeks of tutoring passed and Maggie felt cursed, for Marcus never cut her a break. He wanted to tame her and she resented him. She also couldn't deny her attraction to the dark and mysterious Italian. She learned about relationships through hers with him. And she learned about sex through his expert knowledge. And finally, fatefully, she learned about love by falling in love with a man who claimed love is unconditional, without possession. And she was to teach that to others.

Maggie felt her ability to shape shift had been a blessing and it had also been a curse, for she now had a debt to pay and the interest on it never seemed to end.

Every few years Marcus gives her assignments . . . men needing to recover from loss . . . cynical men, fragile men, angry men . . . rich and powerful men . . . and poor men too. She finds out all about them by shape shifting and then entering each life and turning it around. Of course they think they are falling in love with her, and her challenge is to show them that love must be free, that the tighter they hold it, the more they will lose it. She isn't the one . . . she's the one that comes before the real one can enter their lives. And she can't move on until the men are healed.

Fourteen years she has been in service. To Marcus. To love.

Surely she has balanced the scales and her debt is paid.

At thirty-four she has learned her lessons well. She knows the difference between romance and love, how difficult real love can be as her feelings for Marcus swing between irresistible attraction and frustrated annoyance. In truth, she knows it really doesn't matter how she feels since Marcus isn't a man to plan any kind of normal life.

And she so wants that.

Normal.

The sound of it as she repeats it in her mind is so sweet, yet so unattainable.

Dear God, how she longs for what so many take for granted.

ONE

"I love this place, Maggie. I don't know . . . I just always feel good when I'm here." Tammy Kline slid a twenty-dollar bill across the counter to pay for the latest mystery paperback to hit the best-seller list, along with a large caramel skim milk latte. "What kind of magic do you have to keep this place so busy?"

"You ask that question every time you're here," Maggie said, grinning as she rang up the sale. "And I keep telling you that envy is one of the seven deadly sins. Be happy I'm so busy, Tammy. You're my stockbroker. If I make money, you make money."

"Speaking of investments, we need to go over your portfolio." Tammy dropped her change into her Bvlgari purse, a perfect match to her dark gray Armani suit. "What about dinner next week?"

"Sounds great," Maggie answered, placing the book into a shiny white shopping bag with white corded handles. "How about Fidel's? We'll mix business with a little Cuban food?"

"Right. And I'll watch as you fight off all those Latin types you attract like honey to a queen bee."

"Tammy, it's the drones who bring the pollen for the honey to the queen. I happen to think drones are highly underrated. They're actually quite beautiful. The queen couldn't survive without them."

Tammy shook her blond curls as she stared across the counter. "Honestly, the way you get so passionate about animals and creepy crawly things and you don't even own a dog." Sipping her latte, she waved. "I'd better get back to the office. I'll call later in the week and we'll set a date."

Maggie nodded and then smiled at her next customer, who was placing three CDs, a hardcover book on owning and managing time that had been touted on *Oprah*, and four scented candles onto the counter. "I don't think I need to ask if there's anything else. It looks like you're ready to claim some downtime."

The middle-aged woman grinned, almost self-consciously. "About time too. Thought I could do it all. Motherhood. Working. Now the kids are in college and I'm exhausted." She picked up a hyacinth-scented candle Maggie had already scanned and sniffed before adding, "My friend told me about this store and I thought I'd just browse, but it's hard to leave a place like this without buying something. It wasn't until I was sitting down with a cup of your delicious coffee that I thought it was time to take care of me for a change." Holding her wallet, waiting for the total cost, she said in a strong voice, "I'm going to light the candles, run a bath, listen to music *I* like for a change, and read that book."

"Well, good for you," Maggie answered from the cash register. "You've done your job, and now it's your turn again. I hope you enjoy everything."

The woman paid for her purchases, thanking Maggie while vowing to come back.

Staring after the woman as she joined the pedestrian traffic on Chestnut Street, Maggie experienced a rush of satisfaction. It wasn't unusual for people to bare their souls to her. She couldn't claim magic. It was the effect of the place. All her hard work of the last few years was paying off.

Soul Provisions was the kind of store you didn't want to leave.

The front door opened to a delight of the senses. A customer first encountered the scents of frangipani, lavender, narcissus, lemongrass, and hydrangea before coming to the fruitier candles of apple, ginger spice, and honeydew melon. Then glass display cases dazzled the eye with unique jewelry for women and men. A few feet beyond that began the book section followed by display racks of CDs, music that soothed the soul while the taste buds were aroused by exotic coffees and a tempting arrangement of muffins and pastries, ranging from walnut raisin oat cakes to homemade Milano cookies. Tables and chairs were provided for the customer who wanted to read a book, newspaper, or magazine while munching. And plenty of them did, though it was rare for anyone to be satisfied with simply coffee. Maggie O'Shea had created a space amid the high-powered office buildings on Chestnut Street in Philadelphia for people to regain their breath, to stop the frantic rushing and blood-pounding speed of their days and experience a few moments out of time. A sanctuary.

Perhaps people felt free to tell parts of their own story because while they had been browsing, little signs an artist friend had designed would pop up in the most unusual places:

STUDY MEN, NOT HISTORIANS.

ACCEPTING WHAT YOU ARE IS CONTENTMENT, AND THERE IS
NO WEALTH TO COMPARE WITH CONTENTMENT.

IF YOU SPEND YOUR LIFE WITH YOUR NOSE TO THE
GRINDSTONE ALL YOU'LL END UP WITH IS A FLAT SORE NOSE.

REAL FRIENDS ARE THOSE WHO, WHEN YOU'VE MADE
A FOOL OF YOURSELF, DON'T FEEL THAT YOU'VE
DONE A PERMANENT JOB.

IF YOU STILL DON'T BELIEVE IN MIRACLES,
CONSIDER YOUR MIND.

These bits of wisdom, over thirty of them, were tucked into all sections of the store and every now and then Maggie would hear someone laugh out loud and her own heart would lighten along with the reader's.

Soul Provisions was the kind of place she had always wanted to find. When she couldn't, she created it for herself.

She spent the next half hour at the register and then handed over that responsibility to one of her assistants when a customer wanted to see a piece of jewelry. She unlocked the case and brought out a moonstone pendant with a teardrop tanzanite stone atop the gold setting.

"Oh, it's so beautiful," the young woman breathed as she held out her hand.

Maggie placed the piece onto the woman's palm and smiled. "The tanzanite almost matches your eyes."

The woman looked up from her hand and smiled back. "I've been looking at this for weeks and trying to talk myself into it."

"Well, you're the only one who knows if you can afford it and if you feel you deserve it. All I can do is offer what attracts you."

The young woman appeared almost startled for a moment. "How did you know that's what I've been struggling with? If I deserve it?" She looked down to the pendant and murmured, "I broke up with my boyfriend of three years and . . . I don't know . . . I don't even know why I'm telling you."

Maggie's smile softened as the customer's voice broke with emotion. "This won't heal a broken heart, but I do know of a book that might help. Why don't we put this back on the shelf and I'll show you the book?" Maggie replaced the pendant inside the glass case. Locking it, she said, "Maybe after you take a look at the book you can come back and see if it still attracts you, okay?" She grinned at the younger woman and gestured with her head toward the back of the store. "C'mon, it's now in paperback, so it's a lot cheaper than the pendant," she said, as they walked through the aisles of books. "Besides, if that piece is really meant for you it will be here when you're ready."

"Excuse me, Maggie. There's a phone call for you."

Maggie had just handed the book to the woman when Mark, who worked the stockroom, came up behind her. "Can you take a message?"

"They said it was important."

Turning back to her customer, she nodded to the last section of the store. "Why don't you have a cup of coffee and
read a few pages? I'll be back in a couple of minutes."

Heading for the stockroom, Maggie figured she just might
have talked herself out of a two-hundred-dollar sale, but she
couldn't resist the pain in that woman's eyes. No piece of
jewelry was going to fill the gaping wound in her soul. A
long time ago Maggie learned the answer wasn't a Band-
Aid, even one as pretty as that pendant. The only way to heal
that wound was to go inside . . . and not everyone had the
courage to do it. She wondered if her customer would go for
the ride into her soul or give herself a temporary fix with a
glittering jewel. Soul Provisions offered both.

She picked up the phone on the desk and punched the
blinking light on line one. "Hello, Maggie O'Shea."

"It's good to hear your voice again, Magdalene."

It was as though a cold wash of energy descended onto
her shoulders, pushing her down onto the chair in front of
the desk. Her eyes scanned the many invoices in front of her,
yet she wasn't really seeing them. Instead her mind pictured
a tall, dark, and painfully handsome man.

"Marcus." She said his name in a whisper, more to herself
than in acknowledgment of him. "Where are you?"

"Right here in the City of Brotherly Love," he answered
in his slightly accented voice that was a deep baritone . . .
low, sexy, and feral, winding its way from her ear to travel
down her body. "And I'm inviting you to lunch with me this
afternoon. I'm staying at the Four Seasons. I had dinner in
my room last night when I arrived and the service and food
are quite good."

"I can't," she answered automatically. "I have plans."

"As much as I love spending time in your company, *cara
mia*, I am here to discuss something of importance with
you."

She knew what it was. "Perhaps tomorrow."

"Perhaps you can change your plans. Mine are not flexi-
ble, I'm afraid."

She hated that a part of her wanted to flee the city to get

away from him and yet another part was irresistibly drawn to him. This man had been her teacher, her mentor, her lover, and she could feel his presence over the ten city blocks that separated them. "I'll meet you in the restaurant," she said, trying to bring strength into her voice.

"Do you not trust yourself to dine in my suite?"

She could hear the amusement in his voice. "I don't have time for this, Marcus. I will see you at one o'clock in the hotel's restaurant. You can have one hour and then I must get back. I have a business to run."

"Ah, yes . . . Soul Provisions. It is doing well?"

"You know it is." He always seemed to know everything about her. She wouldn't be surprised if he'd seen her tax returns and her bank statements. "I take it this lunch is because you have an assignment for me."

"You always were intuitive, Magdalene, even when you didn't know what you were doing. I think that is why you have made such a good student." He paused. "So, yes . . . I have your next assignment."

"Then let's forego this trip down memory lane, Marcus. I have to get back to work. One o'clock." She hung up the phone without saying good-bye. Somehow, some way, she had to stay one step ahead of his magnetic charm.

Staring at the papers on her desk, Maggie tried to calm down, to slow the slamming of her heartbeat against her rib cage. She had foolishly hoped she would be free of him, that her obligations were fulfilled. It had been two years since she'd seen Marcus, at least in his human form, though he probably had been spying on her during that whole time whenever his curiosity got the better of him. That last time, though, as she'd left him sleeping after a night of exquisite lovemaking, she had vowed to break free of him and the power he held over her. She could still picture that mass of dark curls falling away from a face that was classically beautiful . . . deep brown eyes that easily scanned the soul, a fine sculpted nose, and full lips that spoke of a profound sensuality. His body was lean and hard and he could use it with elegant grace or an animal's captivating power. But

Maggie knew it wasn't his dramatic good looks. He could be short, fat, and balding and still women would spend a few moments in his presence and be charmed into his arms. Marcus Bocelli had true charisma.

At least she had never told him that she loved him.

She could hold on to that small measure of power.

At exactly one o'clock she walked into the restaurant and bar at the Four Seasons Hotel. Dressed in an Yves Saint Laurent white blouse and chocolate brown slacks, Maggie felt casually chic enough for the upscale locale. She had refused to go upstairs to her apartment over the store and change into something better, although she did borrow a gold omega necklace with a large amber pendant from the jewelry case. And she did carefully reapply her makeup and fluff out the auburn wisps that framed her face. Looking into the bathroom mirror and staring into her blue eyes, she had tried to tell herself any woman facing lunch with an ex-lover would do the same. Unfortunately, there was this small part of her that still wanted to appear attractive to Marcus, and it was that traitorous piece she needed to keep under control.

She took off her sunglasses and scanned the restaurant while wondering who the hell she thought she was, giving out advice to customers about healing wounds when she was obviously still picking at scar tissue. *Heal thyself* echoed inside her head as the maître d' approached her.

"Good afternoon, madam."

She smiled politely. "Good afternoon. I'm meeting one of your guests for lunch. Mr. Bocelli?"

The man looked down at his podium and scanned his list. "Ah, yes. You must be Miss O'Shea."

"I am," she confirmed. How like Marcus to give her name.

"If you'll follow me, I'll show you to his table."

Walking through the elegant restaurant with its lunchtime diners in business suits, Maggie squared her shoulders and lifted her chin as she spied Marcus at a corner table sipping a glass of red wine while perusing the leather-bound menu. As though sensing her, he looked up and held her gaze as she came to him, before breaking into a smile as the maître d' approached.

"Magdalene, how good to see you," he said, smoothly rising from the table and holding out his hand.

It seemed automatic that she would place hers in his and watch those sensuous lips barely graze over the skin below her knuckles. "Marcus. You're looking well," she answered, pulling her hand away and smiling at the maître d', who was holding out her chair. Seated, she picked up the crisp white napkin off the table and carefully placed it on her lap before looking up to the man across from her. How did he do it? He ate whatever he wanted. She'd never seen him exercise beyond lovemaking and yet in all the years she had known him, he never seemed to age.

His smile was warm and inviting and she steeled herself against it.

"It is you who are looking well. Beyond well, *cara mia*. You look beautiful." He poured her a glass of wine and then sat back surveying her closely. "Were you conscious of how many men were watching you as you came to me? Your aura draws them and they cannot help but notice you. Cool. Detached. Classically lovely and innately sensual. Even now they cast envious glances in my direction." His smile deepened. "I wonder how many would make the connection if they knew your given name. Or would they hear Magdalene and think of a courtesan?"

She wasn't about to let him take her down that road. "I'm not a courtesan, which is merely your polite way of saying *whore*, even if I am here to discuss my next assignment. So let's get to it, shall we? Who is he? What's his story?"

Shaking his head slightly, Marcus' expression appeared filled with sadness and regret. "Never would I use such a term and you should never allow it to cross your lips. What you give of yourself is repaid with the healing of another. Mary Magdalene wasn't a whore, though she has been labeled one for thousands of years by those who envied her intelligence, her powers, her closeness to the One who—"

"Save the history lesson, Marcus," Maggie interrupted, opening her menu. "I learned it years ago."

"Then you will remember she descended from the royal House of Benjamin. Your namesake was a high priestess, the most honored student, and a great teacher of unconditional love. You should feel privileged to carry her name."

"I do," she answered, just as a waiter came to their table. Before he could recite any house specials, she smiled and handed him the menu. "Hello. I'm in a bit of rush. I'll have the baby spinach salad and the salmon." She looked at Marcus. "You must have decided, since you were studying the menu when I arrived."

He stared into her eyes for just a moment before opening his menu and giving his selections.

"Can I interest you in appetizers? The chef has prepared several new offerings and—"

"I'm sorry," Maggie interrupted with another apologetic smile. "This is a business lunch so we won't have time."

Thankfully, the waiter seemed to understand and made a quick exit.

"That bordered on rude," Marcus observed dryly, picking up his glass of wine.

"I was trying to make a point."

"You made it."

"And I thought I was very polite. Now, let's move on, shall we? Who do I have to research, and why?" She lifted her glass and sat back in the good reproduction of a Louis XIV armchair.

"Again, to the point, I see."

"Exactly. That is the reason I'm here, after all."

Marcus leaned in to the table and stared at her. "Why are you insisting on putting distance between us, Magdalene? Why can we not enjoy each other? It's been two years since I've seen you."

Staring out the window to the city below, she tried to come up with an appropriate answer. "I know how long it's been, Marcus."

"I like the new haircut."

"It's just a haircut."

"You have grown into the fullness of your beauty and wear it with grace." He paused for a moment. "And I have missed you."

Despite her resolve, Maggie relaxed and shook her head. "You never give up, do you?"

"Not with you, *cara mia*. Never with you."

She would not let his words past the barrier of her mind. She couldn't allow it again. "So who is he? I really do have to get back to the store."

Marcus sighed and reached for a leather portfolio resting next to his elbow. "To business then."

Maggie raised her glass slightly. "To business."

He slid a black-and-white photograph of an attractive man in his mid forties across the table. "This one should be quite a challenge, but also you can delight in designer props. You'll need them with him."

Remembering her last assignment with a fireman whose only love in life had been a machine, a Harley Road King, she picked up the edge of the photo and stared at the picture of a light-haired man with penetrating eyes. "Who is he?"

"Julian McDonald. Entrepreneur. Workaholic. He built his financial empire by running managerial seminars for Fortune Five Hundred companies and then increased his fortune by becoming a venture capitalist." Marcus placed a copy of *Forbes* magazine on top of the photograph. "I'll give you the research I've put together on him so you can study it. He's invested well, even in today's market, and there's a very good cover story on him in that magazine."

In color Julian McDonald was even more attractive. His light blue eyes stared into the camera lens, yet the smile on his face didn't quite seem to be reflected in his eyes. Instinctively, Maggie knew this one wasn't going to be easy. "What's his story?" she asked, noticing the fine lines around McDonald's eyes and threads of gray hair beginning at his temples. She paid attention to her emotions as she studied his face. This man was cynical, to be sure, but there was something else . . . maybe bitterness or intense sadness or perhaps weariness of the world.

Marcus placed another photograph on top of the *Forbes* magazine. It was a picture of McDonald, a pretty woman, and a child, relaxing on the bow of a luxury yacht. "He lost his wife and son in a private plane accident nine years ago over the mountains of Colorado. He wasn't aboard. The wife and child were heading for Aspen."

There it was, Maggie thought, staring at the picture of a once happy family. "What am I working with?" she asked without looking up. "Grief? Guilt? Bitterness? All of the above?"

"I told you it was going to be a challenge. He's rich, cynical, bored with life. His money and power easily attract women that he uses to satisfy his needs. He's also considered suicide, having conquered everything he wanted, so he keeps working in order not to be alone. He likes the chase, but becomes bored quickly thereafter. He spends his precious spare time aboard his yacht, *Stardancer*, which he keeps in Bermuda where he also has quite a spectacular home overlooking the sea. I told you there would be parts of this one you'd like."

Maggie glanced up, refusing to take the bait. "So, as always, my mission, and I have no choice but to accept it, is to help McDonald open his heart again? To heal?"

Marcus flashed her a pleased smile, filled with warmth. "Exactly. He will be in this very city in three days to attend a charity function and receive an award for donating computers to inner-city schools throughout the country. Philadelphia is one of them." He dropped an engraved envelope on top of her stack of research. "Here is your invitation. I would suggest wearing something exquisite, though I'm sure I don't have to tell you that you need not wear a single article of clothing to be divine."

The expression on his face let her know he had not forgotten their last time together either. It was almost too much to bear. Maggie looked back down to the invitation. "It says a silent auction. How much am I to bid?"

"Whatever it takes to get his attention and keep it. The foundation will repay all of your expenses, as always."

She bit back the question that was always on her lips: Who else, besides Marcus, was in this foundation? She'd asked before, many times, and Marcus had always evaded. "And they can afford this kind of assignment? We're talking about big money here. Clothes, first class travel and—"

"Have you ever been questioned about your expenses?" Marcus interrupted.

She shook her head. "I'm just asking if the foundation is prepared for what this one will cost."

"The foundation is prepared," Marcus answered as the waiter approached the table with their food. "This is a major investment that has been carefully researched and it has been decided you are ready. You are the one who can best help this man. It is important for several reasons that I am not at liberty to divulge. Thank you," he added to the waiter as his plate of porcini ravioli with a light rose cream sauce was placed in front of him.

Maggie gathered her material together and placed it face down on the nearby wide windowsill. She then smiled up to the waiter as her salad and grilled salmon was carefully presented to her. "It smells wonderful," she added to make up for her earlier haste in ordering. When the waiter left, Maggie realized how hungry she was. She seemed to always develop a heightened appetite whenever she was around Marcus. All her senses felt elevated in his presence. She tasted the salad and appreciated the distinct flavor of the spinach and the balsamic dressing.

"He has a dog. An old one. That might prove useful."

She glanced up. "What kind of dog?"

Marcus closed his eyes for a moment, either savoring the taste of his ravioli or thinking. He swallowed and said, "A Labrador retriever, I believe it is called."

Maggie grinned. "What color?"

"The color is important?"

"To me, it is. Is the animal brown, black, golden?"

"Ah, yes . . . golden. An old soul and faithful companion. The name is Maxmillion. McDonald calls it Max. It was his son's dog. I think it might be the only thing from his past that he has kept around. He sold the family home years ago and gave away everything that would remind him of his wife or his son. He not only closed off his mind, he also closed off his heart. Except to that dog. That would be the direction to take, I would think."

"First I have to get close enough to even meet the dog."

"Yes, and that is why you have an invitation. In three days you will meet McDonald at this charity function. The rest is up to you."

"I'm not independently wealthy, Marcus, and I do have a business to run. I'll do what I can."

Marcus tapped the corner of his mouth with his napkin and sat back in his chair. He stared at her across the table. "You have a good staff you can trust. This is an important assignment, Magdalene."

"They're all important, aren't they? Is Julian McDonald's heart more valuable than Tommy Clinesmith's? One is a fireman, the other a multimillionaire businessman. Both souls in need of healing. How can one be more important than the other?"

Marcus smiled. "You are right, of course. Neither one is more important. All I can tell you is that McDonald has been given a high priority by the foundation."

"The mysterious foundation." Maggie jabbed at her salmon. "Why is it after all these years I know nothing about it and they seem to know everything about me? If I work for them, I shouldn't be kept in the dark like this. I'm tired of it, Marcus. Very tired. When asked, I give. Now I'm asking, and I deserve some answers. Who or what is this so-called foundation?"

"That I cannot tell you. Even I don't know the entire picture."

"Then tell me about the part of the picture you do know about. You can't ask me to take on something this big, possibly jeopardize a business I have worked very hard to establish, and then keep me in the dark."

"It's safer that way. For all concerned."

"Damn it, just stop." She had to control her anger and

carefully place her fork down on her plate. "You and this foundation have been entwined in my life for almost fourteen years. I go through my life never knowing when I'll hear from you . . . will it be in a couple of months or a couple of years . . . I can never make plans, have a normal life because of you and this foundation. I have never refused you, Marcus, because I've seen that people can change, their hearts can change, differences can be made, but it's time to either know fully what this foundation is or to say my debt is paid and we go our separate ways."

She hadn't planned to make that speech and when it poured out of her mouth she could see Marcus' eyes narrowing. "I deserve to know. I've proved my loyalty," she added with conviction.

He nodded slowly. "You are loyal, Magdalene. For years I have given you tiny pieces of the puzzle, troubled men, and you make them fit. You round out the rough edges, the splintered parts of the piece so it can fall into place. But even I do not have the total picture. It is far too large to even imagine. To answer honestly, I do not know if anyone has that immense viewpoint at this time."

Maggie leaned into the table, crossing her arms on its edge, and whispered, "Then who the hell are we working for? Don't tell me even you don't know!"

"I don't know the name, the label you want to give it, but I do know you and I and thousands of others on this planet are working to balance out the scales. Right now there is a vast imbalance." Marcus sat back and gazed out the window. "Look about you, Magdalene, away from this elegant room. Look down there into the streets. Something very dangerous is gaining power. You know this on an instinctual level or you would not have opened your business to counteract it. People are becoming hypnotized, sleepwalking through their lives. They spend most of their time rushing to make enough money to survive, to work for a two-week holiday when they can feel alive again. They feel empty inside. Something vital is missing. Many are becoming immune to violence, having been exposed to it every day of their lives, either in person or through their news and entertainment, and those who aren't immune can't feel safe without taking antidepressants to get through the anxiety of a day. The darkness is gaining because so many are not awake in their very own lives. You know it. You can *feel* it. And so can every other human being who has not closed off their heart."

Maggie stared at him, knowing he was speaking the truth. The world was in turmoil, as was just about everyone she talked to. Everything and almost everyone was being challenged. Ways of handling problems no longer worked. Something fundamental had changed in people's lives.

No one felt safe anymore.

No one was sure of what to believe anymore.

"So this foundation," she murmured, "is trying to balance the scales?"

"*Has* been since the Dark Ages," Marcus corrected. "Ever since the teachings were altered and used to create fear. We call it a foundation in this modern age, but it was known by different terms throughout the centuries. What we're working for is a sublime balance, not domination by either side, for that would be working against life. You know the teachings. Now don't ask me anymore. Know that what you are doing is required of you because you are a piece of this most important puzzle. As am I. As is Tommy Clinesmith and every other person you and I have helped. And so is Julian McDonald. But we need to know if his heart can be opened again before his piece can fit in with the bigger picture."

No longer hungry, Maggie looked back out the window and felt her throat tightening with emotion, her eyes beginning to burn. "How is it possible, Marcus, to really turn things around? There's so much cynicism and fear out there, all over the world . . ."

He reached across table and tenderly held her hand. "It is possible, *cara mia*, because love is much stronger than fear. You know this . . ." He touched his chest with his other hand. " . . . in your heart."

Blinking back tears, Maggie slowly lifted her gaze and saw what was reflected in Marcus' beautiful eyes. That bond they had created all those years ago was still there, pulling at every vital organ, especially her heart. "Yes," she said, managing to push the word through her throat. "Love is stronger."

He patted her hand and then pulled away. "Now, let us continue to enjoy this most delicious food before you run away from me again. That was very rude to leave while I was asleep and never say good-bye."

Immediately, Marcus had switched off the charge of energy that was growing between them and turned it around, knowing she would push her protective barrier back up with his words.

Annoyed with him, but more with herself, Maggie demanded, "Will it ever be possible to say good-bye to you? To never see your face again?"

Marcus chuckled. "I sincerely hope not, *cara mia*. We make such a good team."

TWO

She began pacing about a half hour ago, taking her glass of Chablis with her as she roamed the large apartment, though it was more like a loft above her store. All the walls had been removed and replaced with support columns of rounded glass blocks, creating an open airy space she filled with palm trees and white tulips, her favorite flower which she paid dearly to be flown in when out of season. Original paintings by unknown artists hung on her walls, adding color to the mostly white room. Her furniture had been picked carefully for comfort. She'd wanted the kind of home she could sink into after a tough day, a place that nurtured her, yet didn't feel overpowering. An overstuffed cream-colored, down-filled sofa sat in the middle of the living room space before the eight-foot-tall windows that offered a great night view of the city. On the opposite side of the large cocktail table were two massive chaise lounges, each able to accommodate two people. Silk accent pillows of cobalt blue and pale yellow broke up the whites and creams with one raspberry pillow thrown onto the sofa that she'd bought in Santa Fe on one of her assignments. The wall connecting to the next building was filled with built-in bookcases and in the middle was a Georgia O'Keeffe–like, unframed four-foot canvas of a red poppy flower that slid down to reveal a television behind it.

It was her sanctuary, and rarely did she invite another to share it for more than a few hours. She liked having dinner parties, listening to the opinions of others, laughing at their jokes, sympathizing with their problems, but no one stayed the night. Not ever.

It wasn't an easy life . . . being a shape shifter.

She infrequently dated, but had never been in a real relationship, for Marcus had left his mark on her, an invisible tattoo of possession. Or maybe that was just her imagination, she thought as she wandered into the kitchen and threw open the subzero refrigerator. He was the one who had taught her that love was the exact opposite. Didn't she pass on that teaching to others? Love, real love, was without possession.

So what was it?

Obsession? On her part?

Taking out a container of banana yogurt, she placed her wineglass on the granite countertop and closed the door of the fridge with her hip. She pulled out a spoon and sat on a stool at the breakfast bar. She wasn't obsessive about Marcus, she told herself. She didn't even think about him for months at a time. Staring into the pale yellow centers of the white tulips in a glass vase, Maggie admitted it was only when he called upon her for an assignment that she was conflicted. How was she supposed to open McDonald's heart when her own seemed to be calling out to a man who could never give her what she wanted?

How many times had she sworn never to see Marcus again, to have him fax over her research? Too many times to count over the last fourteen years. To never be in his presence, ever again, would feel like an amputation. Even if she did refuse to see him, she knew she would still feel the phantom pain. Irritated with herself, she scooped up a spoonful of yogurt and swallowed, realizing no other man she had met compared to Marcus. It was physical. It was spiritual. It was hopeless.

Flipping open the *Forbes* magazine that was lying on the counter, she paged through it until she came to the article she wanted. She had an assignment. Julian McDonald. She would concentrate on him. She read a few paragraphs and then stared at a photograph of McDonald in his New York

City corporate office, standing before a window that over-looked the graceful steel arches of the Chrysler Building.

"What are you going to teach me, Mr. McDonald?" she whispered, because they all did. She left each assignment a bit wiser about human nature. She understood men and liked them—at times more than women, who tended to take longer to heal. But then, women were more in touch with their emotions and, when their souls were deeply wounded, they could bleed profusely for years. That was Marcus' department. The women she found herself friends with were as imperfect as she was, but they weren't bitter or resentful toward all men. That type of woman drained too much power and she had learned to recognize energy vampires—of both sexes—and stay clear.

She turned the page and blew her breath out in a rush of appreciation as she saw McDonald's yacht anchored in the waters of Bermuda. Most of the other boats looked dwarfed next to his. She leaned forward and looked more closely. Well, damn if there wasn't a golden retriever on the aft deck. It must be Max.

Immediately, her brain started to think of shopping and what kind of dress she could find tomorrow. It had to be elegant, yet spectacular. And Marcus did say designer props were approved. Haute couture was called for here. She couldn't get into New York City to go to Escada or Versace. Forget a couture house—she'd have to get something *prêt-à-porter,* ready to wear. Neiman Marcus should have something high end in a size ten, something limited edition that no one else would be wearing. She'd already talked to her staff and told them she might be distracted with a private matter for a few weeks and they had all agreed to pitch in and help. She could trust the people who worked for her. She paid them a good salary, plus commissions, decent benefits in an age where health care was as costly as a car payment and, well, she knew their hearts. Each one of them felt they had found a working home at Soul Provisions.

Throwing the empty yogurt container into the plastic recycling bin in the pantry, she picked up her research and

turned off the kitchen lights. She would forget about
Marcus, forget the past.

It was late, time to get to bed with Julian McDonald.

At precisely eight forty-five on Thursday evening Maggie
handed her invitation to the doorman at the Art Museum. She
was ushered to the private elevator which would bring her to
the main hallway that would serve as the ballroom for this
charity event sponsored by the Dalton-Rhymes Foundation.

"Would you be so kind as to take me to the mezzanine
level?" she asked the man working the elevator.

"Certainly, madam," he replied, punching in the proper
button.

Maggie smiled her thanks and she also couldn't help
noticing the way the uniformed younger man had stared at
her as she'd entered the lift. He was probably working for
the catering company that was running the event, maybe a
graduate student at one of the many universities nearby who
supplemented his income serving the wealthy of the city.
Still, it did lift her spirits to have such a good-looking
younger man appreciate all the trouble she'd gone through
to appear as though she belonged at this socialite party. Even
the photographers outside had taken pictures of her as she
walked up the steps to the entrance. It must have been the
dress, she told herself, for they had no idea who she was.
And that was just as well.

She ran her hand over the skirt of the gown and grinned.
What a find, she thought as the elevator stopped and, thinking the younger man who held the door open, she made her
exit. Shopping was the female equivalent to the hunt, and
when you're hunting a rare object and money is not in question, it becomes a glorious pursuit.

Originally she had been searching for something black
and exquisite, something sophisticated that would, at first
glance, make her appear to fit in with the rest of the people
from Philadelphia's society pages, yet also allow her to
stand apart. Then she came across a dress that made her stop
and she knew with every molecule in her body that it was

the dress, that rare find that literally makes you inhale with awe, sucking in your breath and mentally pleading with the fashion gods that it fit.

It did.

Oscar de la Renta seemed to have made it for her, with a slight alteration of the hemline. It was a deep copper brown silk-faille with a high neckline, long fitted sleeves with one hundred and ten tiny covered buttons that ran down the front from the neck to the sweeping full skirt that skimmed over the floor. After she had slipped the half-buttoned gown over her head, she had actually counted them, and that didn't include the buttons that ran down her forearms to her wrists. It was at once delightfully demure and sexily sophisticated with a tiny ruffle of silk around the neckline that fluttered around her earlobes. It almost matched the color of her hair which was pulled up and back with careless, yet artfully arranged, auburn tendrils escaping. Her only jewelry was diamond drop earrings. Okay, the diamonds weren't real, but quite good reproductions. If Julian McDonald could tell the difference, she would resign the assignment. At least she'd have a once in a lifetime ball gown in her closet.

Looking down the sweeping double staircase to the glittering crowd below, Maggie listened to the string quartet that was entertaining those who were bidding on objects around the perimeter of the ballroom. There must be well over three hundred people milling about. Sighing deeply with resignation, she tested her Robert Cavalli heels, wished she'd had a few days to break them in, and then tightened her fingers around her matching moiré clutch bag. Inside was a platinum American Express card. She'd already put over six thousand dollars on it with her shopping spree and wondered how much more tonight would cost.

Time to find out.

She slowly descended the left staircase and nodded to a few people who were coming up to the mezzanine level. She acted as though she belonged among the denizens of high society, that she wasn't more comfortable in her Levi's and a cotton sweater on South Street amid the skateboarders and goths and aging hippies with their unique shops. A part of her thought the whole thing ridiculous, that some people actually believed a pedigree gave them admission to The Lucky Sperm Club or, if their background tended toward that of a mongrel, their accumulation of money was the ticket. Marcus had taught her everyone had a story and they were all interesting. It didn't matter whether a person had pulled themselves up from modest beginnings to live a life most would envy, like Julian McDonald had done, or spent the majority of time sitting in front of a television. Obviously McDonald's story was interesting, but to Maggie so was the man's who sat staring at a television screen, lost in his own life. He didn't start out that way. Once he had dreams, hopes, desires. Something put the man in the chair. That something, whatever it was, interested her in his story.

Maggie O'Shea didn't have a religion, but one of her deepest beliefs was that human beings came to this planet and interacted with each other to learn more about the only thing we take with us when we leave . . . love. Without conditions.

Which was why, to her way of thinking, this gathering of The Lucky Sperm Club leaned toward the ridiculous. For people to believe that the accumulation of money and status made them special and was the driving force in their lives meant that in the end they would leave life bankrupt of the only commodity of real value. Granted, not many shared her belief, but she had seen too much in her thirty-four years, things that convinced her without a shred of doubt that something far more powerful than what we all perceived as the physical world existed. Her abilities were living proof that there were mysteries still to be solved.

Now . . . what would a man like Julian McDonald silently bid on?

Walking through the throng of well-dressed people to the bidding tables, she had to bite the inside of her cheek at the thought of this crowd suddenly receiving an epiphany, a startling revelation that they just might have been using all their energy striving for an illusion of wealth and good standing. How many would be willing to seek real love? It wasn't an easy quest. To see faults and still remain a loving person, without judgments, went against everything most humans had been taught.

"Excuse me, have we met?"

Maggie turned to her side and saw a man in his thirties, dressed in a well-cut tuxedo. He looked rich, slightly bored, and already half tanked on the champagne being offered to the guests. She smiled and held out her hand. "Hello, I'm Maggie O'Shea, and since I arrived late you'll have to excuse me or I'll miss the bidding entirely." Withdrawing her hand, she moved on to the tables. She wasn't interested in finding McDonald yet, but she was very interested to find the object he desired.

The draped tables were filled with crystal, china, and silver amid tickets for the opera, certificates for exclusive spas and golf resorts. There was a week at the Phillies training camp in Clearwater, Florida, and a cameo appearance in the next Bruce Willis movie to be shot in Philadelphia. So far the bidding on that one was at over seven thousand dollars. *An awful lot of money for twenty seconds of screen time*, she thought as she moved down the table, yet she could just picture some social butterfly retelling his or her "charity" story all next season. Mentally shaking the cynicism out of her mind, she reminded herself that, for tonight, she was supposed to fit in. She needed to be attractive, in the truest sense of the word. She was here to attract to her the one person who—

All thoughts came to a freezing halt when she read Julian McDonald's signature, or rather his scrawl that she could barely make out as J. McD— and then a long line of scribble. How surprising, she thought as she looked up to the small watercolor of flowers by a local art student. It was very good, but also very feminine. Hmm . . . he might be buying this for a woman. Did he bring someone with him? She hadn't counted on that. Maybe she should have.

She refused to look around for him. Instead, she took a step back and clasped her hands behind her as she studied the painting. She unconsciously squared her shoulders and lifted her chin as she pictured it in her apartment. McDonald had bid six hundred dollars. His was the only amount written down. Now either no one wanted the watercolor by an unknown artist, or they were being polite to the man they were honoring tonight. Social gaffe or not, she had less than a half hour to make sure she took it home with her or at least got McDonald's unwavering attention. She wrote down eight hundred dollars and, grinning triumphantly, she moved into the crowd.

Accepting a glass of champagne, she mingled while all the while watching the space in front of the watercolor to see if McDonald would counter her bid. She met Prudence and Karl Aston and Muffie Potter Bancroft and Cornelia Perry. They seemed fascinated that she ran a retail store on Chestnut Street and introduced her to Deborah Stark, a local news anchor who actually had heard of Soul Provisions. Stark was dressed in an interesting combination of a tuxedo jacket with satin lapels and a gorgeous dropped-waist full black chiffon skirt. If nothing else, tonight was a good networking experience. Just when she thought McDonald had forgotten about the painting, she saw him standing over the bidding sheet and reading her name. Taller than she expected, he looked around him and then grinned to no one in particular. And then he picked up the pen and wrote down his next bid.

"Excuse me for a moment, Deborah. I think someone is trying to outbid me."

The anchorwoman laughed. "I understand completely. I'm dying to get the weekend in Bermuda."

"Well then, I hope your bid is the winning one," Maggie said with a smile.

"You too. And, by the way, your dress is absolutely stunning. Yves Saint Laurent?"

"Oscar de la Renta," Maggie answered, moving away. "And thank you. You look lovely yourself."

She came back to the watercolor and saw next to McDonald's name a bid for one thousand dollars. Smiling widely, she picked up the pen and raised him five hundred dollars. Really, she was fortunate McDonald had picked the painting and not the cameo role in the movie. This wasn't too bad at all. How much more could it rise in the remaining ten minutes?

She was pretending to be fascinated with the conversation of the three men around her who were talking about an older gentleman's recent remarriage to a much younger woman. They were speaking as though Maggie knew all parties concerned. She nodded and raised her eyebrows appropriately, while watching McDonald sip his champagne and wander over to the watercolor.

Without hesitation, he picked up the pen and, obviously, raised her bid. A younger man came up to him and he walked back into the crowd, kissing the cheek of an attractive woman in a black dress that clung to every inch of an almost painfully thin body with a black scarf artfully tied around her head, the ends draping over one shoulder.

With no time to lose, Maggie excused herself and deliberately walked up to the bidding table. When she looked down she could barely believe her eyes.

McDonald had written five thousand dollars next to his name.

He really wanted this and his bid was to put her out of the game quickly. Or so he thought.

She hesitated as she picked up the pen. It wasn't her money and she had already spent so much on this one evening . . .

"I realize this is supposed to be a silent auction," a deep male voice said above her shoulder, "but I think it's only fair to tell you I intend to have that painting."

Contact.

"And so do I," she said with a grin without turning to the speaker. She lowered her hand and raised the bid to eight thousand. "It is after all for charity, Mr. . . . " she hesitated, pointing to his name with the pen. "Mr. Mc . . . something. I'm sorry," she said, turning and facing him with her best smile. "I'm afraid I can't read your signature."

"McDonald," he answered with an amused expression, holding out his hand. "Julian McDonald."

Within a few seconds her brain assessed him, comparing him in person to his photographs in the magazines. They didn't do him justice. He wasn't beautiful like Marcus, yet his smile seemed quite charming. His light brown hair had streaks of blond, probably from spending time in the sun on his boat. His face was weathered from the same exposure, creating lines around his intelligent eyes, or maybe that was from intense concentration on business. His nose had the slightest bump on the bridge, as though he had it broken at one time. It was an interesting face, bordering on handsome, and one she was very pleased to see in such close proximity.

She placed her hand inside his. "Well, Mr. McDonald, we seem to have a dilemma. We both want the same painting. Surely there's something else here that could interest you."

"My interest has already been captured," he answered with a look that spoke of a possible double entendre. "For the painting, of course."

She almost laughed. "Of course," she agreed.

McDonald looked over her shoulder to the bid when a voice announced over the microphone that only three minutes were left for bidding. "Very nice handwriting, Miss O'Shea. I had no trouble reading your name."

"Eight years of Catholic schooling will do that to you. The nuns called it Palmer Method." She didn't move, blocking the bidding sheet with a serene smile.

"Sister Ignatius said I was hopeless, that I'd end up with chicken scrawl. It appears I've proved her right." He raised his eyebrows and tilted his head to the table. "Will you excuse me? As we've just been reminded, only minutes remaining . . ."

She stepped to one side, looking over the expensively dressed assembly as others crowded around the tables, laughing at the fun way to spend money, acquire something of value, and write it off on their taxes all at the same time.

A pen appeared in front of her face.

She closed her eyes for a moment and opened them slowly, staring at the pen and then raising her gaze to McDonald's face. He was enjoying this.

Accepting the pen, she looked over her shoulder to the number he had written. Ten thousand dollars. She turned and wrote down twelve, sincerely hoping he intended to raise it again. This was getting out of hand and whoever was going to reimburse her would surely raise their eyebrows on this type of expenditure. Straightening, she inhaled for calmness, and then turned to hand the pen to the man behind her. "Time's running out, Mr. McDonald."

He accepted the pen. "You realize we're making the reputation of this art student."

"It's a good watercolor. Reminds me of Dawna Barton."

"Do you think it's worth this kind of money?"

Maggie looked back to the painting. "The point of our counter bidding, Mr. McDonald, is to raise money for charity. It isn't a personal contest, is it?"

"Isn't it?" he asked, bending down and writing a figure.

An announcement reminded everyone one minute was left and then all bidding would be closed. McDonald handed the pen back to her with an inviting, yet challenging, smile.

She had to remind herself to keep a straight face as she looked down at the paper. He liked to play hard ball. Fifteen thousand dollars. She didn't move, could barely breathe. Maybe this amount of money was pocket change to him, but it certainly wasn't to her. She'd gotten McDonald's attention. The introduction had been made. How much more money would it take?

He reached out his arm and showed her his gold watch. "Fifteen seconds, Miss O'Shea."

Turning her head, she stared into his eyes, saw that he was thoroughly enjoying himself. She wondered if this was the way he conducted business too. Did he always have to come out on top, the winner? Was his ego that big? Marcus was right, despite the designer props, this assignment wasn't going to be easy.

"Five seconds."

She bent down and held the pen poised over the bidding, trying to make her decision. And then she wrote.

"*All bidding must end now.*" Groans could be heard all around.

She straightened, looked briefly at the painting and then to her bidding companion. "Good evening, Mr. McDonald," she murmured with a smile and walked away, knowing his gaze was following her. She could actually feel it.

Deborah Stark was waving for Maggie to rejoin her and, grateful for a direction, Maggie quickly came to the newswoman's side. "So will you be walking barefoot on Bermuda's beaches?"

Deborah crossed her fingers. "Unless some Philistine outbid me in the last thirty seconds. In which case, I'll just have to do an in-depth investigation of their family tree and come up with a good skeleton, like a bloodthirsty pirate or an opium smuggler."

Maggie laughed. "If you looked far enough I'm sure you could find one or two skeletons in everyone's closet, including mine."

"Oh, do tell, Maggie O'Shea," Deborah demanded with relish. "Even though I only report hard news, I do so love gossip."

Grinning, Maggie said, "Well, usually I get to know someone a little bit better before revealing that my great-great-grandfather was a shape shifter."

Deborah stared at her for a second and then burst out laughing. "Good one. I can't wait to introduce you to someone and casually throw out you descend from a long line of werewolves. I'd better watch your fangs, girlfriend."

Maggie took another glass of champagne from a circulating waiter and raised her glass to her companion. "They rarely come out," she said with a chuckle.

Holding her own glass out in the direction of a group of beautiful young women, Deborah muttered, "Well someone else's have been making an appearance for the last few minutes. See that blonde over there, with the neckline that comes down to her waist? I swear she must use duct tape to keep that material over her breasts."

Maggie looked at the three women, dressed in the latest designer fashion, backless dresses with narrow panels barely covering the large, firm, rounded, and most probably bought breasts. "Which one? They're all blonde."

"Good point," Deborah answered. "Hard to tell the difference when they run in packs. The one in the baby blue with the necklace that looks like she hijacked a chandelier."

Again Maggie laughed.

"It's like she's wearing a neon sign," Deborah added, obviously on a roll now that she'd found someone who appreciated her sense of humor. "Saying *look at my breasts! They're brand-spanking-new! Daddy bought them for me.*"

Maggie couldn't help laughing. "Now whose fangs are showing?"

"You're right," Deborah said in a contrite voice. "How do I know she's into spanking? Could be bondage. Anyway, she didn't miss a move you made, especially after Julian McDonald walked up to you at the table. I would say Miss Implants there was none too pleased to see his interest in you."

"I think his interest was in the painting we were both bidding on, not me."

Deborah looked at Maggie for a few seconds until she fully got her attention. "Now you're either really naïve, which I don't think is the case, or you're as decorous as that dress. Which, by the way, doesn't fool me for a second."

Intrigued, Maggie asked, "Doesn't fool you?"

Deborah's smile was knowing. "There's nothing sexier than a gorgeous gown that looks like it costs a small fortune with so many damn buttons that it would frustrate Job to undo them all. That dress screams bodice ripper."

Maggie threw back her head and laughed, her voice capturing the attention of those around her. Smiles returned in her direction. "I love that, a bodice ripper."

Looking well pleased with herself, Deborah asked, "Well, am I right?"

Maggie paused for only a few seconds before nodding. "You're right, Deborah. I thought, well . . . not bodice ripper . . . but intriguing."

"Intriguing, my great-aunt Gertie!" She shook her head and added. "Who *was* a flapper and *did* operate a speakeasy with an *upstairs*, if you catch my drift. So there, I've outed one of my skeletons at this ritzy gathering." She paused. "Listen, if you're going to play with my head, at least don't call me Deborah. That's for the television crowd. My friends call me D. Period. Not Debs or, god forbid, Debbie. Just like the letter D, no cutesy double *e*. And, if I'm not mistaken, I think we are going to be friends, Maggie O'Shea."

"Okay, D." Maggie extended her hand.

D. shook it and then asked, "Did you come with anyone tonight?"

"No. I came alone."

"Me, too. Station wanted me here. Good for publicity. Do you want to sit together for dinner, and then we'll see if we walk home with a painting and a certificate to Bermuda? I mean, I'm not . . . how do I put this in PC language? Let's just say I thoroughly enjoy . . . oh, to hell with PC! I like a good hard dick. I'm not into women, or anything."

Maggie almost spit out her champagne. Swallowing, she answered, "Good to hear that, D. Me, either. So shall we just follow the crowd?"

D. looked around her to the others slowly walking into another room. "Honey, I never follow the crowd," she said, linking her arm through Maggie's. "We may not be lesbians, but let's mess with their heads anyway."

Together, arm in arm, they walked into a hall that was set for dinner with paintings by masters hanging on the walls. It was quite a grand affair and Maggie was staring at a real Monet when D. jerked her arm to get her attention.

"Look to your right. The dress seems to have worked. Julian McDonald certainly looks *intrigued*."

Maggie found herself staring right into McDonald's eyes. He was seated next to the woman in black he had kissed earlier, yet his attention was definitely not on his dinner companion. His expression looked confused, perplexed, and Maggie tore her gaze away as D. steered her to a table with a few empty seats.

It wasn't until she sat down that Maggie got it.

D. was dressed in that tuxedo jacket and McDonald did look like his sense of perception and his ego had just taken a blow. She could see it in his face. The questions. The uncertainty. D. had accomplished her mission and had messed with someone's head.

It would have been humorous, save for the fact that she just might have blown the entire purpose of the evening. And, somehow, she had to fix it.

THREE

"**G**ood luck," D. murmured as the person announcing the winning bids came to the last two items, the ones that had generated the most money. The cameo role in the movie and the watercolor.

"I don't believe in luck," Maggie answered, again feeling that spidey sense between her shoulder blades that told her McDonald was staring at her back. She had, in fact, felt it all during the dinner. She could almost feel his uncertainty, wondering if he had misjudged his initial impression of her.

Somehow, she had to get things back on track.

"Of course there's luck," D. insisted, waving her envelope with a certificate for the Bermuda trip inside.

"I'm happy for you," Maggie answered, remembering how D. had yelped with delight and bolted out of her chair when her name was announced. "And I can't deny more than a twinge of envy when I think about tropical breezes and massages on pink sandy beaches, but it's not like they picked your name out of a hat. You just bid the highest." She gave the woman at her side a pointed look. "Can you tell I want to rip that envelope out of your hand and run to the airport? I am so due for some pampering."

"I like that. You're jealous."

Maggie laughed. "What woman wouldn't be? I'm just trying to make the point that it wasn't luck."

"You're taking all the fun out of this. I won. I don't care how I won, even if I overpaid for it. I get to spend four glorious days in Bermuda. *And* it's a business expense, just like everything I'm wearing tonight."

Applause broke out when Muffie Potter Bancroft jumped to her feet and made her way to the podium to claim her prize of a brief movie appearance with Bruce Willis.

"Can ya picture that? Muffie and Bruce?" D. quipped. "Now if they made her the gangsta bitch of a drug lord, I'd pay to see it."

Maggie almost choked as immediate laughter bubbled up in her throat. "You have such a way with words, D."

"That's why I'm in broadcasting."

"The trouble is I don't think I'll ever be able to look at you on the six o'clock news again and take you seriously."

"See? That's just it," D. insisted. "They force us to be too serious. We're news readers, that's all, and we all sound the same. Now if they'd let me say something like, 'Thatcher Willingsworth was shot last night making a booty call to his main squeeze,' you'd sit your behind down and listen, wouldn't you? Oh, wait . . . Muffie has finally stopped gushing. Now it's your turn. Let's see who walks off with the painting."

"The object that received the highest bid of the evening was, surprisingly, a watercolor by Cynthia Cummings, an art student at Moore School of Design," the emcee announced. "It was quite an intense bidding war between two people and I'm happy to announce the winner is . . ." He paused for effect. "Our honoree this evening, Mr. Julian McDonald!"

"Tough luck," D. said through the loud applause.

Maggie smiled, clapping along with everyone else. "I told you I didn't believe in luck," she answered as McDonald came up to the podium, waved to the crowd and collected his painting. He really was a nice-looking man, interesting face, still decent body, and appeared very comfortable in the spotlight, Maggie thought.

He looked briefly in her direction as he left the stage, but it was long enough for D. to once more lean closer and mutter, "The man is definitely interested."

Smiling, Maggie shrugged her shoulders, both to D.'s comment and to McDonald, who walked past her table back to his seat, presenting the painting to his lovely dinner companion. The woman appeared overjoyed and threw her arms around McDonald's neck, which gave rise to another round of applause. Perhaps she had misjudged McDonald. Was this woman his current interest? Maggie didn't like the thought of competing for McDonald's attention with a woman who might be falling in love with him. No one was supposed to get hurt, and the least Marcus could have done with his research was to make it current. This could put an entirely different spin on things.

"Easy come, easy go," D. said, pushing her chair back from the table after the emcee thanked everyone for their generosity and announced the evening was far from over.

"You can't miss something you never had, can you?" Maggie answered with a smile, as she rose along with the rest of the assembly. During dinner the quartet in the main hall had been replaced by a twelve-piece orchestra.

"I think I'll skip the dancing," D. said as they left the dining room. "I'm beat, and it isn't as if my dance card is filled. This is the portion of the evening where it pays to come with a date, or split." She paused for a moment, staring out at those already dancing. "Though I would have liked to celebrate my Bermuda victory with a twirl around the floor." She glanced at Maggie and added, "Don't worry, I'm not about to ask you to dance."

Grinning, Maggie nodded toward the crowd standing around the main floor and said, "C'mon, Ginger, let's see if we can find someone in this bunch to sweep you off your feet. Oh, look who it is!"

"Who is it?" D. demanded, following Maggie up to an attractive man.

"I'm not sure," Maggie muttered. "Just come with me."

Maggie walked right up to the man. "Hello, we met earlier when I was rushing to the bidding tables. Do you remember me? Maggie O'Shea?"

The man seemed confused for a moment and then his face brightened. "Of course. Maggie O'Shea."

He obviously didn't remember her, but that lapse didn't

matter. It appeared the digestion of a meal had sobered him, and he was doing a good job of covering for his faulty memory. "How did you do? Win anything?"

"I lost," Maggie answered and then her voice lightened. "But my friend Deborah won. She's looking forward to a weekend in Bermuda. Deborah . . . I'd like to introduce you to . . ." Her voice faltered. "Was it John?"

"James," the man corrected. "James Coulter. And, of course, I recognize Deborah Stark. How do you do?"

The two shook hands and Maggie could see that D. wasn't averse to the introduction. "Now, James, Deborah is just dying to celebrate winning that trip to Bermuda out on the dance floor, and I couldn't think of a better partner."

James looked well pleased to have captured the attention of the two women. "Absolutely," he exclaimed, offering D. his arm.

Watching D. accept the offer, Maggie had to bite the inside of her cheek not to grin broadly as D. raised her eyebrows in approval and proceeded to be escorted away. Deborah Stark had made the evening thoroughly enjoyable and Maggie was glad the woman got her wish to celebrate on the dance floor. She could easily see herself friends with D. Deborah's sense of biting humor foretold she would be the type of girlfriend who would refuse to allow you to feel sorry for yourself and would soon have you laughing at your own self-pity.

"Excuse me, Miss O'Shea?"

She turned away from the dance floor and came face to face with Julian McDonald. "Congratulations," she said, recovering quickly and holding out her hand. "I hope your friend enjoys the painting for many years."

McDonald automatically shook her hand. "I'm sure she will."

Maggie nodded, staring into his eyes expectantly. It was obvious he had something else to add.

"I have to ask you . . . why?"

"Why what?"

"Why, at the end of the bidding, did you write *Enjoy*,

instead of an amount? I thought you really wanted the painting."

"It became obvious to me that you wanted it more."

He grinned. "But that's not the reason, is it?"

She grinned back. "No. What would you say if I told you the artist is a cousin of mine and this seemed the perfect opportunity to get her work and her name known?"

He seemed startled for a moment, as though he had never thought of someone outsmarting him. "Is she?"

Maggie tried not to show her amusement at his expression. "What would you say?"

He looked around the room and then back at her with a measure of regard. "I would say congratulations. To you and to your cousin."

Maggie grinned. "Well, she's not my cousin. But it would have been a brilliant scheme."

His expression softened and, for a brief moment, Maggie could see he was relieved. He also seemed to be enjoying himself.

"So you still haven't answered my question, Miss O'Shea."

Inhaling deeply, Maggie figured she might as well tell him. "Perhaps the simple truth is my pockets are not quite as deep as yours, Mr. McDonald. That was a lot of money to spend on an unknown artist. Even for charity, I'm afraid."

"But you did want it."

"Of course I did. I knew exactly where I would hang it."

"Where?"

She looked back out to the dance floor and could see D. was enjoying herself with James Coulter. "What does it matter now? It will hang in another woman's house. I could tell she was very pleased by your gift."

"Normally I wouldn't explain myself like this, but I . . . well, you did really want the painting and I just came over to tell you that you made someone very happy tonight. Emma is my sister-in-law and she's recovering from ovarian cancer. She, too, fell in love with the watercolor and that's why I didn't back down in the bidding."

In that moment Maggie could see the potential in Julian

McDonald, what he must have been like before his family's accident, before he became cynical, bitter, and bored with life. She stared into his blue eyes, trying to see past his discomfort at explaining his actions. Instinctively, she leaned up and gently kissed his cheek.

"You're a good man, Julian McDonald," she whispered, inhaling the expensive scent of his cologne. "Don't be so afraid of showing it."

He was embarrassed as she pulled back from him and Maggie laughed to ease the moment. She stuck out her hand and said, "Even though we encountered each other at the bidding table, I suppose we should be properly introduced before I make such a statement. I'm Maggie O'Shea. It has been a pleasure to meet you tonight."

"The pleasure has been mine, Maggie O'Shea." His eyes narrowed slightly. "I mean that."

Their gaze connected for a moment longer than was polite, but in that time Maggie felt a frizzle of electricity race up her arms and down her back. It was a solid connection of attraction. "I know you meant it," she murmured. "So did I."

They stared at each other, neither willing to break the gaze, and it felt like the rest of the room receded. The music became muffled and distant. The people around them seemed to fade into a rainbow haze of colors. For a timeless moment nothing seemed to exist but the two of them, connecting, feeling drawn to each other.

It was Maggie who pulled the plug, breaking the connection. "So the painting was for your sister-in-law. Thank you for telling me."

McDonald blinked several times, as though forcing himself to concentrate. "Yes. Emma Madden. Do you know her?" He took a deep breath, pulling air into his lungs like it might clear his head.

"No. I don't."

"She . . . she's in remission right now."

"I'm happy for her."

It finally dawned on him. "Oh, my sister-in-law! It's not

what you think. I'm not married. Widowed. We're still very close."

Maggie smiled. "I knew you were a widower."

"You did?" He seemed surprised by her answer.

"It appears your reputation precedes you. You're the talk of the evening, Mr. McDonald. The point of the auction was to continue the good work you started with your contribution of computers to schools, wasn't it?"

McDonald had the graciousness to look embarrassed. "Yes, of course, it's just that . . ." He paused, staring into her eyes. "Are you enjoying this, Miss O'Shea?"

Her grin widened. "Enjoying what?"

"Making me feel like a teenager. I'm not usually this awkward in conversation. It is *Miss* O'Shea, isn't it?"

"It is. Everyone calls me Maggie." It was her turn to pause when she thought of Marcus. "Almost everyone."

"Now that intrigues me. What other names are you called?"

"That would depend upon who's calling me. My mother sometimes called me by my given name, the people who work for me might sometimes call me something quite different after a long difficult day."

"You have a business . . . Maggie?" He used her name hesitantly, as though asking for permission.

"Yes, I do, Julian. On Chestnut Street here in the city."

"The name of it?"

She could tell his interest was even more stimulated. "Soul Provisions."

He didn't answer, but she could almost see the gears in his brain working, trying to figure out what type of business she conducted. "And what do you provide for the soul?"

Her smile softened and she looked directly into his eyes. "Nourishment. Sustenance. Sometimes, just a safe haven to catch your breath and remember the reason you came to the planet."

He didn't answer her, but she could feel the withdrawal of his energy as her words seemed to knock against a quickly resurrected steel barrier.

"I'm not a religious person," he finally stated, looking

around him as if to find a drink or make a quick departure from her presence.

She laughed. "Oh, don't be so afraid, Mr. McDonald. As it happens, I'm not a religious person either. I sell candles, jewelry, books, CDs, and the best damn coffee in Center City."

His shoulders actually relaxed as the tension left. "I'm sorry. I didn't know if you were some New Age cult goddess and into recruitment."

"Well, thank you for the goddess compliment, but it's rare for me to even advertise. People seem to find their way into the store by themselves. As a successful businessman I'm sure you'd agree that good word of mouth is better than a full page ad in the *Sunday Inquirer.*"

His smile was back, accompanied by something new . . . the tiniest dimple in his left cheek. "I'm impressed. A businesswoman who is beautiful and takes risks. That's a powerful combination."

"Flattery, at least tonight, will get you nowhere," she said with a slight laugh as she looked at D. and James ending their dance and walking toward her and McDonald. "I took a risk in bidding for that painting and you beat me. We don't always win." Turning back to him, she added, "And, for me, the night is over. I'm a working woman and it is getting late."

"It's not even midnight," he protested, checking his gold watch. His expression was definitely flirtatious as he added, "Do you really have to leave? Not even one dance to show you're a good sport and not upset about the painting?"

"You already know I'm not upset about the painting." Her hand lifted and she was about to lightly touch the lapel of his tuxedo when she stopped, surprised by the return of attraction so strong she felt like intimacy had already been established. Her fingers curled away from him to rest at the base of her throat, touching a tiny button. "If you'd asked me when you first came up to me I would have gladly danced with you. Now, I'm afraid, it's too late."

"You're actually leaving?" He appeared shocked that she

was turning him down. Obviously, he was a man who was used to getting his way with women. "You won't join me for a single dance?"

She lifted her chin and captured his gaze. "Haven't you realized we've been dancing all evening?" Taking a step back, she added to his confused expression by saying, "And it was exquisite. Thank you. Now I must be leaving."

Just as she turned to D. and James, he called out, "Wait! Can I see you again? I'd . . . like to . . . to discuss" He seemed embarrassed by his words, the sound of desperation in his voice.

"You sound as though you want lessons, which I'm sure you don't need."

"Maybe I do."

She liked him. Even if he wasn't her assignment, she would have enjoyed the mental tango they had been doing. "Dance lessons, huh?"

He pulled her aside, away from the approaching couple. "Look, you've got me talking like a self-conscious seventeen-year-old. Why do you have to leave right now? Are you going to walk up those stairs and drop a glass slipper? Does your car turn into a pumpkin? That gorgeous gown into rags? Why can't you stay for ten minutes?"

Maggie opened her purse. "I could stay, but I won't because you don't just want ten minutes." She handed him a business card. "You are charming, Julian McDonald, and I would enjoy being charmed, but we don't always get what we want exactly when we want it. And I have a very busy day tomorrow." She pressed the card into his hand. "If you're ever in the market for a great cup of coffee, stop in."

He looked down at the business card. "Soul Provisions."

Staring at his expression of defeat, she couldn't stop a giggle from escaping. "Exactly."

She walked away to say good-night to Deborah Stark and exchange numbers.

For her the evening was over and a success.

Besides, her feet were throbbing in pain. Four-inch heels. Who did she think she was, a runway model? She should have known there's always a price to pay for fashion and she couldn't wait to take them off, but thought it better if she absorbed the pain and kept her shoes on.

Knowing Julian McDonald was watching her exit, Maggie figured walking up the stairs barefoot after his references to Cinderella would definitely be overkill.

Insomnia was his curse. He'd tried reading the reports on different companies that his department of acquisitions had recommended, but had thrown them aside in disinterest. He'd browsed through *Forbes, Time, The New Yorker, Town and Country* and *Philadelphia Magazine*, all of which had been provided by the hotel, but nothing caught his interest. Each time he tried to concentrate, his mind started to wander back to earlier in the evening to a certain woman.

Maggie O'Shea.

Who was she and why the hell couldn't he get her out of his head?

He picked up her business card. There was a residential number. It was too late to call, though he wanted to, just to hear her voice again. Damn, he *was* acting like a teenager. Part of him was annoyed at himself for not keeping his mind occupied with business details. It was always the details that fascinated him, where he could find the illusive key that unlocked the doorway for an acquisition. Some people read mystery novels, trying to unravel a tapestry of clues. He read business prospectuses with the same determination. But tonight those details didn't provide the customary comfort for another part of him felt too energized for reading. He wanted . . . What did he want? He searched his mind for an answer, and found one— and it wasn't entirely unexpected. He wanted to know more about the woman who had captured his attention when she gracefully descended the staircase like a breath of fresh air in a crowded room. He couldn't believe his luck when he watched her stop in front of the painting he had earlier bid on for Emma. It was the perfect opportunity to meet her and when he did, he couldn't stop his heart from hammering inside his chest as he looked into her hauntingly beautiful eyes.

He'd liked the bidding war. He'd liked the way she surrendered so gracefully in the end. He'd liked that she and that newswoman had seemed oblivious to the opinions of anyone around them. And he most certainly liked the way she had flirted with him.

She had been flirting with him, hadn't she?

That's what she'd meant by that remark about they had been dancing all evening, right? Mentally dancing with each other?

God, he really was reverting back to adolescent insecurity if he couldn't even be sure about a woman coming on to him. But was Maggie O'Shea coming on to him, or just gracefully . . . *dancing* with him, keeping pace, but never allowing him to actually take the lead?

He shook his head, as if the action could also shake the image of her out of his mind. Damn . . . that dress. How many times had he stared at those buttons, imagining his impatience to see the creamy skin of her shoulders? He already saw her in his bed, under him, surrendering.

He looked at the digital clock on the night table and then down to the business card in his hand.

Soul Provisions.

Throwing back the linens of the bed, he got up and went to the closet. He pulled out gray trousers and dropped them onto the mattress, then went to his opened suitcase and picked up a black cashmere sweater. What the hell, it was past three o'clock and he wasn't the least bit tired. He felt, in fact, energized. Like a young kid.

Twenty minutes later he was standing in front of a tastefully decorated store window and wondering about the woman who owned the establishment. He'd taken a cab to the corner of Sixteenth and Chestnut Street and had walked the rest of the way through the business district of the city. More cop cars passed him than cabs and the only thing open was an all-night deli and coffee shop filled with those customers who also couldn't sleep—cops who had finished their shift, waitresses who were eating before heading for home, maybe writers or musicians whose carnal hungers finally overcame creative urges.

Looking back into Maggie's store window, he felt ridiculous for staring, seeing the shadow of his own image reflected back to him by the streetlamp. He told himself he wasn't going to sleep anyway and he might as well have satisfied his curiosity, but the only thing he could tell was that Maggie sold exactly what she said she did—books, CDs, and jewelry—though the books in the window display seemed a mixture of current offerings and self-help, the CDs were by artists he had never heard of, and the jewelry was an eclectic presentation of silver and gold with stones he couldn't recognize in the dark. Still, the place did look successful in a great part of town and . . . hell, what was he doing here at almost four in the morning? Because some woman made him feel like he was twenty again? He could almost sense the strong pull of attraction when she'd stared into his eyes, the sound of her voice when she'd whispered that he was a good man.

A good man.

How many years since he'd felt like that?

Distracted from his musings by the purring of a cat, he looked down at the scruffy feline who was slowly walking up to him. "Couldn't sleep either, huh?" he muttered, realizing that he needed to get back to the hotel and catch at least a few hours' sleep before leaving the city. Maybe he'd come back in the morning and get a cup of coffee, he thought, turning to the corner. And maybe he should just get back to work and forget about being attracted to a woman who was, to say the least, unusual.

Standing on the corner, waiting for a yellow cab to show up, Julian looked down and saw the cat had followed him. When it began to rub against his pant leg, purring, he stepped back. "Look, buddy, I'm not a cat person, okay?"

He jammed his hands into his pant pockets and looked up and down Chestnut Street. Twenty minutes ago several cabs had been in the neighborhood, yet now that he wanted one they'd disappeared. Unlike the cat. It continued to purr while walking back and forth beside him. It was gray and black with white feet and looked like it lived on the street.

Sighing, he glanced into the coffee shop window before once more checking for a cab. The street was deserted, save for himself and the cat.

"Hungry?" he asked, and when the cat stared up at him he felt a strange compassion for the animal. Suddenly he remembered what it was like to be hungry, to be alone, trying to make your way in an unfriendly world. His mother had died when he was seven and his father, an appliance salesman, had been overwhelmed by a son who was scared of being abandoned again and was desperate for attention. Even negative attention was better than pretending his mother hadn't died and his father didn't drink his way into oblivion every night. By seventeen he was on his own, but by that time he'd already figured out using his brain was easier than using his fists and he'd laid out his own plan. A scholarship at Yale followed by Wharton School of Business gave him the credentials he needed. The eighties gave him his first million and by the nineties he was married, a father, and richer than he'd ever dreamed. But he never forgot what it was to be hungry, that fist in the stomach that grabbed at the muscle walls, producing a distinct cramping pain that must be assuaged.

"Wait here," he said to the cat and pulled open the door to the coffee shop.

He was looking over the display of Danish when a young woman asked him in a tired voice if he wanted coffee.

He smiled. "No, thanks. I'm looking for something to eat."

"Well, we have that," she said, pointing to the trays of fried chicken under hot warming lamps.

It looked unappealing, dried out, as though it had been under the lamps for hours. Julian walked toward the deli case and saw exactly what he wanted. "I'll have half a pound of your liver pâté."

"Liver pâté," the girl repeated, grabbing a plastic container.

There was a man sipping a cup of coffee and reading the paper, and when Julian looked at him he raised his head, gave him, cursory glance and then returned to his paper. Things were different in the early hours of darkness, bringing out people whose internal clocks, whether by nature or necessity, were active while the rest of the world slept. The man probably stayed and watched out for the girl until her shift was over.

Julian paid for the liver and walked back outside. Just as he'd figured, the cat was tenacious and was waiting. He stooped down and pulled off the lid to the plastic container. "Here ya go, pal. Eat up."

Watching the sad-looking animal devour the pâté, Julian straightened while wondering what the hell was getting into him tonight. Why did he feel that rush of recognition when the street cat looked up at him? And why the trip down memory lane? He hadn't thought about his parents in years or his rough beginnings. Looking up, he saw a cab coming down the street and he rushed to the curb while holding out his hand and whistling.

He glanced once more at the cat, still busy cleaning out the round container, and shook his head at being so sentimental. Opening the cab door, he gave the driver the name of his hotel, got in, and leaned his shoulders against the leather seat.

Hadn't he learned long ago you don't look back?

Maggie wandered into her kitchen and turned on the soft lighting over the counters. She opened a cabinet and searched until she found the box of antacids, burping as she dug her fingernail into the foil container and popping out two pills.

Damn, he had to pick liver pâté.

Bad liver pâté, at that.

FOUR

"She's made contact."

"Where is McDonald now?"

Marcus, sitting across from Gabriel Burke, his old teacher, answered, "He's in New York City, at his office."

"And Maggie is in Philadelphia. Distance is not exactly a conduit for intimacy." Gabriel paused, running his long tapered fingers down the carved arm of his chair. "Are you sure she's ready for this assignment?"

"I trained her," Marcus said. "I've watched her mature and refine her skills. She's more than ready."

"You know the importance of this one, Marcus. I'm trusting you. How are you doing with Victoria?"

Marcus thought of the woman waiting for him at his apartment. "I'm in the last phase now, convincing her I'm not the one she's been searching for her whole life. You know how difficult it is . . . letting go, that surrender of a hungry will. It can be even more challenging than the desire for possession."

Gabriel nodded. "The fact that I am relegated to an office now doesn't dim my memory. I haven't forgotten my many years in the field."

"Do you miss it, Gabriel?"

A small smile played across the expression of the older man. "Marcus, sometimes my desire to be out there is overwhelming. Then sanity kicks in and I know my level of energy couldn't sustain it. I'm in the exact position where I can facilitate the most good." Gabriel suddenly straightened in the chair and stared at the door to his office in Washington, D.C.

Gabriel Burke was one of the most distinguished men Marcus had ever met. His thick gray hair was impeccably cut. His blue eyes seemed as sharp as ever. He looked to be about sixty, claimed to be sixty-seven, yet Marcus wanted to ask Gabriel how old he actually was. He knew such an inquiry would be highly disrespectful, and his curiosity quickly faded as two short beeps sounded from the phone on the desk. Gabriel's expression required immediate attention. "What's wrong?"

"You must leave now. And not, my good friend, in your present state." Gabriel nodded toward the closed door. "You have very little time to make yourself scarce."

Marcus immediately rose and hurried to the corner of the large office. He hated to be rushed and resented whoever was about to open the door. It was only because of his training that he was able to master the elements and rearrange them quickly, thus changing the shape of matter, including his clothes. Blocking out everything from his mind, especially the knock on the door, Marcus concentrated on reducing his energy, shrinking the molecules and the space around them. Just as the door opened, a fly rubbed its back legs together with relish before lifting off the Berber carpeting.

"Senator Burke, how good of you to receive me without notice when I know your time is—" The senior senator from Texas halted his drawled greeting as he batted a large horsefly away from his face. "Goodness, I do believe we have an infestation problem in the Senate building. Two of those nasty buggers insisted on squattin' in my office this mornin'."

"Come in, Senator Robertson," Gabriel said, effortlessly hiding a smile of satisfaction as he held out his hand to the chair Marcus had occupied only moments ago. "What can I do for you?"

"I'll come right to the point. No sense in beatin' round the bush, as the sayin' goes in my neck of the woods. As you know, Gabe," Senator Robertson began, easing his ample bulk into the chair across from the desk, "tomorrow night there are scheduled special-order speeches in the House. Three hours of them. Your boy from Delaware is plannin' on bombastin' my boys on C-SPAN and I'm askin' you, my old friend, to persuade young Jackman to lighten up. The talk on the hill is that Jackman plans to go public with what was simply a memo from our friends in the pharmaceutical industry."

Gabriel didn't even try to hold back his smile. "Now, Senator Robertson, they may be your friends, but they're not mine." He was pleased to see Robertson appear unsettled by the remark. "Why should I ask Representative Jackman to bury the fact that your friends in the pharmaceutical industry have earmarked one hundred million dollars to be used by their lobbyists for advocacy here in Washington?"

"Because it's bad for business, that's why," Robertson countered.

"Whose business, Senator? The pharmaceutical companies? The six hundred pharmaceutical lobbyists here in the capital, many of whom are our former colleagues? The campaign contributions that may be questioned?" Gabriel settled back in his chair. "Now you and I both know it's only a matter of time before this whole nasty business becomes public anyway. You can't ask the taxpayers to finance the cost of research yet pay six times more for prescriptions than someone in Europe. I've always been an advocate for free enterprise, Senator, but gouging the American public crosses the line. We're the only country in the world that doesn't regulate drug pricing and we pay the highest in the world. Are you aware, Senator, that twenty-nine percent of seniors let prescriptions go unfilled because they can't afford medicine and food? And now the FDA, who gets over five million from your friends, is trying to stop them from obtaining their medicine from Canada and Mexico?"

Robertson held up his hand. "I didn't come here, Senator, for a lecture. I came to see if there is some way we can make peace on this issue. I don't think I have to remind you that as an Independent, you can't count on majority support on either side of the aisle. And you do sit on the Government Reform Committee. You convince your boy to back off on this and I can assure you of support when campaign finance comes up next year." He sat back, looking pleased with himself.

Gabriel laced his hands together and stared across his desk to the man. Jedidiah Robertson was typical of the politicians who had no conscience, handing over the government to corporations and their lobbyists. Gabriel thought of the axiom of keeping your friends close and your enemies closer. He'd lived by it for much of his life. In his mind he pictured Alan Jackman, an honest man in a town where honesty was regarded as naïveté. He wouldn't withdraw his support for Jackman now, even if it meant distancing an enemy.

"Jed, by the time campaign finance reform comes up your friends will have already put a hundred million into the pockets of Congress. How do we explain that to those who put us in office? How do we explain to the American people that one CEO walks away from a pharmaceutical company with a compensation package of seventy-two million plus seventy-six million in stock options? That's over a hundred and fifty million dollars that your friends pay their top man in one year, but they can't lower the cost of medicine so some elderly woman in Kansas can have her breast cancer medicine *and* eat that month?" Gabriel drew a deep breath to allow the anger to leave his body. Anger never solved anything. "This isn't about one side of the aisle against the other, right versus left. This is about right versus wrong. Jackman has my support. Let's see if the rest of us have the guts to stand up and say no to over one hundred million dollars."

Robertson rose from his chair and shook his head, causing his gray hair to fall over onto his broad forehead. His face turned a darker shade of red, which was rather alarming since his complexion already showed his years of fondness for bourbon. "You're makin' a big mistake, Gabe, on this one. Too many have a vested interest in not airin' our laundry on C-SPAN tomorrow evenin'. This isn't a partisan issue, you understand. Both sides of the aisle are against it."

Gabriel stood up and held out his hand. "Thank you for coming to discuss this with me, Jed, but you know where I stand."

"Sad day when two gentlemen from the old school can't come to a compromise."

"Sad day, Jed, when two elected representatives can't stand together for the American people."

Robertson stared into Gabriel's eyes for a fraction longer than was necessary. In that moment Gabriel could read the other man's anger and resentment, hidden beneath his "good ole boy" demeanor. "Good day to you, Senator," he said pleasantly, yet firmly.

Robertson nodded. "And to you, Senator."

When he was once more alone, Gabriel sat back down and looked out a tall window to the stately halls of government that surrounded him. Dear God, but he was tired of this place and its illusion of power. He was old now and found himself dreaming at night of retiring to Maryland, to his farm south of Rock Hall on the Chester River, fishing for dinner with his grandson, living out his time on this planet more simply. No more Washington. No more politicians. No more wars of wills or ideologies. A few more years and he could retire from office and remain only in an advisory position within the foundation. He'd served both as well as he could, but he had been truthful with Marcus. His energy was dwindling with each year.

That charming Italian had better be right when he'd insisted Magdalene O'Shea was qualified for this assignment. Too much depended on her being successful with McDonald. Remembering the angry look in Robertson's eyes, Senator Gabriel Burke prayed there was enough time to put into play a very intricate plan. He only knew his part of the puzzle, but it was a big enough piece to realize the foundation was preparing for a worldwide shift in consciousness and at this point it could go either way. Human beings would either wake up and take back their innate authority, or sublimate their fears with the illusions of safety. Sometimes he wished he didn't know what he did. It had been so much easier when he was sleepwalking, before he had awakened into his own life and saw how he had given away his greatest gifts for that illusory concept of safety. But there was no going back. You can't not know, anymore than it was possible to blow up a balloon, let the air out of it, and expect it to be the same size. It's altered. When you know, you know. Something beyond the conception of most humans was at work on the planet. And he was a part of it, playing out his role, adding his weight on the side of balance.

He could only pray Marcus was right about the O'Shea woman.

Maggie had driven to New York City, parked her car at Port Authority right out of the Lincoln Tunnel, rode down the elevator to the lobby, and walked outside to join the queue for a taxi. She'd given the driver the address on the Upper East Side and had stood across the street from Julian McDonald's apartment, a few blocks off Central Park. She hadn't heard from him and it had been five days since he'd left Philadelphia. Obviously, the man needed a bit more of a push in her direction. She had thought about how she could get into the apartment and then saw a window opened to receive the warm breeze in an early summer of mostly rain. Her eyes had searched the area for a vehicle, a way to get her inside. She'd spied how to accomplish that when she had looked up to the apartment building next door, to a fifth-floor window ledge.

Perfect.

All she'd needed was a few moments of privacy and then she had been flying, a glorious peregrine falcon in a city of pigeons. It took her almost a half hour to pull away the screening at the window, using a powerful beak that was not meant to tear tiny threads of metal. She squeezed her body through the opening and caught a wing on the sharp metal. That added another few minutes, freeing herself. Once inside, she sat on the windowsill and stared at the bathroom of green marble. The sinks were a high-gloss brass as were the fixtures. The crystal lights caught the rays of late afternoon sunlight and cast prisms around the beautiful room. She looked at the huge shower stall of green marble and saw eight strategically placed shower heads. McDonald was a man who liked his luxuries. She hopped off the windowsill and stood on the cold marble countertop. Not knowing who else might be in the apartment, she decided to remain as she was and explore by flight.

His bedroom was minimal, yet comfortable in shades of tan and white. She landed on a white down comforter and sank at least four inches. Struggling to get out, she finally thrust herself to the top of a rosewood armoire. No pictures sat on dressers or night tables. No papers or magazines out of place. It looked like an expensive hotel room.

Exiting the bedroom she flew down a hallway and found herself in his office. Landing on his desk, she was pleased to see at least here was a bit of clutter. The man wasn't a complete neat freak. It took less than a minute to find what she wanted. Placed facedown next to the telephone was her business card. So he had thought of calling. Good sign, but not good enough. She'd take that card and place it in his bedroom where it couldn't be missed.

Just as she was about to pick up the business card between her beak, a loud bark startled her so much that she dropped the card and screamed as she flew up to a bookcase. Her little heart was pounding so hard she thought it might just stop, in which case she would die. She tried to calm down as the big golden dog kept barking at her. She didn't know what to do. If anyone else was in the house, she'd be dodging towels and brooms and a very excited dog. He wasn't called a retriever for nothing!

Should she change into herself and try to calm him down?

Nothing was going to sedate this old hunter, so she decided to just go for the business card and pray she was faster than the dog. She swooped down to the desk, and held the card with her claw. Just as she was about to lift off the desk, she felt the wet mouth of the dog around her wings.

She was trapped.

The animal didn't bite down tightly and, listening to his growl, she knew she had only moments to make a decision. To fight for her life she might severely wound the old dog with her strong beak and razor sharp claws. Without hesitation, she gathered her energy and focused, expanding her awareness of Oneness, finding that center of balance, slowing her metabolism, reweaving the threads of molecules that made up the DNA of feathers into skin and fur.

Sorry, Max, she mentally apologized, taking over his body and watching as the falcon appeared before her, stunned, shaking off the transformation. She sat up and could feel the strain in the old dog's bones, how every movement in his hips was accompanied by pain. The falcon flew to the highest point, the bookcase, and Maggie wondered how she was going to free him. Maybe she shouldn't have used the falcon. Out on the street, it was just simpler and much quicker to have a host than shape shift without one. Now she had another animal to worry about. Well, she couldn't think about that now. Later, after she'd accomplished what she came here to do, she would concentrate on the bird.

It took some effort, but she was finally able to get the business card and place it on McDonald's night table. Right next to the phone. He wouldn't miss it. He would wonder how it got there and that would bring his thoughts back to her.

In the office, she sat on the rug and gazed up to the terrified falcon atop the mahogany bookcase. She tried to communicate with it, but the poor thing was too frightened to be open to receive. All it saw was a big dog. Having shape shifted twice in the last hour, she knew trying to get back into herself right now could prove dangerous. She could be too weak to even open a window for the bird. Might as well explore the rest of the apartment while she waited. The falcon wasn't going anywhere.

She wandered into the living room and saw that McDonald's taste was traditional yet elegant with some very good paintings

on the walls. It looked like the cover spread for an issue
of *Town and Country*, everything in understated good taste,
perfectly balanced and in its proper place. The kitchen was
a wide galley with black marble countertops and white cabinets on either side. She went over to the twin stainless-steel
bowls and drank some water while thinking the kitchen
looked like it had been a long time since someone actually
cooked a meal in the room.

It was then she heard a door opening.

"Max! Where are you, fella?"

McDonald was home.

She hadn't counted on this, but decided it just might prove
fortuitous. She headed back to the living room, hearing her
nails tapping out her entrance on the marble flooring.

"There you are," McDonald announced, throwing his
briefcase onto a hall table. "Give me a minute to change and
we'll be on our way."

She tagged along behind McDonald into his bedroom and
watched with interest as he began to undress. He took off his
shoes and placed them in his closet. He hung up his suit
jacket, threw his shirt into a laundry bin and folded his
trousers over a wooden hanger. The man liked to follow a
routine and neatness seemed to be a priority in his life.

She might be inhabiting the body of an old dog, but she
could still appreciate the fact that McDonald kept himself
in decent shape. And he was a boxer man. Baby blue ones.
She sat down and watched. He scratched the side of his
hip as he walked into the bathroom. She could hear him
relieving himself and her own bladder, or Max's, gave off
warning bells.

She whined.

"Okay, okay . . . I'm coming," he announced, walking out
of the bathroom and back to his closet. He took out a pair of
jeans and a light blue Polo shirt. Throwing the shirt onto the
bed, he pulled on the jeans. Maggie watched his every
move, waiting to see if he would notice the business card on
the bedside table.

He didn't.

Walking into the closet, he came back into the room wearing a pair of brown penny loafers. He picked up the shirt and pulled it over his head. "Okay, boy, let's head out. I have plans later."

She followed him from the room, into the hallway, then was startled when McDonald headed into his office. She stayed at the doorway and watched in dismay as Julian yelled out in fright as the falcon spread its large wingspan and screeched in terror.

"Jesus! How the hell did *that* get in here?" he demanded, half falling back against his desk.

Maggie automatically tilted her head to the side, wondering why people ask animals questions as though the animal could speak back to them. *Just open the window*, she kept thinking, hoping he could pick up her thoughts. She watched as Julian inched his way along the desk toward the window, all the while keeping his eyes on the falcon who was keeping its sharp glare completely on the man. It would have been comical, save for the possibility that the falcon might strike. She'd have to interfere and then Julian would see her shift and her assignment would be blown.

Not knowing what else to do, she kept sending out tranquil, calming thoughts to the falcon.

Julian slowly eased the window open, and then the screen. She could tell he was holding his breath as he walked backward out of the room, never taking his eyes off the bird. When he reached the door, he grabbed the handle and closed it so quickly she had to scramble out of his way.

McDonald stood in the hallway, his hand against the wall as he caught his breath. Glaring down to her, he muttered, "Great watch dog."

She merely blinked.

"C'mon," he said, jerking his head toward the living room. "If it's not gone by the time we get back, I'll call the police."

She followed him, wondering what he thought the police were going to do. Shoot it? The falcon would leave by the open window. It had to. He stopped at the hall table and picked up a red lead from the drawer. Attaching it to her collar, he opened the front door for her and she walked out.

"What a day," he murmured, running his fingers through his hair and then punching the elevator button.

She couldn't agree more, she thought, stepping into the elevator along with Julian. She looked up at him as they rode down to the street level. He appeared tired, strained, and she didn't think it was all due to nearly being attacked in his own home by an animal of prey. He carried the stress of his work home with him.

They walked out the building and turned right toward the park. Her legs immediately began to ache, especially her hips. Poor Max, she thought. He was an old soul . . . with arthritis. When she entered McDonald's life as herself, she would have to make sure something was done for the animal. They proceeded to the park and Maggie had to say she wasn't too pleased having a collar on her neck. It was a first for her, to be so constrained, and it made swallowing difficult when someone was yanking on the lead.

"C'mon, Max," Julian urged with a hint of impatience. "Let's get on with it."

She wanted to yell out her frustration to him that her hips were killing her and it wouldn't hurt to walk a little slower. Maybe at one time McDonald had used Max for daily exercise, but Max was no longer a frisky pup. Was he so preoccupied with business that he'd failed to notice his dog limping in pain?

When they got to the park, she thought she would squat down as soon as she approached grass, yet found herself compelled to sniff every few feet, as though reading a calling card from every other animal who had passed by the vicinity. A male dog. A squirrel. A female dog in heat. She seemed to spend a lot of time there, sniffing the essence of a primal urge to reproduce.

"Max!"

Annoyed to be yanked away—it wasn't like she could help it—she walked beside him and then stopped at a tree. How very odd. Without any thought on her own, her left leg automatically lifted in relief. She was embarrassed to be performing this act in front of McDonald and looked away, to the bike path and the skaters and joggers.

"Julian!"

She glanced over her shoulder to a woman walking a skinny little Pomeranian, with tufts of long reddish fur coming out of its ears and tail. Not an attractive sight, she thought.

"What a coincidence! I was going to call you later tonight," the woman gushed. She was tall and thin and looked like a pampered socialite. Her cashmere jogging suit seemed like it had been pressed and had never been soiled by a droplet of actual sweat. What woman wears cashmere, full makeup, and perfectly coiffed hair to exercise in the park? During the summer?

"Good to see you, Margot," Julian answered, pulling the lead closer to him.

Maggie stood next to McDonald and stared up at the woman, who actually appeared to be preening in front of him. "I was going to tell you about a dinner party I'm having next week. The Randolf-Cramers will be there, along with Sam Watersman from the Met with his wife. I'm thinking eight all together, just a small gathering, and I'd just love to have you join us."

"Well, thank you, Margot. I'll check my schedule and get back to you."

"It's next Wednesday . . . or if that's not convenient I can make it later in the week."

Sheesh . . . even she could see McDonald was uncomfortable being backed into a corner.

"I'll call before the weekend and let you know," he answered.

Maggie, who was trying to pay attention to the conversation, was distracted by the Pomeranian sniffing around her tail. Without thought, she snarled at it and it whimpered while backing up to its owner.

"Max!" McDonald scolded her, yanking again on the lead, as though in punishment. "He's not usually unfriendly," he apologized to Margot.

"Oh, that's all right," the woman muttered, scooping up her pet and cradling it in her arms. Though anyone could see she was not pleased as her precious pup started shaking.

For heaven's sake, it's not like she bit the overbred, little no-manners monster, Maggie thought indignantly. And she was really getting tired of being yanked around on the lead. How would McDonald like it if every time he didn't say or do exactly what she wanted, she jerked on his neck to pull him in line? Why do some people forget that animals have feelings too?

"I really did enjoy our evening together, Julian," Margot murmured, stroking the dog in her arms. "I was hoping we could do it again."

McDonald simply nodded and his smile was a bit strained.

Obviously, Maggie wasn't the only one to pick up on Julian's discomfort, for Margot couldn't let well enough alone and tried to fill the empty space with conversation. "I mean you were a delightful dinner companion and . . . well, afterward . . . I was hoping to hear from you."

"I've been very busy, Margot. With business. A lot of traveling . . ."

"Of course."

This was really awkward, Maggie thought. Was Margot one of the women he dated and then dropped? Men who had commitment phobias, like Julian, left a woman's self-esteem wounded and it was obvious Margot was one of them. To end the scenario, Maggie started to pull on the lead. She barked. Whined. Strained against McDonald's hold.

"I'd better get going," Julian said. "This old guy seems impatient tonight."

"You'll call and let me know?"

Maggie felt sorry for the woman. The last-minute plea sounded so desperate, she wondered if Margot had not been waiting for Julian in the park all along. McDonald's deep trauma when his family died had left him severely wounded. And his wounding attracted women whose own self-esteem issues were struggling to be healed. She always marveled that we seem to be attracted to the person who can mirror our problems for us, giving us the opportunity to work through them. *It's too bad*, she thought as they left the park, *that so many of us never even saw the opportunity*.

When they arrived back at the apartment, Maggie was grateful to be off the lead and followed McDonald as he walked down the hallway to his office. She stood in back of him as he hesitantly opened the door a few inches and looked inside. He stuck his head in and then opened the door all the way.

"Well, there's a break," he muttered.

The falcon was gone.

Watching him close the screen and then the window, she realized now she would have to remain as Max until Julian either went out or fell asleep. He rummaged around on his desk, found a feather and stared at in his fingers for a few seconds before tossing it into a pewter wastepaper bin. Now see, she would have saved it. How many times did a person find a magnificent peregrine falcon in one's home? Clearly, he wasn't the sentimental type. That was obvious by the lack of personal effects in the place. She followed as he went into his bedroom.

"How the hell did it get in here?" he muttered, staring at the windows.

She thought she could be a bit helpful and redeem Max in his master's eyes. She stood by the bathroom doorway and barked.

Julian looked at her. "What is it, Max?"

She barked again, then whined.

He walked up to her, turned on the crystal lights above the sinks, and looked around. "Well, I'll be damned."

She followed him into the bathroom as he walked up to the window and stared at the mangled screen. He shoved the screening back into place and closed the window. "Have to get that fixed," he said, patting her on the head. "Good boy, Max. Guess there wasn't much you could do, huh? Pretty scary though. Did you see that wing span? Those claws?"

Before she could think, she nodded.

Julian stopped stroking her head and stared.

"You didn't just answer me, did you?"

She shook her head and smiled, or at least dropped her jaw with pleasure.

Julian shook his head, as though not quite believing what he'd seen, and walked out of the bathroom. She followed. When it appeared that he was walking out of the bedroom, she stood next to the bed and barked again.

Standing at the doorway, Julian turned around. "What is it?"

She barked again.

He came up to the bed, stood next to her, and asked, "What's wrong, Max?"

Frustrated that the only means of communication was barking and whining, she whined. Julian looked around the bedroom and saw the down comforter was messed. He fixed it.

"Okay? The bird was in here?"

She moved closer to the night table and whined.

"I don't know what you want . . ." He saw the mangled business card and picked it up. Turning it around, he stared at it and then at her and then back to the card in his hand. "How did this get in here?"

She barked happily, now that he'd finally discovered it and she found herself dancing around in a circle of happiness. Even the pain in her hips didn't bother her as much.

"Maggie O'Shea," he murmured, reading her name. "You'd like her, Max."

This time she barked twice in approval and then did another little circle dance. Staring up at him, she barked again. "What do you *want*?" he demanded. "We went for our walk. You have food and . . ."

His words trailed off as she walked over to the phone on the night table and nudged it with her nose.

"And now you're freaking me out," he finished in a whisper.

Frustrated, she barked once more. She couldn't *be* more blatant! If she could dial a phone and hand it to him she would!

He sat on the bed and stared at her business card. "I don't know, Max . . . she's different." Sighing, he added, "There's something about her that makes me feel things I haven't even thought of in years. Scares me too. All that talk about nourishing the soul . . ."

She came closer and licked his hand, nudging him toward the phone.

"What is it with you? You're acting weird, boy." He rubbed her neck and she stuck her muzzle under his hand and pushed it again toward the night table. "If I didn't know better . . ." he didn't finish his thought. Instead he picked up the phone.

She barked in approval.

"Okay, shut up so I can hear," he ordered, dialing her number.

She sat patiently, watching him as his eyes widened with anticipation and then his shoulders slumped as her voice messaging came online.

"Hi, Maggie," he said, and she watched his Adam's apple bob in nervousness as he swallowed. "This is Julian McDonald. We met last week at the charity auction and you graciously allowed me to give my sister-in-law the watercolor. I believe we spoke of dance lessons, if I remember correctly. I . . . ah . . . I'm going to be back in Philly this weekend and was wondering if you'd like to meet for dinner on Friday or Saturday night. I'll leave my cell phone number and you can call me back, or I'll stop in at Soul Provisions and take you up on the great cup of coffee. Entirely up to you." He hesitated and Maggie could sense his awkwardness. "My number is area code six-four-six, five-five-five, seven-eight-two-one. Hope to hear from you."

She barked and again did her happy circle dance.

Julian laughed as he placed the phone back on the night table. "You are one strange animal today. What did that falcon do to you?"

She pranced out of the bedroom and headed back to the kitchen. Later tonight when he went out she'd shift back into herself, console poor Max, and then quietly leave the apartment. Her mission was accomplished. She would be seeing Julian in a few days, on her home turf.

So, he wanted to discuss dance lessons?

Well, let the music begin.

But right now, she was hungry.

FIVE

Julian walked into Soul Provisions at seven thirty on a busy Friday night and was impressed. Not only that Maggie had left a message on his voice mail saying she would welcome his opinion on her coffee Friday night, but that she also invited him to join her for dinner after the store closed. Added to that, for some strange reason, even though the store was crowded, he felt most of the tension in his body easing away.

There was something about the place, a feeling of calmness, of quiet welcome.

Listening to an overture from Bach, he inhaled the scents of the candles as he slowly walked through the store. He stared into the jewelry case and then looked at a young woman with red curly hair who was showing a silver necklace to a man. She shifted her gaze and simply smiled at him and he found himself smiling back. He passed the best-seller rack of books and noticed as he walked to the back of the store the subject headings ranging from health and philosophy to humor.

He read a hand-lettered sign: EVERYTHING WILL BE OKAY IN THE END. IF IT'S NOT OKAY, IT'S NOT THE END, and chuckled as the scent of coffee led him to the rear of the store. He had yet to see Maggie. He stopped in front of a blackboard and read the different offerings and his taste buds began salivating in response to looking at a glass-enclosed display of tempting sweets.

"Can I help you?"

He jerked his attention away from the goodies and said, "A cup of coffee, please. Black."

"Yes, sir," a middle-aged man answered. "For here, or to go?"

"Here." Julian watched as the man, dressed in jeans and a chambray shirt, picked up a white mug and poured out the coffee. His long dark hair was pulled into a ponytail and when he turned around, Julian noticed a tiny ear stud. He placed the coffee on the counter and then wrote out a tab on a small piece of paper.

Julian reached into his pocket and withdrew a five-dollar bill. He held it out.

The man handed him the coffee and said, "You pay at the register."

"Oh . . ." Stuffing the five back into his pocket, he took the coffee and the bill. "Thanks."

"You're welcome. Sure I can't interest you in something to go with that? Here," he said after a moment's hesitation, taking out two Milano cookies and placing them on a plate. "We're getting ready to close soon, and I have to clean out the case anyway. You'll save me a few seconds."

"Thank you," he answered, taking the plate while wondering if Maggie knew her staff was giving away inventory. And how did she know everyone who drank coffee in the store actually paid for it? There should be point-of-sale collection. Anyone could simply pocket the tab and walk right out.

He was the only one in the coffee area and he sat at a table, watching the customers lining up at the cash registers at the front of the store. He still hadn't seen Maggie. She did say Friday night, right? It was then he picked up the mug and took his first sip.

Damn, it *was* good coffee!

He couldn't suppress a smile as he read a sign tacked onto the side of a bookshelf. IF YOUR DREAMS TURN TO DUST, VAC-UUM. AND THEN BEGIN TO DREAM AGAIN. He had to admit he liked Maggie's store and so, it appeared, did the public.

She should branch out into other cities, even franchise or—

A shiny copper penny hit the table and he jerked his head up to see her smiling down at him. Looking just as pretty as he remembered, she took his breath away as she said, "For your thoughts. How's the coffee?"

He started to rise, but she waved off his politeness as she sat down opposite him. "You were right. It might just be the best damn coffee in the city."

She laughed, tilting her head back and exposing her neck. "I forgot my boast. Nothing like having your words thrown back at you. Fortunately, in this case, you seem to agree with me." Her smile softened. "How are you, Julian? How has the corporate world treated you in the last week?"

He settled back in his chair and returned her smile, trying to get his emotions under control as he watched her arms gracefully cross and lean on the edge of the table. "I and the corporate world are just fine, thank you. And how are you? You look wonderful, by the way."

Her smile turned into a grin. "Why, thank you, I'm doing well. It's good to see you again. I'm glad you received my message."

He didn't know how to answer that, except with the truth. "So am I."

She looked over her left shoulder. "So what do you think of Soul Provisions?"

Taking in her appearance of a long, flowing, pale buttery yellow skirt and a tissue-fine white cotton blouse, revealing a silky camisole underneath, he muttered, "I'm impressed." She looked remarkably fresh after putting in such a long working day.

She turned her head back to him. "Good," she said simply.

He noticed that her piercing blue eyes had a sparkle to them now, a friendliness that he found inviting. She wasn't flirting with him, or messing with his head as she had at the charity auction. There was nothing in her open expression that was intimidating or challenging. He suddenly felt awkward by the lapse in conversation and cast his gaze down to the table. Seeing his bill for the coffee, he cleared his throat and said, "Though I would make a comment about this area. A small bit of advice."

Her eyes widened and her smile increased. "You have my complete attention. I would never turn down advice from such a scion of business."

He wasn't sure if she'd just complimented him or was putting him in his place. Her smile was throwing off his instincts. He picked up the tab for the coffee. "Why don't you have customers pay for their coffee here, at the point of sale? Anyone could just walk out of the store without paying and you would never know."

Nodding, Maggie said, "I can see your point." She hesitated a few seconds and then continued, "Here's mine, Julian. I might never know. But that person would."

"Of course they'd know and, for most people, they wouldn't care."

"You really think most people don't have a conscience?"

"I think most people would try to get away with whatever they could. Anything else is naïveté."

Still staring at him, she sat back and folded her hands in her lap. He noticed that her blouse had tiny tucks stitched down the front and it fell open at her neck to reveal a threadlike golden wire with a small diamond hanging from it. Now that she was leaning back the wisps of auburn hair no longer framed her face and he could see diamond studs in her ears. Yet it was her eyes, once again intensely blue as they stared into his own, that had him fighting to keep his gaze steady. What was it about this woman that rattled his composure?

"I'm not naïve, Julian," she finally said in a low voice as she took his bill and crumpled it into a ball. "I realize some won't pay, but I know most will. If you haven't figured it out yet, let me enlighten you. The entire place is geared toward communicating with what is known as conscience. Sometimes it's heavy and deep, and grabs the bowels and shakes it into shedding old garbage. Sometimes it's light and airy and joyful, even downright funny. It's about balance, I guess. I lose some, but my profit margin allows it."

Wanting to bring this conversation back on track, he picked up the penny and rolled it between his fingers. "I stand corrected. I suppose I was seeing it strictly from a business point of view."

She startled him by laughing and standing up. "Of course you were. You *are* a businessman. A very successful one. But certainly that's not all that you are and success can be defined many ways, I suppose. Now, since you've sampled my coffee and you seem to like my store, I say we eat now. C'mon, I'm starving!"

He stood up and watched as she walked up to the coffee man. "Alan, I'm leaving now. There should be no problem closing. You know where I am if you need me."

"See you tomorrow, Mags. Gonna be a big Saturday with Father's Day on Sunday."

She nodded. "Right. Tina and Charlie are coming in early, so we'll be fully staffed. Thanks for closing for me tonight."

"No problem," Alan said, then looked at Julian. "You didn't eat your cookies."

For some weird reason Julian felt a twinge of guilt, so he grabbed one off his plate and bit into it. "Delicious," he muttered and then realized they were. Moist, buttery, sweet. He lifted the plate and brought it back to the counter to save the man work. Nodding to the other Milano, he added, "Don't want to spoil dinner, but they're very good."

"Students at the Culinary Arts Institute make them for us," Alan stated, lifting the plate and biting into the remaining cookie. "You should try them with ice cream," he mumbled through the crumbs in his mouth. "Heaven on earth."

"I bet," Julian answered with a laugh and then saw Maggie heading toward the front of the store. He followed. Watching her waving good-night to her staff, he wondered why she didn't get her purse. Not that she was paying for dinner, even though she had invited him. He had reservations at a very good restaurant, but most women wouldn't go out without carrying one. He also couldn't help staring at her back, the way that silky skirt was swaying with the movement of her hips. Having only seen her in a ball gown, he admired her ankles, the high wedged espadrilles with pale yellow silky fabric covering the front and back of her foot and matching ribbons crisscrossing up her legs. A sudden vision of him unlacing her shoes, of slowly lifting the hem of her skirt to touch her skin seemed to flood his brain and he actually shook his head, as though the movement might also shake out the image. He could already feel his juices stirring, that unmistakable rousing and whipping up of hormones urging him to do whatever was necessary to bring about submission.

He tried to think of anything safe, of leaving his office in the midst of a sudden wrinkle in an otherwise smooth acquisition proposal. He hadn't done that in years. Business came first, then pleasure. So why the change? he asked himself.

Because this one is different.

The answer came up to his consciousness with sudden clarity and it didn't sit well. He didn't want different. He wanted a safe, predictable encounter with no strings or heavy emotions attached. He wanted fun, the chase, the patient building up of attraction and the ultimate satisfaction of surrender. He wanted a playmate for a short while until the fun went out of the play. And it inevitably did. He then simply picked up his toys and went home . . . but not all his toys. He always left a trinket in his wake.

Thinking of his modus operandi now made him feel almost immature, so he struggled to push it too out of his mind. Why should he justify the way he lived his life? It worked for him. Noticing Maggie had been stopped by a customer in line at the cash register, he also stopped and looked at a display of candles, trying to appear disinterested. But really, he couldn't help overhearing the conversation between Maggie and the younger woman.

"I just wanted to thank you for recommending that book last week. I read it and loved it. You were right. No piece of jewelry would help heal a wounded heart." She showed Maggie the book in her hand. "I've come back to get the other book by the same author. Seems I have some work to do."

Julian was rattled a bit as he watched Maggie give the woman a hug.

"Good for you," Maggie answered. "When you're ready I just bet you'll find the perfect piece of jewelry for you, and who knows, it might mean something even more special."

What were the chances of him thinking about leaving trinkets for redundant lovers and this woman coming up to Maggie and repeating Maggie's words that no piece of jewelry heals a wounded heart? How bizarre. If he did become intimate with Maggie, he'd have to remember not to leave jewelry.

"Have a good night, everyone," she called out at the cash registers. She returned waves, adding, "I'll see you all tomorrow morning. Get some rest. It's going to be another long one."

Her staff seemed cheerful, even though they were still working at almost eight o'clock at night. He couldn't help but remark when they were outside, "You have a great place here, Maggie."

She looked into his eyes and they almost sparkled with good humor. "Why, thanks, Julian. Now, are you ready for dinner? I'm starving."

He laughed. How refreshing for a woman to state her hunger. Most of the women he'd dated treated food as a social commodity, to be ordered and then played with to get to the next step in the evening. "I'm hungry," he answered as she walked about ten feet and then stopped in front of a dark teal green door with urns of graceful trailing flowers on either side of it.

She took out a key from her skirt pocket and inserted it. "Good, because we're here."

"Here?" he asked, staring at the door and then at her. "Where's here?"

She grinned. "My home. I did invite you to dinner."

"Wait, Maggie, you've worked all day," he protested, touching her arm. "I've made dinner reservations."

She looked at his hand on her arm and then up into his eyes. "Cancel them, Julian. The very last thing I want after working all day is to sit in a chic restaurant. It is chic, isn't it?"

"I'd hoped so," he admitted. "It was recommended to me."

"Then that would account for the chic attire. You do look very *GQ*, by the way, in that beautifully fitted suit. C'mon . . ." She tilted her head toward the door as it opened. "Cut me a break tonight. I can't guarantee anything chic, but I can promise relaxation. I won't even mind if you take off your jacket and that handsome tie."

He followed her into a narrow hallway with black-and-white checked marble flooring. A hall table under a mirror was the only decoration. She dropped her key into a bowl on the table and nodded to the long flight of stairs ahead of them.

"It helps work up an appetite."

"Also a good cardio workout," he added, walking toward them. "This is unexpected. Not the stairs," he answered her quizzical expression. "Dinner in your home."

She shrugged as she began ascending the stairway. "Expect the unexpected is my motto. Maybe it's just me, but I've found that most of my expectations in life always seem to be blown away anyway."

He followed her. Again. He seemed to be doing that a lot around her. It was like the tables were turning and he wasn't sure how comfortable he was not being in the lead. "What were your expectations in life?" he asked. Good God, there had to be twenty steps. This probably helped her to have such sculpted calf muscles. Thinking about her legs was again turning him on and he had to—

She stopped suddenly and he almost tumbled onto her. Holding out her hand to his chest to steady him, she said, "That's more of an after-dinner question when the belly is full and the conversation turns deep, don't you think? Right now all I can reflect upon is an excellent bottle of chardonnay that's chilling in my fridge." She looked down to her hand on his chest and removed it. "Only a few more steps and then we're home."

He knew she had felt his heart hammering against his chest wall and hated that she might think it was because he was out of shape. Of course that could be better than her knowing his heart had immediately responded to her touch, jumping into second gear by the mere contact of her skin against him. He'd felt the heat of her hand through the material of his shirt and undershirt. He could almost feel it, that residue of electrical warmth, even though she was now walking up the last few stairs.

She turned around and waited for him to join her. "Welcome to my home, Julian."

He looked around him and swallowed deeply. He didn't know what to expect, not having entertained the idea of dinner in her home, but it wasn't this beautiful space of glass and light, tall plants and big cushioned furniture that was so inviting he wanted to sink into it. Watching her walk to a bookshelf and press a button, flooding the place with music, he entered the huge room. Toward the opposite end he saw the dining table had been set for two. For some reason, he felt a lump in his throat and it was totally unwarranted. He'd been in women's apartments. He'd had dinner cooked for him. He'd even been in better apartments. Lots of them.

Swallowing down the unwelcome emotion, he ran his hand over the back of one of the large chaise longues. "Very nice, Maggie. It suits you."

"Yes, it does," she said, sitting on the edge of the other longue and hiking up her skirt to her knees. She crossed her legs and began untying her right shoe. "It took me a while to get it the way I wanted," she added, pulling on the bow at her shin.

Yes. Legs. Her legs. He didn't realize until that moment how much he had wanted to see them. Every time he'd thought of her he had pictured her in that gown, legs well hidden. God almighty, he really was reverting to teenage fantasies again!

"There were lots of little rooms with hallways that reminded me of a rabbit's warren." She slid the ribbons apart and looked up at him. "I have a good friend who is an architect and he helped with the structural aspects so I could flood this place with as much light as possible. Plus," she said, sliding her foot out of the shoe. "I wanted open living, save for the bedroom that's behind that glass wall. It works for me."

Her toenails were painted apple red.

The effect of them seemed to travel straight from his eyes right down to his groin.

What the hell was happening? He was never into feet.

Legs, yes. Feet were functional.

Looking away as she began untying her other shoe, he walked over to the bookshelves surrounding a large painting of a red poppy flower. Needing to do something to take his mind off her legs and those red toenails, he read some titles. Fiction, mostly mysteries. Lots of biographies. A section of philosophy ranging from Aristotle, Thomas Aquinas, Descartes, Jung, and Kierkegaard, to Mother Theresa. His gaze rested upon an odd title. *Overview of the New Physics.*

Yes, Maggie O'Shea was certainly different from any other woman he had ever met, he thought, walking to the other side of the painting and seeing three shelves dedicated to books about animals. He looked around the apartment for signs of a pet, didn't find anything, and then saw that she was watching him.

She didn't say anything and he felt he had to fill in the silence. "Quite an interesting library."

"You think so?" she asked, standing and holding her shoes. The long yellow ribbons trailed onto the wooden floor. "You can tell me why in the kitchen." She walked away from him and, again, he followed. He watched as she stopped beside the glass wall that separated her bedroom from the rest of the apartment and threw her shoes onto the floor. Barefoot, she led him into her kitchen.

It was obvious this woman liked to cook.

He stood at the entrance to the room and admired the hominess of pots hanging from a brass rack, fresh herbs in decorative pots on the windowsill and some drying out, hanging by a cabinet. Flowers, the same white tulips that were in the living area and on the dining table, were also in this room, on the breakfast counter where woven-seated stools invited him to sit down. He did.

"I like your kitchen," he stated with a smile. "Sort of a combination of contemporary and French country."

Her smile widened as he loosened his tie. Might as well get comfortable, he thought, suddenly liking the fact they were going to have dinner here at her place.

"That's what I wanted," she announced, opening the refrigerator and taking out the chilled bottle of wine. Placing it before him, she then pulled on a drawer, removed a simple corkscrew, and handed it to him. "I love country French, but the rest of the place was too contemporary to not follow with the flow. I thought perhaps in here I could indulge myself a little."

"It works," he said, winding the corkscrew into the top of the bottle.

"Thanks," she answered while picking up a white apron and lifting the top over her head. She let it hang down in front of her, not bothering to tie the back.

Julian continued to watch her take dishes out of the refrigerator that she'd obviously prepared earlier. She was quite a sight . . . barefoot, in the kitchen, as though they had known each other for months instead of one week. And only one meeting at that. "Glasses?" he asked.

Peeling plastic wrap from a large glass dish, she answered, "Cabinet over the dishwasher." Then she looked back at him. "Do you mind?"

Grateful for something to do, he slid off the stool and walked around the counter into her kitchen. "Not at all. I'm still feeling somewhat guilty about this. You must be tired," he said, opening the cabinet and taking out two crystal wineglasses.

She stopped examining what appeared to be salmon and looked at him. "Didn't you also work today?"

"Yes."

"Didn't you drive an hour and a half to get here? That is if you missed rush-hour traffic?"

"An hour and forty-five minutes, and I missed most of it."

She grinned. "Then take off your jacket, Julian, and relax. Dinner will be ready in twenty-five minutes."

He liked her answer and put the glasses next to the bottle of wine. Taking off his jacket, he slipped it over the back of the stool and then pulled the knot of his tie down even farther to undo the first three buttons of his shirt. He started smiling and then his lower jaw dropped slightly of its own accord as he watched Maggie bend over to place dishes into the oven.

Again those hormones began to stir.

She had a nice ass, real nice. Rounded, like the rest of her. He could imagine the soft curve of her thighs, the fullness of her breasts . . .

Suddenly she turned to him and he felt as though he'd been caught with a dirty magazine.

"What were you just thinking?"

"What?" He could actually feel his cheeks heating up. He simply had to get himself and his thoughts under control. He was a grown man, not some adolescent.

"I just felt something," she murmured, running her toes backward over the terra cotta tile flooring. "Like a rush of energy sweeping over me and . . . " She shook her head. "Never mind. It was silly."

"Actually . . ." He cleared his throat as she opened the refrigerator. "I was just thinking that we know very little about each other. We met under unusual circumstances, and only briefly, and yet here I am back in Philadelphia. I didn't expect this."

She placed a plate on the counter containing chilled chunks of thick white lobster meat and pink prawns surrounding a bowl of red sauce. "Actually . . .," she cleared her throat in a good imitation of him, "I do know more a than little about you."

Surprised, he asked, "You do?"

She laughed as she picked up the plate and nodded to the wine and glasses. "Don't look so surprised. You're on the Internet. Let's both get off our feet and relax and I'll tell you what I know."

Picking up the wine and glasses he followed her to the large white sofa. He placed them down on the square coffee table by her plate of appetizers and then poured them each a glass as she opened a drawer in the table and took out square white serviettes. She sat in the corner, pulling her legs up under her skirt. He handed her a wineglass and sat down, putting a good three feet between himself and her toes peeking out under the silk material.

She raised her glass. "To friendship," she stated.

He saluted her with his wineglass and repeated, "Friendship."

They enjoyed their wine in silence, until Maggie sighed and turned to face him, her arms wrapped around her knees. The comfortable down-filled sofa seemed to cradle her in the corner.

"You're allowed to relax now," she murmured. "You can even kick off your shoes, if you'd like." Her smile was soft and inviting. "There's no pressure here, Julian, and my only formal rule is no shoes on the white furniture."

He didn't realize how tense he was holding his body until she pointed it out and, considering her bare feet and informal attitude, he did seem overdressed. Still, he felt uncomfortable taking off his shoes. The jacket and tie were okay, but how much more disrobing was required before dinner? Usually, he would be all for it, but here, in her home, seeing how open she was, he felt like an inexperienced schoolboy. "Nice music," he commented. It was soft, soothing, yet slightly primal and sexy.

"It's called 'Still Life with Lions' by Tim Storey. He lived in Philly before moving to Ohio."

"Did you know him?"

"Yes. I knew him. Good man."

For some odd reason he felt a twinge of jealousy. Not only that she knew this talented musician, but that she described him as a *good man*. Somehow those words she had whispered to him the night of the charity auction had haunted him. He realized he wanted her to think of him as such. Maybe she said that to every man she met. What did he know? He actually knew very little about this unusual woman who sat across from him.

"Oh, go ahead," she said with a chuckle, nodding to his shoes. "You know you want to. Just relax, will you? I'm not going to attack you or laugh at your feet, or whatever you're worried about."

"I'm not worried about anything," he protested, maybe a little too strongly. Shaking his head, he bent over and untied a shoe. "I'm only doing this because you seem to be insisting." When his shoes were off he lifted one leg and sat sideways, facing her. "Happier?"

She grinned. "Absolutely. And you?"

"Ecstatic." Wiggling his toes inside his socks, he muttered, "Happy feet."

"Oh wait . . . I forgot something!" She jumped up from the sofa and hurried back in the direction of the kitchen.

Just when he was beginning to relax, she'd startled him by bolting from the room. She certainly kept throwing him off balance. He heard her opening cabinets and when she returned she placed a tray on the sofa. Taking the dish of lobster and prawns off the coffee table, she put it on the tray and then sat back in her corner. Looking down, he saw she had added small plates for the appetizers and extra napkins.

"Now we can dig into this in comfort," she said, picking up a prawn by the tail and dipping it into the sauce. She placed it on a plate with a chunk of lobster meat that appeared glazed with a buttery substance and handed it to him. She laid a napkin on his knee and then she served herself. "Been thinking about this all afternoon," she said. Placing the lobster in her mouth, she closed her eyes as she savored the taste.

He couldn't help smiling at her pleasure.

"Go ahead," she encouraged. "You must be hungry too."

Since he'd skipped lunch in favor of extending a meeting, Julian picked up a prawn and eagerly devoured it. "Delicious."

Maggie settled back with her wine and sighed again, this time with satisfaction. "So I was going to tell you what I know about you . . . from the Internet."

"Right." Finally relaxing, he leaned his shoulder against

the sofa and tasted the lobster meat while waiting to hear what she'd discovered.

"Well, I already knew the obvious. You're a very successful businessman. You're self-made. Neither noblesse oblige nor nepotism helped you along the way. You went to Yale and then Wharton here in Philly. Where did you live in Philly when you were at Wharton?"

"Ninth and Pine. Right near Wills Eye Hospital."

She grinned. "There's something I didn't know. Okay, you started at Kholmann Brothers and worked your way into being the youngest vice president in the company's history and then you went out on your own in the late eighties, investing in troubled companies and building them up to sell at a profit. Your main company, the one you still hold on to, is your baby, ICBE, Institute for Collective Business Explorations. You're also a philanthropist, giving money to charities and organizations that, to quote a cliché, don't give man a fish, but teach man to fish. Like the computer program you put together for urban schools."

He couldn't help chuckling. "That's pretty good. I should check out myself on the Internet."

"That's not all," she stated, picking up another prawn and biting into it.

"There's more?"

She nodded as she swallowed. "Oh yeah. You have a boat that you keep in Bermuda where you own a house overlooking the sea."

"You got that from the Internet?"

"Don't worry. There weren't any pictures."

"And you did this research . . . ?"

"To find out about you. I don't invite just any man into my home and cook him dinner, you know. Have to be careful these days."

Grinning, he nodded.

"Lots of weirdos out there, Julian. Had to be sure about you."

"So I've passed the weirdo test?"

"You've passed the he's-not-a-serial-killer test. You still

might be weird. In fact, I'm coming to believe there's a bit of the weird in all of us."

He laughed. "You're admitting you're a bit weird?"

Her giggle was endearing. "Oh yes, Julian. I'm definitely a bit weird, but I'm harmless."

"Okay, now it's my turn," he said, liking the way her eyes crinkled when she giggled. "So I know you're a bit weird and you like art which, by the way, that watercolor would have looked great here . . ."

"It went to a better home," she interrupted, saluting him with her wineglass.

"And you own a successful business, offering provisions for the body and soul. I won't talk to you yet about expanding and opening in other cities."

Her shoulders sagged. "Sometimes I can barely handle this one. I'm not greedy."

"We'll talk about that another time, not tonight," he said, grabbing another hunk of moist lobster. "I know you like good clothes, good furnishings, good music, good food, and I think you like to dance." He popped the meat into his mouth and resisted licking his fingers.

Her eyes lit with delight. "I *love* to dance!"

It took him a few seconds to chew and swallow. "Are we talking about real dancing here, or mental dance lessons? I believe I was promised those."

"You don't forget much, do you, McDonald?"

He smiled. "Not much." He seemed to be smiling a lot since he'd arrived.

"Well, you're right about all of it. I also love picnics, swimming, flea markets, sky diving, though I only did it once. I love rainy Sundays in the fall when I can curl up with a good book and—"

"Wait a minute," he interrupted. "Sky diving? Are you serious?"

She nodded.

"I think you're tilting the weird meter over the line there. What kind of person jumps out of a perfectly good plane?"

Before she could answer, a buzzer sounded in the kitchen.

Maggie gracefully slid her legs off the sofa and stood up. "I'll tell you during dinner, but how would you like to help me get said dinner onto the table?"

"Sure," he answered, standing and bringing his wine along with him as they went back into the kitchen. "What can I do?"

She opened the refrigerator and brought out two plates of artfully arranged baby spinach, watercress, grape tomatoes, and curls of cheese. "You can put these on the table and light the candles. There're matches out there."

"That I can do," he answered, taking the plates from her and then heading toward the dining table. He placed them on the big white embossed ceramic chargers at each place setting and then noticed how carefully she had set her table with crystal and sterling silverware. He picked up the small box of wooden matches off the white linen tablecloth that matched the rolled napkins she'd tied together with a pale green ribbon. He struck a match and set about lighting the many candles. Long white ones, over two feet in length, sat in tall silver candle holders on either side of the bowl of white tulips, cut short and kept in place with glass pebbles to maintain a clear view between them. Tiny circles of candles, no more than an inch in height, were in crystal containers and scattered around the table. Being a man who appreciated details, he could tell that the seemingly casual arrangement had been carefully placed for effect.

He glanced at her in the kitchen, busy pulling together their dinner, and couldn't remember the last time he'd been this relaxed in someone's home. Even his own apartment in New York didn't seem as inviting as this one. If he wasn't socially engaged, he usually ordered out or went to the restaurant on his block where the owners knew him and always had the same table ready for him. But this . . . this was a home. A beautiful, serene place that invited intimacy, safety. A sanctuary.

He had the sudden desire to show Maggie his place in Bermuda. She'd like it.

"I hope you're hungry," she called out, expertly drizzling

some kind of sauce over the plate in front of her. She then caught a drip from the ladle with her index finger and stuck it in her mouth, slowly pulling her finger out as she savored the taste.

Immediately, his body seemed infused with such an intense charge of sexual energy that his soldiers went on red alert as he felt himself becoming aroused.

She turned her head. "You are hungry, aren't you?"

He had to swallow down his desire. "Very," he answered. And it was the truth.

SIX

"**O**kay, so you jumped out of a plane for the experience. Your favorite city in the world is Prague, not Paris, and you own no pets. By the way, this is delicious," he added, picking up a forkful of nectarines, strawberries, and blueberries in a Grand Marnier sauce with whipped cream over a delicate sponge cake.

Maggie was very pleased by the way this dinner was progressing and also by the way Julian seemed to notice every little detail about it. "I have to be honest. I didn't make the cake, but I did pull together the fruit and that's homemade, hand-whipped cream I'll have you know."

"Again, I'm impressed," he said, digging into the dessert. "I thought the salmon and Gruyère potatoes were exceptional, but this . . . it's excellent. Where did you learn to cook?"

She grinned. "Trial and error over the years. More errors than I'd like to admit, I'm afraid." Sipping her wine, she looked at him enjoying her efforts. Now that dusk had passed, the only lighting was from the candles and she had to concede Julian McDonald was one attractive man. She liked this version of him better, without the perfectly tailored jacket and expensive tie. He'd rolled his sleeves up when he'd helped her bring the food to the table and had filled their water and wineglasses. He seemed much more relaxed, happier, less guarded.

And he was definitely attracted to her. She'd felt it in the store when she'd met him and it had only increased during the evening. She knew if she made the right moves he wouldn't object to being led into her bedroom, but she also knew she'd have to proceed very slowly and carefully with him. He might want her tonight, but this was a man who enjoyed the chase, the challenge, the ultimate victory of surrender. When she did surrender it would be on her terms, not his. Besides, she was enjoying his company and she couldn't help wondering if he had any female friends. Not business associates. Not lovers. Not family. Just friends. Probably not.

He placed his fork on his plate and sat back in his chair. Rubbing his stomach, he said, "Thank you, Maggie, for a wonderful meal. I can't remember the last time I ate so much."

"I'm glad you enjoyed it."

"Now tell me the truth . . . when did you have the time to prepare all this?"

She laughed. "Ah, so you don't believe I'm superwoman?"

"Not for a moment," he answered with a grin.

"Okay, the truth . . . my claims of being starved were because I worked through my lunch hour and at sixthirty came up here to throw this meal together. But, c'mon, you have to admit I did a pretty good job of making it appear effortless, right?"

"Was that to impress me?"

She hesitated. "Yes, Julian, it was."

Now it was he who hesitated. His face looked so serious. Finally he said in a low voice, "Thank you for all your efforts. You were right. I enjoyed it far more than dinner in a restaurant. Next time it's my turn to impress you."

"Are we agreeing to a next time?"

"I hope so."

She smiled. "So do I. Now, would you like your coffee and brandy here, or back at the sofa?"

"First," he said, rising from his chair, "I am going to clear the table and do the dishes."

She sat back and watched as he picked up his empty dessert plate and then reached for hers. "You are?" she asked with surprise.

"You don't think I know how to do dishes?" He tried to appear insulted.

"I would think you did your share when you lived at Ninth and Pine. I just don't imagine you've done many since then."

"I have a good memory. And, besides, you have a dishwasher. Didn't have that at Ninth and Pine, so this should be a breeze," he said, walking into the kitchen.

Taking her glass of wine with her, she rose from the table and followed him. She perched on a stool at the counter and said, "This I have to see."

He found the light over the sink and began scraping the dishes. She watched as he carefully stacked everything in her dishwasher . . . the dinner plates, salad plates, bread plates . . . everything placed according to size. She forgot he was a neat freak. Fortunately, there were no pots or pans so within a few minutes he had completed his job.

"There," he declared in triumph, wiping his hands on a dishtowel. "Done."

"Not bad, Jules," she answered, lifting her wineglass in tribute. "Very efficient."

His jaw seemed to drop slightly as he stared at her.

"Something wrong? Don't like nicknames?"

He shook his head. "I just haven't heard that one in a long time."

She knew immediately his wife had called him that. "Sorry, didn't mean to upset you."

"You didn't," he said, folding the towel and placing it on the counter. "Now, what about that coffee and brandy?"

She pointed to the double coffeemaker. "Regular and decaf. Too late for real coffee for me. Unlike some people, I work a six-day week."

He checked his watch. "It is late, Maggie. Maybe I should leave so you can get to sleep. I heard you telling your staff tomorrow is going to be a long day."

She slid off the stool and came into the kitchen. "That's very sweet of you, Julian, but I insist that we end the evening after coffee and brandy. Can't offer you a cigar, though. Do you smoke cigars?"

"Can't stand the smell of them," he answered, leaning against the counter as she filled the coffee cups with decaf.

"The brandy is in the other room," she murmured, picking up the cups and leading him out of the kitchen. "Would you bring one of the tall candles from the dining table? And the brandy is over there on the table between the windows."

She settled herself on the sofa and watched as he placed the candle on the coffee table and then went to where she'd directed him. He picked up her decanter and poured them both a glass. "Thank you," she said, taking her brandy.

Her gaze followed him as he sat down at the opposite end of the sofa and turned sideways to face her again.

"So is now the time you tell me about your life expectations, or is it too late for deep conversation? Because my belly is certainly full . . ."

She grinned. "Are you going to hand all my words back to me?"

"Probably," he answered, then sipped his brandy. "Sign of a good communicator."

"Well, I can give you the condensed version or perhaps we can postpone that communication until another time." She had hoped he'd forgotten all about her blown expectations.

"I choose the condensed version . . . for now."

"Okay." She took another sip of brandy and tilted her head back to rest against a pillow. "I'm thirty-four, and I suppose one of my expectations was that I'd be more settled. That I'd be farther along the path to being a grownup. Marriage. White picket fence. Children. All those things I'd been programmed to expect in life. Instead I find myself single, independent, a businesswoman. And I like it. I like my life."

"You don't want the picket fence and the children?"

She straightened her head and stared at him in the candlelight. "The truth is if it came along I'd welcome it into my life. Though it would have to be extraordinary, the person *and* the fence, but I don't expect it anymore. I'm happy right here, right now. That's all that's real anyway. This very moment.

Neither one of us knows if we'll wake up in the morning. This," she waved her arm out to the room, "life, all of it, could be gone in a split second. There are no guarantees."

He nodded. "September eleventh taught us that."

"Right, *carpe diem*. I think we did that tonight. Thanks for accepting my invitation, Julian. I had a very good time."

"So did I," he admitted with a slight smile. "So we're going to do this again?"

She smiled back at him and nodded. "I'd like that. What are you doing tomorrow evening? You're not driving back to New York tonight, are you?"

"No. I'm having lunch with Emma and my nieces tomorrow." He put his brandy glass on the table and waved away a moth that fluttered its wings near the candle flame. "You won't be too tired tomorrow night?"

"I'll be fine."

"No chic restaurants, I promise. What time do you close?"

"Usually we close at five on Saturdays, but because of Father's Day on Sunday we're staying open until six. I should be ready by seven, if that's not too late."

"Not for me. I'll pick you up at seven and then it's my turn to pamper you."

"I can hardly wait," she answered, and found that she meant it.

"Now, it's time for you to get some rest," he declared, putting his shoes back on. "Never let it be said I stood in the way of profit."

"You're a very considerate businessman and an excellent dinner guest. Thanks for all your help tonight. I was impressed by the way you stacked those dishes."

He rose and held out his hand to her. Pulling her to her feet, he looked down and stared into her eyes. "And you're quite a woman, Maggie O'Shea," he whispered, as his fingers cupped her face.

He was going to kiss her. She hadn't planned on this yet and—

Thoughts ceased as he lowered his head and planted a light kiss right between her eyebrows. It was a mere brush of lips against skin, yet its effect was electrifying. "I'm going to thank Emma tomorrow for choosing that painting," he murmured against her skin. "I might never have met you if both of you didn't have the same taste in watercolors."

She looked up into his eyes. "Thank her for me, too. I'm glad I met you that night. Even if you did take that painting away from me."

He pulled away playfully. "Hey, you were the one who gave it to me. You had the advantage and could have out-bid me."

She patted his arm as she walked away. "You play to win. I gave it to you so you wouldn't sulk at being beaten. Nothing worse than a sulking man in a tuxedo." She brought his jacket from the kitchen and held it out to him.

Turning around, he slipped his arms into it and said, "Just so you know, I never sulk. I get even."

"Good to know," she replied, leading him to the stairs. "I won't walk you down, if you don't mind. The door locks automatically."

He adjusted his jacket and shook his head. "You are tired, aren't you, Maggie?"

"I am," she admitted, holding out her arms.

He slid his arm around her waist and brought her close to his chest. She avoided his face and kissed his jaw line, right below his ear. "Drive carefully. And have fun tomorrow with your nieces and sister-in-law."

He squeezed her slightly when she pulled away. "Good night, Maggie. Sleep well."

She winked. "I rarely have trouble sleeping."

She knew he would be awake for hours. And it wouldn't be because he suffered from occasional insomnia. Not entirely. She watched him descend the stairs and when he opened the door, he looked back up at her.

"Good night. Tomorrow at seven."

She waved. "I'll be ready."

When the door closed and the locking mechanism clicked into place, she turned back to the room. "Okay, Marcus, show yourself," she commanded. "Now!"

The moth flew up from the coffee table and hovered in the air for a few moments until the molecules surrounding it began to intensify and form. It was like looking at a stack of pictures that was quickly flipping, showing a moth altering and expanding into a human being. In less than ten seconds, Marcus Bocelli stood before her.

"How did you know it was me? You did leave the windows open."

"Never mind how I knew. How dare you spy on me?" she demanded, hands on her hips to keep from slapping him. She had felt his unique energy the moment he'd entered her living space. "You've never done this before! How *could* you?"

"You're angry, *cara mia*," he began. "And I was—"

She wouldn't allow him to continue and waved her hand to stop him. "Drop the *cara mia* crap, Marcus, because I'm beyond angry. I'm *furious!*"

Dressed in black slacks and shirt, he held up his hands in a placating manner. "Do calm down, Magdalene. I was not spying on you, as you claim. I was . . . simply checking on you."

"*Checking* on me? I don't believe this!" Shaking with indignation, she marched over to her bookshelf and stabbed the CD player into silence. "How *dare* you check up on me like I'm some novice who needs your help?"

"You must listen to me, Magdalene," he pleaded, running his fingers through his dark hair. "This assignment is the most important one you've ever had. I have put my reputation on the line with the foundation in recommending you for it. I have more than a passing interest in how it is progressing."

She spun around to face him. "As you observed, it *is* progressing. What is the big deal with McDonald? So he's rich. Aside from that, he seems remarkably similar to most of my assignments. He's a man with unhealed traumas buried so deep it's going to take a metaphysical excavation to bring it to the surface."

"This one is different, that's all I can tell you. For whatever reason the foundation has put a high priority on it. I was called onto the carpet, as you Americans say, and had to report on your progress."

"What the hell is going on, Marcus?" she demanded, sitting on the edge of a lounge chair. "If you or this mysterious foundation don't trust me, then we can stop it right now. Give the assignment to someone else. I'd be thrilled to be done with all of you."

"I saw the way McDonald was looking at you, *cara mia*. It has already begun in a most favorable fashion. Your approach to him is excellent, and that is what I shall report. You are seeing him again tomorrow night. The ball, so to speak, will be in his court and his actions will tell you how quickly you can proceed."

Her body was immediately infused with indignation and she had to force herself to rise slowly, instead of jumping to her feet. "Do you think I need instructions from *you*? I'm not some naïve young girl any longer who looks up to you with adoring eyes, Marcus. Get it through your head I am not your student. I know what I'm doing, and I like McDonald. I *like* him as a human being. Even if he wasn't my assignment, I would want him to open his heart again, to live his life with the possibility of some real joy in it. I certainly don't need you to tell me what I should be doing."

Marcus nodded slowly. "I understand your anger, Magdalene. I have never done this before and it appears to you that I do not trust your instincts or abilities. Perhaps I was overzealous because of the pressure I feel from my superior."

"Well, you can go back and tell your superior that I do not need that kind of pressure put on me or this assignment *will* fail, because I will not tolerate spying or mistrust or the questioning of my abilities." The anger had taken the last reserves of her energy. She took a deep breath and pointed to the window. "Now leave the way you came in. I have work tomorrow."

Appearing chastised, Marcus shook his head. "I apologize if I have offended you. That was never my intention. You know I have the highest respect for you and—"

"Just go," Maggie interrupted in a tired voice. "And don't ever do it again. I mean it, Marcus. Not ever again. Neither you, nor this foundation owns me. Tell them that. Tell them they either trust me or they don't."

He began his transformation back into the moth by saying, "Sleep well, *cara mia*. I am sorry I have upset you."

When he flew out the window, she slammed it shut.

And locked it.

What absolute arrogance! Marcus Bocelli could take himself and his insufferable condescension straight into the nearest electrical light and fry himself into oblivion!

It had been the kind of day that had started off well and then went downhill. She'd arrived at the store feeling optimistic. The sun was shining and the streets were already beginning to fill with early shoppers. Alan had coffee waiting for her and when they opened their doors the customers began streaming in within minutes. Then she found Kelly in the back room, doubled over in a chair with cramps. She'd sent her home. Two hours later Mark fell off a stool, twisting his ankle, and she'd taken him to the emergency room for X-rays before depositing him at his girlfriend's apartment. By the time she returned to the store, she was exhausted and yet had to face another six hours shorthanded. She took over restocking what was left of the Father's Day cards, filling in for Tina and Charlie so they could finally take their delayed lunch breaks. Finally, she used up the last of her diplomatic energies trying to reason with a man who insisted the candles he had bought for his wife's anniversary present had triggered such a formidable allergic reaction that he wanted to sue her and the manufacturer for his wife's alienation of affections. She'd fought the urge to tell him that it wasn't the candles that was alienating his wife, that it would help if he trimmed his nose hair or didn't wear brown socks with shorts and sandals and a T-shirt that stated A HARD MAN IS GOOD TO FIND. Instead, though there had never been such a claim before, she refunded him the money for the naturally scented candles and told him to give his wife her apologies.

The day didn't end soon enough for her to rush upstairs, take a hurried shave-legs-armpits-etc. shower, blow out her hair, apply enough makeup to look fresh and dewy instead of agitated and sweaty, and then slip into a black-and-white dotted sundress. No sooner had she picked up a pair of strappy high-heeled sandals when the doorbell rang. She grabbed a black shawl and her black straw purse and nearly ran out of the bedroom.

Rushing down the stairs, she stopped at the hall mirror, blew out her breath and fluffed out her hair, then she straightened her shoulders before opening the door.

"Hi," she breathed, not trying to be sexy. It seemed she had been running ten hours straight to get to this moment.

"Hi," Julian said with big smile. Dressed in tan slacks, a cream-colored shirt, opened at the neck, and a navy blue blazer, he looked relaxed and quite handsome. "Ready for some pampering?"

"Oh, Julian, you have no idea how appealing pampering would be tonight. But first let me put on my shoes." She handed him her purse and her shawl.

He held the door open as she walked back to the stairs and sat down.

"You really don't like to wear shoes very much, do you?" he asked.

She looked up and saw he was grinning. "If you were on your feet every day as long as I am, you wouldn't either." Holding out a leg to show off the sexy Moschino sandal, she grinned. "See what I'm willing to do for friendship?"

"Hmm, well maybe you won't have to wear them all night."

Finished, she straightened her dress and walked back up to him. "Now, that's intriguing. Where are we going? You promised no upscale restaurants, remember?"

"My lips are sealed until we arrive," he said, holding the door open wider to allow her to pass through to the street. He waved his hand to the left. "This way, madam."

Grinning, she slipped her arm through his. "I love surprises."

"Good," he answered, looking almost mischievous as he led her down the street.

"You're enjoying this, aren't you?"

"Immensely."

"And you won't even give me a hint?"

"And ruin the surprise? No way."

She liked this playful side to him. "Okay, then tell me about your lunch with Emma and your nieces."

"The lunch was delicious and my nieces seem to have been taken over by preteens who cannot stop giggling and tagging everything they like with the ridiculous term of bling-bling, whatever the hell that means."

Maggie laughed. "It's a good thing, as Martha used to say."

He turned his head. "You've heard of this?"

"I'm not *that* old, Julian," she protested.

"Are you hinting I am?"

"You're not old," she told him with a soft elbow jab into his side. "You're just not into hip-hop."

"And *you* are?" he asked in disbelief.

"Some of it. The poetry can be exceptional. You should listen sometime."

"Another time," he answered, stopping at a dark blue Lexus convertible. "Right now you can get off your feet," he added, walking her to the passenger side.

"Nice car," she murmured, sliding onto the leather seat, glad the top wasn't down for the sun was still brightly shining. The last thing she needed was a scorched bottom from sun-baked seats.

He walked around the car and got into the driver's seat. "Do you have a license to drive?"

"You want me to drive?" she asked, wondering why he had just deposited her into the passenger seat.

"No, I just wanted to know if you have a driver's license on you."

"In my purse. Are you planning on getting loaded and looking for a designated driver?" How very odd.

He chuckled. "Not exactly. Just always better to be prepared for any eventuality." Leaning across her, he opened the glove compartment and took out a white Hermès silk scarf. "This is Emma's," he said, handing it to her. "When I told her my plans, she insisted I keep it for you to borrow."

He started the car, pushed a button, and the top slid away. Then he put on his sunglasses.

Grateful for Emma's thoughtfulness, Maggie wrapped the scarf around her head, tied it at the back of her neck, and put on her sunglasses. "Bless Emma's heart," she said as the car pulled out of the parking space and joined the early-evening traffic.

Once they were on I-95 heading south, speeding along with the rest of the traffic at seventy miles an hour, they really couldn't talk because of the wind. She settled back and closed her eyes, listening to classical music and letting the world pass by. Wherever they were going, it wasn't in Center City and she was glad. Maybe he was told of an intimate Italian restaurant in South Philly. But as they passed the South Philadelphia exits she began wondering if he was taking her to Delaware.

"Where are we going?" she nearly yelled as they crossed the Pratt Memorial Bridge.

"Not too far now," he yelled back.

He had that mischievous grin again and she had to admit that with the wind blowing his hair back, he looked much younger and much happier than when she'd seen him waiting for her in Soul Provisions the previous night. It was obvious he, too, liked surprises, especially if he was springing them on others.

They came off the bridge and Julian got in the far right-hand lane. He left the traffic on the interstate and Maggie's jaw dropped when she saw him taking the exit for the airport. "What are you doing?" she demanded, trying to figure out his plans.

He held his hand up. "Few more minutes. You'll soon see."

She sat back and watched him turn into General Aviation. "Julian, really . . . what are you doing?"

He parked the car and she stared at him in disbelief.

Turning off the engine, he said, "There's Bill."

"Bill *who?*"

He laughed. "Bill Myers. He works for me. C'mon. I'll introduce you."

She got out of the car and wrapped her shawl around her more tightly, not that it was windy or cool any longer, but almost for added protection against whatever wacky plan Julian was hatching.

"Good to see you, Bill," Julian said, shaking the man's hand. "This is Maggie O'Shea. Maggie, meet Bill Myers, who tries to keep my life running smoothly despite my sometimes quirky impulses."

She shook hands with the man. "Nice to meet you, Bill."

"A pleasure, Miss O'Shea." He turned to Julian and held out his hand. "Everything's prepared. I'll drive the Lexus back to the city tonight. Max is spending the rest of the weekend with me and Allie."

She watched as Julian handed over the keys to the Lexus and then patted the man's shoulder. "Thanks for everything, Bill. The traffic shouldn't be too bad this early in the evening."

Bill nodded. "Enjoy yourselves." He got into the car, turned over the ignition, then waved to Maggie and Julian before backing the Lexus out of the parking space.

"C'mon, Maggie. The plane is waiting."

Watching the Lexus takeoff, she took off her sunglasses and turned to stare at Julian. "What the hell are you talking about? What plane? Ready for what? Where are we going?"

He put his arm around her shoulders and steered her toward the glass door of the building. "Now that I can't tell you until we arrive. It's my plane. A Gulfstream. I had it flown in for us and we have a seven forty-five takeoff scheduled so we have to hurry. Listen, it's a short flight. A little over an hour. And I promise you can relax."

"Julian McDonald, I cannot just get on your jet and take off without any idea of where I'm going."

He stopped and put his sunglasses on the top of his head as he stared at her. "You could jump out of plane for the experience, but you won't sit in one for an hour without having every single detail? What happened to *carpe diem?*"

That stopped her. "I'm going to have to be very careful what I say to you, aren't I?"

Grinning broadly, he nodded toward the aviation building. "Come on. We can discuss this on the plane, if you insist. Now, either you simply talk a good game, Ms. O'Shea, or you really mean what you say. Where's your spirit of adventure?"

Okay, he had her.

SEVEN

She had never been in a private jet before and tried hard not to appear taken aback as she was introduced to the pilot and copilot who would be flying the Gulfstream to an unknown destination. The inside of the cabin was simple, yet elegant. The walls and ceiling were covered in a beige micro-suede and the six cream leather recliner seats were wide and inviting, as were the cashmere throws folded neatly on each. Not to even mention the sofas at the back of the plane.

"Take a seat," Julian offered as they walked down the aisle. "Would you like a drink? A glass of wine?"

Maggie picked a seat, holding the cashmere blanket in her arms. Julian sat down in the seat across from her. They were facing each other.

"Listen, Maggie, I can almost promise you will enjoy this. I'm not one hundred percent positive because right now you're a little unnerved, and I don't know you well enough yet to guess how long that's going to last. Hopefully, it won't be for too long. Now, what can I get you to drink?"

She looked out the window to the tarmac and heard the door to the plane closing. "I think I could use a drink," she murmured. "I'm being kidnapped, aren't I?"

Laughing, Julian stood up. "You are not being kidnapped. You are being whisked away for some pampering. There's a difference. So what do you drink, besides wine?"

She looked up to him standing in the aisle, casually lean-ing his forearm on the tall backrest. "You wouldn't happen to have bourbon on this plane, would you?"

"I believe we do. On the rocks?"

"Ginger ale, if you have it. If not, the rocks will be fine."

He grinned. "Back in a minute."

She listened as the plane engines began building up power, and her stomach muscles clenched. Not with fear. She wasn't afraid. Maybe with a mixture of anticipation and something else. Not being in control, she thought, finally able to identify the source of the emotion. For the first time on an assignment, she hadn't a clue as to the game plan.

Julian McDonald had turned the tables on her.

"Here you are," he announced, placing a short, cut crystal glass into the holder at her armrest. "When it comes to hard liquor, Scotch is my preference." He sat back down opposite her and held out his glass as Maggie picked hers up. "To pampering," he suggested as a toast.

"And surprises," Maggie added, clinking his glass.

"I think you'll like this one, Maggie," he said, relaxing into his seat. "I promise nothing will be required of you, save to enjoy whatever you choose."

"Are we going to some exclusive spa?"

Julian shook his head. "I'm not giving you any hints at all."

The plane began moving and, sitting backward, Maggie watched the General Aviation building receding from her vision. So they were on their way, though she had no idea where they were heading. She looked at the man across from her and began to relax since there was nothing else to be done. She granted him a small smile. "Well, Julian, I have to give you credit. As far as second dates go, this has to be the most surprising."

"I told you last night I was going to try and impress you. It's my turn."

She burst out laughing. "Good lord, Julian. Dinner in my home hardly compares to *this*!"

"You're wrong, Maggie. Last night was unexpectedly wonderful—the food, the surroundings, and the company. I was prepared for dinner at a good restaurant and I was given a very peaceful, relaxing night. I thoroughly enjoyed it." He looked down her legs. "You can take off your shoes now."

She felt suddenly self-conscious and gulped her drink. "It's okay. I'm sitting down so my feet are fine."

"C'mon, you know you want to."

She knew exactly what he was doing. He was letting her experience what she'd done to him last night. Wanting to show him she was a good sport about all of this, she reached down and unbuckled the thin straps around her ankles. She then slipped her feet out of the high-heeled sandals.

"Happy feet?"

She grinned. "Not yet ecstatic, but getting there."

"Good," he answered as something beeped on his armrest next to the cabin wall. He flipped open the armrest and revealed a phone. "Yes? Right. Thanks." Hanging up, he looked at her. "We're second in line for takeoff, so if you'll finish your drink I'll take the glasses back to the galley." He tilted his own glass and emptied it.

Feeling like she needed all the relaxation she could get, Maggie did the same and handed her glass back to him. Within less than thirty seconds he was back in his seat and buckling his seat belt. She found hers and followed suit.

It was a very odd sensation to be sitting backward as the plane raced down the runway. She felt like she was on an amusement ride as the ascent began, for instead of being thrust backward into the seat, she felt herself propelled forward and had to stop herself from reaching out to brace her hands against Julian's knees. Looking out the window, she saw they were turning toward New Jersey and wondered if Atlantic City was Julian's destination. The gambling town wasn't her idea of relaxing.

"Are you cold?" he asked, as the plane leveled out and the air-conditioning inside the cabin seemed to lower.

Her feet were suddenly chilled. "A little," she conceded.

"Sit back," he said, leaning forward and pressing one of the many buttons on the side of her armrest.

Maggie found herself reclining in the chair with her feet resting up on an ottoman attached to the seat. Julian took the blanket from her and covered her feet.

"There. Now do you want another drink? Something to eat? There should be something light in the fridge."

Maggie smiled. "I'm fine, Julian, thank you. And you're a wonderful host. If you ever get tired of the business world, you would make an excellent flight attendant. Very solicitous."

He chuckled. "I'll keep that in mind."

"You're allowed to relax too, aren't you?"

"Of course. I am relaxed."

"You know where we're going," she said dryly. "I, on the other hand, am kept in the dark. However, I've surrendered. I'm no longer going to pester you about it. I am, in fact, going to just close my eyes and relax. Wake me when we get there."

"You really don't handle prolonged surprises well, do you?"

She couldn't help laughing, though she didn't open her eyes. "Guilty as charged, yet I should be cut a break for this one. It's not every day that I get whisked away on a private jet."

"I'm glad."

She opened her eyes and stared at him. He was smiling.

"I want this to be special. Something you'll remember."

"I don't think I will ever forget this. So, thank you in advance, Julian . . . as long as we're not going to Atlantic City. We aren't, are we?"

He didn't even glance out of his window. "Clever, Maggie, but there won't be any hints. You're just going to have to wait and see for yourself. And trust me. Why don't you take a nap? You must be tired after working all day."

Closing her eyes again, she said, "Now that might be the second great idea you've had today, Mr. McDonald."

"And my first?"

"This pampering," she murmured, pulling the cashmere blanket up from her knees and snuggling under it. "No matter where we land, Julian, or what we're going to do, you'll never know how much I appreciate winding down right now. It was a challenging day to get through."

She felt him patting her feet. "Relax, Maggie. It's your turn now."

Oh yes . . . she could get used to this.

"Wake up, Maggie."

"Huh?" She blinked several times and tried to focus on the man smiling at her. "Julian," she breathed his name and closed her eyes again as it all came back to her. "Are we there yet?"

"Almost," he answered.

She opened her eyes. "How long have I been asleep?"

"About forty-five minutes. Look out the window, Maggie. Here's your first clue."

Now that alerted her brain into complete attention. Stretching as she pushed herself up from the reclining position, Maggie looked out her window. The most beautiful water was below them, almost like an impressionist's painting of the dark water over coral reefs contrasting with shades of turquoise over sand. "Dear God, it's beautiful!" she murmured. "Where are we?"

"Guess."

She glanced at him and could see he was very pleased with himself. "The Caribbean?"

"Not technically," he answered. "Though some consider it to be the northern most part of it and there are Caribbean cricket matches. It's the Gulf Stream."

She looked out the window again and saw an island of pink beaches and the roofs of pastel colored houses. "*Bermuda?*"

"Well done, Maggie."

She tore her gaze away from the window. "For our second date, we're having dinner in Bermuda?" It sounded too incredible to be real, yet it was happening.

"In my home." He looked out the window. "We're approaching the northern part of the island and the airport. If you look across that bay there, Castle Harbour, you'll see a piece of land jutting out. That's Tucker's Town. The house is there."

Still in awe, she shook her head. "This is unbelievably beautiful. I can't wait to tell D. I got here before her."

"D.?"

"Deborah Stark. She's a news anchor in Philly. I met her the night I met you. She won the bid for a trip here."

"Oh, yes. The tall brunette who walked you into dinner."

Maggie reluctantly pulled her vision away from the gorgeous view outside the window. "Had you confused there for a while, didn't we?"

He shrugged as his eyebrows lifted. "I thought I could have picked up the wrong signals from you earlier in the evening."

"Oh, Julian," Maggie said with a grin, "it must be so confusing for men when women are allowed to be more affectionate in public. It's a shame men feel constricted with their emotions."

"C'mon, Maggie," Julian protested. "What would you have thought if I had walked into dinner arm in arm with another man?"

"I would have thought, there goes a liberated man who's sure of who he is and doesn't feel the need to prove his manhood to the world." At his look of disbelief, she grinned and added, "Okay, maybe it might have crossed my mind you enjoyed the company of both men and women. Or that perhaps you'd had too much to drink and needed the support of a steadier arm to make it to the table."

He laughed. "Are you always so willing to look at two sides?"

"There're always two sides, Julian. I've found that the truth lies somewhere in the gray area in between the polarities."

"I can see the benefit of your extensive philosophy library with that answer."

Now it was she who shrugged her shoulders as the phone under his armrest sounded. "I was just answering your question honestly. Now I have one. A question that can wait until you answer that."

Julian picked up the phone. "Okay. Thanks." He reinserted the phone back into its place and then looked at her. "We're making our approach to the airport. Now, what's your question?"

"Exactly how am I going to get into Bermuda and pass customs without my passport?"

His grin widened. "You have your license. I come here at least once a month, more if I can arrange it, and I know the customs officials well. It's already been arranged with faxes. There shouldn't be a problem."

"It must be nice to be so powerful you can circumvent ordinary procedures. I'm impressed."

"That's what this is about, isn't it? Making an impression. You did that last night and now it's my turn."

"You have more play toys and you're raising the bar to a level I can't even begin to compete with, so it's not really a fair playing field."

"Hey, Maggie," he said, suddenly serious. "Let's forget about competitions tonight and playing any games on any field. Let's just enjoy ourselves. I wanted to impress you as you had done to me last night with a relaxing evening in your home. And I couldn't think of a better place than BellaLuna Cottage."

"That's the name of your home in Bermuda?" When he nodded, she looked out the window and saw they were about to land. "BellaLuna," she repeated. "Beautiful Moon Cottage. It sounds wonderful, Julian. Thank you so much for this fabulous surprise."

"So I take it you're no longer upset?"

Unable to stop the giggle as the plane's wheels touched back down on earth, Maggie's cheeks almost hurt from smiling. "I can't believe I'm here in Bermuda! You are definitely an uncommon man, Julian McDonald. It's not every day someone can pull off this kind of surprise."

"And that's a good thing, right?"

"It's a very good thing," she conceded as a feeling of gratitude almost brought tears to her eyes.

He unbuckled his seat belt while the plane slowed down. "I'll be right back. Just want to speak to Peter and Will about a few things before we leave the plane."

Nodding as he left for the cockpit, Maggie freed herself from the seat belt and put her sandals back on as she looked out the window. The airport was small, but charming. She could see tall palm trees and even larger pines with soft long needles that swayed in the breeze. She was in Bermuda! To have dinner! Who would believe it?

She giggled again as she ran her fingers through her hair. How thoughtful of Julian to spoil her like this, and that's what she felt like . . . a woman who was being spoiled, cared for, pampered. She wasn't used to such treatment. Being single, independent, and self-employed didn't leave much time for spoiling herself. She quickly opened her purse and took out her compact and a tube of lipstick. Touching up her makeup, Maggie could feel butterflies in her stomach.

How long since she'd felt like this?

Excited by a man.

She'd have to be careful and not forget this was an assignment, no matter how glamorous or inviting it might seem. Her purpose was to help Julian open his heart again.

"Okay, are you ready?" he asked, holding out his hand.

"Absolutely," she declared, picking up her shawl and draping it over her arm as she rose. "I can't believe that in a little over an hour I'm in paradise."

"Believe it, Maggie, because it's true. At least this is my little slice of it."

She thanked the pilot and after walking down the few steps, she took the hand of the copilot, who was standing and waiting to assist her to the ground. "Thank you so much. It was a wonderful flight."

"Enjoy your evening, madam," he responded with a smile, looking very smart in his uniform of a white short-sleeved shirt with epaulets and navy trousers.

"I believe I will," she replied, watching as Julian patted the man's shoulder before holding his hand out to her. She put hers inside his and let him lead her to the terminal with its clock tower. It was an hour later than on the East Coast. "I feel so decadent without luggage, like I'm merely stopping for dinner on this exotic island."

He turned his face to her. "Maybe you deserve to feel decadent once in a while?"

She thought about it for a split second and then chuckled. "Now there's the third great idea you've had today."

His laugh was spontaneous and very sexy. "Ah, Maggie, the evening has just begun . . . and I'm full of ideas."

She didn't give a response or make any comment, for her brain was repeating over and over *this is just an assignment, this is just an assignment* . . .

They breezed through customs after Julian spoke with the official. All she had to do was show her driver's license with its photo ID and sign a piece of paper, and then they were walking through the airport terminal.

Julian waved to a man standing by the exit doors. "There's Alastair."

Alastair was a tall stately Bermudan man, dressed neatly in a navy blazer, white shirt, and shorts. He also wore navy blue knee socks and Maggie was reminded of all those proper school uniforms the children wore in England.

"Good to see you, Alastair," Julian said, holding out his hand.

"Good evening, Mr. McDonald. It is good to see you again. Welcome back home," Alastair added in his lilting, melodious adaptation of a proper British accent.

The men shook hands and then Julian turned to her. "Alastair, this is Miss Maggie O'Shea. She will be our guest for dinner tonight."

Maggie extended her hand in greeting. "Hello, Alastair."

"Welcome to Bermuda, Miss O'Shea. You have picked a perfect evening. It will be a spectacular sunset."

"I'm very excited to be here," she answered. The man's expression was formal, yet kind. His complexion was the handsome color of café au lait and she thought he had the eyes of an old soul and the smile of an angel. She couldn't help smiling back.

"Shall we depart then for BellaLuna?" Julian asked.

"This way, sir. The car is parked very close."

They followed Alastair outside and he walked up to a small white BMW. He held open the back door. Maggie slid in and Julian followed. She felt like a small child as she gawked through the window, taking in all the sights. They crossed a causeway made of coral and, staring at the water, she wanted to pinch herself to make sure she wasn't dreaming. They passed quaint storybook villages and unspoiled natural wonders and Julian allowed her to take it all in without conversing. He seemed relaxed, happy to be back in Bermuda. And who could blame him? It truly was a paradise, only an hour's plane ride from the East Coast. Amazing.

They were on Harrington Sound Road. She could tell by the street signs on the sides of buildings and houses. They passed places called Church Bay and Shark Hole, and Maggie couldn't help but notice how clean and cared for everything was.

"That's the famous Swizzle Inn, a favorite watering hole," Julian said, pointing to a two-story building on the right. "They say you swizzle in and stagger out."

"I'm already staggered by the beauty of this place," Maggie remarked as they turned to the left. "I'm in awe."

"I know how you feel," he answered. "I felt the same way when I first came here. There's something . . . I don't know, magical about this place."

"I agree," she whispered, gazing up at stately palm trees that lined both sides of the road. They had to be eighty feet tall. And some of the homes they were passing were spectacular mansions. "Why are the roofs like that?" she asked, seeing each home had a unique design of gables and tiles.

"Water here comes out of the sky, not the ground. So instead of wells, there are roofs of whitewashed limestone. They're built that way to collect rain water, several sloping gutters that guide the water toward internal gutters that pipe water into a holding tank containing twenty to thirty thousand gallons. Water is a precious commodity here."

Nodding as they approached what appeared to be a beautiful golf club, she asked, "Do you play golf?" She really knew so very little about him.

"Sometimes. When friends come out for a holiday. Do you?"

"Oh, no. Though I appreciate the game, I'm afraid I don't have the patience it requires to be any good. I sort of whack 'em and walk. Lots of whacking, to be honest, which is not the point of the game."

He laughed. "Okay, there will no whacking on this trip."

"Good lord, I hope not!" she exclaimed. "Hardly my idea of relaxation. And not very relaxing for the people I've played with either." Chuckling, she added, "I seem to remember a distinct aura of frustration in the air."

"I'll remember that."

She sat silently, taking in the sights as they turned onto the South Road.

"Not far now," Julian commented.

She simply nodded as her head filled with stunning bits of scenery and also with what seemed like Julian's casual comments about their future meetings. This could be really easy to get used to and she had to remember to keep that place inside herself free from expectations. It's what made loving without the need of possession possible for her.

"There're private beaches here," Julian said, pointing out her window.

The homes were huge, nestled into impeccably maintained foliage and gardens. In the background she could catch glimpses of the turquoise sea.

Alastair turned into a driveway and Maggie's jaw dropped in awe. "*This* is BellaLuna Cottage?" she demanded in a shocked voice. "What kind of cottage is *that* size?" It was a long one-story, pale yellow home with white trim, white roof, and a portico over the huge front door. Flowers were in white stone urns, in hanging baskets, on windowsills, even lining the circular drive. It looked like an oasis in an exotic fairy tale. "Oh, Julian . . . it's beautiful," she said sincerely as the car stopped under the portico that had blooming jasmine climbing up the front columns.

"I'm glad you like it," he answered, opening the door and helping her out of the car. "The original BellaLuna Cottage is now the kitchen and home for Alastair and his wife. I've added on over the years."

Her hand was on her upper chest, as though to contain her heart from bursting with joy. She felt . . . in the strangest way . . . like she was coming home. Realizing such a feeling was silly and downright dangerous, Maggie immediately shook off whatever it was that seemed to capture her and thanked Alastair for the scenic drive.

"It has been my pleasure, Miss O'Shea."

"Please, call me Maggie," she insisted.

"If you should need anything, please let me know."

"Thank you." She turned with Julian and headed toward the front door.

"He won't call you Maggie," Julian whispered. "I've been trying to get him to call me by my first name for years. Here in Bermuda there's a genteel civility that has nothing to do with servitude. They are simply a gracious people and stand on long-held customs."

Before they reached the front door, it was opened by a middle-aged woman with bright eyes and a broad smile to match her hips. She was wearing a white blouse with a navy blue skirt and a white apron. "Welcome home, Mr. McDonald. BellaLuna has been missing you."

"Thank you, Elizabeth. I've missed being here." Julian held out his hand and added, "May I introduce Miss Maggie O'Shea, who will be joining us tonight. I take it by the fabulous aroma dinner is cooking?"

"How do you do, Miss O'Shea. Welcome to BellaLuna."

No hand was offered to shake, so Maggie simply smiled and said, "Thank you for your welcome, Elizabeth. It's a pleasure to meet you."

The woman looked closely into Maggie's eyes and then nodded once before turning her attention back to her employer. "Dinner will served on the terrace as you requested in twenty minutes. I have prepared a carafe of rum swizzle. It is waiting for you outside."

"Thank you, Elizabeth. The place looks great. Did everything arrive that I had ordered from town?"

"It has all been taken care of, as you requested."

"Thank you. I think I'll show Maggie the house now."

Elizabeth nodded. "I'll announce dinner. It should be a lovely sunset."

"I was counting on that," Julian said, touching Maggie's elbow as Elizabeth turned away.

Maggie took her first look around the interior and had to stop her jaw from dropping in admiration. The home was built in a squared, elongated U, with the wide-open living area connecting the two wings on each side. Looking through the glass doors that formed the walls leading out to a large stone terrace and a pool, Maggie murmured, "It's just lovely, Julian. I can see why this is your slice of paradise. It must break your heart to leave."

He smiled. "It's always nice to know it's here waiting when I can get the time to visit."

It was a beautiful beach house, and she tried to take it all in, the cool, soothing mixture of whites and the palest aqua blue that matched the pool water and the sea, the contemporary sofas facing each other in front of a wide fireplace, the mixture of antiques, of nautical accents and books, the collection of shells and corals and watercolor artwork depicting Bermuda's gorgeous scenery.

"Let's go outside," Julian suggested, leading her through the opened sliding glass doors that each had to be eight feet wide.

A large stone terrace faced the pool and the sea beyond. It was a spectacular view, gazing at the pool that seemed to be dug out of the stone and surrounded by lush flowering plants in shades of lavender, deep purple, white, and pink. A thatched roof pavilion was nestled into the foliage as it thinned out toward the turquoise sea. "Did you design this?"

"I had a hand in it, but a project manager oversaw everything for me," he answered, approaching a round table set for dinner with crisp white linens, crystal, and sterling silver. In the center of the table a crystal vase held together a beautiful arrangement of cut flowers from the garden. "Now, you simply must taste this," he added, picking up a silver carafe and pouring out a dark-colored drink. "You can't come to Bermuda and never have a rum swizzle."

Accepting the drink, Maggie waited until he had poured one for himself. She lifted her glass. "To relaxation, and to surprises. I believe this is the best one I've ever had, Julian. Thank you."

He raised his glass and looked very pleased as he took his first sip.

"This is wonderful," she announced, tasting the cool drink that quickly frosted the sides of her glass. "What's in it?"

"Black rum, Demerara rum, apricot brandy, limes, honey, and a dash of bitters. Now you've been officially welcomed to Bermuda with Elizabeth's recipe." He took off his jacket and hung it on one of the backs of a grouping of chairs.

"Are they a couple?" Maggie asked, sitting down in a cream cushioned chair. "Alastair and Elizabeth?"

Joining her in the opposite chair, Julian said, "Yes. Alastair and Elizabeth Edwards have been with me ever since I bought the place years ago. I'd be hard-pressed to replace them. Elizabeth can be protective, which I'm sure you noticed at your introduction. Give her a few hours to check you out and she'll come around. Then she'll start being protective of you."

Maggie grinned. She wanted to ask him how many women he had brought to BellaLuna, but knew it wasn't any of her business. Still, she wondered what the proper Alastair and Elizabeth really thought about their employer's extracurricular activities and his guests over the years.

"Perhaps after dinner we could take a walk on the beach," Julian offered. "It really can be spectacular at sunset. I remember when I first moved in, I think I took twenty rolls of film trying to capture each one."

"And you don't anymore?"

"I have a digital camera now so I still take pictures, but only save the really good ones."

"I've always meant to come here," Maggie said, staring out beyond the property to the gorgeous sea. "I've taken vacations to the Caribbean, Bahamas, St. Thomas, but never made it here. I'm sorry I waited so long."

"Well, you're here now, that's what's important."

"It's so beautiful, so clean and unspoiled."

"The government makes sure it stays that way. There's

no pollution, no illiteracy, no unemployment, and no income tax."

Maggie laughed. "I feel like I've landed in the tropical version of Oz!"

"Shh," Julian whispered with a grin. "We're trying to keep the magic a secret."

"Dinner is served."

They both turned to Elizabeth. Alastair was holding out her chair for her.

Feeling totally pampered, Maggie rose and walked over to the dining table. "Thank you," she said to Alastair, who pushed her chair in for her. "The table looks beautiful, Elizabeth."

"Thank you, madam. I hope you enjoy your dinner."

"I'm sure I will," she answered, inhaling the delicious aroma emanating from the soup bowl in front of her.

"Thank you, Elizabeth," Julian added, picking up his napkin and placing it on his knee. "I've missed your cooking."

Elizabeth's smile widened, as though she had been waiting for Julian to say those very words.

"I told Elizabeth to prepare a Bermudan meal for us. This is fish chowder, made with Bermuda black rum and Outerbridge cherry peppers. If you like the taste of the peppers, there's more in that cruet to enhance the flavor."

Maggie placed her napkin on her lap and picked up the soup spoon, seeing her reflection in the polished sterling silver. Elizabeth's soup was delicious, as was the baked red snapper that followed accompanied by a sweet potato pudding that was light green, instead of the orange yams she was used to. A distinctly flavored ragout was the other side dish. There was an exotic savory zest to the entire meal, stirring her taste buds with new flavors. She and Julian spoke leisurely about the island and Maggie had to admit it was a fabulous dinner with an even more fabulous view and her dinner companion was turning out to be pretty fabulous too. The fact that she was on her third glass of rum swizzle only added to her feeling of relaxation and fabulousness. But who was counting in paradise?

As the dinner plates were taken away, Maggie sat back and exhaled with appreciation. "Julian, you and your staff have outdone yourselves. I'm already dreading leaving, getting back on the plane, and returning to the busy city. This will all seem like a dream."

"C'mon, Maggie," Julian said, rising and pulling back her chair for her. "Take those shoes off and let's go for a walk on the beach. I'm sure we're going to need it if Elizabeth has prepared syllabub, a monster of a dessert."

She unbuckled the straps of her sandals and slipped them off as Julian took off his shoes and socks and rolled up the cuffs of his cream-colored trousers. "Ready?"

"Oh, yes," Maggie answered, holding out her hand.

He took it and led her around the long pool and into the thriving garden, abundant with blossoms. They passed the thatched roofed pavilion and she saw a wide double hammock facing the sea. If she were to lie down there, she knew she'd fall fast asleep. They walked down stone steps, around a tall pine tree and then there it was in all its glory—a magnificent private beach with its uniquely pink sand flecked with coral. In the fading rays of sunlight, the sea seemed to capture the last of the light and sparkle in exquisite shades of blue. Soft waves were lapping at rocky cliffs and Maggie stopped in her tracks to take it all in.

"Oh, Julian," she breathed, unable to tear her vision away from the unspoiled cove.

He bent his head and stared into her eyes. "Are you . . . crying?"

"Don't worry, I'm not about to fall apart on you." She sniffled and blinked hard several times. "Haven't you ever seen something so beautiful it resonates with your soul, and you feel . . . I don't know . . . like you're filled up, bursting with joy, so you release it with tears?"

He looked back out to the cove. "Do you feel everything so deeply?"

She shrugged. "Sometimes. I guess it can depend upon what I'm feeling. Oh, I have to put my feet in the water," she exclaimed, letting go of his hand and hurrying down to the surf. She lifted the hem of her sundress up above her knees and laughed as she turned around to him on the beach. "Come in," she yelled, kicking up spray in his direction.

Julian smiled back at her and held out his hand. She looked so delightfully happy, holding up her dress like a young girl and playing in the surf. There didn't seem to be anything affected about her. She appreciated everything with the sincerity of someone who didn't take anything for granted, and she appeared to tell the truth, even if it put her in an unfavorable light. She seemed . . . real. Not pretentious, bored with life, or cynical. In that moment, he realized why he'd been attracted to pretentious, cynical women: They'd been safe.

Watching Maggie walking back up to him from the surf, he felt his attraction deepening into something more than physical. He liked her. Really liked her. Liked spending time with her. He wasn't thinking about getting her into bed as quickly as possible and then wondering how long he could keep her there without making any moves toward a commitment of time or emotions.

She was different.

"C'mon, Julian, you rolled up your trousers for a reason. The water's wonderful."

"Listen, Maggie," Julian answered, moving forward, taking both her hands and pulling her to stand directly in front of him. "I have another great idea. At least, I hope you'll think it's a good one."

"What's that? I can't wait to hear it, since you're batting a thousand tonight."

Her happiness was contagious and he resisted pulling her closer into his arms. "What would you think of spending the night here? We could fly back to the States late tomorrow afternoon."

She merely blinked back at him, her smile frozen in place.

"There's no pressure on my part," he hurried to add, not sure if she was surprised or shocked by his suggestion. "I have a guest bedroom and it's all yours . . . if you want to stay."

"Do you mean it?" she whispered and then broke into a giggle of excitement. "We can stay overnight? I'll have all of tomorrow here?"

He nodded. "I already told Peter and Will to book a reservation at Grotto Bay just in case we decided not to fly back tonight."

"Oh Julian!" She threw her arms around his neck and hugged him tightly. "This is the best, I mean the *very* best date I've ever had!" She pulled back and pushed the hair away from her forehead, looking back out to the sea. "I just wish I'd brought a bathing suit with me."

"Well . . ." He drew out the word as she turned to look back at him. "With the possibility of extending our stay, I had Elizabeth purchase a few things. They're in the guest bedroom."

She looked deeply into his eyes and he knew, somehow he *knew* she was wondering if he did this sort of thing all the time. It embarrassed him that this wasn't an original idea, and he could feel his cheeks actually heat up with an adolescent blush as he shifted his gaze to the smooth skin of her shoulders. What was it about this woman that brought up feelings he hadn't experienced in years?

"So shall we both get changed and then we can take a swim later?"

"Thank you, Julian. You're a very good host."

As he watched her walk back toward the stone steps, he suddenly realized he wanted to be more than a host to her. He wanted to be her friend, someone she could trust. And he also wanted to see her in a bathing suit.

All lofty aspirations aside, he was still human.

EIGHT

She fell in love with the yellow-and-white bedroom, its four-poster bed and the French doors that opened onto the courtyard and pool. In the bathroom was a corner Jacuzzi and a long, thick terry cloth robe, along with an array of Molton Brown products in a white wicker tray that made her feel she actually was at a spa. On the bed was a deep green iridescent bathing suit. A one-piece maillot, thank God. Along with a matching sheer pareo. Picking up the suit and checking it out, Maggie wanted to kiss Elizabeth when she saw it had tummy control. It was also the right size. Julian McDonald must be very good at describing women, or there was a wide range of bathing suits in this house for just such an occasion.

She didn't want to think about that right now. It really was none of her business how many women Julian had entertained exactly as he was entertaining her. It shouldn't matter to her, so why then had she looked into his eyes on the beach and seen something that bothered her? Julian's embarrassment that this was something he did often was clear. This wasn't something special. And even though she knew it was dangerous to even think differently, Maggie had to admit she'd wanted it to be special.

And that was extremely stupid.

She pulled the tags off the suit, thankful that it was new and not worn by another woman Julian had been seducing, No point in even thinking about anything except the assignment. All else could lead to ruin. Besides, there was a gorgeous sea waiting for her. She deserved this and it didn't matter how many others had slept in this room or swam with Julian before. She had something they didn't possess.

Magic.

She had wrapped the pareo around her waist and was holding her tummy in, feeling reasonably attractive as she joined Julian at the water's edge. She was, after all, thirty-four years old, not some young chickie whose body was sculpted by Pilates and weight training. Still, she felt she could hold her own in the present circumstance, though it would have been nice to have known about this and have applied some tanning cream so she wasn't fish-belly white all over. Oh, well . . . she could only be herself and there was no point in hiding or pretending, she rationalized, as the moment of the big reveal was upon her.

Julian didn't look too bad himself, she thought, seeing him turn around and watch her making her way down the steps to the sand. Thank heavens he favored swimming shorts and not those French bikinis some men of a certain age paraded on beaches. Julian didn't have a six-pack torso, but he wasn't out of shape. He appeared solid, as though he could be counted on in a physical situation. He also looked very pleased to see her.

"Ready for a swim?" he asked, throwing a towel onto a bamboo mat on the sand.

"Absolutely," she answered, dropping her towel and then untying the pareo. Not willing to wait for his reaction, she headed straight for the surf and began swimming when it reached her hips.

It was simply heavenly. There was no other way to describe that feeling of weightlessness in water so clean she could clearly see the sand ten feet below her. When she stopped swimming and treaded water, she watched Julian's powerful strokes as he joined her.

"So what do you think?" he asked, grinning like a kid.

Seeing his hair slicked back and the happiness in his expression, Maggie laughed, feeling more than a twinge of attraction for this man. "I think surely this is heaven on earth. Thank you so much, Julian, for this gift of the sea."

"You're a pretty good swimmer. I take it you like the water."

"I love the water. Have since I was a little child. My mother said at three I swam underwater like a fish. There's something . . . I don't know . . . almost primal about it for me. Like I'm home." And with that, she dove under the salty water and wished the light wasn't fading so quickly. Tomorrow she would have to come out here in full sunlight and explore the beauty of the reef.

She spun her body in a tight pirouette, almost giggling with pleasure, and found she had to resist the urge to turn herself into a creature of the sea. The desire was so strong that she headed for the surface before the image of a dolphin could take shape in her mind. She turned onto her back and floated, allowing the water to support and cradle her. Until that moment she didn't know how much she'd needed a break from the city.

"If I had a penny on me, I'd give it," he said, somewhere near her head.

She grinned, still not opening her eyes and relinquishing the absolute peace. "I was just thinking how much I needed this and how grateful I am to you for providing a precious vacation from life."

"I appreciate but don't want your gratitude."

"What do you want, Julian?"

"First of all I'd like you to call me Mac, like my close friends do."

Okay, she opened her eyes. "Mac?"

"As in McDonald? Not the arches. Me."

She laughed, sputtered water, and gave up her peaceful float. "I thought you didn't care for nicknames."

"I'm okay with Mac."

He looked so happy she wasn't going to press him about last night at her apartment when she'd called him Jules. Last night. It felt like weeks ago. "So friends call you Mac, huh?"

"Close friends, people I've known since college."

"Then I'm flattered, Mac, to be included in old friends."

He treaded water closer to her, so that only inches separated their swaying limbs. "I feel like I've known you for a long time. Even though I know very little about you."

She smiled into his serious face. "What would you like to know?"

His hand reached out and rested on her hip. She allowed it, so he pulled her in closer until her breasts were brushing against his chest. "I want to know everything, Maggie. I want to know what you were like as a child. Do you have brothers or sisters? What was your childhood like? Who broke your heart for the first time?"

She looked into his intense eyes, surrounded by lashes that were spiked with dampness. "I think my mother would have said I was a precocious child and teenager," she answered, placing her hand on his upper arm. "I have no brothers or sisters and my mother died four years ago."

"I'm sorry. Your father?"

She sighed and looked at the sprinkling of freckles that dotted his shoulder. "My father . . . he left before I was born. They weren't married."

"So you're alone."

She raised her vision and smiled. "I'm not alone. I have friends, not many since my working hours are restricting, but I'm not a lonely woman."

"I hope you'll include me now as one of your friends." He pulled her even closer and she wrapped both her arms around his neck, allowing him to tread water for them both. "Right?"

"This is kind of close for friends, isn't it?" She could feel herself getting aroused by the grazing of slippery skin again skin.

Grinning, as though he knew exactly how she was feeling, he said, "Well, maybe we could be close friends."

She hesitated answering. "Does this type of seduction work for you all the time, Mac?" Without waiting for an answer, she dove backward, away from him, allowing her legs to slide up his sides as she went underwater and surfaced a few yards away.

"That was tricky," he yelled. "And yes, guilty as charged. It usually does work for me."

"I thought so," she said with a laugh and started swimming for shore.

She was toweling herself off when he joined her. Grabbing his towel, he flung it around his neck and then took her hand.

"C'mon, I want to talk."

He led her to the pavilion and said, "There's room for two on the hammock. Let's watch the sunset from here. There's something I want to say to you."

"Sounds serious," she murmured, sitting down and then swinging her legs up onto the knotted mesh. He laid down next to her and she resisted snuggling against him for it was the closest they had been out of water, hip to hip, leg to leg. Instead, she curled her arm under her head and looked out to the sky turning shades of pink and turquoise and orange as a gentle warm breeze dried off her skin.

"It's not serious, but I am."

"Now I'm very interested."

He sighed deeply before speaking. "This is kind of embarrassing, but I suppose it's obvious I've brought women here before."

She couldn't stop the chuckle. "Ah, yeah . . ."

He shrugged. "Well, there's nothing I can say or do about that, but I want you to know when I thought about bringing you here it wasn't like that . . . to seduce you."

"You don't want to seduce me?" she interjected in a joking voice.

"Stop it, I'm serious."

"Oh, okay."

"I watched you last night preparing dinner in your kitchen and well, I wanted you to see BellaLuna, to enjoy it."

"I am."

"Good. I don't know how to explain this, but I feel as though we've known each other before. I don't believe in reincarnation or anything like that, and I realize what I've just said sounds crazy, but I can't seem to shake this feeling.

It's natural. I'm so comfortable around you, relaxed. There's no pressure, no agenda . . ." His words trailed off and he sighed. "I like you, Maggie."

"I like you, too."

"I mean I'd like to see you whenever you're free. I know there're ninety miles between where we live and work, but there're weekends." When she didn't respond, he added, "Look, I know this is only our second date, so to speak, and I must sound like a complete jerk. Here I'm saying you don't put any pressure on me and I'm pressuring you. I'm probably saying everything wrong. It's been so long since I felt . . . comfortable with a woman, and I just want you to know I didn't bring you here for selfish reasons. Not entirely, anyway."

Maggie smiled and turned her head. "Julian?"

"Hmm?"

"When are you going to kiss me?"

The muscles in his face relaxed as he stared into her eyes. "Right now."

And then he did.

The temptation had been too great. Every atom in her body seemed to be crying out for it, that irresistible craving drawing her to proceed against her better judgment. There were so many reasons not to, but she hadn't been able to resist.

The moon was full.

The air was still warm.

And the house was quiet.

Unable to wait any longer, she exited her bedroom by the French doors, walked carefully around the pool and found the steps leading to the sea. She left a towel on the sand and slowly walked up to the water's edge. A moonlit swim. She wouldn't get another chance. No one would know. Alastair and Elizabeth had retired to their room and Julian was in his. She'd locked her bedroom door, just in case he decided to pay her a nocturnal visit. He was the one who'd called an end to their making out in the hammock when he'd rolled over onto her and had stared down into her eyes saying he wanted to wait to take her to bed to prove to her he had meant not inviting her to Bermuda for selfish reasons. Maggie realized Julian wanted to prove it not just to her, but also to himself. He wanted her to know she was different.

Still, just thinking about Julian's body covering hers, his arousal pressing against her, his lips possessing her and traveling down to her breasts was reason enough to immerse herself in cool water. She swam out, following the moonlight's trail upon the surface of the sea. When she was deep enough, she plunged under the water and allowed her imagination free reign. She felt her body and spine transform, her limbs and shoulders receding as her face elongated. Within moments she burst through the surface in a perfect arc with absolute joy. She built up speed and raced through the water, reveling in being at one with the world, her lungs filled with ample air, sensing objects when she couldn't see them. It was an exquisite experience.

She dove deep, knowing she should end this pleasure soon. She was preparing to soar toward the surface to jump just once more when she suddenly felt something tugging at her tail. She moved sideways forcefully to free herself and it was then she realized she was caught in a fishing net.

She wasn't sure what to do.

She stayed calm, floating in the water, trying to move her tail slowly, to find some escape. Nothing was working, and she couldn't remain underwater much longer. Something had to give. Either the net or her lungs . . .

Panic started to build as she realized she was forced to stay as a dolphin. Should she return to human form her lungs would be empty and begin to fill with salt water before she could work herself free. She flailed back and forth, desperate to liberate herself from what was surely a death trap now!

Time was meaningless in the dark space that earlier had seemed so magical and welcoming. Now it was enclosing her in what felt like a wet tomb. She would die here and her mind screamed out for help. Knowing she had to conserve what little air remained, she concentrated and moved her tail slightly, still attempting to free herself.

She was not about to check out like this without a fight!

Suddenly the sonar in her head told her of something approaching. Unable to see any distance in the dark she was stunned to make out a huge fish coming closer to her. God, was it a *barracuda*? She couldn't even defend herself!

She didn't know if she was hallucinating, but she would swear that fish was using its teeth to break the net around her tail. She felt the movement, the tugging on the net. Maybe this is what happens when you're dying, when you take too many risks, when you are cursed with the ability to shape shift, and drawn into working for someone who'll use you and . . . her mind ran images of Marcus. She cursed him. She loved him. She cursed him again. She thought of her staff, her friends, of Julian. Dear God . . . Julian! He would never forgive himself. He finally opens a crack of the barrier that's surrounded his heart and another woman he lets in dies on him.

She couldn't allow that to happen!

Using every ounce of strength remaining, she flailed her tail with such force that, miraculously, she was free. She propelled herself to the surface, drawing in air, and then swam to more shallow water. There she settled herself, calmed her frantic thoughts and called upon any reserve of willpower to assist her. She moved closer to the beach and when she could feel her belly touching sand, she finally transformed. It was slow and she had to concentrate very hard to spin the molecules and constrict her energy.

She nearly crawled out of the water, gasping for breath.

"That was very foolish. You could have died out there."

Stunned, she raised her head to see Elizabeth standing before her, dripping wet.

"I . . . I shouldn't have gone for a moonlit swim. Couldn't help myself . . . looked so inviting." Dear God, what was she supposed to say to the woman if she saw her shape shift from a dolphin into herself?

"Here, let me help you stand up."

Maggie accepted the woman's strong hand and rose to her feet. She was still unsteady as Elizabeth led her to the steps.

"Sit down and rest for a few moments," the woman instructed, wrapping the towel around Maggie's shoulders.

Maggie wiped her face and huddled under the towel. "Why are you wet?" she asked, seeing the cotton nightgown sticking to Elizabeth's muscular body.

"I am wet because I came after you. Didn't anyone teach you the danger of shifting in water?"

Maggie couldn't speak. Her jaw dropped open and she stared at the dark woman in front of her. She did not just hear that. Elizabeth couldn't have just talked about *shifting*!

"Why are you surprised?" Elizabeth asked. "Did you think the foundation wouldn't have a plan already in place?"

It took her some time to find her voice. "You . . . *you're* a shape shifter?" Maggie asked in disbelief, feeling her heartbeat slamming inside her chest and strumming in her eardrums. The foundation! She knew about the foundation!

Elizabeth nodded. "For many years, child. And I know never to do what you just did alone. At night the fishermen lay their nets. It was only a matter of time before you became entangled, playing the way you were."

"It was you? You helped me?"

"Surely you must have realized no ordinary barracuda would have assisted you." Elizabeth shook her head, as though in disapproval. "Now come with me into the house. I will make a cup of chamomile tea to calm you and I can get into something dry."

Maggie obediently rose from the step and allowed Elizabeth to have a tight hold on her elbow as she was led up the stairs and around the pool. She didn't know what to say. So many things were racing through her mind. Elizabeth was a shape shifter. She knew about her and about the foundation, so she must also know about her assignment. What the hell was going on?

"Go into your bedroom and get changed. I will bring you tea in a few minutes."

Maggie started to do as she was instructed when she suddenly turned. "Thank you, Elizabeth," she whispered. "You saved my life."

The stately woman nodded toward the French doors. "We will talk about that and many other things. Now I must get dry and make sure Alastair is still asleep. Be very quiet."

Maggie measured each step as she rounded the pool and chairs. She knew the end bedroom facing the sea was Julian's so she was very careful until she made it to her door. Once inside, she hurried into the bathroom and stripped off the bathing suit. Wrapping the thick terry cloth robe around her, she looked at her reflection in the mirror.

So Elizabeth was expecting her.

It would have been very nice if someone had told her about Elizabeth!

She towel-dried her hair and then ran a brush through it, anxious for Elizabeth to show up. What a complete shock! Prim, proper Elizabeth Edwards was a shape shifter!

A soft knock sounded on her bedroom door.

Maggie hurried to open it and smiled politely as she held the door open for Elizabeth, dressed in a pale yellow robe that zippered up to her neck, and holding a tray with a bone china teapot painted with flowers and two cups. There was also a plate of what looked to be shortbread cookies.

"You sit down in bed and I'll bring you a cup," Elizabeth said, as Maggie took a vase of flowers off a small table by the wide wing chair.

Placing the vase on the dresser, Maggie answered, "You don't have to serve me, Elizabeth."

The woman straightened and leveled Maggie with her gaze. "You are a guest in this house, Maggie O'Shea, so sit down. I know what I have to do and also what I don't have to do."

"Yes, ma'am," Maggie said, automatically sitting on the edge of the bed while feeling like a misbehaving adolescent in the presence of her elder.

Elizabeth poured out the tea and handed the cup and

saucer to Maggie. "Well, someone taught you manners, even if they didn't instill in you common sense."

"I'm sorry for . . . well, for what I did tonight," she answered in a humble voice. "I know I shouldn't have, but the thought of a moonlit swim was irresistible."

"You should have resisted," Elizabeth replied, sitting down in the wing chair across from her. "And you certainly should have resisted shifting at such a crucial time on your assignment. What if Mr. McDonald saw you?"

"I was careful," Maggie murmured, then blew on her tea. "How did you know I was swimming?"

"Very little happens in this house that I don't know about, Miss O'Shea. When I realized you had left the courtyard, I followed you."

"Thank God you did." She sipped her tea and felt the heat of it warm her inside. "Surely, Elizabeth, considering that you just saved my life, I think you could call me Maggie now, don't you? Especially since we share something . . . unusual. Is Alastair also a shifter?"

Elizabeth shook her head. "No. But he knows about me, and about you. I prepared him when the foundation notified me that you had made contact with Mr. McDonald."

Maggie held the saucer tightly in her hands. "Elizabeth, what *is* this foundation? Marcus doesn't tell me anything. I think if I'm working for them I have a right to know who they are. How I came to be like this and what exactly they want from me."

"Marcus Bocelli?"

"Yes. He was my teacher."

Elizabeth shook her head then sipped her tea. "Mr. Bocelli should have taught you better than to ask such questions. But you shouldn't be left in the dark, so to speak. There is an ancient lineage that is followed. Somewhere in yours was a shape shifter, as was someone in my lineage."

"It has to be on my father's side."

"Then you have your answer."

"I have a part answer. I never saw my father and when I tried to explain to my mother what was happening to me, she became very angry saying I was as crazy as my father. He must have told her about himself when she was pregnant with me. My mother didn't believe him, thought he was, well, unbalanced and refused to even listen to me speak about shape shifting. She never married and wouldn't tell me my father's name or if he's even alive. Those answers died with her, so I really don't have much information about my lineage."

Elizabeth's eyes softened. "Then listen to me, child. Mr. Bocelli should have explained this to you. You are part of a very old tradition that goes back before any organized religions. There are those who have always remembered the power of nature, all nature, seen and unseen. There is power to be harnessed and you have become skilled at how to use that in shape shifting. Those who have kept this mysterious tradition alive through the centuries have learned to be guarded and cautious. People fear what they do not understand. Many hundreds of years ago, in what is now Europe, a group of like-minded souls met and became organized, vowing to work together to help balance the energies that keep this world from destroying itself. Did you think it was only by chance that civilization came out of the Dark Ages and into the Renaissance? In times of growing darkness, light workers are called upon to play their part."

Maggie listened with rapt attention. "What does all this have to do with Julian? Why is the foundation so interested in him?"

Elizabeth shrugged. "That I cannot tell you. I was asked four years ago to make myself and Alastair available for Mr. McDonald. I was to watch out for him while he is here in Bermuda. And I have and I will continue to do so." Elizabeth held out the plate with the cookies. "He is falling in love with you."

"I know," Maggie whispered, picking up a small square of shortbread. "That's my assignment with him. To open his heart again to love. I think it's going to be difficult though, when I leave him so he can go on with his life."

"For him or for you?"

"For him," she answered automatically, not wanting to think about her own reactions. "That's what I do, have been doing for fourteen years. I'm the one who comes before the real one can enter their lives."

"So you prepare men to love another?"

"Yes." She bit into the dry cookie and had to sip the tea to swallow it. "I've been invited to weddings, declarations of partnerships, christening of babies. They even send me Christmas cards to keep me updated on their lives."

"And you haven't wanted those things for yourself? Wedding and babies?"

Maggie looked down to the soft yellow rug under her feet. "I've given up wanting, Elizabeth. I'm thirty-four now. I don't know if it will ever happen."

"Why?"

"Why? Because of who I am and what I do. How many men would accept either?"

Elizabeth nodded. "I see. However, Alastair has accepted who I am and works with me. If a man did accept your gift, you would consider working for the foundation in another way?"

Maggie stared at the older woman. "Of course, but I didn't think I had a choice."

Elizabeth straightened her back. "Who told you such a thing? You have free will. You always have free will."

"But Marcus always makes each assignment seem so important, especially this one."

"Marcus Bocelli!" Elizabeth pursed her lips. "I met him once many years ago in France. He has been given beauty and possesses charisma, I will grant you that. Now I will tell you again, Maggie, that you always have free will. Is it not difficult for you to love and then leave?"

"Sometimes," Maggie answered truthfully. "I just didn't know any way out of this life."

"Maybe there is and maybe there isn't. The gift you give must be given with a full heart. If your heart is full and over-flowing, it is easy to give. You want to give. You need to give away the overflow for it is too much for the body to contain. You have felt this?"

Maggie nodded.

"And if your heart is not full, if it is depleted for whatever reason and you still give, then is it not a half-hearted gift?"

Again, Maggie nodded.

"And who would want such a gift? Would you? Would you want to take from someone who needs to restore themselves?"

"But I thought if you give when you think you can't, then it was . . . well, honorable. A good thing."

"And who taught you that?"

"My mother. The nuns at school. It's in our culture."

"A common misconception. You came to this earth school for a purpose, like the rest of us. Your first obligation is to yourself. What good are you to the rest of us if you don't take care of you? If your heart is not full of light energy? Wonder? Joy? Gratitude? Appreciation? Love? Who would want a gift that is dense with resentment, bitterness, fear?"

"You're right, Elizabeth."

"The foundation would defeat itself if it forced you to continue giving such a gift. That's why you have free will to accept or decline any assignment. If your energy is not full, if you cannot give from a full heart, the gift you bring to others is really no gift at all." She paused for a moment. "You are doing well on this assignment. I have seen Mr. McDonald's expression when he looks at you. It is different. You are different from the women he has brought here in the past."

"There've been a lot?"

"I don't gossip about Mr. McDonald," Elizabeth answered. "He is a very good man who has experienced great sorrow in his life, but you must already know this."

Maggie nodded. "His wife and son."

"If you can help Mr. McDonald open his heart once again to the lightness of love, then I support you in your assignment. But you must promise never again to do what you did tonight. You endangered both our assignments."

"I promise," Maggie said, angry with herself for putting everything in danger. She also tried to suppress her anger with Marcus, feeling beyond annoyed that he hadn't given her all the information she so clearly needed.

"You've been given a great responsibility," Elizabeth stated, while rising from the chair. She took Maggie's near-empty cup. "There are many thousands of us in the world who are working in whatever capacity we hold to balance the darkness. Now get some rest and enjoy your time here."

Maggie rose, watching as Elizabeth placed the cups back onto the tray and picked it up. "I enjoyed our talk," she said in a shy voice. "I've never spoken to any other shape shifter, except Marcus. Especially a woman."

"Tomorrow morning," Elizabeth whispered when Maggie opened the door, "you will be a guest in this house and I will be the housekeeper. I take my job very seriously. I suggest you also remember how important your job is."

"We can talk again?" Maggie asked, hating that her voice sounded like a pleading child's.

"Not on this trip. Perhaps on the next."

"What if there isn't a next one?"

Elizabeth smiled for the first time that night. "Oh, there will be. I think there will be many trips here for you now. BellaLuna has accepted you and so have I."

Maggie's heart lifted, feeling she'd been given a seal of approval. She didn't know why it meant so much to her, but it did. "Thank you, Elizabeth."

"Sleep well."

"You, too," Maggie whispered back. She wanted to hug the older woman, but didn't think Elizabeth would have appreciated it. Shutting the door, she turned back to the bedroom.

In the silence of the night, Maggie walked over to the French doors and looked up at the moon. She'd met another woman shape shifter, one who'd saved her life and told her she had free will, that even the foundation recognized she could terminate her assignments and work in another capacity.

It was a taste of freedom that was sweet. There was hope.

Marcus hadn't counted on her meeting another and finding out the truth.

She could make this her last assignment.

She could be free.

NINE

"**I** don't believe it! You got there before me!"

Maggie couldn't stop grinning. She felt like Cinderella, retelling her story of Prince Charming sweeping her off her feet and taking her to a magical island. "Believe me, D. it came as a complete shock. I thought maybe dinner at a nice relaxing restaurant, not flying in a private jet to Bermuda!" She sighed, remembering her weekend trip. "God, it's so beautiful, D., and Julian's house . . . it's enchanting. I fell in love with it the moment I saw it."

They were seated at an outside table, having lunch. D. picked up her iced tea and pointed to Maggie. "Watch it; sounds like you're falling in love with the place *and* the guy."

"The place, yes," Maggie admitted. "The guy would be easy to fall in love with, but . . . it was just a spectacular second date, that's all."

D. dressed in a white blouse and tan linen skirt in preparation for reporting that evening's news, sat back in her chair, and stared across the table. "Don't make the mistake countless women before you have made. Julian McDonald is a great playmate, but the minute playing becomes entangled with emotions, he's a runner. Disappears so quickly he doesn't even leave dust in his trail."

"I know that."

"But you think you're different?"

Maggie shrugged. "I think he's different now. We spent Sunday reading, talking, and strolling the beach. He didn't even make a serious move on me."

D. leaned in closer and said in a low voice, "Listen, in my mother's day they would have called Julian a playboy—rich, lots of toys, loves the company of beautiful women to showcase on his arm. Oh, he can be serious—about business, about influential friends in right places. He puts his money where his mouth is in philanthropic causes and I'm sure he's a real nice guy to boot. I'm just saying watch out and remember he's simply playing. Anything else can lead to a broken heart."

Maggie couldn't explain to D. that she knew all those things, that Julian was the one now who seemed to want to bring emotions into play. She couldn't tell her friend that on Sunday as they strolled in the surf, Julian had held her hand and made plans for this coming weekend. "I can promise my heart won't be broken."

"Honey, I wish I could believe that. You should see yourself when you talk about him. Your eyes light up like a Christmas tree."

"I'm just excited. It was the best second date I've ever had."

"I can imagine. When are you seeing him again?"

"He's coming on Saturday after the store closes. He's bringing me to New York, to his apartment."

D. looked impressed. "My, my . . . he's taking you to his turf again, this time his cave. If I didn't know better I would think he is serious."

"What exactly do you know about him?" Maggie asked, checking her watch and seeing she had about ten minutes left to chat.

"Let's see," D. murmured, looking up to the sky peeking in between the tall buildings. "Outside of the business world, he's mainly known for the money he gives to charities. He's never been in a real relationship that I've heard of, save for his marriage. Shame about that. There's been talk that he's been approached several times to turn his attention to politics, but doesn't seem to be interested. Not that I blame him. Why should he? He's already got everything he wants."

Except happiness, Maggie thought. It was time to put an

end to the Julian McDonald discussion, so she said, "Well, I had a great time. Bermuda is stunningly beautiful and Julian's a wonderful host."

D. laughed. "I bet. Oh, don't mind me, Maggie. I'm just jealous. I won that trip to Bermuda and it'll probably be Fall before I can get away. Did I tell you James Coulter has been calling me?"

"James Coulter?"

"That man you practically made dance with me at the charity affair. Remember? Tall, reasonably attractive and . . . hey, not quite as attractive as that gorgeous man who's about to walk right up to this table, I believe."

Before she could even check out the guy, she heard the voice.

"Magdalene, that is you, isn't it?"

Maggie couldn't believe her ears were hearing that damn Italian accent! She spun around and was stunned to see Marcus right at their table. "What are you doing here?" she demanded.

Dressed in tan slacks and a tan silk shirt, and wearing his sunglasses on top of his dark curly hair, Marcus looked at D. and smiled. "I am afraid I have startled our mutual friend. I am Marcus Bocelli." He extended his hand and when D. looked quite pleased to put hers in his, he lowered his head and kissed her knuckles.

"Deborah Stark," D. answered in a near breathless voice. "Won't you join us?"

"Why thank you, Deborah," he answered, gracefully slipping onto the empty chair at their table. "What a surprise running into you, Magdalene, when I was hoping to see you. It is . . . how would you say it . . . fate?"

"Not quite," Maggie answered, trying to keep her temper under control. "And what a pity, too. I really have to be running back to the store."

"Oh, but you can sit with me for a few minutes, no?"

"No," Maggie stated emphatically and looked around for their waiter. When she saw him, she raised her arm and indicated she wanted the check.

"Well, what a shame I cannot share a few minutes with two of the most beautiful women here. I would be the envy of every male who passes." He smiled at D. and watched her eyes widen with delight.

"Maggie, surely we can have a cup of coffee and you can catch up with your friend."

"Sorry, D. I really have to be getting back."

"Since I interrupted it, allow me to pay for your lunch," Marcus said, rising with their waiter's approach. "Then I can walk you back to Soul Provisions, Magdalene. It will give us a chance to," he gave D. another devastating smile, "catch up." Without waiting for a reply, he walked off with the waiter.

"My God! Who *is* that hunka hunka burnin' love?"

Maggie had to relax her jaw in order to speak. "He's just an old friend. Nothing more."

"Well, he looks at you like it was something more."

"That was a very long time ago."

"How did you ever let that man get away? I'd have him hog-tied and branded in less time than it would take to yell out a fake orgasm!"

Maggie shook her head. "He's not one to be hog-tied, D. so don't even waste your time or your breath." She didn't want to add that with Marcus there had never been a need for a fake orgasm, but Maggie shook that stupid thought out of her head. How dare he interrupt her private lunch with a friend? She had *told* him to leave her alone. Oh yes, she'd walk with him back to the store and she'd definitely let him have a piece of her mind.

"How greedy can one woman be? Julian McDonald *and* Mr. Gorgeous-with-a-sexy-Italian-accent Bocelli? The man's oozing with charm and the air is positively crackling with pheromones. I swear when he kissed my hand, I almost swooned! The hair on my arms stood straight up! C'mon, Maggie, didn't your parents ever teach you about sharing?"

"There's nothing to share, D., honestly. Marcus Bocelli and I are simply friends. In my case, a reluctant friend."

"Then you wouldn't mind . . . ?" D. asked.

"Believe me, D., Marcus would only break your heart. Besides, he doesn't even live in the city."

"It's been broken before, kiddo, for far less a specimen of manly pulchritude. And what does it matter where he lives? May I remind you Julian McDonald lives in another state and that doesn't seem to be a problem."

"Fine," Maggie stated, watching Marcus return to their table. "Do whatever you want, just don't forget I warned you."

Rising from the table, D. leaned down and whispered to Maggie, "Thanks. Give him my number, and let's see what happens."

Maggie pushed her chair away and stood up. She leaned forward and gave D. an air kiss. "Good to see you again."

"I'll call you," D. replied with a pretty smile as she turned her attention to Marcus. "And it was a sincere pleasure to have made your acquaintance, Mr. Bocelli. I hope we meet again."

"Ah, Deborah, you have brightened my day. Who can tell what the future may hold, eh?" His lips brushed her hand. "*Ciao, bella bambina.*"

"*Ciao,*" D. answered in a breathless voice.

God, it was sickening to see how Marcus could turn an intelligent woman like Deborah Stark into a walking hormone. Maggie left the restaurant and waited until they were on the sidewalk before speaking.

"I thought I'd told you never to do that again, Marcus. How dare you interrupt my lunch and fawn all over my friend like that! Why can't you listen to me?"

"I thought I behaved charmingly. You didn't say I could *never* see you, so what is your complaint now?"

"My complaint is that you have no right to just barge into my life all the time."

"I went to your store and was told you were at lunch. When I explained it was of grave importance that I speak with you immediately, a young woman with red hair told me where to find you."

Maggie stopped walking and stared at him. He turned around to her slowly.

"You are not to insinuate yourself with my staff, is that understood? You play no part in my life, Marcus, save for my assignment."

"It is about the assignment, cara mia, that has caused me to seek you out in such a way. Why is it every time I see you, you strike out at me? What have I done to you that you would treat me with such hostility?"

"What have you done? How far back do you want me to go, Marcus?"

"Listen to me, Magdalene, I have heard about Elizabeth Edwards and your escapade in the sea."

"*What*?" Maggie couldn't believe that Elizabeth would report their talk to anyone. And so soon!

"I have heard from my superior. It appears Elizabeth is very pleased with you, but she claims you were not tutored in all things and that affects me. What did you do and what did you say about me?"

Maggie had to force her mouth closed in order to swallow. "Wait a minute. You're here because I got you into trouble?"

"That is correct."

She burst out laughing.

"I do not see anything humorous about this," Marcus protested, as she began walking again.

"You wouldn't," Maggie said, suddenly feeling much better. "You should have told me about shifting in water, how dangerous it is."

"Why would I *think* you would shift in water?!" Marcus demanded, truly upset.

"I should have been told about the dangers. If it were not for Elizabeth I would have died." This was a new aspect, seeing Marcus unraveling beside her.

"Perhaps this assignment is too much for you, Magdalene. I believed you were ready, but I may have been mistaken."

Again, she stopped walking and faced him. "Now wait one minute. Let's see if I've got this straight. You get in trouble and now you're thinking about pulling me from the assignment? When I'm making great progress? When

McDonald is ahead of schedule in opening up? When Elizabeth, who happens to be a shape shifter and knows about the foundation and that our assignments obviously coincide and are connected, is pleased with me? On what basis are you forming your decision? Pride? Because your feelings were hurt by a reprimand?" She tried to keep her smile from being condescending. "Now, now, Marcus. Pride is a deadly indulgence. You were the one who taught me that."

"I am serious, Magdalene. This is the most important assignment either one of us has ever worked on and . . . there are those who are very interested in each step we take."

"We? I thought this was *my* assignment. Where do you come into it?"

"I trained you. And I am on assignment myself with someone . . . " His words trailed off, as though he had already said too much.

"Someone? What is it, Marcus? Who is your assignment?"

"Suffice it to say it is someone who is important to your assignment."

She thought about that for a moment and then her jaw dropped. "Are you telling me your assignment is the woman Julian will fall in love with after me?"

"We can only hope."

Normally, such a revelation wouldn't have bothered her. In fact, it shouldn't have bothered her. It should have made her feel even better, knowing that after she left Julian he would find real happiness with another. So why did she feel as though Marcus had just punched her in her solar plexus?

So many feelings were swirling around inside of her that she knew she had to get centered. She couldn't let Marcus know how his words had affected her. "So who is she?"

"You don't have to know that. It isn't important to your assignment. What I need to know from you is if you think your training has prepared you properly for what you have to do. I do not want any more negative reports."

"But, Marcus, the reports about me weren't negative.

Yours were." For the first time she had something on him. He didn't seem quite so all knowing now.

"Do not play games with me, Magdalene. Remember it was I who taught you how to play."

"I wish I could forget," she said, turning the corner onto Chestnut Street. "You might as well know, this is my last assignment."

"What are you saying? Don't be ridiculous. You are a valuable member of the foundation."

"I'm not a member of the foundation. How can I be a member of something I know nothing about? Elizabeth told me I have free will in this. You can't make me do anything I don't want. And I don't want any more assignments." She stopped a few stores away from hers. She didn't want to end the conversation in front of her display window where they could be overseen by her staff.

Marcus looked up and down the street before saying in a low voice, "And then what do you intend to do, eh? Get married and live happily ever after?"

"Maybe. I don't know, but I want the chance for a normal life."

"What is wrong with you, Magdalene?" he asked, his eyes dark with irritation. "You of all people know you will never have a normal life. There is no such thing for you."

She felt the emotion in her chest and the burning in her eyes. What he said couldn't be true. It would be too cruel to help others for so many years and be denied the possibility of finding happiness herself. "I suppose I'll have to figure it out for myself, won't I?"

"Neither one of us are what is considered normal. You understood that and accepted it. You have a gift and—"

"It feels like a curse, Marcus," she interrupted. "I'm tired of helping others to heal and find real love. I want to try to have a normal life. I deserve it."

"*Cara mia*," he said in a low voice that was meant to be comforting. "I know the stress of this assignment is causing you great discomfort. I know how you feel. I have felt it myself . . . with you. Did you think I did not love you deeply? That I don't still? That I would have given anything to take you for my wife, to live what you call a normal life?"

"Stop it!" she ordered, pushing him away from her. "How dare you talk to me like that? It was *you* who said you would never marry, have children, be any woman's husband. It was you who taught me the rules, Marcus, and they were false. I know now I have free will. I can no longer be ordered on any assignment. This *is* my last."

"Magdalene, after this one you and I will go away together for a little holiday. It is past time for us, no?"

She closed her eyes briefly and tried to still her anger. "Forget it, Marcus. Don't try to use your charm on me. I'm immune to it now. You can't manipulate me any longer. Don't tell me you love me, or insult my intelligence by claiming you wanted to take me as your wife. And don't ever again think dangle a holiday with you as if it is some treat that I'll grab, as though you're throwing me a bone and I'll be ever so grateful to spend time in your presence. Those days are over."

His eyes narrowed for only a few seconds before they softened again. "You are truly upset. And I didn't mean for that to happen. Forgive me, Magdalene, I meant only to help you see reality. I do care for you most deeply."

"You overestimate your charm, Marcus." She looked down the street. "And I have to get back to work."

He took her wrist and raised it to his lips, softly kissing her pulse. "You and I are alike, *cara mia*. You may try to find normal, but you will come back. We are, as you say, two of a kind. And you know my arms will always be open to receive you."

She pulled her hand free. "You're wrong. I'm not like you. You enjoy the chase, the seduction, the surrender to love. It's starting to break my heart." She would not cry and allow him that satisfaction. "Good-bye, Marcus."

She was afraid Max would run away from her in fear, yet when she walked into Julian's apartment on Saturday evening, the old retriever's tail was wagging as he came up to greet her and Julian. "Hi there, boy," she said, crouching down to his level and scratching his head. "Good to meet you, Max."

"Well, he seems to like you."

She looked up to Julian and smiled. "I think we're gonna be pals. How old is he?"

Julian thought for a moment as he put his sunglasses and keys into a pewter tray on the hall table. "He's . . . eleven. We've been together for a long time, right, Max?"

Hearing its name, the dog left Maggie and walked up to its master. Julian petted Max's head. "He was a Christmas present for my son. I know they say you shouldn't get pets during the holidays, but it worked out well."

Maggie slowly rose. "What was your son's name?"

She could see the muscle in Julian's jaw tighten right before he said, "Morgan."

"Morgan McDonald," Maggie whispered. "A great name."

He simply nodded and held his hand out to the living room, inviting her to enter his home. Save for a terrace in the back overlooking a small garden, Maggie already knew the apartment, but made all the right comments as Julian gave her a tour of the place. This time it was thorough and she suddenly realized there was only one bedroom.

"Julian?"

They were in the kitchen and he had opened the refrigerator and was taking out platters that had already been prepared by a cook or a caterer. Smiling, he popped his head over the refrigerator door. "Yes?"

"Um, I couldn't help but notice there's only one bedroom."

He placed the platters on the counter, then turned around and leaned against it. "If that's a problem I can sleep on the sofa."

She moved closer to him, using her finger to gently push back a stray lock of hair from his forehead. He was so cute, so willing to wait for the right moment. "I didn't say it was a problem," she whispered, staring at his lips as they formed a sexy smile after hearing her answer.

His arm came around her waist and he pulled her against him. "Good."

It wasn't planned, for it was hardly the room for the first real taste of intimacy.

His lips came down on hers in a hungry possession. She answered his claim by meeting the thrust of his tongue with one of her own, as her arms circled his back. It seemed that was the invitation he'd been waiting for and he moaned as his hands roamed over her breasts, around her back. When he squeezed her behind and then slid his hand down to pull her leg up, Maggie obeyed willingly, wrapping her leg around his thigh. He lifted her up and turned himself around, placing her on the edge of the counter. Standing between her legs, he stared into her eyes. "Do you know how long I've waited, how patient I have been? How much I've wanted you?"

She pulled him in closer and ran her fingers through his hair as she whispered against his mouth, "I do believe, Mac, your patience and your waiting has come to an end."

And that's when it happened, when neither one of them gave thought to anything save surrendering to a passion kept too long under control. He opened her blouse as his lips trailed the skin from her ear to her shoulder, to her nipple. She pulled his shirt over his head and ran her nails down his bare back, savoring the feel of his skin and the way he responded to her touch. His hand reached under her skirt, slowly, agonizingly slowly, as though memorizing the feel of her thighs, her hips, the small of her back until he sank his hands beneath the silk panties and Maggie raised her hips as he pulled them off.

And then he knelt down, his lips and tongue teasing her ankle, her calf, her knee, her thigh . . . branding her as he left hot imprints of petition upon her skin. No thoughts of denying him access even entered her mind as her blood began to thicken, to rush to wherever his lips were. Supported by her arms, she leaned back, her head thrown backward, waiting, wanting, biting her lower lip not to command him to hurry. When he finally reached her, she cried out.

Her arm also slipped and the platter of food went crashing to the floor.

"Oh, God. Julian! I'm so sorry!"

He raised his head, saw the damage, and laughed before returning to his mission. "To hell with it," he muttered, as his hands grasped her hips and he pulled her back into position. "Sweet Maggie, it ain't food I'm hungry for at the moment . . ."

She couldn't stop the giggle, but laughter was quickly replaced with a gasp of shock, then glorious desire, as he branded her with his tongue. "Julian," she whispered, as he continued to explore her, finding her core and making her shudder with need. She gave herself over to it, caressing his hair, allowing each stroke of his tongue to tear down her defenses until she thought she'd die if he dared to stop. From some faraway place she heard Max attacking the food on the floor and she forced that outrageous image out of her mind as Julian expertly drove away all thoughts of anything, save the ways he was finding to drive her over the edge. She was so close, so very close. And Julian must have known it, for as he stood up she cried out with denial. But such disappointment was short-lived as he yanked down his zipper and pulled her against him, finding her open and wet and so very much in need.

"Oh, God," he cried out as he entered her.

She clung to him with one arm and supported herself with the other as they began the ancient dance of lovers, a dance that was wild and primeval and Maggie had to restrain herself from shifting right out of her body and into an animal. She wanted to take him deep inside of her, to devour him, to make him hers. He stirred something profound within her, some small hidden place that had been disturbed by only one other man and she had to fight to clear her mind of any image that wasn't human.

"Julian," she cried out. "Julian. Julian." She kept repeating his name, making sure the object of her passion was

clearly and firmly in her mind. And the more she said his
name, the more the desire built. Again she could feel herself coming closer to the edge and her focus was so clear,
so centered, that nothing else existed in that moment save
the man making love to her. Nothing else was real. Together
they stopped time and thought. They were driven by a need
as old as the universe . . . the rhythm of the dance, the cul-
mination of body heat, the friction and grazing of sensitive
nerve endings all coming together in one explosive burst of
exquisite creativity.

"Oh, my God!" he cried out, holding her so close she was
supporting him. He threw back his head and the sound that
came out of his mouth was a mixture of agony and ecstasy,
of release, triumph, and sheer joy. And then she joined him,
soaring in that timeless, powerful space where the miracle of
pleasure was too great to contain within herself so she
released it, taking him with her as her essence expanded
beyond the room, the apartment, the city, the planet. She
became one . . . with Julian, with all space. With nothing, no
thing, and every thing, all at once.

Moments passed in silence as they both tried to come
back into this world, to the mundane, the ticking of the wall
clock, the sound of Max slurping up food from the floor, the
sound of the traffic on the street below.

"What *was* that?" he gasped. "I've . . . never . . . damn . . .
that was unbelievable!"

She kissed his damp temple and smiled, even as the
aftershocks of pleasure continued to make her shudder
and, in response, so did he. "That was making love," she
murmured.

"Holy shit," he muttered, still trying to catch his breath.

Feeling his heartbeat pounding against her, she ran her
shaking fingers over the side of his face. "It was beautiful,
Julian. Thank you."

He raised his head and stared into her eyes. His face was
flushed, beads of sweat were trickling down his forehead and
temples. His eyes looked wide and wondering, as though he
still hadn't recovered. "You aren't upset? I mean . . . here . . .

in the kitchen . . . Jesus, Maggie, my legs are shaking so bad right now I don't know if I can stand up by myself."

She chuckled. "Wanna come up here on the counter with me?"

"I haven't the strength!" he said and laughed. "I should do something romantic now, like carry you into the bedroom and wash you with hot towels, but damn . . . woman, you've taken all I have to give."

She slid down in front of him and wrapped his arm around her shoulder. "Lean on me, Sparky, and I'll get you to bed," she said, grabbing his belt to keep his pants up. "You're too big to carry."

"This isn't the way I planned it, you know," he said as they walked out of the kitchen. "I wanted it to be something special, not attacking you like that."

"Who was attacked?" she demanded with a laugh. "I do believe I was more than a willing partner."

"I'll make it up to you. I promise," he stated, holding onto the hall wall to steady himself. "Jesus, this is embarrassing, but I feel as weak as a kid."

"Why is it embarrassing? If you were helping me into the bedroom, would you think less of me?"

"I'm the man!" he exclaimed and then chuckled. "I should be carrying you. Then I'd feel like I was ten feet tall having rendered you weak with lovemaking." He ran his chin over her temple. "It's not supposed to be like this."

She laughed as they neared the bedroom. "What? So I'm not allowed to feel ten feet tall? Hell, I feel twenty feet tall. So there! Deal with it." She brought him to the bed and shoved him onto it.

He lay down, his bare arms outstretched, his pants unfastened. He ran his fingers through his hair and moaned. "What have you done to me, woman?"

She laughed as she walked into the bathroom. Pulling a towel from the brass rail, she turned on the water at the sink. "Are you complaining, Mac?"

"I don't know what I am," he yelled back. "Nothing like that has ever happened to me before."

"Like what? Tell me," she stated, wringing out the towel and bringing it with her into the bedroom.

He turned his head. "Maggie. Honest to God, I've had good sex before. Great sex even. But that . . . that was unbelievable!"

"Believe it," she whispered, sitting down next to him. Taking the wet part of the towel, she softly began blotting the sweat on his face to cool him down.

His hand grabbed her wrist, pulling the towel to his chest. "I felt like . . . I don't know how to describe it . . . like I was out there . . . you know? As though a part of me escaped like a . . . a rocket into space. I know it sounds crazy."

"It doesn't sound crazy at all," she said, staring at his expression of wonder.

"No?"

She shook her head and smiled. "It sounds, Mac, as though for a timeless space you left the human experience and experienced a touch of the Divine."

He didn't say anything, just continued to stare deeply into her eyes.

Maggie stared back, allowing him entrance into her soul. She smiled again, letting him know it was okay to search for whatever he wanted, that there was safety in her. She didn't want anything from him.

"Who *are* you?" he whispered. "You come into my life and turn it around. I had structure, a routine. I knew what tomorrow was going to bring."

"You mean you were a control addict. You forgot about spontaneity, how joyful it can be when you just allow life to unfold before you. Like you did in the kitchen."

"That was definitely spontaneous," he agreed with a chuckle. "And combustible."

"And was it joyful?" she asked, unable to stop her pleased grin.

"God, yes!"

"Good." She rose from the bed. "Now I'm going to take a quick shower as you contemplate the many joys of not knowing what the next moment can bring. May I use your robe on the back of the door?"

"Maggie, in this moment you can do whatever you wish. I am helpless to put up any resistance."

She laughed as she went into the bathroom. "Don't tempt me, Julian."

Turning on the water in the shower, Maggie sighed with exhaustion. Even though she'd like nothing better than to snuggle up next to Julian she wanted to refresh herself and clear her head. She pulled off her skirt and blouse and left them on the floor. They were ruined anyway. Thankful for the clean clothes in her overnight bag, she entered the shower and reveled in the many jets of cool water that came out of the marble walls. Really, all she had to do was soap herself and then just stand there.

So she did.

With the water soothing her muscles, she closed her eyes and just allowed the water to run over her. Making love with Julian had been far better than she'd expected. He was a very good lover, so good he'd been able to take her out of herself in record time. She remembered having to fight her imagination to stay in human form. Only Marcus had been able to do that. Without warning, her brain ran images of that dark-haired Italian, of them making love, her shifting into a lioness, him into a lion biting her neck. The wildness of their lovemaking had been exhilarating, but Maggie shook those thoughts out of her head. It seemed almost a betrayal of Julian to be thinking about Marcus so soon after such an incredible experience. Julian, when he'd lost his inhibitions and self-image, possessed an astonishing ability. He was quite a man, a man who Maggie knew could accomplish great things in his life beyond his business endeavors. His heart was opening, and if he could leave it open and unprotected, some woman was going to find herself married to an extraordinary man.

At the thought, Maggie's stomach clenched in rebellion.

What was that? She couldn't be jealous.

She'd never been jealous before. She'd always felt blessed to have been a part in revealing the man's potential, in knowing that her gift was also a gift to others, to the man, to the woman he would attract, to the children he might have, the friends who would enter his life, the community he would interact with. Why didn't she feel like that now? It was too confusing and she turned off the thoughts as she also turned off the water in the shower. She didn't have time for such introspection. Now that Julian's heart was opening, the opportunity for him to heal was within his grasp.

This was going to be an intense night and tomorrow might be just as demanding.

She toweled off and slipped into Julian's thick white terry cloth robe. She had to roll the sleeves up and when she tied it, the hem still dragged on the floor. She opened a drawer on the wide vanity and found a comb. Surely, Julian wouldn't object since they'd just shared far more intimate things than toiletries. She ran the comb through her damp hair and then walked out of the bathroom.

Just as she'd expected, Julian was fast asleep.

Smiling, she quietly left the bedroom and made her way into the kitchen. It was a disaster. Max was lying on the floor, obviously satiated with forbidden food.

"Well, we've got quite a mess here, don't we?"

The golden retriever lifted his head and wagged his tail, but didn't get up.

"I bet your tummy is hurting, huh?" Maggie bent down and rubbed his head. "I guess since I caused this, it's up to me to clean it up." She grabbed the roll of paper towels from the counter and opened the cabinet door under the sink. Finding a hidden garbage can, she took it out of its holder and brought it with her. What a shame, she thought, as she picked up the remains of what looked to have been a fabulous pork roast with mashed potatoes and gravy. Max had left the vegetables alone.

It took her twenty minutes to clean the floor thoroughly. When she finished, she opened the refrigerator, found a dessert, milk, light cream for coffee, eggs, cheese, and not much else. She opened a few cabinets and was surprised by the lack of staples in the place. Obviously, Julian ate out a lot. Well, she was hungry and didn't know the local Chinese takeout, so she decided to make omelets. Doing a search of his kitchen she managed to find everything she needed, including Pepto-Bismol for Max.

She felt very comfortable in his kitchen, barefoot, wearing his robe, talking to his dog. Maggie didn't want to face the fact she was becoming very comfortable around Julian. Perhaps too comfortable. She brought the omelets into the bedroom and sat cross-legged on the mattress next to him.

"Wake up, sleepyhead," she whispered in his ear.

His eyelids fluttered open and he tried to focus. "Maggie?" he asked in a rough, sleepy voice.

She handed him a glass of water from the tray on the night table. "Here, you must be thirsty."

He slowly rolled over onto his side and leaned on his elbow. "Thanks," he muttered, accepting the glass.

She watched him drink. His hair was tousled and he looked much younger bare-chested. "You must be hungry. I'm starved," she exclaimed, taking back the empty water glass and handing him a plate. She placed napkins and forks on the bed and then took her own plate. "We kind of ruined our dinner. And what we didn't ruin, Max ate. Poor thing has a bad tummyache. I gave him some Pepto-Bismol."

"You shouldn't have had to clean that up by yourself. How long have I been asleep?"

"About forty-five minutes. Just a nap." She picked up her fork and dug into her omelet. "And I made that mess. It was only fair I cleaned it. I'm just thankful whoever made it didn't use glass platters. That would have been a nightmare."

"Someone arranged it for me. I was supposed to transfer everything to the oven." Julian bit into his omelet and moaned in appreciation. "This is delicious," he stated. "I'm sorry you had to cook. You must be exhausted. You worked today and well, after everything . . ." His words trailed off.

She grinned and bent down to kiss the tip of his nose. "Thanks for thinking about me, but I'm fine."

He grinned back at her and then used his hand to hold the

nape of her neck, to keep her there. Nose to nose, he said, "Lady, you're more than fine. You are brilliant." He paused as he let go of her head. "You kinda scare me a little."

She laughed as she straightened. "I do?"

Nodding, he grinned back at her. "I've never met anyone like you before. You make me think about stuff I haven't even considered since I was young. And I cringe thinking about being so weak you had to walk me in here. And then I fall asleep on you while you clean my kitchen, tend to my dog, and make me dinner. You're intimidating, Maggie O'Shea."

"Get over it, Mac," she declared, right before stuffing her face with more omelet. "Besides, this isn't dinner," she added after swallowing. "This is to keep us from starving. Do you ever keep food in this house?"

"I eat out a lot."

"I guessed. Well, if we get hungry later, I hope you have the number of a good takeout joint."

His hand slipped under the fold in the robe and caressed her knee. "What if I'm hungry right now?"

She narrowed her eyes. "Finish your omelet."

"Maggie, you were fantastic."

"What? A little power nap and you're superman again? I think not, Mr. McDonald. Somebody's going to have to walk that dog after all it's eaten, and it's not going to be me."

He laughed. "You're right."

She watched him regain interest in his food and then said, "You know, Julian, I think Max has joint problems. Maybe it's arthritis. Have you noticed him limping when you walk him?"

"Not really." Then he nodded. "Well, maybe a couple of times."

"He should be checked. I believe they have medicine for that now."

"I'll tell Bill about it on Monday."

"You won't forget?" She pictured Bill Myers, the man who Julian said kept his life organized, who drove away and left them at the airport in Philly. That seemed so long ago.

"I promise. Bill will get Max to the vet and I'll report back to you."

"Well, you don't have to do that. I was just concerned. I know how much Max means to you."

He didn't say anything, just continued to eat.

She figured now was as good a time as any to begin.

"You don't talk about them, Julian."

He glanced up. "Who?"

She stared into his eyes and smiled. "We haven't played games so far tonight; let's not start now. You know exactly who I'm talking about."

He dropped his fork onto his plate and sat up. Placing the plate onto his night table, he leaned back against the pillows and said, "What do you want to know?"

Finished with her omelet, she sat back and turned on her side to face him. "Whatever you want to tell me."

"I don't want to tell you anything. I don't talk about them."

Reaching out, she stroked his upper arm and felt his muscles tighten with defense. "Relax, Julian. If you haven't figured it out yet, I'm not someone you have to be on guard with. I'm asking because I care about you."

He turned his head to look down at her. His expression was serious. "I care about you, too, Maggie. And it makes no sense. I've only known you existed for a few weeks and . . ."

"And what?"

"And you've turned my world upside down."

"I didn't do that, Julian. If your world is upside down, you're doing it because who you are is changing, things you've believed to be true are shifting. Most people get rattled by change."

"I know that, but this is major change for me."

"In what way?"

He sighed. "I should get a shower."

She grinned. "You're probably right, but I'll still be here, waiting for you to answer that question."

"You are relentless, aren't you?"

She shook her head. "Nah. Just persistent."

"So I should just surrender?" His right eyebrow lifted with his question and a smile played at his lips, bringing out that dimple in his cheek.

"Surrender's a choice. I simply would like to know why this is a major change for you."

"Because it *is*."

She laughed. "Now you sound like a child who doesn't want to tell the truth. If it's so important to you, keep your answer and take your shower. I'll just draw my own conclusions."

"Oh, you're good," he said, shaking his head. "I'm glad you don't sit across a conference table from me." When she didn't answer him, he looked at her and said in a low voice, "Maggie, you're making me think things I thought were impossible. And that's scary for someone like me."

"Someone like you?"

"Someone who . . ." He took a deep breath. " . . . who didn't believe someone like you would come into my life."

"Again?" she offered, reaching out to once more touch his arm.

This time his muscles didn't resist her. "Again," he repeated in an emotional voice. "You have to understand. I closed myself off to it, to even the possibility of you."

She waited a few moments before asking, "What was her name?"

He waited a few moments more before answering. "Catherine. Cat. She was a good wife and mother."

Maggie nodded. "She must have been for you to still grieve for her."

"Okay, is that enough?" he asked with false brightness. "Can I take my shower now?"

"You can do whatever you want, Julian. Thank you for telling me."

He hopped off the bed and headed for the bathroom. "I'll be quick and take Max for his walk. If you want to order anything, there's a pile of menus in my desk drawer."

He shut the bathroom door and Maggie stretched out on

the bed. Well, he'd successfully closed her out, but there was the rest of the night and tomorrow to get through. This was always the most difficult part, even more difficult than the parting. And Julian had years to build that wall around his heart. It would take more than a few minutes to pull it down.

TEN

They both got hungry about eleven o'clock and Julian ordered takeout from an Italian restaurant. Even in Philly, a city of considerable size and amenities, finding a good Italian restaurant to deliver at such a late hour was highly improbable. Only in the city that never sleeps was such a treat commonplace.

Maggie had changed into beige capri pants and was wearing one of Julian's white shirts with the sleeves rolled up. She was sitting cross-legged in bed and when the doorbell rang and Max barked, Julian sprang off the mattress.

"Be right back," he said, grabbing his wallet from the night table and following Max from the room.

"I'll pause the movie." She picked up the remote, causing Kevin Kline's face to be frozen in an endearing smile. Lying back against the pillows, she sighed with contentment. They'd decided to stay in and watch a video and Maggie had picked *The Emperor's Club*. It was turning out to be a great choice. The movie, and staying in.

They'd cuddled together against the pillows, leisurely exploring each other, making love again with tenderness and awe. They'd also showered again, though this time together, and it was then Julian had taken his time drying her, enfolding her into his thick robe and taking her to the bed. When she stated she had to dry her hair, he took the hair dryer, made her sit between his legs, and brushed her hair dry. She almost fell asleep with his gentle ministrations. It had been her idea to relax and watch a video and Julian had seemed grateful, telling her he rarely got the chance to catch up on the ones Bill bought. He had then revealed a television hidden in what she thought was an armoire and had called out the titles of videos.

Everything fell into place and even Julian remarked as they'd settled into the bed that it was as though they'd known each other forever, how easy and relaxed it was to be together.

She'd told him it was because they'd gotten the sex out of the way and he'd laughed and insisted it was more than that, otherwise he wouldn't be able to tell her to shut up so he could hear the movie. She'd acted insulted and they had started wrestling for the remote until he'd pinned her to the mattress and she had surrendered after being thoroughly kissed into silence.

"Okay, madam," Julian called out, ending her recollections. He was carrying a big tray into the bedroom. "Our dinner is served."

"Oh, goody!" she exclaimed, her taste buds salivating at the close proximity of food. He looked so cute, dressed in his gray sweat pants and a white T-shirt, his hair messed up, and barefoot, as he carefully placed the tray on the bed.

"Wow," she whispered, seeing he had transferred their food onto good china and was using crisp white napkins and, if she wasn't mistaken, sterling silver cutlery. "I'm impressed."

"Hey, I promised you a dinner, didn't I?" He sat back in his place, cross-legged, and added, "And now you get the addition of a movie. Don't ever tell me I don't treat you to the best."

She turned her head. "You treat me very well, Julian. Thank you."

"I was kidding," he said, picking up his knife and fork.

She smiled as she pointed the remote at the television and resumed their movie. "I wasn't," she murmured.

His attention focused on the television set, he leaned over and kissed her temple, smelling like the lemon-butter sauce of the chicken francese they had both ordered. "Thanks, now let's eat and watch the rest of the movie."

Maggie grinned at his casual behavior and she was glad he was so interested in this film about young boys learning about honor and serving their fellow man through a remarkable teacher. Obviously Julian was happy, and she realized how much she had needed such a night. Great company. Great sex. Great food. A great movie. And her feet were up.

Yes, indeed, it would be so easy to get used to this, to him. Maybe for tonight, just tonight, she could pretend it didn't have to end.

They returned to Philadelphia with Max in the back of the car, the top off, listening to oldies blaring from the CD player and singing along when a favorite song brought back memories of being younger and filled with dreams. Both she and Julian were surprised when they arrived in the city, feeling like the drive took less than half the time they'd expected.

"You're sunburned," she said, grabbing her overnight case as Julian helped Max out of the car.

"So are you," he answered. "We should have used sun block."

She put her bag down on the sidewalk and held Max's lead as Julian fixed the roof into place. "I have some lotion we can put on."

He grinned. "I can't wait."

"Well, you're going to have to," she called out, as Max squatted down by a tree. "You're going to have to come back here and clean up this."

Julian shook his head, as though he couldn't blame Max, who'd suffered through being windblown and stuck in a car for an hour and a half. "I'll do it," he said, locking the last part of the roof into place. He grabbed a small leather bag, put it on the sidewalk, and then opened the glove compartment and pulled out a package of wipes. Luckily there was a refuse container about ten feet away.

"Always prepared, I see," Maggie commented, as Julian picked up both their bags and she continued to hold Max on his leash.

"Have to be with an old dog. But you're worth it, aren't you, Max?"

The dog heard his name, but was more interested in sniffing each and every door and corner they passed. When he seemed particularly interested in one spot, Maggie heard Julian say, "I think we look good together."

She glanced up to see their reflection in an ornate mirror displayed in an antique store's window. She was wearing a white blouse with a pale yellow sweater thrown over her shoulders, and jeans. Julian was wearing jeans and a robin's-egg-blue Polo shirt. They looked . . . like a couple. A well-matched couple, returning home after a great weekend.

"What do you think?"

Maggie didn't want to admit what she thought. Instead, she said, "I think I need to take a brush to my hair. Good God, I look like a wild woman."

He leaned over and murmured against her cheek. "Your wildness is an aspect of you that I love!"

Laughing, she shoved him to continue walking and tugged on Max's lead. "Come on, boy. Your master is going to have to carry you up the stairs. Let's see how much energy he's got left after that."

"Oh, you underestimate me, Maggie O'Shea."

"Hey, Mac, I seem to remember assisting you down a hallway and dropping you into bed."

"And I suppose you're never going to let me forget that, are you?" he asked in a teasing voice.

"Probably not. Face it, it's too good to forget. Any time you get too puffed up with testosterone, I have this terrific thing to bring you back down to size. What sane woman would let it go?"

"One with a little bit of compassion?"

She inserted her key, opened the door, and walked in with Max. "Oh, I have compassion." Nodding to the stairs, she bent down and unhooked the dog's lead. "I'll have a glass of wine waiting for you when you get to the top."

"I think he can handle the stairs, Maggie."

"No, he can't," she insisted, taking the bags from Julian's

hands. "He needs to be carried until he's on medication. You don't want to aggravate the situation." She began walking upstairs. "White or red?"

Julian bent down and grunted as he picked up Max, who had to weigh over sixty pounds. "Red," he growled. "I'll need to build up my blood after this."

Maggie put their bags into her bedroom and went into the kitchen. She found a bottle of red wine and was opening it when Max came walking into the room. "Welcome to my home, Max," she said cheerfully. "Where's your human?"

Julian came into view and leaned over the counter while trying to recover his breath. "I'm right here and I'm wondering just who is the master in this man/canine relationship."

Popping the cork, Maggie laughed. "Didn't you know, Julian, that a true master serves?" And she served him his glass of wine.

"Is there some significance to your words I should know?" His voice was teasing, but his gaze was intense.

Maggie shrugged as she poured wine for herself. "Just referring to the words in the Sting song. The servant is the master." She held up her glass. "Thanks for a fabulous overnighter." Leaning across the counter, she kissed his chin. "And I do mean fabulous. I can't remember when I've had such a great time."

He sipped his wine as Max began exploring the apartment. "You mean that?"

"I try to always say what I mean. Don't you?"

His head tilted slightly. "Sure, but I don't want you trying to flatter me or—"

"Hold on there," she interrupted. "Are you implying that I don't flatter you? That I didn't jump out of bed and do cheers and you had to wait until now to hear how fabulous you are?"

"Maggie . . ."

Giggling, she put down her glass and stood in the middle of the kitchen as he came around the counter. With her hands on her hips, she began, "Julian, Julian, he's our man. If he can't do me until my knees are weak then—"

He quickly pulled her into his arms. Staring into her eyes, he muttered, "Finish it. Say it, Maggie."

She read the desire for possession in his eyes.

"Say it," he challenged.

"Then no one can," she whispered, right before his mouth came down on hers.

He kissed her long and thoroughly, holding her head in his hands, and when it ended he rested his lips against her forehead. "What have you done to me, Maggie? In three weeks you've made me feel . . ." His words trailed off.

She turned her head and rested it against his shoulder as they stood wrapped in each other's arms. "That's a good thing, right? To feel again?"

She could sense him nodding.

"It's scary," he admitted.

"I know. But if you don't feel, you aren't fully alive, are you?"

"It seems safer to protect myself."

"From hurt? Julian, do you really think life should only be about what we consider good things? Would you appreciate all your advantages now if you hadn't worked hard first? I'm sure it was scary then, too. I bet you had to hustle to pay your rent, buy your textbooks in college, pay for your electricity. And I bet you ate more peanut butter and jelly sandwiches than you care to remember."

She could feel his chest move as he chuckled. "I swore I'd never eat them again."

"So they were tough times, but you used them as challenges or opportunities to accomplish great things. Many people don't, Julian. They feel defeated by life and settle for less than their dreams because they're afraid of risk. You're a risk taker." She kissed his jaw and moved out of his arms. Picking up their glasses of wine, she handed his to him. "In most areas of your life."

He leaned back against the dishwasher and studied her as he sipped his wine. "It sounds like there's a follow-up to that last statement."

It was time. She knew she could take his hand and lead

him into the bedroom and delay this talk. So much of her wanted to do just that, to pretend and take comfort in his arms, but she had to remind herself that Julian McDonald was her assignment. She didn't have the right to dream of a future with him. He belonged to a faceless woman who could give him everything he desired, or at least one who didn't shape shift right out of her body. Julian was an intelligent man and, even though he may be starting to fall in love with her, he could never accept her gift and her curse. What normal man would?

"C'mon, let's get comfortable." She took his hand and led him into the living room. They sat down on the sofa and she cuddled up next to him when he put his arm out in invitation.

"So what did you mean 'in most areas'?"

She took a deep breath and exhaled slowly. "You surprise me, Julian. I didn't think you would be open to this discussion."

"I'm open to your opinion. That doesn't mean you're right."

She grinned. "No wonder you're so successful. You must be a great negotiator."

"I am."

She nodded. "Okay, here's my opinion, for what it's worth. You are afraid to take a risk with your heart because you have been so traumatized by the deaths of your wife and son."

She felt his muscles tighten with defense. "Is that what you think?"

"Yes. And it's understandable," she said as Max came and lay down by their feet. "You have everything any man could ever want, save real happiness. You've closed off your heart for protection. If you never love again, you can never be that hurt again."

"You have no idea what it was like." His voice sounded dull, without feeling.

"You're right. I don't. But I know you're scared because you're beginning to feel something you promised yourself you never would again. I just want you to know that you're worthy of real happiness again, Julian. You deserve that."

He didn't say anything for a long time. Maggie respected his right to his thoughts. She resisted lifting her head to see his expression, but she could feel his turmoil, how he wanted to take his arm away from her, pick up his dog and his bag, and leave this discussion. And her.

"So that's your opinion of me," he finally muttered.

She nodded. "That's my opinion of why you are afraid of love, but my opinion of you is so much more." She took his hand. "I admire your intelligence, your instincts, your generosity, your compassion for those not as fortunate as you. I love your hands, strong hands that feel as though they can protect me, yet can also be exquisitely gentle. I love your spirit of adventure, in life and in making love to me. I appreciate your taste in food, clothes, art, the way you've decorated your homes. And I love the way you can make me laugh. You are, frankly, quite a man, Julian McDonald. One that I respect."

"Wow," he murmured. "I swear I wasn't hunting for compliments."

She laughed. "I know you weren't. I was serious. This is a serious discussion, even though you are trying to lighten it up with humor."

His arm tightened around her. "I know. It's just that I've only known you such a short time and I wasn't ready for this to happen."

"For what to happen, Julian?"

"You know what I'm talking about."

"I think you need to say it, to make it real."

He sighed, blowing his breath out in a frustrated rush. "Do you know what I do during the week? Instead of concentrating on business, I'm daydreaming about you, about the way you looked coming out of the sea at BellaLuna. Or I'm picturing you coming down those stairs at the charity ball, or flirting with me in front of the painting in that gown. Or the way you looked asleep on the plane. I can be in the middle of an important deal and I can hear your infectious giggle in my head. I can envision that beauty mark right above your breasts and I find myself getting hard. I'm wondering about men coming into your store and capturing your attention. I'm even irrationally jealous of that musician guy whose songs you play. And for the first time in years I'm not having trouble sleeping. This is *not* me, Maggie."

"Who is it then, if not you?"

"This is some guy who's infatuated, who isn't thinking clearly."

"And that's what you think this is, infatuation?"

"Well, yes. I mean, I have all the signs."

She pulled out of his arms and sat back to look into his face. "Okay, let's tap dance our way all around this. Let's pull this discussion every which way, except where you're afraid to go. Is that what you've planned?"

He stared at her. "You *are* relentless, aren't you?"

"About this, yes. What do you expect me to do? I care about you, Julian, but you already know that. Am I supposed to just ignore the fact that every time we get close to discussing your wife and your son you manage to divert us?"

"I don't *want* to talk about them!"

Now she was getting somewhere. "I know that. I think you have to."

"Or . . . ?" He left the challenge out there, daring her to proceed.

"Or you will live the rest of your life too damaged for any woman. You will continue to live half a life, terrified of loving someone who might one day leave you, and then years from now you'll be an old man, alone, without—"

"Half a life?" he demanded, putting his glass on the cocktail table. He rose and stared down at her. "You just said I have everything any man could want. I have a great life. A *great* life!"

"I said you had everything any man could want, save happiness. Who are your friends, Julian? I mean real friends, the ones you can talk to in the middle of the night about your fears? I'm not speaking about business acquaintances or influential people where the conversations are on the surface.

I think maybe Max is your best friend because the two of you survived something you thought would kill you. I think that dog is the only one you can be honest with about your true feelings, but Max can't answer you. He can't tell you that life is about joy and also pain, about loss, about the courage it takes to be vulnerable, to open yourself up to something that scares the hell out of you, to love again. Because without love somewhere in your life, Julian, you're playing at life on the surface. All your advantages and toys can keep you busy ignoring what's really missing, someone, anyone, who can look at you, all of you, and reaffirm you are beautiful and worthy of real happiness."

He was breathing heavily, working his jaw muscles, blinking rapidly.

"You don't have to stay the night, Julian," she said, feeling his hostility. "It doesn't matter what we planned. I know you don't want to be here right now."

"Well, thanks for your permission, Maggie. It must be nice to have all the answers to everyone's problems. You make a good living out of that downstairs, but I don't appreciate your amateur psychological analysis of me. I'm not some poor creature that needs one of your books to get me through the night, thinking some guru has all the answers to my problems."

She couldn't help smiling slightly. "Any guru worth his love beads would tell you all the answers are within you."

He closed his eyes briefly, as though gathering his patience. "You're right," he said, turning around and heading toward her bedroom. "I should go. No point getting up early to miss rush-hour traffic in the morning."

She watched him get his bag from her bedroom and walk back into the kitchen for the leash.

Holding it in his hand, he said, "Come on, Max. We're going home."

Max didn't move from Maggie's feet.

"Max!"

"He knows you're angry," she said, petting the dog's head. "Give me the lead and I'll walk him to the stairs."

Maggie rose and took the leash from Julian's outstretched hand. "C'mon, Max," she urged when she'd fastened it to his collar.

The dog rose and walked with her to the stairs. She handed the lead back to Julian and said, "Drive carefully. I know you're upset."

"I will," he answered, then turned his attention to his dog. "Let's go, boy."

He started down the stairs and tugged on Max's leash to pull him along.

"Maybe you should carry him," Maggie called out.

"He doesn't need to be carried," Julian insisted and Maggie winced with what she knew was Max's pain as he tried to keep up with the irritated man ahead of him.

When the door closed, Maggie wrapped her arms around her waist and sighed deeply. That hadn't gone as well as she'd expected. Well, he'd either think about what she'd said and contact her, or she'd have to resort to more direct methods.

There was a part of her that strongly wanted Julian to return to her because he missed her so much that he would do whatever it took to heal himself and this distance that now existed between them. She didn't want to go back to New York and shape shift into his life again to remind him that he was worthy of someone's love.

And then it hit her like a baseball bat to the back of her head. For the first time in fourteen years, she wanted this assignment to be different.

She really, honestly, wanted to be that someone.

ELEVEN

"**H**ow long have I known you? Ten years?"

Julian looked up from his desk to his PA. Hannah Green, dressed in her usual impeccable gray business suit, stood before him with her fist on her hip along with her Day-Timer. At the moment she didn't look prim and proper, all business, which was the way he preferred seeing her. That image was comforting and reassuring. It was a sign of business as usual. However, right now, he could tell she was into her mothering mode and he sighed before sitting back in his chair and waiting for the lecture. They came on average of one every three or four months. He'd figured it was a small price to pay for a highly accomplished personal assistant who could put up with his propensity for last-minute changes in schedules, meetings, flights, dinner reservations, and late nights at the office.

"Yes, Hannah. I believe it is ten years," he answered, wondering what he'd done this time to bring about this talk. And Hannah, once she got her teeth into a subject, could *really* talk. Julian braced himself.

"Then I wouldn't be stepping out of bounds to ask what the hell is wrong?"

His eyes narrowed. Hannah rarely used profanity. "I don't know what you mean."

"Don't fool with my head, Julian. At least not right now. You're distracted, short-tempered, making mistakes any junior executive would pick up and you just asked for the Domingo sugar file again and it's right there by your elbow. Are you forgetting you passed on it a month ago?"

Julian looked to the right and there it was. "I was going to take another look at it."

"Why don't you just level with me about what's going on? Are there problems I should know about?"

His spine straightened. "Problems?"

"Within the company."

"The company's fine."

"So you didn't just bite off Jack Millner's head because he's a day late with his assessment of Biolog?"

"I didn't bite his head off," Julian stated, realizing he had done just that.

"Yes, you did. What's highly out of character for you is that you did it in front of me and several department heads. What's wrong with you?"

Julian didn't say anything for a few moments, knowing Hannah was right. He prided himself on being a good manager of people. Whenever he had a problem with an employee, he always discussed it in private. He never gut reacted and embarrassed anyone publicly. "I'll apologize to Jack," he said. "I was distracted."

Hannah slapped the edge of his desk for emphasis. "That's what I'm talking about. *Why* are you distracted? For the last week you've been acting like you're dealing with some terrible news. Are you okay physically? Did you go to the doctor recently?"

He grinned. "I'm fine, Hannah."

"No, you're not fine, Julian. I've known you too long for you to try to pull that with me. I was here when things were bad and I've been here to watch you turn everything around. If it's not business and it's not health, then what?"

Hannah really had been there for him. She'd helped him pick up the pieces after Cat and Morgan died, had helped him to focus on work, to get through one day at a time. She'd called him at home and had covered for him when he'd drowned his sorrows in a bottle of gin and could barely function the next day. Through the years she'd encouraged him to look toward the future, to take care of himself, even to date. He owed her some explanation.

"Max has joint problems. Bill took him to the vet and his hip is deteriorating."

Hannah sank into a chair. "Oh no, poor Max. What can they do?"

"He got a cortisone shot and I'm giving him supplements with something called glucosamine. I'm supposed to talk to the vet next week about alternatives. But Max is a little old for anesthesia, so I'm not sure yet what the strategy is going to be."

"Oh, Julian, I'm so sorry. He's your last link to . . ."

She didn't have to finish her statement. It was true. Max was the last tie to Cat and Morgan. When he went, Julian knew he'd be all alone. It didn't matter how many people worked for him, how many acquaintances he interacted with during the day or night, once Max was gone he would be truly alone in the world. Maggie had been right, painfully accurate in her assessment of him, and it distressed him to realize he'd shut her out without hesitation because he couldn't handle the truth.

He forced a smile. "We're going to do everything possible for him. He's a tough old guy." He didn't mention his guilt at not having noticed Max's problems, or for dragging him down Maggie's stairs because he was too mad to even think about carrying him. That woman had gotten way too close and he wasn't ready to rip off an old scar to examine a wound he'd never been able to truly heal.

But he missed her, damn it.

He hated to admit he missed hearing Maggie's voice at night, anticipating seeing her face on the weekends. Every time he watched the weather on television, he always checked to see what it was like in Philadelphia. He wanted to call her, but held back because he knew she had started something and wouldn't let it go until it was all out in the open, exposed to air and inspection. He had to question if he even wanted to heal. He was used to it now, to that raw feeling in the middle of his chest. It was like a toothache: not bad enough to send you to the dentist, but a strong enough pain to make you aware.

Did he really want to go around wounded, to never open himself to another again? Was Maggie right? Would he wind up an old man, all alone? The last question haunted him. It was what had caused him, every now and then, to wonder if it was all worth it, the push to move forward each day through life. Until he'd met Maggie. Then he'd found himself anticipating each day, knowing it was bringing him closer to the weekend and to her.

"See? That's what I mean by distracted. You're not even here with me in this room right now."

Julian blinked. "Sorry, Hannah. I have a lot on my mind."

"Okay, so Max is worrying you. I understand, but that's not all of it, is it?"

"Hannah, do you ever think you're wasting your time here in the business world?"

"I am?"

Hannah Green was the closest thing he had to a real friend and, even though she was always open to him, he couldn't just dump his mess on her. She was fifty-nine years old and just recently had begun taking medication to lower her blood pressure. Still, she knew more about him than anyone else. "Maybe you could get yourself a crystal ball and hang up a sign."

The older woman laughed. "I knew it! What's up, Julian?"

He hesitated only a moment and then blurted it out before he lost his courage. "I met someone."

Hannah sat back and crossed her arms over her chest. "Are you going to elaborate? You're always meeting someone. I take it we're talking about a woman here."

He nodded.

"And what's new about that? It's your pattern, Julian. You meet a woman. It lasts about a month and then you send her a fabulous gift and move on. Are you debating what kind of gift to send? Because I told you years ago, I'm not doing that anymore. You dump someone, you take care of it."

"It's not like that, Hannah. If I sent this woman a gift, she'd lecture me on my immaturity. She'd probably send it back with a self-help book to discover my inner child and heal him."

Grinning, Hannah said, "I like her already. Who is she?"

"She's from Philly. Name's Maggie O'Shea. And she's driving me crazy."

"This is a first, you seriously talking to me about a woman. Where did you meet her?"

"She was at that charity auction at the Art Museum in Philadelphia last month. I've been seeing her . . . like every weekend and, well, things were going so fast and—"

"And you did your disappearing act," Hannah finished, shaking her head.

"It wasn't like that," he protested. "She kept pushing me to . . . to talk about Cat and Morgan, and I don't see why she felt she had to do root canal on my psyche."

"So you ran away, instead of having an adult conversation." Shaking her head again, Hannah unfolded her arms and sat up straighter. "I swear, Julian, I don't know how you can be so intelligent about so many things and so dense about human nature. She sounds like a woman who's got your number, and who's not willing to let you get away with your usual diversions."

Julian didn't answer, so they sat in silence for almost a minute. Finally he said, "I can't stop thinking about her, Hannah. I haven't felt like this since . . . since Cat." The admission made his throat tighten with emotion and he could feel his stomach muscles constrict with that dreaded guilt.

"Well, so that's it." Hannah sighed deeply as she rose. She leaned on the edge of the desk and stared directly into Julian's eyes. "Okay, I understand why you're distracted, but since I feel I have more than a passing interest in your well-being, I will risk the boss/employee relationship and talk to you as a friend."

Julian smiled slightly. "I thought that's what you've been doing."

She ignored his remark. "Ten years ago when I came to work for you I thought you were the luckiest man alive. You had a business that was soaring and a family life that I thought was idyllic. A beautiful wife who supported your every move and an adoring son. When they died I watched a part of you die with them. Oh, you've done a very good job pretending to be alive, fully alive, but I knew there had to come a day when you got tired of acting, pretending for those around you. There were times I was afraid of getting a phone call, telling me about a car or boating accident, yet you pushed through your grief and you plunged yourself into work and good causes, anything to take your mind off the true state of your heart."

She paused, collecting her thoughts. "What you had with Cat never got the chance to really be tested, so it's always going to seem perfect in your mind and nothing and no one will ever come up to that perfection for you. But you know that's not realistic. People aren't perfect. Relationships are messy and sometimes torturous, but if it's the right one it's worth it. I've watched you amass a fortune and you know what, Julian? You're not really happy. The money and all it buys isn't doing it for you. What you really want can't be bought. What you want takes work and it takes risk. And this is one deal you can't manipulate. You've got to be honest to make it happen."

Julian bit the inside of his cheek, wishing what Hannah was saying didn't resonate with truth. "You and Abe are happy, right? What's it been, thirty years?"

"Thirty-two. And if you think it's been easy with me working for you and him stuck down there in the district attorney's office, think again. It takes work, sometimes lots of work to stay on track, to make our marriage a priority." She looked up to the ceiling, deep in thought, before adding, "It's sometimes like those old vinyl records we used to have. When it's smooth everything is clear and harmonious. But every once in a while there's an irritant and the harmony is interrupted. If it's really serious the needle jumps out of its groove and then nothing makes sense. The trick is for someone to either remove the irritant or place the needle back into the proper groove so harmony can return."

"That's your trick?"

She shook her head, almost in sympathy. "There's no trick, Julian. We couldn't do it without communication. But then I think about all we've been through, the kids, colleges, the roller-coaster ride of any relationship, those moments when I felt so connected to another human being, and I know then it's all been worth it. I see myself as an old woman in a rocking chair, sitting next to Abe Green on a porch somewhere warm, with him wiping the spittle from my lips as he makes me laugh at myself. See, Julian, I'll know at the end of my time on this earth that I was loved, well loved by a man who saw all my warts and stayed at my side anyway. That, in a nutshell, my friend, is what we come here to find. Unconditional love. It's the unconditional part that's hard, day in and day out finding no matter what is thrown at you, you are capable of loving someone who's perfectly imperfect."

"Wow, Hannah, I didn't know you were so deep." Julian felt he was seeing a whole new side to this woman who worked with him. He wanted to give her a vacation to take Abe away to someplace warm so they wouldn't have to wait until they were truly old to rock in chairs and relax with each other.

"I've always kept my life outside this office private, but you asked a serious question and deserved a truthful answer. And I answered you as a friend who's concerned about you."

He grinned to lighten the discussion. "So you think I should call her?"

Hannah laughed as she picked up her Day-Timer. "Do what your heart tells you, Julian. I know you've ignored it for almost a decade now, but start listening again. You'll know what to do."

"Thanks, Hannah. Sorry I've been such an irritant lately," he said with contrition and watched her grin. "Remind me to give you a raise for your consultant fees."

Walking to the door of his office, Hannah called out, "It's already in the works. And don't forget to see Jack Millner. It would be nice if you went to his office, so it's seen."

"Yes, ma'am," Julian replied as the door closed. Spinning around in his chair, he gazed out his window to the Chrysler Building. He actually felt better after talking to Hannah. Even though he'd taken care of her financially with a healthy portfolio, and he knew she probably made twice the salary of her husband, he still felt the urge to do something special for her.

Looking at the clock on his desk, he pulled out his personal address book and found what he wanted. Punching in the numbers on his telephone, he waited until he heard the voice of a very overworked assistant district attorney.

"Abe? This is Julian McDonald. Yes, yes, Hannah is fine," he quickly cut in when the man questioned whether anything had happened to his wife. "I know I don't ordinarily call you, but I was wondering if you're up to surprising her this weekend." He listened as Abe's voice brightened a bit as he asked how. "I realize it's Friday afternoon and a holiday weekend, and I know this is last minute and you'll have to scramble to pull this off, but how would you and Hannah like to spend the weekend in Bermuda? Could you manage to pack a bag for her and meet her here at the office by, say seven o'clock tonight? I'll have the jet fly you there and bring you back on Sunday, but I don't want her to know."

He listened as Abe tried to figure out how to pull off a surprise for a woman who seemed to know everything about everyone.

Julian chuckled. "And that's exactly why we have to do it. It's about time someone turned the tables on her. You'll stay at my place. Bring your passports and just pack enough for two days. If you forget anything my people there will take care of it. So what do you say?"

Grinning widely at the man's excited responses, Julian nodded. "Okay, Abe, I'll see you here at seven. Enjoy yourselves."

He hung up the phone and dialed Bill's number to get the ball rolling. He'd have to contact the pilots, Alastair and Elizabeth, and get a car to take them to the airport. Money may not be the answer to everything, but it was certainly useful in arranging a surprise for a friend.

Hannah Green was going to be struck speechless, and he wouldn't miss witnessing that minor miracle.

"As you can tell, Magdalene, I am contacting you through the telephone, through the proper channel, for I have no desire to stir your anger again."

Maggie unclenched her teeth. "Fine, Marcus. What is it you want this time?"

"I would like to arrange a meeting with you."

"I have nothing more to say to you. I thought I had made that clear," she replied, feeling her jaw muscles tighten once more.

"The meeting is not with me, not directly. Someone wishes to meet with you."

"Someone?"

"Someone of considerable importance. They have asked me to arrange such a meeting as quickly as possible."

"From the foundation?" She couldn't imagine who else Marcus could be talking about.

"Yes."

That intrigued her. "When? You know I'm a busy woman."

There was a pause, and then Marcus said, "We are here already, Magdalene, and are hoping you would find it convenient to see us this evening."

She looked down to her bare feet. So much for a Friday night of pampering. "Fine. Give me an hour."

"Thank you, Magdalene. We will be at your home by nine."

"And use the front door, Marcus," she threw out at the end.

"As you wish, *cara mia*," he murmured before hanging up the phone.

Well, well, Maggie thought, *something important is happening*. The foundation, or a representative of it, was coming to her. She figured Marcus had relayed her statement about this being her last assignment and the big guns were coming to recruit her into reenlisting. No such luck. Whoever was being sent was wasting his or her time.

She jumped as another firecracker went off close by. Fourth of July weekend was always wild in the City of Brotherly Love, which took great pride in housing the Liberty Bell, Independence Hall, and the Betsy Ross House. Tomorrow night cars would pull over onto the shoulder of Interstate 95 and crowds would gather at Penn's Landing to watch the breathtaking display of fireworks out on the Delaware River. For Maggie it was a holiday and a rare Saturday that she didn't have to open the store. Two blessed days off. She could put up with cherry bombs and M80s going off throughout the night for, outside of this impromptu meeting, her calendar was clear.

She headed into her bedroom and pulled off her soft worn cotton pajama bottoms and threw them onto a chair. She planned on getting back into them as soon as Marcus and his friend left. After taking off her old T-shirt, she looked into her closet and chose a pair of jeans and a pale blue silk shirt. She wasn't about to dress up for this meeting, though she would put on a pot of coffee and she had some leftover cookies from the store she could offer. That was as far as she planned on entertaining.

Besides, her mood wasn't that expansive.

Not hearing from Julian this past week had bothered her far more than she'd imagined it could. She should have been used to it. Every time in the past that she'd zeroed in on an assignment's Achilles' heel they always backed off in anger, an obvious manifestation of their fear. Sometimes it took weeks before they made contact again, so why was she so disappointed that Julian hadn't? A part of her didn't even want to contemplate the answer. She knew that Julian wouldn't just disappear. He would deal with her one way or the other. Each day she feared receiving a package delivered by a personal messenger with some kind of kiss-off gift inside.

She didn't want to fail with him.

Not only would it be the first time she had actually failed in an assignment and that wasn't the way she wanted to end her affiliation with Marcus and the foundation, but she really, honestly wanted Julian to heal his old wounds and find happiness. Even though it would never be with her.

She loved him.

There. It was admitted, at least mentally. She had loved them all, wanting what was best for them, cheering them on to discover true happiness. But this was the first time she had fallen in love.

She ran a brush through her hair and stared at her reflection in the mirror.

"You're the one who comes before the real one can show up."

She'd been telling herself that for fourteen years and it had always felt right before. Why now, with Julian, did those words ring hollow? It wasn't because he was rich and handsome. It wasn't all those things that came with his wealth. It was much more simple and basic.

She felt at home in his arms.

He could lose everything tomorrow and she would still feel as though after a long, lonely journey she had finally come to rest in an oasis of blessed contentment. There was ease being in his presence, the intimacy of acceptance, the shared laughter and the comfort of shared silence. She felt happy to know he was alive on this planet and it didn't matter what he did or what he owned.

He was a man with a good heart.

The doorbell rang and she ended her introspection by slipping into her sandals and rushing downstairs. When she opened the door, she saw four men: Marcus, an older man who looked vaguely familiar, and two men dressed in dark business suits, who stood behind Marcus and his guest. Those guys, one blond and blue-eyed and the other dark as black coffee, stared at her while holding their hands together at their abdomens.

Damn, they could have guns inside their jackets for all she knew.

"Magdalene, may we come in?"

Maggie blinked, turning her attention to Marcus. "Of course, come in." She held the door open to admit them. "I didn't expect . . . so many," she added lamely.

The older gray-haired man, dressed in khaki pants, a white shirt, and a casual navy linen jacket, extended his hand. "I do apologize for this surprise visit. Thank you for seeing us."

Placing her hand in his, she heard Marcus make the introduction. "May I present Senator Gabriel Burke."

That was it. She'd seen him on television. He was an influential politician on Capitol Hill. What the hell was he doing in her home? Regaining her senses, she said, "How do you do, Senator?" She looked at Marcus as if he were from another planet.

"Very well, Maggie. You do prefer to be called Maggie, don't you?"

The man had a charming smile, but she still felt rattled as she nodded and glanced to the other two men, who stood like silent soldiers by the closed front door.

"We'll explain everything if we could just sit down," Marcus said, looking pointedly toward the stairs. "I seem to remember your excellent hospitality."

She blinked several times and resisted shaking her head to clear it. "Absolutely," she answered in a high voice that sounded weird even to her ears. Lowering it, she added, "Please, follow me."

She was so very aware that right behind her, probably staring at her behind, was a very important man who must be involved in the foundation in some way and nothing was making any sense. She thought the foundation was run like some esoteric club, whose members did good deeds without recognition. Light workers, Elizabeth had called them. What did politics have to do with that? You couldn't get more public than that, except if you were a movie or rock star.

At the top of the stairs she waved them into her living room, wishing she had prepared better. Coffee and old cookies might not do it. She noticed as Marcus and Senator Burke walked toward the sofa that the ebony and ivory team remained at the front door. "Please, won't you sit down? May I get you coffee and something to eat?" she offered, though she hadn't a clue what she could prepare quickly.

"We're fine, Maggie. Please join us," the senator answered, as though waiting for her to land her agitated body somewhere.

Maggie sat on the edge of the chaise longue and clasped her hands together in her lap, rattled by this man's appearance at her front door. She waited for someone to begin the conversation and prayed she would find the right answers to whatever was going to be discussed.

"I want you to know how much I appreciate you seeing us on such short notice," the senator began. "Marcus assured me it could be arranged, but I know how hard you work and I wouldn't intrude unless I thought it was important."

She simply nodded, refusing to even look at Marcus.

"Let me begin by saying the foundation is indebted to you for the excellent work you have done in the past. By all accounts you are a remarkable woman and we are honored that you've given of yourself so unselfishly."

Again she nodded, not knowing what else to say.

"You must be wondering why a United States senator has shown up on your front door and how all of that fits in with your assignment."

"Yes, sir. It's certainly confusing, to say the least." She glanced at Marcus, who was giving nothing away by his expression.

The older man smiled gently. "It has to do with your current assignment. Julian McDonald."

"Why? Is he in trouble with the government?"

"Not at all. From what I gather he's an upstanding citizen. Even pays his taxes on time. The government, at this point, isn't interested in him. I am. Or, I should say, the foundation is. I represent the foundation at this meeting."

"I'm sorry," Maggie blurted out, unable to stop herself. "I'm trying to piece together what the foundation and politics have to do with each other. Having only recently learned more about the foundation, I'm confused when I try to put the two together."

"Yes, your visit with Elizabeth Edwards. She likes you very much."

"I like her, Senator, and I don't mean to be rude, but what does my assignment have to do with you, or the government?"

"You aren't rude. You're direct. I like that in a person. As a politician, I find it refreshing and rare in the circles I travel within Washington." He smiled again and then nodded. "So, to provide you with an answer I will have to tell you something about myself. I, like you, Maggie, discovered very young that what I was being told about the world didn't fit in with my own experiences. You were given a gift and more than likely it was ridiculed, so you no longer spoke of it with others."

She nodded.

"The same thing happened to me. I felt all alone, a freak of nature, if you will pardon the pun. When I was in college I was approached by the foundation and you can imagine how grateful I was to know I wasn't alone. Like you, I underwent a period of tutoring and it was mutually decided that my gift and my innate talents could best be used by entering politics. That was to be my service."

While he was speaking, Maggie tried to remember everything she could about the man. He was an Independent, well respected for his views and highly regarded by the media and his home state of New York. She also remembered his name had been mentioned as a possible running mate as vice president in the last election. He'd turned it down.

"I have served my country and the foundation for almost forty years and I would like to begin thinking about retirement. However, I would feel much better if I knew my place would be filled with a person of integrity, someone who wouldn't owe his position to the power brokers in Washington. I am speaking about Julian McDonald."

"Julian?" she asked in shock. "He's not interested in politics."

"He hasn't been interested in the past. We are hoping once his heart is opened, his mind will follow. May I ask how you are progressing with him?"

She glanced at Marcus and then back to the senator. "Last Sunday, I broached the subject of his family's death. It went as I expected it would. He couldn't get past his fear and he left in anger. I'm giving him time to think about it. I'm sure you know this is the most fragile part of the assignment."

Senator Burke nodded. "So you haven't heard from him?"

"No," she admitted. "I haven't. But I've found that isn't unusual. Sometimes it can take weeks. Julian's had nine years to build up and fortify that wall around his heart."

"How confident are you that he will initiate a meeting?"

"Fairly confident," she answered, hoping she was right. "But I still don't see why you would think Julian is the man to replace you. As far as I know, he has no experience with politics."

"And that's exactly why he would be the perfect candidate. You see, Maggie, people all over the planet are beginning to wake up and realize that safety has always been an illusion. They have given over their power to men who promised security and cannot deliver, because none of us knows for certain what will happen in the next moment. None of us ever really did, but that was the illusion. People are starting to realize the struggle isn't between people so much as between old ideas and new thoughts, between the concepts of yesterday and those of tomorrow. Distrust of politicians is growing and, in our fear, we have created a life that is very violent with itself. We accept the violence as normal and that's very frightening. The foundation stands for balance. Not good over evil. Evil is simply the absence of goodness. And even stating that is creating dogma, something the foundation is very careful to avoid. Yet what label would you give to any society that, through technology, can eliminate the entire population on this planet in one afternoon?"

"Terrifying," Maggie whispered.

"Exactly. So far the millions who are awakening from the hypnosis of false security and becoming convinced the old ways are no longer working are, for the most part, not influential people. They are ordinary people who are looking for a voice to be heard above the shouts of fear. What is needed now, what the foundation hopes to begin doing, is to assist people in positions of influence to open and awaken their hearts and discover how they can be of service during this most crucial time in the history of humanity."

"That's why Julian was chosen?" Maggie asked, seeing more of what Marcus had called the big picture.

"Yes, and also despite the spin us politicians and the media would like to put on issues, the most important one in the next election is going to be the economy. This country's greatness cannot be measured by the size of its military. It will be measured by the quality of life of its citizens. Unemployment is rising at an alarming rate, and states from coast to coast are now reaching depths of desperation unseen since the Great Depression. When people are frightened about their financial security, they can't even begin to envision a bigger picture. This is where Mr. McDonald comes in. He has an excellent background in taking over failing businesses, cutting excess costs, and turning them around. He's a man that came from humble beginnings and became highly successful, the embodiment of the American Dream. He would appeal to the working man and also to the wealthy. He's a free man who doesn't owe his position in life to anyone, and when the truth is told by a man of freedom it can be heard clearly. He's also made a name for himself as a philanthropist in the arts and in inner-city programs. And what's most important, he isn't owned by the lobbyists. He would be a clean candidate with a persuasive platform. The only thing working against him is his reputation in his private life. And that, dear Maggie, is where you come in."

"I see," she murmured. And she did. It was all coming together. "And Marcus is on assignment with the woman who would possibly be his wife?"

Senator Burke nodded. "As you know, nothing is certain. We always respect free will, but the woman comes from an excellent family. To use a distasteful term, her pedigree would be a great asset in a political career."

"So now you understand, Magdalene," Marcus said, "why I have been telling you this assignment is most important."

She nodded. "I get it, Marcus. The foundation wants

Julian to replace Senator Burke. He's accomplished everything he's wanted in the business world and this would give
his life a dynamic purpose. It's a very good idea."

"I'm glad you agree," the senator said with a sincere
smile. "Once his heart is opened and his mind is free of fear,
I will take over the assignment. It will be up to me to present Mr. McDonald with the concepts of the foundation. We
can only pray he will be open to listen."

"Magdalene has never failed in an assignment," Marcus
said, with a smile toward Maggie.

Uncomfortable with his praise, she stood up. "Are you
sure I can't get you a cup of coffee?"

Gabriel Burke shook his head. "We're fine, Maggie.
There's one more thing I'd like to discuss with you before
we leave."

She nodded. "Would you mind if I got myself a cup? I
need one."

"Certainly," the older man said with a smile. "I understand."

She knew her answering smile was strained, but she
needed some time to compose herself. In her kitchen she
stared blindly at the granite countertop, resting her hands
on it, trying to bring her thoughts together with some kind
of clarity. *Gabriel Burke was part of the foundation?* She
felt rattled, unsteady, remembering seeing the man on television being interviewed. And all the time he has been
working to bring about the intricate harmony of light and
dark. And Julian . . . Somehow she had to keep her true feelings masked.

Knowing she was leaving her guests for too long, she
quickly poured herself a mug of coffee and brought it with
her back into the living room and sat down.

The senator leaned forward, resting his elbows on his
knees. "Marcus has told me you want this to be your last
assignment. Is this true?"

She placed her coffee on the table in front of her and
straightened her back. "Yes."

"And I suppose there's not much I could say to talk you
out of it?"

"Not much, Senator. It's been fourteen years and I want a life of my own. Even though you have served many years longer, I'm sure you can understand why I wish to retire. My service has been very emotional."

"I do understand, Maggie. In truth you've done a double service with your store downstairs."

"I'll continue with the store, at least as far as I can see right now, but the time has come to find my own personal happiness."

"Of course. I am wondering, and please forgive me if I am out of line, whether your feelings have manifested at this time because of this assignment?"

"I'm afraid I don't understand," Maggie answered, sensing his probing eyes searching for the truth.

"To put it bluntly, are you falling in love with Mr. McDonald?"

She had to be very careful how she answered, or they would take this assignment away. Inhaling deeply, she said, "In order for me to be successful, I have loved each and every one of my assignments. Otherwise, I would be manipulative and false in what I am hoping to accomplish. Mr. McDonald is no different in that respect. I have come to love him and, when you are dealing with such fragile emotions, my own heart has to be strong enough to survive when he moves on to whomever will bring him real and lasting happiness. It's what I do, Senator. And I do it very well."

The older man's smile was so gentle as he gazed into her eyes that Maggie found herself tearing.

"I can see how much this is costing you, dear child. On behalf of the foundation I want you to know how important your work has been. When you succeed in your last assignment, all of us will hold you in the highest light and envision you finding your own real and lasting happiness."

She swallowed down her emotion. "Thank you, Senator Burke."

"Please, my friends call me Gabe." He stood up and opened his arms to her. "I hope you will consider me a friend."

She rose and walked the few steps into his arms. His hug

was oddly comforting, almost paternal. When it ended, he looked into her eyes and nodded. "You're a good woman, Maggie O'Shea. I hope we meet again."

"Thank you, Gabe." She moved out of his space and felt suddenly awkward. "Are you sure I can't get you that cup of coffee now?"

He chuckled. "We've kept you long enough. I will be in town tomorrow for a ceremony at the new Constitution Hall." He reached into his jacket pocket. "Here's my card with my private cell number. Call if you are free. I'm not sure what time I'll be through the more formal part of the planned activities, but I would like to see you again. If not, you have my number should you need anything."

"Thank you," she answered, realizing she would like to see him again. "I don't have any plans this weekend."

Gabe Burke motioned Marcus to the stairs for their departure. "Then we shall wait and see how tomorrow unfolds. Thank you for giving up your time tonight. It was a sincere pleasure to have met you, Maggie."

She could see why Gabriel Burke was so admired. He certainly knew how to work people. And, somehow, she hadn't minded being worked.

Now, that's a politician.

TWELVE

Saturday mornings were generally taken for granted. After working five days, it was time to unwind or take care of things left undone during the work week. For Maggie it was a precious gift and she didn't intend to do anything productive. She was so grateful not to be working downstairs, catering to customers or smoothing away the inevitable wrinkles in the day, that she'd decided when she woke up to stay in her old, soft pajama bottoms and just throw on a sleeveless T-shirt that she'd cut at the neckline in a deep V. She hadn't brushed her teeth or even combed her hair. At least not yet. It was rare when she could veg out, catch up on her reading with a cup of coffee, and forget about a healthy breakfast while munching away on cookies. At a little past eleven o'clock, she was totally into relaxing and didn't even know if she would take a shower that day. She couldn't remember the last time she'd done nothing.

Guilty pleasures, it was called.

Why is it, she thought, *that we believe we always have to be productive? When did we forget how to relax and do absolutely nothing?* Well, she was getting back into practice. Reading a magazine, she glanced at her fingernails. After that remarkable visit last night, she'd given herself a manicure and pedicure, while playing over in her mind the conversation she'd had with Senator Gabriel Burke. She'd felt stunned when her company had left. Her brain wouldn't stop dissecting each sentence, even when she'd tried falling asleep. Once again, in the midst of doing nothing, her brain ran over the facts.

They wanted Julian to enter politics, to eventually take Senator Burke's place. He needed a wife to end his playboy reputation and they'd found one with the right pedigree. It could work and would be a brilliant move for all concerned.

Except, of course, for her.

More than ever she could see why her feelings for Julian had to be sublimated. She had to fix in her mind that he was simply her last assignment. She was already more than halfway through it and it should be completed soon enough. Then she could send Julian on his way. She imagined herself watching from a distance as he went on with his life, seeing pictures of him and his new wife, watching on television as he announced his intention to run for Congress and then the Senate. He would be dynamic.

So why did she feel torn in two, wanting him to succeed and yet also wanting to be at his side as he fulfilled his destiny? It was beyond foolish. The senator had been right. For Julian to succeed in politics he did need a wife with a good pedigree. She didn't even know the name of her father. On her birth certificate, the word *unknown* was typed for posterity. Not exactly the ancestry needed for a politician's mate. Oh yes, and let's add the fact she'd inherited shape shifting through her lineage. What more did she need to prove her feelings for Julian were totally improper? If she wanted what was best for him, she would treat him like any other assignment.

That was the right thing to do.

A rebellious streak rose up within her. Damn it, she was tired of self-sacrifice! Doing the right thing was becoming too painful. Thank God, this was her last assignment. She needed to find a normal man whom she could love and raise children with . . . and who would accept her for who she is? Who was she kidding? Even if a man could accept the shape shifting part, how would he feel about her past assignments? Maybe she would just be a single mother. It would be difficult, but she could do it. She could hire a nanny and extra staff for the store to cut back on her hours. The more she thought about it, the more appealing it became.

She didn't have to bother with a man at all.

When she let her mind wrap around the idea, she became excited. She could go to a sperm bank, pick out the most suitable DNA choice, and begin her family. Somehow the thought of not really knowing the father didn't sit well with her. She'd lived that scenario herself and didn't want her child to inherit that particular challenge. It would be better if she knew the father, his health history, his level of integrity.

And, of course, Julian McDonald's image blasted across the surface of her mind.

What if she couldn't have Julian, but she could have his child?

Immediately she wondered about the ethics of such a plan.

How fair was it to use Julian as a sperm donor without him knowing about it?

She allowed the heavy magazine to fall off her lap onto the sofa cushion and placed her hand upon her belly. It would be imperative that no one could ever know about it, not Julian or the foundation. She would tell everyone that the father simply wasn't in the picture. No one would pressure her about it. Not even Marcus. She'd already set in motion her intention to have as normal a life as possible and that would include having children.

Thousands of women had done it before her, including her own mother.

No, her mother wasn't a good example.

Barbara O'Shea had been resentful of her role as parent, letting Maggie know how her conception had interrupted her mother's last year of college and her dreams of being a lawyer. Her mother had settled for a career as a paralegal, doing the grunt work for other lawyers, and never missed an opportunity to complain, which always made Maggie feel guilty for her very existence.

She would never be like that. She would consider a child in her life a miracle. Granted her mother hadn't planned on getting pregnant, and before she'd died Maggie had made peace with her, but Maggie vowed any child that came into her life would always know they were cherished.

Excited, feeling as though her life had some direction, she left the living room and walked into the bathroom. Opening the medicine cabinet, she took out the plastic container and stared at it. She'd been taking the Pill off and on for years. Whenever she got a new assignment, she went to her doctor and began the cycle. When she wasn't on assignment, she had no use for them as she rarely dated and never became intimate. It was a tricky juggling act, but so far it had worked.

She thought about flushing them down the toilet and then wondered if it was harmful to the environment. She had no idea, so she decided to take them into the kitchen and dispose of them. Popping each pill out of its container, she dropped the remaining ones into the garbage. She figured if she just threw away the plastic disk, she might retrieve it later when doubts began to surface. And she knew they would. Disposing of them this way meant it was a done deal. She had made a choice, for herself and her possible child.

When that was accomplished, she opened a cabinet and took out her vitamins. Popping one into her mouth, she pulled out a box of cereal, one that proclaimed it was good for the heart. She cut up a banana and thought if what she was doing was right, then she would be given a sign to go ahead. She relied on signs for directions in life. They could come from anywhere or anything, the words on a billboard, something she read in a book or even something she overheard in the store, some words that came at the exact time she needed direction. And they always resonated in her gut, alerting her to pay attention. She'd wait to see and, in the meantime, she'd get as healthy as possible.

Taking her bowl of cereal out to the sofa, she listened to Pachelbel's haunting "Canon in D," envisioning a baby in her life. She would have to do some reconstruction in the apartment, giving up space for a nursery off her bedroom. She could envision a room filled with a crib and a changing table, a toy chest, a comfortable rocker.

Okay, she was romanticizing this whole baby thing. It

would also be stressful, energy draining, and she would lose her independence. Right now that seemed like a small price to pay for experiencing love every day.

When the doorbell rang, she resented the intrusion and almost decided not to answer until she figured she might as well get rid of whoever was at the door or they might come back. She blew a strand of hair away from her eyes as she descended the stairs. Straightening her back and resolving to liberate herself of visitors or salesmen or evangelists, she opened the door then stood slack-jawed seeing a huge bouquet of red and white roses, blue delphiniums, and baby's breath. Even Max had a patriotic red, white, and blue handkerchief tied around his neck as he wagged his tail furiously while looking up at her.

"I thought, considering the holiday, I would take my chances that you'd be home," Julian said, lowering the flowers so she could see his face. He extended the bouquet. "I'm sorry I ran out of here last week. We'll understand if you send us packing, but to plead my case I will say the Jersey Turnpike is murderous and it'll be worse tomorrow. We're looking for some sanctuary from the traffic, Maggie. Even for a half hour?"

Shaking her head, she took the flowers and stood aside to allow them to enter. "That's a pretty lame excuse, and you know it," she remarked, bending down to scratch Max's head. "How're you doing, boy?"

"He's much better because he's gone to the vet and got a shot of cortisone. It's like a miracle drug for what's ailing him. Too bad they don't have something I could take." He paused, staring into her eyes. "I've missed you, Maggie. I am so sorry for what I said before I left. You were getting too close . . . to things I've wanted to forget."

She could see by his expression how emotional he was and she nodded toward the stairs behind her. "Come on up. I'm sure I can spare something cold for two victims of road fatigue."

She closed the door and watched as Julian bent down to pick up Max.

"He's getting thoroughly spoiled now, being carried up and down stairs. Thank God my building has an elevator."

She didn't say anything as she preceded him, only now realizing what she must look like, wearing that old T-shirt she'd put back on last night. She could at least have brushed her teeth! She cupped her hand over her mouth and exhaled. Her breath smelled of cereal and banana. "Do you want a cup of coffee? It's still hot."

"Actually, I'd love a glass of water," he answered, placing Max down on the floor. "Lame excuse or not, the traffic really was horrible."

"Water coming up for both of you," she called out while walking to the kitchen. She put the flowers into the sink and ran the tap, then went to the fridge. She opened a big bottle of water and poured it into a glass and a wide bowl. Max was right at her side as she placed the bowl on the floor. She watched him slurp it up and then turned to see Julian watching her.

"Here you are," she said, picking up the glass and handing it to him.

"Thanks," he murmured, bringing it to his lips.

She crossed her arms over her breasts and leaned against the counter, watching Julian's Adam's apple bob up and down in the V of his white Polo shirt as he quenched his thirst. He was wearing jeans and loafers without socks and the casual look appealed to her. She liked the fact that he wore his wealth with ease, without the need to display it. Nothing about him, not his clothes or his homes, was overstated.

Julian placed his empty glass on the counter and smiled. "Thanks."

She simply nodded, waiting for him to take the lead in any conversation.

"You're upset with me, aren't you?" He seemed embarrassed.

"No, Julian, I'm not. I expected you to run and you did."

"You expected it and yet you pushed it anyway?" The surprise in his voice was unmistakable.

"Do you remember the first night we met and we spoke of dancing lessons?"

He nodded. "It intrigued me. Funny thing is we've never danced."

"Not in the literal sense, but we've been doing it in some form every time we're together."

"You're speaking metaphorically."

"Sort of. Actually, the way I look at things, which I'll grant you is not widely accepted, is that every single thing on this planet is made up of energy. You and me and Max, everything, even the flowers you brought me and that glass you just drank from. What we've been doing is dancing with each other's energy. Up until last week, the dance was pleasurable and the steps were easy to follow because we simply relaxed and weren't thinking where to place our feet next. Last Sunday you started thinking and you became afraid you wouldn't know the next step or where to place your feet or, even worse, that I might step on them and hurt you. The dance became awkward, potentially painful. You didn't like the uncertainty, not feeling in control, and you withdrew your energy. You left the dance floor."

"What can I say? You're right," he admitted, shoving his hands into the pockets of his jeans. "I got scared. Of you, I might as well admit."

"Have I ever done anything to warrant your fear?"

"Not intentionally. Just being you is enough. You're one hell of a woman, Maggie. Sometimes I think you're too good to be true. I've heard women are supposed to be more enlightened than men, but you're like . . ." He waved his arm toward the ceiling. " . . . out there. Like the way you just described what happened last Sunday. I came here expecting recriminations, maybe even to take up where we left off, and now I'm feeling what happened was . . . well . . . maybe just a human frailty. That you're not angry and you don't think less of me."

She smiled. "You just said it, my friend. We're merely human and, perhaps, part of that is we make mistakes sometimes. I like that word. Mis-takes. We sometimes miss the mark, but we have the choice for another take on the matter, another opportunity to see it differently this time."

"See? That's what I mean. How many women think like that?"

"More than you're willing to believe," she answered. "So don't think I'm too good to be true, Julian. I'm going to let you down and disappoint you. You're going to be angry with me, frustrated with me, and you'll probably walk away from me again. One of the mistakes we humans tend to make is that we want to believe love is about romance and running through fields of wildflowers, or in a male's mind it might be about conquest and surrender and protection and spreading your seed. We don't like conflict or chaos, yet without it would we ever change or see something differently? I guess I've come to accept life isn't about just the good times. The difficult times might be even more important than we realize. So that's why I'm not upset with you for being human." Her smile increased. "I'm glad you came back . . . though I'm sorry you caught me looking like I just rolled out of bed."

He stepped forward and pulled her into his arms. Kissing her forehead, he murmured against her skin, "You look great. Soft and vulnerable, yet you're also one of the strongest and smartest women I've ever met."

"Well, that's sweet of you to say, but I really would feel better if I could run a brush through my hair." She tried to pull out of his arms.

He held her fast. "I like you looking like you just rolled out of bed. And speaking of beds, can we stay the night?"

She laughed. "You aren't subtle, are you?"

"No, ma'am, not when there's so much at stake. Besides, I'd get a hotel room before I got back on the turnpike."

"Well, if it's to save you from the New Jersey Turnpike on a holiday weekend, I guess you and your dog can camp out here."

"Then I'm going to have to go back to the car and get my bag. Didn't want to assume anything."

She pulled back and looked into his eyes. He appeared

happy. "But we still need to talk, Julian. You understand that now, don't you?"

He slowly nodded. "I'm not looking forward to it, but yes. I know it's coming. I'm just trying to postpone it."

She kissed his chin. "Go get your bag and I'll get a shower and then you can make us peanut butter and jelly sandwiches for lunch. It'll remind you of when you didn't have things so easy, when everything didn't go your way."

"Are you serious?" he demanded, letting his arms drop. "Peanut butter and jelly?"

"Too good for it now, Mac?" she challenged, moving backward out of the kitchen.

Grinning, he tried to grab her and she quickly evaded his hands.

"The keys to get back in are on the table by the door," she said with a laugh. "Now go so I can see to my very necessary ablutions."

"Ablutions? I'd like to see that. Come to think of it," he said with a gleam in his eye, "I'd like to ablute you myself. You're not wearing a bra under that, are you?"

Laughing, she shook her head and pointed to the stairs. "There's no such word as ablute and you know it. Now get out of here before I send you to a hotel. Max, of course, is welcome to stay," she added, looking down at the dog who was following her into the bathroom.

"And I think he would, too, the little traitor. Just tell me to shove off and watch you ablute."

"Okay, I think you're heading toward overkill on the ablutions thing. Get out of here." She blew him a kiss and closed the bathroom door, leaving Max outside to wait for her.

"You need me to pick up anything while I'm out, hon?" he yelled. "Like maybe hot dogs or hamburgers? It *is* the Fourth of July, right?"

"No," she yelled back, pulling her shirt off and trying not to laugh. "Don't try and get out of peanut butter and jelly. It'll be good for your soul."

She heard him mutter a curse before he headed down the

stairs. Turning on the shower, she adjusted the water temperature and then walked inside the square of opaque glass blocks. She lathered her body and then shampooed her hair, wondering what the hell she should do. She hadn't expected Julian to show up today. She thought he'd call first. Now what was she going to do? Should she go through with her plan, or should she hunt in the garbage for a tiny pill and wash it off before popping it into her mouth?

That first weekend at Julian's apartment, she'd told him she was on the Pill. She was probably still protected, but she wasn't sure. She'd never been in this situation before. As it was, eight out of every one hundred women became pregnant during the first year on the Pill, so maybe she should have told Julian to pick up condoms. Just to be sure.

Well, by the look in his eye she was going to have to make a decision.

And he'd called her "hon" so casually, as though it were natural, like they'd been together for years. He was ready to open his heart now, willing to take down his carefully constructed barriers. Her assignment was almost over and she didn't have much more time with him. She should make the most of this weekend, in every way.

It was as though she had two angels on her shoulders who would not be washed away with soap and water. One was telling her it wasn't entirely ethical to get pregnant without saying anything to the potential father, especially someone with Julian's issues, someone who had been tapped to be a senator. The other was putting images of a baby in her mind, telling her she had asked for a sign and she'd gotten one. Julian had come to her of his own free will.

That's true. It was a sign she couldn't ignore.

Now did she have the courage to go through with it?

Maybe she wouldn't get pregnant anyway.

And maybe, just maybe, she would.

"I met Cat in the Hamptons. I was staying with friends and we went to a party and there she was . . . the prettiest girl at the party, or so I thought, and she was flirting with me.

She was intelligent with a wicked sense of humor, but there was a softness to her, a vulnerability. She worked in New York City as an editor at *Elle*, and volunteered at a reading program in the Bronx twice a week. Before the night was over I felt like I'd known her my whole life. I wanted to ask her to marry me right off the bat, but I waited six weeks. Her family was old money and I didn't think they would approve, but she told them I was the man she wanted and if they didn't accept me with open arms she would run away to Las Vegas and deprive her mother of a wedding. So we had the big wedding, three hundred guests, pictures in *Town and Country*, the whole nine yards. I thought life couldn't get any better . . . until Morgan came and then I knew it could."

Maggie sat across from him on the sofa. He had a glass of Chivas Regal in his hand that he sipped and he wasn't even looking at her. He seemed lost in time, revisiting scenes in his past he hadn't wanted to recall for many years. He'd begun by telling her about his talk with Hannah, his assistant, and how she'd made him see it was time to move on. Maggie sent a prayer of thanks out to the woman, who was now at BellaLuna.

"She was great with Morgan," he muttered, his voice rough with emotion. "I was so busy with work that I missed so much of his life, but Cat was there for everything. If we had any disagreements it was about time, making better use of my time to spend with my family." His head began shaking slightly from side to side, as though in regret. "Before he went to preschool he knew how to read simple sentences. Cat taught him. Morgan would get up in the mornings and run to the kitchen table to show me a new word he'd learned. I missed his graduation from preschool, his Christmas play in third grade, and most of his soccer games. But I made some of his baseball games and he was good, Maggie. Really good. I remember this one game. Morgan was a shortstop. You need to be good to play shortstop because you have to cover so much of the infield. Well, his team was playing the last year's champions and there's this rule that you can only use a pitcher for two games in a week. The coach had gone through his pitching lineup and so he put Morgan in as the last relief pitcher. Morgan had a great arm, but he hadn't pitched in years since taking over as shortstop. And there was my son, nine years old, on the pitcher's mound, warming up with the catcher. I was so nervous I started pacing. I couldn't sit still. There were two innings to go and so much pressure on him."

"How did he do?"

Julian sniffled back his emotion. "He got out of the eighth inning by throwing to first base for two outs and the outfield got the last out. In the ninth inning, he struck out the side. Honest to God, Maggie, you would have thought my son won the World Series the way everyone went crazy." He pinched the bridge of his nose to stop the tears. It didn't work, for they slid down his cheeks. "When . . . when I put him to bed that night I sat down next to him and told him to remember that day for the rest of his life, that he now had proof he could do anything if he wanted it enough and focused on it. I didn't know the rest of his life would only be a few short months. I should have spent more time with him. I should have made more of his games. I should have been with him and Cat on that damn plane!"

"You're not the only father who missed his child's school play or game, Julian. Most fathers at some time regret not being there for their children. You can't change the past, but you can treasure your memories. And it sounds as though you have great memories of them both."

Leaning forward he placed his glass on the coffee table and rested his arms on his knees. His face looked tortured. "Don't you see? I should have been there! If I only knew how little time I would have with them . . ." He covered his eyes with his hand. "I should have been there," he muttered, trying so hard to keep himself together and not break down.

Maggie inhaled deeply. Now was not the time to wrap him in her arms. He needed to get it all out, to release the guilt, the pain, the anger. She would not contain that energy around him by hugging him, so she fought the urge to comfort him, to take it all away. He, alone, had to do it.

"Julian, none of us know how much time we have. You've been beating yourself up for an illusion. Let me ask you something. Do you believe that Morgan knew you loved him, that you were proud to be his father?"

"God, I hope so," he answered, wiping his eyes and picking up his glass of Scotch.

"I'm not asking what you hope. I'm asking if you believe your son knew you loved him."

He hesitated, staring out into space. "I did everything I could to make his childhood different from mine. I wanted him to know he was loved."

"How old were you when your mother died?"

"Seven."

"So young. Did you know your mother loved you?"

He nodded. "I can remember her. Not the way she looked, but the way I felt when she hugged me. She loved me."

"How about your father?"

He snorted derisively. "How about him?"

"Did he love you?"

"What has this got to do with my wife and son being killed?" He finished the last of the Scotch and stared at the melting ice cubes in his glass.

"I'm just asking a question. Did your father love you?"

He closed his eyes and exhaled in frustration. "I don't know, okay? Maybe he did before my mother died. After that he was too drunk to tell me."

"So, if I'm understanding you, your father couldn't accept the death of your mother and medicated himself with alcohol to block the pain?"

"I guess you could say that. I never asked him."

"So the two of you never got the opportunity to grieve together after losing the person you both loved?"

"Pretty hard to grieve with someone who drank himself into oblivion every night," he answered, a tinge of anger in his voice as he rose and walked over to the table between the windows. He poured himself another drink.

"So you were alone a lot?"

"Yes," he snapped, as though it made no difference. "And before you ask, I've forgiven my father. After Cat and Morgan died I understood the appeal of oblivion."

"Have you forgiven your mother?"

His hand stilled over his glass. "My mother?"

"Yes, Julian. You were a young child dealing with the trauma of losing the person you loved the most. Have you forgiven your mother for dying and leaving you all alone in the world?"

He shot her an angry look as he took his glass and stood in front of the window, staring outside the room as though wishing himself anywhere else. "I never blamed my mother for dying. It wasn't her fault."

"You know that now, as an adult. But wasn't there ever a time when you felt powerless to stop everyone from leaving you, including your father every night? It was all out of your control, wasn't it? It would have been perfectly normal to be scared and angry at the adults who you thought were there to protect you. Your mother dies on you and your father ignores you. You were just a child and you were all alone."

"This isn't about me, Maggie," he stated in a firm voice, still staring out the window. "This is about my wife and my son."

"Of course it's about you, Julian." She could see that muscle in his jaw working as he clenched his teeth. "It's about parts of you that have remained unhealed since you were a little boy."

They were well into it now and she had to continue, even if it meant he would run again. "So here's my armchair perception of what might have happened. As a child you sublimated the anger and pain, bottling it up and probably becoming quite the terror for your father because negative attention is better than no attention at all. Somewhere along the line you decided to rein yourself in, control what you could, yourself, and work really hard to get what you wanted out of life. When you met Cat you saw yourself creating the kind of family you wanted to have when you were growing up, what you thought your parents should have had. Maybe you thought subconsciously if you did that, you could heal your family wounds. You probably vowed never to be like your father. And you did it. You had a beautiful family life until it was cruelly taken away from you. And, guess what? After you absorbed the initial shock, you didn't use alcohol like your father. You medicated the pain away with work. More benevolent, I'll grant you, but just as effective in blocking out what you can't deal with. Did you ever think your father shut you out because loving you, showing love to you, was too damn scary for him? Perhaps he thought he had to protect his heart because he realized none of us know how long we've got, something could happen to you, and he believed he couldn't go through the pain of loss again. He closed off his heart, built a wall against intimacy. He made the mistake of thinking if you never love again, you can't be hurt."

Julian kept staring out the window, clenching his jaw muscles and the glass in his hand.

"Any of this sound familiar?"

It took him a few seconds to answer. "Too much of it."

"Listen, my love," she said gently, "so many of us think we can heal our family wounds. Why else do we vow never to be like one of our parents and find ourselves in situations where we're challenged with the same traumas? Like a young girl who finds out her father is unfaithful to her mother and then as a woman keeps attracting men who betray her over and over. Or the boy who swears he would never be like his abusive father and he'll marry a strong woman who can stand up for herself, and then as a man he attracts women who are addicted to drama and he finds himself rescuing them time and again. Lots of us keep trying to heal our parents' wounds. And most of us don't even realize it."

It hit her with the impact of a baseball bat to the head.

Here she'd been trying to help Julian and her own past was coming to the surface. Was she desiring to get pregnant and become a successful single mother to heal her mother's wounding and prove being a single parent could be done without resentment? Oh God . . .

Neither one of them said anything, each lost in their own thoughts. Maggie was trying to figure it all out in her head, but her heart was telling her the truth. She couldn't get pregnant, repeating her mother's challenge yet thinking she would do a better job of it. It was a pattern she didn't want to repeat.

She'd asked for direction and it had come from her own words.

Pulling herself together, Maggie cleared her mind of her situation and focused once again on Julian. She rose from the sofa and walked up behind him. Wrapping her arms around him, she placed her hands upon his heart. "You are a good man, Julian. You were a good husband and a good father. You didn't do anything wrong. It wasn't your fault." She kissed his back softly and breathed her next words through the material of his shirt. "And you were a good boy who got a raw deal. You can forgive yourself and your parents. You were allowed to be angry with them and hurt by what happened after your mother died, because you can't control feelings, only actions. I'm so sorry someone in your life didn't recognize what was happening to you, but I promise it's not too late. You're not alone, Julian. Not anymore. Please don't become your father and close your heart off to love. It must be so lonely." She focused all her energy on her hand over his heart. "You don't have to carry that burden anymore. It's okay to let it go now, all of it, because deep down, beyond all your pain and anger, there's a place that knows you're worthy of love. You always were. You just forgot."

He clasped her hand tightly to his chest and she placed her cheek against his back as she felt the old pain, anger, all his tightly held fear, rise up within him and transform itself into the release of tears. He rested his shoulder and head against the edge of the window, gulping down sobs. Maggie held him in silence, envisioning the heavy energy he had carried since he was a little boy being discharged, creating a space for love to grow once again.

After a few minutes, he took out a handkerchief and blew

his nose. "I'm sorry about all this," he muttered, stuffing the handkerchief back into the pocket of his jeans.

"Shh," she whispered. "I'm honored you could do this with me."

His hand rubbed back and forth over hers, still at his chest, and she could feel him deeply inhale. "I'm falling in love with you, Maggie." He exhaled quickly, as if in relief. "There. I've said it."

"I know, Mac. But it isn't that scary, is it?"

He laughed through his tears. "It damn well is . . . scary as hell."

"It's not. And you know it." She kissed his back again. "And you also know I love you." When she said the words, it wasn't like before. This time the love was so deep that it cut right into her heart.

He turned around. His face was red and blotched from releasing years of emotion. He looked exhausted. "Even though I just fell apart on you, you still love me?"

She was filled with tenderness. "Listen, Mac, when we stay comfortable, we quit growing. If you didn't just fall apart, as you put it, I don't think I would have been able to tell you I love you. I wasn't being facetious when I said I was honored you could do that with me. I so respect you. It took extraordinary courage to release everything that's been holding you back from real happiness. Many can't. Any woman would be feel blessed now by your love."

He looked deeply into her eyes, his own filling again with moisture. "I don't know what to say to you," he whispered, cupping her face between his hands. His thumb wiped away a tear sliding down her cheek. "You're such a decent person. Far too good for me. Thank you doesn't seem enough."

She grinned and squeezed him. "It's enough. Now, how about I run a bath for you?"

In spite of everything, he chuckled. "I don't take baths, honey. If you're insinuating that I offend, I'll take a shower."

"I wasn't insinuating anything. I want you to relax now. This has been stressful, I know, and a bath might be just what you need."

"Will it make you happy? I've learned not to argue with you when you get fixated on relaxation. I remember that first night here when you forced me to take off my shoes."

"I didn't force you," she answered, standing on her toes to kiss his reddened nose. "But if you take a bath now, I'll bring you a glass of Scotch. I promise you'll feel better."

"Hmm . . . will you take one with me?"

She laughed. "C'mon. I'll surprise you."

She led him into the bathroom, all the while knowing her time with him was coming to an end. She would make this night count . . . for both of them.

Love. Real love was without possession.

Somehow, she had to put aside her feelings and teach him that last lesson.

THIRTEEN

"**O**h-my-God . . ." Julian laid his head back against the edge of the wide round tub.

The bath water was scented with chamomile and lavender oils to relax him. Maggie sat on her Parsons chair upholstered in white moiré to match the drapes in her bathroom. Her fingers were massaging his scalp as she shampooed his hair with green tea and fig soap. "Relaxed?"

"Jesus, if I were any more relaxed I'd sink under the water and drown. You really know how to take care of a guy."

She grinned. "It's the aromatherapy."

"It's more than that. It's you. It's this tub. I like it, and the trees."

"I fell in love with the tub when I saw it and the room was designed around it. The palms make me happy. When I take a bath and look up to a canopy of leaves and the skylights beyond I feel like I'm transported to a tropical island." She played with the soap, making his hair spike out like a punk rocker. "When it's snowing in February and the temperature is below freezing, it can be heavenly."

"You're very creative," he murmured, thoroughly enjoying the attention.

"You want to talk about creative, you should see your hair right now," she answered with a giggle. "You look like Billy Idol. Remember him? 'White Wedding'?" And she started singing the song.

He reached up and grabbed her hand. "C'mere."

She rose and stood over him, looking at his face upside down. "You look funny. Say something."

"I know what I want to say. I just don't know if you want to hear it."

She giggled again. "I had a friend and we used to make each other laugh by doing this. Watch my mouth." She licked her lips and made a face. "What don't you think I want to hear? Go ahead. Say it."

He grinned at her playfulness, but he didn't laugh.

"Have you ever kissed someone upside down?"

"I don't think I have," she answered with a laugh because watching his mouth upside down really was funny.

"Then c'mere." He pulled on her wrist and she bent over him, finding his lips.

There was something so sensual about it, their tongues intertwined, that she moaned with sudden pleasure. "My, my, my . . . we'll certainly have to do that again."

He sank down in the tub, plunging his head under water, and used his hands to push his hair back off his face when he surfaced. He took her hand again and led her around the side of the tub.

Maggie sat on the edge, holding his hand as she smiled down at him.

"What about a white wedding, Maggie?"

She felt her smile freeze. "The Billy Idol song," she answered. "Great dance music."

He stared into her eyes, water dripping from his hair, his nose, his chin. "You. Me. A white wedding, or any other color you want. Will you marry me, Maggie?"

She felt her face crumble as tears sprang into her eyes. "Oh, Mac, now is not the right time to ask me such a question. You're in a vulnerable state and . . . and we've only been dating for such a short time and—"

"It doesn't matter how long we've been dating," he interrupted. "I know what I want. And I want you. I want to make a life with you."

"Julian, listen, you need time to adjust, to get yourself in balance now that you're free of—"

"Don't you get it?" he interrupted her again. "I love you, Maggie. I know I could search this world from now until the end of time and I'll never find another woman like you." He pulled her hand to his lips and kissed her fingers. "I want *you*. I want to spend my life with you."

She couldn't stop the tears from falling down her cheeks. She'd had marriage proposals before. How cruel that this was the only time she wanted to shout out her acceptance. And she couldn't. Love was without possession. She had to let him go and it was breaking her heart. Sniffling, she stood up and kissed his forehead. "I love you, Julian. And I am so honored you want me, but you need time. I need time. Isn't it enough right now to know we love each other?"

"How much time?" he persisted. "A month? Two months? I'm not going to change my mind. I know it . . . in here," he said, placing her hand upon his heart. "You can have all the time you need, but I know we're going to live out the rest of our lives together. I trust my instincts, Maggie, and every single one of them is telling me you're the one."

It was too, too cruel. He would never know how much she wanted his words to be true, how much she wanted to be the one. She pulled her hand away and stood up. It took every ounce of strength to push past the pain and say it.

She wiped her eyes with her palms and looked down at him.

"I'm not the one, Julian." Tears were blurring her vision and she felt her throat tighten, almost choking off the rest of her words. She felt her stomach muscles clenching and her diaphragm twisting off her breath as she began sobbing. "I'm the one who comes before . . . before the real one can show up in your life."

"What?" he demanded in disbelief.

"I'm not the one, Julian. I . . ." She couldn't say it again. Her heart would rip in two if she tried.

When he rose from the tub and grabbed a towel, she shook her head and left the room. "Maggie, what the hell are you talking about?" he shouted after her.

He found her sitting on the edge of her bed, her hands

covering her face as she continued to cry. "Maggie?" he whispered, tucking the edge of the towel in at his waist. "What's wrong, honey? What did you mean?"

She looked up at him and the sadness on her face broke his heart. He knelt in front of her and took her hands in his. "C'mon, talk to me." When she didn't say anything, just kept breathing in hard as though trying to control her tears, he added, "Look, I went too fast. I'm sorry. Hey, I'm on my knees here. Either forgive me or marry me."

He was pleased to see her lips move into a faint resemblance of a smile.

"There's nothing to forgive," she answered in a tiny voice.

"Do you love me?" he asked, staring into her tear-filled eyes.

Her expression crumpled as she extended a trembling hand to his face. Tenderly pushing back a wet strand of hair off his forehead, she said, "Oh yes, Julian. I do love you."

"Then that's all I need to know."

Shaking her head, she pulled back her hand. "You don't understand."

His knees were killing him on the hardwood floor, so he got up and sat next to her on the mattress. "What is it I don't understand? We love each other. That's enough for now, isn't it? Aren't you the one who believes in *carpe diem*? Seize the day? So maybe I seized a little too much back there. Marriage can wait." He rubbed her back in small circles of comfort. "Do you know, Maggie, how long it's been since I was with someone I loved?"

She glanced at him and moaned, then slid her head onto his damp chest as she wrapped her arm around his waist. "I'm sorry, Julian. I didn't mean to ruin everything."

"What's ruined?" he insisted as he hugged her to him. "We're together. Almost in bed. And one of us is undressed. It's looking pretty damn good to me."

She laughed and then sniffled, using the edge of his towel to wipe her eyes. "You've got a one-track mind when it comes to sex."

He was so relieved to hear her laugh that he could actually feel the tension seep out of his muscles. "No, I have a one-track mind when it comes to sex with you. So let's crawl up farther onto this mattress and I can show you how focused I can be."

"I need to tell you something first," she said.

"And what is that?" he asked, grateful to have his Maggie back. It was the first time he'd seen her cry like that and it really rattled him.

"I stopped taking the Pill, so I don't know if I'm protected."

"You stopped?" He couldn't figure why. "You didn't think I would come back after last week?"

"I just stopped. It doesn't matter why. I don't even know if I'm still protected, but I think, to be sure, we should use something if we make love and I don't know what's open on the Fourth of July and—"

"Hold on," he interrupted, taking her shoulders and moving her away. "I have no desire to be combing the city looking for condoms, but I just might save the day yet." He got up and pulled his overnight bag onto the bed. Shoving his hands into the inside pocket, his fingers searched the contents. When he withdrew a small wrapped package, he announced, "Prepare yourself to be ravished, Maggie O'Shea."

"I'm not even going to ask," she replied with a laugh, standing up and unbuttoning her blouse.

Throwing the pack onto the bed, he stood before her. "None of it matters anymore, honey." Her nose was still red, along with her eyes, but she seemed so much better now. He would make love to her, casting away her doubts, and they would be back on track. She just needed some reassurance. He placed his hands over hers and continued what she had started. "That was then, before I knew someone like you would come into my life. Thank God, you did," he muttered, pulling on the edges of her opened blouse and trapping her against his chest. "Ready to seize the day?"

Her answer was to slip her fingers under the towel at his

waist and rip it away. "What do you think, Mac?" she countered, throwing the towel behind her.

"I think you've got too many clothes on." He yanked the sleeves down her arms, trapping her.

"So do I," she answered as he pulled the blouse away and dropped it to the floor.

She unbuttoned her jeans and he moved back so she could take them off. Watching her undress, he felt his arousal build and when she bent down to pull the legs off, he stared at her bottom and was unable to resist slipping his hand under her panties to cup her. Hearing her moan of pleasure only excited him more and before he realized what he was doing, he grabbed her hips and pulled her back against him.

"I love you, Maggie," he murmured into her hair as she straightened and arched her back in an age-old invitation.

"Thank you for loving me," she whispered, reaching behind to stroke his thigh. "You will never know how much I have come to love you."

One moment they were grinding against each other, building up exquisite tension as his hands roamed freely over the front of her body and in the next when she bent over the mattress to get the condom he thought he might explode with a passion that seemed primal and immediate. She opened the wrapper and handed the condom to him and he put it on so quickly that he almost growled with frustration. "Don't move," he muttered. "Please . . . don't move."

Something came over him, seeing her bent over before him, some primitive urge to make her his alone and when he entered her a guttural groan of satisfaction escaped his lips. He knew he should be thinking about her, being more tender, but it was as if he couldn't help himself. When she flicked her hair to one side, he bent over her and kissed her shoulder, but even that wasn't enough. He wanted to taste her skin, to run his teeth over it, to leave his mark on her. He started kissing her flesh harder and harder, knowing he was going to leave a mark. He hadn't done such a thing in years, but he couldn't seem to stop himself, especially when he heard Maggie's growl of pleasure.

He straightened to penetrate her more fully and that's when it happened, when his eyes played some kind of crazy trick on him, for instead of Maggie's precious face turning to look over her shoulder, he would have sworn it was the face of a . . . lioness!

He blinked, hoping to clear his vision.

He blinked again and then closed his eyes tightly, thinking his imagination was just overactive. Maggie was a great lover, a fantastic lover, taking him places he'd never been before. But this was just . . . *crazy!*

He had trouble keeping up the rhythm, telling himself it was the aromatherapy. The tub water had been too hot. The blood vessels in his brain had been contracting or something. Breathing hard, he slowly opened his eyes and his relief was immense to see everything was normal. He was making love to gorgeous, beautiful, sexy Maggie, a woman who made him feel like he was twenty again.

But what a bizarre fantasy!

It took every ounce of control for Maggie not to shift again. She couldn't even give in to her pleasure for fear that Julian would trigger her imagination. When he bit her shoulder, it was like an electrical charge traveled right to her brain, releasing the image of a lioness.

This was too dangerous, for he was more than her match in passion and she couldn't chance it happening again. Dear God, if he had seen her shape shift, he'd never recover. She needed to see his face, to concentrate on him. "Julian."

"I know, honey . . . me too."

"Wait. Let's get in bed. I want to see you."

He withdrew and she turned around, clasping her arms around his neck. "Make love to me, Julian. I want to see your eyes. I want you to look into mine so you'll know this is real."

It was a plea for tenderness and his lips came down on hers in the sweetest kiss, filled with reverence. *I must memorize this*, Maggie thought as tears came into her eyes once again, for it would be the last time they made love.

• • •

The room was in darkness, save for all the candles that were lit. They were together on the chaise longue, wrapped in each other's arms.

"Oh! Look at that one!" Maggie exclaimed for the tenth time as another firecracker exploded in the night sky over the city. It started as a single burst of white that faded into tiny twinkling stars.

"You're like a little kid," Julian remarked, kissing her temple.

"I love fireworks. The first year I was here, I couldn't believe what a great view I had. How many other people can just sit in their living room and get this kind of show?"

"Not many. Great way to spend the holiday . . . with you in my arms." His fingers absently traced a line up and down her arm. "What do you think about going to BellaLuna next weekend? Can you get free?"

"I work on Fridays and Saturdays. You know that. Seems a shame for you to miss out though, Julian. You should go on Friday and enjoy yourself."

"Now I wouldn't be enjoying it half as much without you there beside me. I can wait until Saturday."

Maggie stared at another brilliant display in the night sky, this one of pink and then green, and knew she couldn't postpone it any longer. "Julian, I think you should go alone. Without me."

He looked at her. "Why?"

She deeply inhaled. "Because you have to start to live your life now. Who knows who is going to cross your path, who you'll attract to you now that you've released what's been holding you back."

"Maggie O'Shea, you want to start speaking English, or at least some form of it I can understand? I *am* living my life. This is the first day in almost ten years that I am completely relaxed. I'm here with you, the woman I love."

She moved away from his arms and sat on the bottom of the chaise. Holding his hand, she said, "Listen to me, Julian. Please. Listen very carefully. I love you. I think you know that. But love is without possession. It isn't a prize that you capture and then hold tightly in fear of losing it. The love I feel for you exists. It doesn't matter what you do or where you are. It's unconditional. What I said to you earlier in the bathroom is true. I'm not the one, Julian. I'm the one who comes into your life before the real one can show up. You wouldn't have attracted her before because you were carrying around too much baggage. You would have continued to attract to you women with the same kinds of issues. I helped you to heal old wounds so you could live your life fully. But it won't be with me." Maggie felt her heart breaking as she added, "She's out there, Julian, waiting for you."

Just as she expected, she could feel his energy withdraw along with his hand. He sat up straighter. "What kind of psycho-babble bullshit is this?" he demanded. "You're not the one? Well, I say you are! What do you think you are? Some kind of soul healer?"

"In a way," she murmured, crossing her arms over her chest to protect her heart and stiffen her resolve.

"Don't flatter yourself, Maggie."

Her smile was weak as she raised her head and looked at him in the candlelight. "I'm not flattering myself. I'm just telling you the way it is. There is a woman out there who has healed her wounds, who will cross your path, who will share your life and bring you great joy. But it isn't me."

He didn't say anything for a few moments. "Is all this because I asked you to marry me? Because you think you're the rebound relationship?"

"In a way I am your rebound relationship and everybody knows they never last." She shook her head. "But it was going to be this way, no matter what happened. I can't marry you, Julian. I don't know if I'll ever marry."

"So we'll live together. I just thought you'd want marriage and that whole white picket fence you talked about. Doesn't matter to me if we have a fence or not."

"I can't live with you either. I know you don't understand this yet, but you will one day. When you meet her, you'll know exactly what I mean."

"Will you shut up about *her*? There is no her. There's you.

You're her!" He shook his head. "Jesus, I feel like I'm in a Marx Brothers movie. This can't be happening. I've heard of guys freaking out about the concept of marriage, but you've beaten that, Maggie."

"I'm not freaking out," she answered gently. "I'm trying to convey to you that I love you, but it will never work between us and no amount of arguing is going to change that. I'm not your one, Julian. You'll meet her soon enough."

"Oh, and now you're a fortune-teller? Did you get that extraordinary ability from those damn books downstairs?"

"I know this is difficult, but there's no reason to be rude."

"Really? Well, excuse *me* for fighting for us. One of us has to. You're quite willing to let it all go."

"Julian, it *has* to go. I'm not going to prolong what's inevitable. My heart . . ." She shook her head and stood up. Walking to the window, she added, "You will never know how sorry I am to hurt you like this, but I'm doing the right thing. You'll know that soon enough. I have to believe that."

She heard him move off the chaise.

He stood behind her. "What were you going to say about your heart? Finish it."

She had tried so hard to keep the tears at bay. Once more she willed them away, yet her eyes burned with the effort. "My heart isn't at issue here."

"When is your heart the issue, Maggie? How many boyfriends are you going to have before you grow up and make a commitment?"

Her head hung in misery as the finale to the fireworks began. Each explosion felt like a shot to her heart. "I'll accept your anger, Julian. You have a right to it, but I have a right to make a commitment when the relationship is right. So far, that hasn't been the case."

"What's wrong with our relationship? Answer me that."

"There's nothing wrong with you. I told you earlier that any woman would be blessed to have your love. I meant that."

"Just not you."

She nodded. "Not me."

He grabbed her arm and turned her around. "Are you seriously telling me that you don't want to see me again? Ever?"

"Not for a while. I can't. It would be too painful."

"So you're Saint Maggie, sacrificing yourself for the love I'll find in the future?"

"I'm not a saint."

"Damn right, you're not," he shot back angrily. "You're delusional if you think I'm going to just forget about you, about us. You know what it took for me to come here and open a vein for you? To dig up things I never wanted to confront? *That's* how much I love you, how serious I am about us. Let's get to you now, shall we? What is it in you that makes you attract men with problems? Do you get some kind of weird metaphysical high off helping them heal their wounds and then releasing them back into the world? So that they can find *the one*? What is it, Maggie? When are you deserving or worthy of being the one? When's it your turn, huh?"

"You don't understand," she cried, no longer able to stop the tears.

"You're right!" he nearly shouted. "I don't! Explain it, because I'm not getting out of your life. Maybe the others did what you wanted, allowed you to get away with this, but I'm not. You think you *know* something all intuitive about me and my future? Well, let me tell you something. I didn't make a fortune by just using my head. I trust my gut. My instincts are every bit as good as yours. And my gut instinct is that you're scared of something, something that's holding you back, has been holding you back for years."

He laughed, as though incredulous. "Maybe I should be glad of it because you haven't married yet, but we are going to solve it tonight. You are my one, Maggie O'Shea, and nothing you can do or say is going to change that. That's what my instinct tells me and I've learned to trust it."

She lifted her head, knowing what she had to do. "What you have failed to understand, Julian, is that you don't have the ability to change everything. Your persistence, while admirable, will get you nowhere. I didn't just meet you accidentally at the charity auction."

He stiffened and raised his chin. "What do you mean?"

She didn't want to do this, to hurt him like this, but knew he was serious. He would persist in trying to create something that never could be. In the end it was kinder this way. Still, she felt sick to her stomach as her heart broke in two. "What I mean is that I came to that auction to meet you."

"Go on . . ."

"I knew things about you. About the state of your heart. You were my assignment."

He actually leaned backward, as though steeling himself against a strong gust of wind. "Your *assignment!?* What the hell are you talking about?"

At that moment the grand finale of fireworks exploded, filling the sky with a brilliance of color and sound. When it was over, the silence was deafening. Maggie imagined it was like the sickening stillness after a bomb explosion, where your heartbeat still pounds in your head and your solar plexus is twisted with dread because you just know there is collateral damage.

"I asked," he said in a deadly calm voice, "what the hell you are talking about."

Observing his expression of shock, Maggie swallowed down her pain and continued. "I would have told you eventually. I was hoping it would have been later, after you'd met someone."

He sank to the arm of the sofa, as though too stunned to keep standing. "You'd better explain this, Maggie. *How* was I your assignment? And who gave it to you?"

She could see how she was hurting him, but Maggie knew from past experience that it was better to do it quickly. Like all the others he would be angry and shocked, but would recover when the right woman came along. It's what made them release her and go forward in their own lives. It worked, had worked perfectly in the past. She had the wedding invitations to prove it. Still, it broke her heart to do this to Julian and she felt sick to her stomach that he would leave her and find happiness with another. Taking a deep breath for courage, she said, "In the last fourteen years I've had seven assignments, men who are struggling with the past, who've closed off their hearts. It's my job, so to speak, to help them heal. When they leave, they then are able to attract someone they can truly love."

"You do this as a part-time job? I've been a *job* to you?" His voice matched his incredulous expression.

How could she tell him he had been different, that she would give anything to spend her life with him? It would only encourage him and prolong the pain. "What can I say, Julian? It works. I've been invited to the weddings, the christening of child—"

"And you loved these men?" he interrupted angrily.

His words felt like a knife slicing through her and she knew her answer would hurt him even more deeply.

"Answer me!"

She nodded. "It wouldn't have been possible unless I loved them. There are many shades of love; what's important is knowing the person is worthy of receiving it and remembers again how to give it to others."

"And what shade am I?" There was now bitterness added to the anger.

"The brightest shade, Julian. You're going to go on to much greater things."

"I don't give a damn about your crystal-ball predictions. What I want to know is how you can make love to me, tell me you love me, and then say it's a part-time job. You know what that job description says about you?"

"Don't, Julian," she pleaded. She couldn't stand that accusation coming from him. "It stopped being a job in Bermuda. I came to love you, but that doesn't mean I have to possess you. I am always going to love you. Nothing you can say or do is going to change that. My love just *is*. Once born, it exists. I want what's best for you. And it isn't me."

He didn't say anything. He couldn't even look at her, and Maggie felt his pain. After a while, he asked, "So all of it, us, was nothing more than an assignment?"

She should say yes. That would be the final blow. But she couldn't do it. She couldn't lie to him. "You, Julian

McDonald, are so much more than an assignment to me. I treasure each moment I've spent with you. I wish I could say something to make you understand that in time you will see what I'm saying is true. Whoever she is, she's out there waiting for you to show up."

"And you think I can just walk away from you? You think you're doing me some favor by breaking it off? Who do you work for?"

She swallowed deeply. "That I can't tell you, but your best interests have always been a priority. Everything you feel I've done to you has been with the intention of healing a broken heart, freeing a heart to discover real happiness again. You were happy, Julian, until you pushed to make it more."

"So everything about you has been a lie."

"I've never lied to you," she quickly answered. "If you think back, you will see I spoke the truth. You deserved it. Even the first night I met you, I told you I knew certain things about you. I didn't elaborate, but I didn't lie. And that's why I can't lie to you now. My full name is Magdalene. Why my mother named me that I'll never know, but it certainly guaranteed I would be picked on in Catholic school. I never understood Magdalene in the stories I had read. They had so misrepresented her. She was a woman of intelligence and great love, and was the beloved. To put it kindly she was resented by the males of her time, so instead of being the greatest student of unconditional love she has been portrayed throughout the last two millennium as a repentant whore."

She sat on the edge on the chaise again and faced him. "Think what you will about me, Julian. I can't control your thoughts or feelings. I have loved you unconditionally, and will continue to, but I want you to know I never bartered or sold my love. I never tried to manipulate your feelings. Had we not been attracted to each other, I never would have accepted the assignment. I knew I would fall in love with you. And I knew I would have to let you go."

When he didn't respond to her words, the muscles in

Maggie's chest tightened. She so wanted him to understand. Maybe not tonight, but later, when he was with someone else he would remember. "Listen, Julian, when I was young I did some things I'm not proud of, nothing illegal, but I did manipulate others for my own benefit. I stopped when a young man full of promise paid the price for my actions. I was taken under someone's wing and became a student of life. There I learned the natural law of cause and effect. It was then I realized I had to balance the scales, to make reparation for what I had done. I am in service to love. I know that sounds strange to you and I'm probably not explaining it well, but it is the truth. Every two years or so I'm given the name of someone wounded by life, someone who has forgotten how healing love is, and I help them remember. Your name was given to me two days before the charity auction. I knew that night I met you I was going to love you, Julian. No crystal ball needed. You are so easy to love and you make me feel like the most blessed woman to have received your love in return. Please remember I do love you, more than you realize right now. And if you think I am unaffected by this, or that what I am now doing comes easily, then you don't really know me at all. My heart is being torn in two."

"Then *why*, Maggie? Why are you doing this to us? It doesn't make sense."

She couldn't believe he still wanted her after what she had told him. Usually at this point the man accepted it or left in anger. Why wasn't he? It would be so much easier if he didn't continue to fight her.

"Because I know from past experience that I'm not the one. There will come a day when you realize this and you'll be grateful I didn't accept your offer. I know asking you to trust me, considering everything I've just told you, must seem like I'm asking for a slice of the moon. All I can say is wait and see. You are going to be happy, Julian, with a woman who is more appropriate for you. That woman isn't me."

"I suppose at this point, if I'm like all the rest, I should leave."

She cringed when she heard the dullness in his voice. "Perhaps it would be best," she murmured. "You'll think about all this and soon see it was for the best."

"Boy, you really underestimated me, Magdalene." He turned and slid down the sofa arm onto the cushion, facing her. "Even if you really believe everything you just told me about making reparations, I say your debt is paid in full. Whatever you did in your past, before me, is your business. I'm not going to find anyone more appropriate than you. Get that through your head. Your assignment with me isn't over. It will never be over until one of us dies. And even then, if it's possible, I would watch over you."

"God, you're making this so hard, Julian. Please just accept what I've told you. I'm not the—"

"I never want to hear that coming out of your mouth again," he interrupted. "You may think that now, but I'm going to prove you wrong. I'm *your* one, Maggie. And there isn't a damn thing you can do to change that."

She burst into tears, holding her hands over her eyes and her mouth. He was right. Her debt was paid. After this, she would never have to endure such pain again. It was too cruel to love someone this much and know they were meant for someone else. How much more would she have to sacrifice?

"Normally I would take you into my arms and try to soothe you," he said from the sofa. "But maybe you need to cry. Maybe you, Magdalene O'Shea, need to release fourteen years of guilt. Whatever you did, whatever price that man paid, it's over. And I'll give your words back to you. It wasn't your fault. You can stop blaming yourself."

"There are things you don't understand," she cried out. "And I can't explain them to you. Please, Julian . . . please accept what I'm telling you. There's someone else out there waiting for you."

"I don't want someone else. I want you."

She lifted her chin and wiped the tears away from her eyes. "You can't have me. No one can. I'm not willing to give up my independence to be possessed by any man. You'll get over your disappointment with me soon enough, but you should go now. We can rehash this all night long and it's not going to change my mind or the fact that I'm not the one for you. My assignment with you is completed."

The silence in the room was broken only by sounds from the street.

"I'll go," he said, standing up and walking into the bedroom. "Come on, Max. We're being asked to leave."

Maggie steeled herself against the urge to run into his arms and tell him everything, the truth about her, the foundation, the woman who might one day be his wife. When he walked out of the bedroom with his overnight bag and Max at his side, she felt what was left of her heart breaking with sorrow. "I'm sorry, Julian. One day you'll understand."

Attaching the leash to Max, he straightened and looked at her. "I'll never understand why you're so willing to end us just when we're getting started." He headed for the stairs and put the shoulder strap of his overnighter over his head. When he picked up Max, he added, "Just you remember, Maggie O'Shea, I didn't run away from this or you. I stayed and tried to work through it. You tell me, which one of us is being guided by old patterns?"

She listened as he left her, each step he took being imprinted upon her brain with the sound of him beyond her reach. The door opened . . . and then clicked shut, locking into place the finality of her decision. She didn't move, hardly breathed, for she didn't know if her legs would support her. She felt dizzy with pain and the enormity of what she had just done. Julian McDonald loved her, really loved her, and she'd turned him away. What was worse was that she loved him. He was right. He was her one, and she would have to live out her life knowing that.

The tears slid down her cheeks as she remembered him accepting her story, insisting her debt was paid. He'd accepted her past, something she never thought would happen. Still, there was so much more he didn't know about her. He would never be able to accept the shape shifting, no man would, so she was destined to live out her life alone. No husband. No children who were born of love.

She crawled up the chaise and pulled the cashmere throw over her curled body.

She felt so alone, robbed of happiness, cursed by something she'd inherited from a father she'd never known. This was to be her life, watching from afar the only man she'd ever wanted to build a life with fulfill his destiny with another. The universe must love irony.

Emotionally exhausted, she closed her eyes and prayed for sleep to claim her, to wipe out the image of Julian's hurt expression, the sound of the door closing, the way her heart felt lacerated like an open wound. She couldn't make herself move off the chaise and, besides, she couldn't bear to sleep in the bed.

It would only remind her of what she'd just let go.

FOURTEEN

Each year New York City's best and finest came together for the benefit of cancer research. The Red and White Ball was a fund-raiser and also a grand party where the A list of society, film, music, theater, government, and business gathered together for a good cause and to reaffirm their positions. It was an invitation-only event and ticket holders were the envy of those up-and-coming individuals who had not quite measured up yet to the standards of the city's A list . . . which meant either their publicist hadn't done their job or their financial portfolios were not yet impressive enough. It was a social climber's dream to receive that thick cream-colored envelope with engraved red printing and more than one individual considered its appearance in the mail as the sign of having *arrived*.

Julian wasn't in the mood for a party and for some reason wearing his tuxedo was annoying him. The tux had been custom made in London, yet it felt confining as though he'd outgrown it, which was ridiculous. His weight rarely varied. Still, he fought the urge to yank on his collar. Nodding his head in acknowledgment to different groups, he made his way through the dazzling crowd to the bar. He didn't want champagne. Scotch was on his mind.

It took him a few moments to get the bartender's attention, but with drink in hand he turned to the dance floor observing a sea of expensive gowns. Unbidden, his mind ran a picture of Maggie in that brown dress with all those buttons, slowly descending the staircase at the Art Museum in Philly. He closed his eyes tightly for a moment as though to shut out that image. He didn't want to think about Maggie, had been banishing her from his thoughts for the past three weeks. She'd told him to leave and he'd convinced himself that if what she said was true, that she was in service to love to make reparation for some past transgression, then she was definitely unstable. None of it made sense. In service to love! He had convinced himself it had been a close call. Simple infatuation with a kook. She'd fascinated him with her eccentricities, her unique way of looking at life. What scared him was he'd almost married the woman.

"Julian, good to see you," a voice announced from his side.

He turned to see Christopher Armatage extending his hand. Shaking hands with the United States ambassador to Spain, Julian smiled. "Good to see you again, Ambassador. How are you?"

"Fine, fine. Glad to be home for a visit. Vanessa insisted we return for this." Christopher Armatage looked out to the crowd for a moment and then turned his attention back to Julian. "From everything I read and hear, the world of business is treating you well. You're on your way to becoming this city's new Golden Boy."

Julian laughed. "Hardly, Ambassador. But thank you for the compliment."

"You know, McDonald, you're approaching a position in life where you might want to think about politics. The foreign service can always use another man to promote the American agenda abroad."

"Well, thank you for thinking of me, Ambassador, but politics isn't my game. I think I'll leave promoting the American agenda to those better informed than myself."

"Nonsense, you'd be perfect. The American agenda, my boy, is capitalism. Not many here tonight who would be better informed than yourself on that subject. Ah, here is Vanessa, along with my daughter Victoria, and our guest Senator Burke. Have you met him?"

Shaking his head, Julian said, "I haven't, but I'm an admirer."

The trio approached and Julian accepted a kiss from the ambassador's wife as Christopher Armatage slipped his arm around his daughter's back, presenting her. "May I introduce my lovely daughter, Victoria? Victoria, this is Julian McDonald. Surprised the two of you haven't crossed paths before now."

Smiling, Julian extended his hand. "How do you do, Victoria?"

She was pretty. Tall, blonde, thin, and her smile was reflected in her hazel eyes. Dressed in a chic white dress with a wide scarlet bow at her waist, she looked to be about thirty years old. Victoria placed her hand inside of his and said, "I'm doing well, Mr. McDonald. Why *haven't* we met before this?"

He chuckled as he let go of her hand. "I'm sure I don't know. I'm usually aware of such a lovely woman in any crowd."

"Ah, and there's that famous McDonald charm showing itself," she answered with a grin before stepping aside.

Gabriel Burke extended his hand. "Good to meet you, sir."

"The pleasure is entirely mine, Senator," Julian answered as he accepted the handshake. "I was just telling Ambassador Armatage I've been an admirer of yours for some time."

The distinguished politician grinned. "I can see what Victoria meant about the McDonald charm."

"My words," Julian said, "are sincere. I've followed your illustrious career for years now, Senator."

"As I have followed yours. And please call me Gabe. Perhaps after you have danced with Victoria I might engage you in conversation?"

To her credit, Victoria Armatage looked highly embarrassed by the senator's suggestion. Placing his glass of Scotch on the bar, Julian allowed his gentlemanly nature to kick in and he held out his hand to her. "Shall we?"

"Thank you," she murmured, inserting her hand inside of his.

The band was playing "The Way You Look Tonight" and when they reached the dance floor and Julian took Victoria into his arms, she blushed prettily and said, "Please believe me, I didn't pay Gabriel Burke to say that."

He laughed. "I believe you. Besides, I would have asked you to dance myself. He only got us out here a few songs earlier."

"Well then, I'll forgive my godfather for embarrassing me," she answered, following him easily as he led her through other couples.

She was lovely, with her straight, shoulder-length hair held back by a red satin band. "Seriously, why haven't we met before?" he asked.

She sighed, stared at his shoulder for a moment, and then raised her gaze to his. "I was married for six years and I lived in Texas."

"And now?"

"Now I no longer live in Texas, and I'm no longer married." Her eyes held a hint of sadness. "I'm sorry," he said.

She smiled. "So am I. Sorry about a lot of things." Her expression brightened. "But that's the past. Tonight is my coming out party. Well, my second coming out I should admit. I'm a woman free of the past."

For some reason her words reminded him of Maggie and he immediately dismissed the thought. Instead, he smiled and remarked, "That sounds liberating."

"Oh, it is!" she rushed to say. "Someone helped me to see I no longer needed to carry all that baggage, so I'm starting my life over."

"Well, congratulations," he replied, as a shiver of something raced up his spine to his brain, reminding him that Maggie had done the same for him. It was then the words to the old-fashioned song seemed to play out in his head, about feeling as though you've known someone before. Victoria smiled up at him and he simply blinked while staring into her eyes.

It wasn't her. This song reminded him of Maggie, of meeting Maggie, of being in Maggie's presence. He'd known right away she was *the one*.

How could she send him away?

"Are you all right?"

He blinked again, bringing himself back to the present. "Sorry," he said with a self-conscious laugh. "Just listening to the music."

"It's a wonderful song, isn't it?"

He only nodded, trying to concentrate on his dance partner and not a woman who was beyond eccentric.

"It always reminds me of my parents dancing on the patio of our home in Rye. Summer evenings. The two of them drinking their vodka martinis, until my mother would insist my father dance with her." She smiled a little. "I used to sit by the French doors in my nightgown and watch them. I thought that was the way marriage, life, was supposed to be."

He felt her sadness again and compassion rose up within him. "Hey, maybe it will be now. I heard someone say that mistakes are simply times we miss the mark. We always get another take, another chance."

Victoria's eyes widened. "I can't believe you said that."

"What?"

"Someone recently said almost that exact thing to me. This is too much of a coincidence."

He was about to say there are no coincidences and stopped himself when he realized it was Maggie who'd said that and the bit about mistakes. He was actually quoting Maggie O'Shea! Realizing he had to say something, he cleared his throat. "Well, then it must be true. You get another chance."

"Yes," Victoria said, looking up at him with wonder. "This is my second chance."

Thank God the song ended. Walking Victoria back to her parents and Senator Burke, he noticed the trio smiling at them as though very pleased. It made him uncomfortable, as though the three of them were delighted with their match-making efforts. He knew how to recognize such efforts for it had been happening to him for years, people thinking he needed a wife and they had the perfect candidate.

"Thank you," he murmured to Victoria as he rejoined the group.

"Thank you, Julian," she replied. Her gaze was searching his face. For what, he wasn't sure.

He smiled politely and then picked up his glass from the bar. Turning to the older man at his side, he said, "You wished to speak with me, Senator Burke."

"Well, if I can tear you away from this lovely creature," the senator remarked, nodding to Victoria, "then, yes, I would ask for a few moments of your time."

Julian finished his drink, then nodded his acknowledgment to the Armatages and their daughter and held his hand out to the crowd. "Perhaps we can find some privacy on the terrace."

"Good idea," Gabriel Burke answered.

The two men made their way toward the edge of the crowd and once on the terrace they moved in silent agreement to a secluded spot in the corner.

"You are probably wondering what I have to say that couldn't be said in front of others."

Julian smiled and nodded. "I'm intrigued, sir."

"I hope you remain intrigued, Julian. May I call you by your given name?"

"Of course."

Julian watched as the older statesman looked out to the city of New York sparkling with lights. "This is a beautiful sight, is it not?"

Turning his head, Julian took in the view. "Yes, it certainly is."

"Yet I think we both know it's surface beauty, underneath is a different story. Like with people. One may observe a person of beauty, though it is only when we search within we find the true state of affairs."

Julian didn't know where the conversation was going. Was he talking about Victoria, or the underbelly of the city?

"Do you agree?"

"I would agree that appearances can be deceiving."

Burke nodded. "Yes, they can. Forgive me if I'm blunt, but out of respect I see no point in prevarication." He paused for a moment. "I am planning to retire, Julian, and I am seeking someone to replace me, someone I can endorse and throw my support behind. I believe that someone is you."

Julian jerked his head to stare at the man's profile. "Me?" he asked in a shocked voice. "I'm afraid you have the wrong man, Senator."

Burke smiled. "I know how you feel about the matter. I'm hoping to change your mind."

"Sorry to dash your hopes, but I don't think my mind can be changed. I'm flattered you would think of me to replace you, but I have no interest in becoming a politician."

"As we've agreed, appearances can be deceiving, Julian. Great abundance has been bestowed upon you and you've handled it with responsibility and respect."

"Thank you," Julian answered, his senses going on alert for this was definitely an unexpected discussion.

"Look out there, Julian. Can you sense the change that is coming? I'm told your instincts are excellent. What do they tell you about the state of our country?"

"I'm not sure I know what you're asking, Senator. If it's my opinion, then—"

"No, not your opinion," Burke interrupted. "What do your instincts tell you is happening to the people who are the country? And I'm not talking about those who are dancing here tonight or working the room for their own advantages. I'm talking about an ordinary family trying to make ends meet when the father loses his job, his pension plan, his 401K to downsizing, and his company's officers walk away with billions. The next election is going to be about the state of the economy. You have an excellent background in taking failing businesses and turning them around. Let's be honest. The United States government is the biggest business in the world. And it needs help from men and women who are not in the pockets of the lobbyists and special interests. They say if you want to find out the truth, follow the paper trail.

Unfortunately, that trail in our nation's capital is littered with corruption. Your trail, Julian, happens to be clean. You don't owe your position in life to anyone. That's a free man. Imagine what a free man could accomplish."

Julian felt overwhelmed. "I don't know, Senator. I'm an extremely busy man and quite happy right where I am."

Gabriel Burke turned his head and looked directly into Julian's eyes. "Are you really? You've accomplished everything you've wanted in the business world. How challenging is it now? Do you remember that excitement when you were starting out? That vitality that seemed to pump the blood through your veins? When was the last time you felt that?"

Julian wondered if the man had the ability to read his mind, for the only thing that truly challenged him now wasn't associated with business. It was a woman in Philadelphia. "But politics? It's the dirtiest game in town."

Senator Burke laughed. "It is that. And it's getting dirtier." His expression sobered. "Right now we are heading for a one-party rule. What I'm about to tell you is confidential. Agreed?"

Julian nodded. "Agreed."

"There are weekly meetings in which a certain senator vets the hiring decisions of major lobbyists. What is happening is that one party's activists are being placed in high-level corporate and lobbyist jobs, excluding the other party. The dominant party boasts that thirty-three of thirty-six top-level Washington positions have gone to that party's members. That senator and his colleagues have also used intimidations and private threats to bully lobbyists who try to maintain good relations with both parties. Even the House Majority Leader has declared, 'If you want to play in our revolution, you have to live by our rules.' These are serious times, my boy. Very serious."

Julian listened carefully. "Isn't that just the way it is? Interest groups want to curry favor with the party that controls Congress and the White House?"

"Yes, but it goes deeper than that. Lobbying jobs are a

major source of patronage, a reward for the loyal, except now many lobbyists owe their primary loyalty to that party and not the industries they represent. There was a time when corporate cash was split more or less evenly between parties. What's happening is that corporations themselves are becoming part of that party's machine, being rewarded with policies that increase their profits like deregulation, privatization of government services, elimination of environmental rules. In return companies like the auto industry and communications use their influence to support the ruling party's agenda."

"So much for an independent press," Julian remarked.

"Exactly. It's frightening that you can hear a more accurate accounting of America's news by listening to the BBC."

"What about campaign finance? You keep hearing it's going to be brought up again before Congress."

Burke shook his head. "Campaign finance is just the tip of the iceberg. This reminds me of the McKinley era when the nation was governed by and for big business. If these people get their way, Julian, it will destroy what our founding fathers fought so hard to achieve. Balance of power. It may be a cliché, but absolute power corrupts absolutely. Did you know Thomas Jefferson once said that every form of government needs a revolution every two hundred years to clean out the corruption? Fortunately, we can accomplish such a transformation with our power to vote. The people out there need a voice, Julian. You came from them. You could speak their language and they would hear you."

"I'm flattered, Senator, that you believe I could fill your shoes. Personally I doubt it. I've stayed away from politics because I don't want to make deals with people who would sell their grandmothers to make a buck. Nor do I want to live under the glare of the media. I'm perfectly happy to remain in the shadows."

The older man nodded. "I do understand. However, to whom much is given, much is expected. May I ask you a personal question?"

Julian stiffened his shoulders, not knowing what was coming next. "Go ahead."

"Do you have a belief system?"

"Are you asking if I believe in God?"

"If that's the label you're comfortable with, yes."

"I'm not sure what I believe any longer."

Burke nodded. "What do you believe in then?"

He thought about it. "Myself. My instincts."

"And where do they come from, those instincts?"

Shrugging, Julian answered, "From within. It's a knowing."

"Ah, yes . . . the unexplainable. Well, my son, may I suggest that you listen carefully to those instincts. All I shall say for now is that the Universe might be knocking on your door. It may be time to be of service to your fellow man."

All Julian could think about were the words the old man had spoken. *To whom much is given, much is expected.*

"Now I think it's time we rejoined our party. We'll talk again at another time. Tell me, what do you think of Victoria Armatage? Is she not a lovely creature?"

"She is," Julian agreed, still floored by the conversation.

"Perhaps the two of you could join me next weekend at my farm in Maryland. Great fishing."

That got Julian's attention. "Are you now playing matchmaker, Senator?"

"Is it that obvious?" he asked with a laugh.

Grinning, Julian replied, "It is. Victoria seems like a wonderful woman, but there would be no point in inviting us both."

"I'm sensing you're too polite to tell me to mind my own business."

"To be honest, my affections are engaged . . . elsewhere, Senator." He had no idea why he'd just said that. It was a good excuse, though, to end any notions of matchmaking.

Burke stopped at the doorway to the ballroom. "Really? And may I ask the fortunate woman's name?"

His answer was automatic. "Her name is Maggie."

"Interesting . . . ," the older man murmured as they entered the ballroom and were immediately engulfed by the cream of New York's society.

It had to be a summer flu that was making her so tired. Maggie forced her lips into a smile as D. walked around her apartment.

"Love what you've done in here. Who's your decorator?"

"No decorator," Maggie answered from the sofa. "Just me picking things that would be comfortable and welcoming after a long day."

"I should get you over to my place," D. declared. "It's in dire need of help. Looks like a warehouse. I just can't seem to get it organized, but then I was never any good with those girly things like knowing just how to place a pillow or make a flower arrangement. If I get flowers I just stick them into a vase the way they come. See, like this," she said while pointing out an arrangement of white flowers on the coffee table. "I bet you carefully placed each one to make it look like that."

"Come sit down and eat," Maggie instructed, patting the sofa cushion. "The food is getting cold."

D. kicked off her heels and hiked up her skirt to sit down. With her legs apart, she leaned in over the coffee table and looked into the white containers of Chinese food. "Smells great," she murmured, picking up a pair of chopsticks and making a plate for herself. "What's the matter? You're not eating?"

Maggie shook her head. "I think I caught a bug somewhere."

D. shifted to the end of the sofa. "No offense, but I'm not taking any chances. That's all I need. It took me eight months to get the anchor chair at six o'clock and I'm not about to let another's arse sit in it."

"No offense taken," Maggie answered with a grin. When D. had invited her to dinner, she'd been so lonely and so tired that she asked her friend to come to the apartment. Normally she would have cooked something special, but she just didn't have the energy. Chinese takeout came to the rescue.

"See, you didn't listen to me when I told you McDonald would be a runner and now you've gotten yourself sick over it."

The last month had been a slow torture, but she hadn't told D. about it. "How did you know I'm not seeing Julian any longer?"

D.'s shoulders sagged. "I suppose you'll find out anyway. I was leafing through *People* magazine and you know how they have those pages with pictures of celebrities at parties, and they always include some society types, Muffie and Puffie and Stuffie and all those women dressed to kill and hanging on the arms of their men?"

Maggie nodded, dreading what was coming next.

"Well, there was a page devoted to the Red and White Ball in New York City and there he was, smiling into the camera lens with Ambassador Armatage and his wife, Senator Burke, and a tall, willowy blonde. Name's Victoria Armatage, the ambassador's daughter, who appeared to be clinging to McDonald's arm with a look of near ecstasy. Kinda sickening, if you ask me. How do men get away with it? Playing with a woman's affections and then when he's had enough, when it means he has to maybe think about the other person's feelings, his commitment phobia kicks in and he gets to move on to the ambassador's daughter. Where's the justice?" She plopped a dumpling in plum sauce into her mouth.

So it had begun. An ambassador's daughter. Gabriel Burke's presence confirmed it. Maggie felt tears well up in her eyes and she forced them down. She was so sick of crying. For the last four weeks she'd been in battle with her emotions. One moment she would be fine, telling herself she'd done the right thing, and in the next moment she'd curl up in bed and cry herself to sleep. She must be depressed. All the crying. The escape of sleeping. Her immune system had suffered and she'd been vulnerable to any virus that walked into the store. Realizing she had to say something to D. to let her know she didn't resent Julian, Maggie murmured, "I hope he's happy." As crazy as it might seem, she really did. It would be a waste of her suffering if he wasn't.

"You, woman," D. said, pointing her chopsticks at Maggie, "need your head examined. You hope he's happy!" She mimicked Maggie. "Get real. Let's hope his dick shrivels up like this chopstick and falls off."

Maggie burst out laughing. "You're a cruel woman, Deborah Stark. I wish no such thing." Though she really couldn't bare to think of Julian with another woman, taking her into his arms and making love to her. That just wouldn't compute in her brain. Probably a survival tactic.

"I may be cruel, but I'm honest. And I'll take honesty any day over being nice." She shivered as though in distaste. "Nice. I don't even like the sound of that word. Who wants to be nice, to say and do the right thing so we don't offend anyone? To pretend and smile when we want to scream? To make the appropriate noises when we're under a man who's been trying to come for a half hour, instead of shoving the loser off your abused body and sending him home? Gimme a break, Maggie. Nice is for people who are afraid to be themselves. I'm no pretender."

"I'm not a pretender and I think I'm fairly nice." Maggie said, feeling like D. was getting carried away.

"You're decent. There's a difference between being a decent human being and pretending to be *nice*."

"You say that word as if it's a curse." Maggie grinned at seeing D. riled up, so she curled her legs under her and waited for what she knew was coming.

"It *is* a curse!" D. insisted. "How many nice people stand up for themselves? How many people take all kinds of shit not to rock the boat? Whoever taught us that being nice is a virtue was a manipulative bastard. What is so wrong with being honest? Expressing how you really feel? If you're pretending to be nice when you don't feel nice, then you're not really being you. So who *is* being you? Nobody. You don't exist." She delicately used her chopsticks to pick up a piece of chicken. "As long as I'm here on this planet, I'm going to be me and make sure I exist."

Maggie smiled at her friend. "I didn't know you were so deep."

D. finished swallowing and chuckled. "Ah, that's just the tip of the iceberg." She sobered, her smile becoming gentle. "I'm just trying to make you laugh, kiddo. I can see how hurt you are."

"That's why you called and invited me to dinner? You saw Julian's picture in the magazine and thought I could use company?"

"Well, I was going to call anyway."

"You know what this makes you, don't you?"

"If you say nice I swear I'll stuff a dumpling down your throat and choke you."

Laughing, Maggie shook her head. "You're a good friend, D., a decent human being . . . despite your bizarre sense of humor. Thanks for coming over tonight."

"It ain't easy, I know, but we make it through each time they leave." She opened another white container, peeked at the contents, and grinned as she stuck her chopsticks inside. "But, seriously, do you think it will ever get better? Is there hope for the future? Will there ever be a man who can put up with me?"

"What about James Coulter? He seemed pretty interested."

D. shivered. "I went out with him once. The man drinks gin and tonic as though it were the elixir of life. Besides, I think he was only into the celebrity thing. I had to drag him away from a photographer outside the restaurant. God forbid a picture of that man slobbering all over me got into the papers. Personally, I think it's hopeless. Did you ever give my number to that glorious man, Marcus something?"

Maggie exhaled loudly. "No, D., I didn't. He would have only broken your heart and then there would be two of us miserable."

"Oh well, he probably is in love with himself, right?"

"He's aware of his beauty," Maggie answered, picturing Marcus' face.

"He is beautiful, isn't he? Now that's unfair too. Wouldn't want to go out with a man who was prettier than I am. I have enough self-esteem issues to deal with as it is."

"You, D.?" Maggie asked with surprise. "You seem like the most confident woman I know."

D. chuckled. "If you saw my high school yearbook picture you'd understand. I wasn't born with these looks."

"You mean . . . ?" Maggie couldn't finish her sentence, though she looked closely at D.'s face.

"Yes, good friend, and I believe you are a good friend who will keep this to herself. The nose isn't exactly mine and the lips are plumped up every few months."

"I never would have guessed."

"It's television, a medium very unforgiving of imperfection. Gotta be perfect, put more pressure on America's women. Get this, they put together a focus group. Six women and six men and it was the women who said my lips were too thin. They didn't know if they could trust someone with thin lips!" D. shook her head. "So collagen got me the six o'clock anchor position. Unbelievable. Not talent. Puffy lips. Go figure."

Every time Maggie was in D.'s presence, she always had trouble reconciling the highly professional newscaster she saw on television with the earthy real woman. "C'mon, your talent got you there, D. There wouldn't have even been a focus group if you weren't talented."

"Yeah, well, enough about me. I say you find a gorgeous man and have him ravish you. Like that Marcus guy. You said you had something once and he certainly looked interested. What's that old saying? The way to get over a man is to get a new one under you?"

Maggie's stomach churned and she crossed her arms over it, willing it to still. The last time they'd been together Julian had announced he was going to ravish her. Why couldn't she stop the memories from piercing her heart, and just get on with her life? "The very last thing I'm interested in is another man. I think I'll just join the new celibacy movement and be done with it."

"I know you're feeling lousy at the moment, but you don't strike me as a quitter. You'll get over this and then some man will strike your fancy and you'll be back in the game. I know men can drive any woman crazy, but we love 'em just the same and—hey, are you okay?"

Maggie bolted off the sofa and ran for the bathroom.

When she emerged five minutes later, D. had cleaned off the coffee table and was putting the leftovers into the refrigerator.

"I'm so sorry for that," Maggie said, clutching a damp washcloth in her fist as she leaned against the breakfast bar.

D. shook her head. "You look like hell. I'm getting out of here so you can rest."

"Please take that food with you," Maggie pleaded. "Just the smell of it is turning my stomach."

D. opened the fridge and took out the white containers. She put them on the counter and asked, "Did you save the bag they came in?"

"Just take a new one. In that cabinet," she said, pointing to the end unit.

D. found a plastic bag to be recycled and was putting the food into it when she said, "How often do you get sick?"

"This is the second time and I haven't eaten anything all day. I don't know what I caught, but I can't wait until it passes." Maggie sat down on a stool and dropped her head onto the cool granite of the breakfast bar. "I'm just so tired."

"Well if you don't feel better tomorrow, see a doctor."

"It's just the flu or some virus I caught. It'll pass." She heard D. getting something out of the fridge and gasped when ice wrapped in a kitchen towel hit the back of her neck.

"Maybe it will pass," she answered, taking Maggie's hand and placing it on top of the pack to keep it in place. "I hate to ask this, but is there any chance you could be pregnant?"

Maggie opened her eyes. "No. I used protection." She didn't want to explain to her friend that she'd thrown away her birth control pills and Julian had come to the rescue. "I work with the public. A customer sneezes or coughs and before you know it somebody on staff is sick. This time it's me."

"All the same," D. said as she picked up the bag with the food, "see a doctor if it persists. All kinds of scary stuff is popping up again. I just reported on Legionnaire's disease."

"Oh please," Maggie moaned. "I don't want to hear any more."

D. rubbed her back in sympathy. "Sorry. I'll call you tomorrow. You'll be okay tonight?"

Maggie nodded, not wanting to lift her head from the granite. "I'll be fine. It's just feels so cool here."

"Shouldn't you get in bed?"

"I will. Sorry about this, not exactly a great visit for you." She heard D. move toward the living room.

"Forget it and take care of yourself. I'll let myself out and if you need anything, call me. I have a PA that can hustle a prescription of Compazine out of a doctor she's dating."

"I'll be fine by tomorrow, but thanks." She raised a weak arm and waved behind her. "You're an angel of mercy."

"Well, just keep that to yourself. I have an image to protect."

"Too late. Underneath that tough exterior is a softie. A *decent* person," she added with a weak smile.

"But not nice," D. answered from far away. "Get to bed and get better."

"I will . . ." She didn't know if D. heard her, but Maggie heard the door click shut and it was a signal to her brain that she could let go.

The silence was wonderful. No need to entertain anyone, though she'd been a terrible hostess anyway. If she could just get past this and get some energy back. She knew she should get up and fall into bed, but the thought of doing it was exhausting. She would just close her eyes and rest for a few minutes, let the ice work on the headache that resulted from retching. A few minutes . . . just a rest . . .

She felt a soothing hand push the hair back from her forehead and then she was lifted and carried like a baby.

She'd never been carried before and relished the dream of someone caring for her, placing her in bed and pulling the covers up around her shoulders. She opened her eyes in the darkness and thought she saw the shadowy face of a man, then wearily closed her eyes, knowing dreams were unexplainable.

Still, for a few moments, she had felt cherished.

FIFTEEN

Gabriel Burke's Maryland farm was situated on a beautiful piece of land that bordered the Chester River. In August the excellent weather brought out the butterflies and dragonflies. Morning glories were climbing up tree trunks in shades of lavender and white. Cicadas chirped out a serenade over the peaceful water as Julian and Senator Burke lazily fly cast, creating the only disturbance upon the surface.

"Perfect day, Senator," Julian remarked, standing in water up to his thighs.

"Yes, you can see why I'm anxious to plan my retirement here. I would keep the family home in New York, but I plan to spend most of my time here. Close enough to Washington across the Chesapeake if I'm needed."

Looking over his shoulder to the trees and the farm house beyond, Julian said, "Seems idyllic." He didn't mention the two large and silent bodyguards standing watch.

"Ah, now, Julian, I thought we'd already agreed that appearances can be deceiving."

"We did, Senator. Are you telling me this picture of serenity is false?" he asked with amusement. He liked the old man. He had a certain charm and Julian wasn't immune to Burke's almost paternal interest in him.

"In the moment, it is serene, I agree. Just like this stream of water where we find ourselves. On the surface everything appears calm, yet we both can agree that below the surface there is an entirely different world evolving. We may only catch glimpses of it, but we know it exists."

Julian nodded, feeling relaxed by the lazy afternoon's quiet and the low timbre of Gabriel Burke's voice. He knew better than to wish for the impossible, but it was moments like these that made him contemplate what life could have been like if he and his father had ever shared such an afternoon. If he thought about it, he could feel the hollow tightening within his gut that he would never teach his son to fish. So many losses . . .

"I'm glad you accepted my invitation, Julian. It means you've given some thought to our discussion in New York."

"I can't deny it. Something you said seems to have stuck in my head."

"And what is that?"

"To whom much is given, much is required. First, not much was given to me. I worked hard to get where I am. And I have tried to give back through organizations I respect. You made it sound as though it were a gift."

Senator Burke smiled as he expertly cast out again, watching the fly he had made himself rest upon the surface of the water. "To my way of thinking, Julian, every one of your talents is a gift. Some you were born with and some you cultivated along the way. Did you ever wonder at how easily you were accepted to a prestigious college? Did you ever investigate thoroughly where your scholarship to Wharton actually came from?" He glanced at Julian and grinned. "Now before you start protesting and giving me facts, allow me to give you a few. There is an organization, I shall call it a foundation, that has been very interested in you for many years."

"A foundation?" Julian was stunned by this information. His scholarships had been through an elite organization, HTURT, the initials standing for five unidentified corporations forming a trust fund for outstanding business students. It had been his favorite teacher's suggestion that he apply.

"I know what you're thinking. HTURT, right?"

Julian could only nod.

"Joseph Morris was an excellent educator."

"You know my high school business teacher's name?" This was too incredible and he looked back to the bodyguards as a shiver of fear raced through his veins. What the hell was going on? Was the man reading his mind?

"I know many things about you, Julian. Relax. There is no need for apprehension. My friends back there," Burke nodded to the men on the shore, "are there for my security."

"They think I would harm you?" How was it that Burke seemed to know what he was thinking and feeling?

The senator chuckled. "Not you, my boy, certain individuals connected with special interests are not pleased with me these days. But getting back to you. Since HTURT is no longer in operation, it is safe to tell you that the scholarships you received were because you showed great promise. You possessed not only a sharp mind for business, but also a heart where integrity could reside. You've proved to those of us who invested in you that we made an excellent choice."

"*You* invested in me? You paid for my education?" This was becoming surreal!

"Well, not me alone, certainly."

"Who or what was HTURT?" Julian demanded, almost afraid of the answer.

Gabriel drew back his rod and expertly cast his line. "People who work behind the scenes, so to speak, for the benefit of those they share the planet with. You. The person who collects your garbage in New York. Your lawyer and the man who sells you the morning paper. We don't discriminate or think one person is more deserving of assistance than another. All are valued for the gifts they bring. Yours happened to be in the business arena. Turn the initials around, Julian. Spell it backward."

In his mind, Julian did just that. *"Truth?"*

The older man nodded. "Exactly. This foundation is comprised of individuals, both men and women, whose interests are in maintaining balance in the world. It was formed during the Dark Ages, when suppression of knowledge by those in power created a great unbalance, which, in turn, created immense fear. You would be surprised at some of the names of those who came together to birth what has been called the Renaissance to bring light back into the world."

The man had Julian's complete attention. "You're saying this . . . foundation, as you call it, is responsible for the Renaissance?"

"Well, not entirely, my boy. It's awesome to behold once seeds are planted in the light how quickly they grow and blossom. Should you be interested in combining your gifts with others, there is much I will tell you. For now, I will reveal that you have been assisted at times in your life by members of this foundation, the right people showing up at the right time, opportunities presenting themselves just when you needed them. Your best interests were always a priority."

Julian felt like a steel rod had just been shoved up his spine. Maggie had said those exact words to him. He stared at the older man, who somehow seemed so very familiar. "Have you ever heard of a woman named Maggie O'Shea? Magdalene O'Shea?"

Burke hesitated, while staring out to the water. "This is the Maggie who has engaged your affections? The woman you told me about at the Red and White Ball?"

"Yes. Do you know her?"

Gabriel Burke waded out of the water and began to switch the fly on his line for another in his opened box. "I was hoping you wouldn't have put that together so quickly. Yes, I know her, though I only recently had the pleasure of meeting her in person. I can see why you love her, Julian. She is a lovely woman."

"When did you meet her?" Julian felt sick to his stomach and he wasn't sure if it was from anger or fear.

"I was in Philadelphia for an appearance at the new Constitution Hall on the July Fourth weekend. A mutual friend made the introduction."

"I was at her home on July fourth."

"It was the night before."

"Is Maggie . . . ," he didn't believe he was asking this, "a member of this foundation?"

"First rule is never to reveal another member's name or participation," Burke answered, successfully tying on a new fly and walking back into the water.

"Answer me this then," Julian persisted. "Maggie talked about me being her assignment, about her being in service to love, to help me heal. Was her assignment from this foundation?"

"Have you healed?"

"You're not answering my question."

"I can't answer your question, Julian. How would you feel if you knew people who cared about you have been looking out for you?"

"I don't know exactly what I'm feeling, Senator. I certainly don't like thinking that my life was predestined by some mysterious foundation."

"Now you've always had free will to make your own choices. Fortunately for all involved, you've made excellent ones. The reason I am bringing this up now is because it is time to mentor someone to take my place in politics. I am tired, Julian. Besides the obvious reasons we discussed in New York, you have been chosen because of your integrity. It is no small honor to become a member of the foundation and to work with your gifts for the good of mankind. You would also make an excellent member of the Senate, an honest independent voice. This is a time of crisis, a time to call into service people who are not hampered by fear." Gabriel Burke smiled as he looked directly into Julian's eyes. "This, my good man, is your wakeup call. It is, as always, your choice whether or not to answer it."

So many thoughts were running through Julian's head that he couldn't reply immediately. He tried to quiet his mind from the jumble of facts that were crashing into each other. Senator Burke belonged to some secret organization that had been influential in his rise in the business world. He wanted him to join. Maggie may be involved, or may not. Burke wanted him to run for the senate. It would mean divesting himself of his business, moving to Washington, starting all over in a field where he would be the novice. How could Burke think he was without fear?

"There is no need for an answer, Julian," Burke said, nodding toward the shore as he pulled in his line. "Take your time and think about it. I'm sure lunch has been organized by now and my staff are probably wondering what's keeping us."

The once idyllic afternoon had lost its charm for Julian. He felt completely rattled, as though his past had somehow altered from the way he had always reviewed it. "I'm more than troubled, Senator, by the secrecy involved in all this. I have questions."

"I'm sure you do. I will answer those that I can at this time, however, without your acceptance of my proposal some of those questions will have to remain unanswered."

"If I did accept, what would be the next step?"

"The next step would involve a period of tutoring in a more accurate accounting of history, which can alter dramatically from what we all have been taught in our institutions of learning. I'm sure you have already gained knowledge of an ongoing battle for power. It occurs everywhere, from relationships to governing nations. The foundation stands for balance. When that power is out of balance, as it is today, then members are asked to step forward and answer a call for service."

"Is that what Maggie does?"

Burke laughed. "You will not trick me into an answer that is not mine to give."

Julian looked deeply into Gabriel's eyes. "You sound just like her." That familiarity was back.

"Perhaps you might listen to her then. She might have words of advice for you."

"I haven't talked to her in over a month."

Burke picked up his box of custom-made flies. "I thought you said your affections were engaged. Doesn't she return them?"

"I don't know what she thinks anymore." Julian unhooked his waders and slipped out of them. "She tells me she's not the one for me and seems convinced I will come across this great woman who can make me happy. She's a bit of a kook," he added.

"And you haven't entertained the possibility she might be right?"

Julian glanced at the older man. "If you mean Victoria . . ."

They began walking back to the farmhouse. "I, too, lost my wife and I know your sudden tragedy doesn't compare with a lingering illness when you know the end is coming. But grief is grief and yet I know neither woman would want us to grieve forever. I learned to celebrate my Amelia and the time we shared together. For you to consider loving another is a great act of courage."

"It seems more like madness," Julian muttered. "I finally am able to love another woman and she tells me I am meant for someone else."

"And you refuse to entertain the possibility she might be right?"

"If you're speaking about Victoria, you need to stop advancing that cause. I can't even think about another woman."

Burke patted Julian's shoulder. "Without seeming too forward, allow me to paint a picture for you. Just suppose you make the decision to accept my offer. What you would need is a good running mate, in the truest sense. A married candidate is more trusted than a single man. I have known Victoria since she was a baby. She married hastily, without her parents' approval. Or, perhaps, it was in retaliation for their lack of approval. She's a good woman who has matured through adversity and would make any man an excellent wife, especially a man in politics when you consider her father's sterling reputation. You could do far worse, Julian."

"You're still matchmaking."

"If putting two intelligent and compatible people together to see if there is any attraction is matchmaking, then I am guilty as charged."

"From our brief meeting, I agree that Victoria would make any man an excellent wife. Unfortunately, Senator, the woman I wish to be my wife is an eccentric owner of a bookstore in Philadelphia called Soul Provisions. Can you imagine what the media would make out of that?"

"But you said you haven't spoken to her in over a month.

Perhaps the intensity of your feelings is more about rejection. Is it possible the love you spoke of has weakened, but since you are focused on the rejection you have misinterpreted your actual motivations?"

"I wish," Julian stated, feeling strange talking to a man about being in love with Maggie. Yes, he admitted to himself. He still loved her, eccentricities and all. "She seems to have captured a permanent place in my heart, whether I like it or not."

"Then take it one day at a time. I'm sure I have filled your mind enough for one day. Perhaps we could meet again next week, if you're free?"

"I was hoping to get over to my home in Bermuda next weekend. Would you care to join me?"

"Ah, that does sound tempting. However, I don't think I can manage to get out of the country right now. There is an important vote coming up concerning the pharmaceutical industry and I must prepare and be available for last-minute negotiations before we take the floor next month. Some other time?"

Julian nodded. "I have many more questions, Senator. You can't drop a bomb like this on me and expect me to just accept it. I need answers."

Senator Burke placed his hand on Julian's shoulder. "I know, son. Let's have lunch and we'll continue our conversation."

Maggie did not want to think about going into work in the morning. All she wanted to do was sleep. Whatever this bug was, it wasn't tapering off as she'd expected. For almost two weeks she'd been fighting it. Some days she felt stronger and the next day she was exhausted and sick to her stomach. *I should go to the doctor*, she thought as she pointed the remote toward the TV. If it was bacterial, she could get an antibiotic. Tomorrow. She'd call on Monday and get the earliest appointment. It was time to get to the bottom of this, for she was sick and tired of being sick and tired.

Ready for a pity party, Maggie sniffled as she grabbed for another tissue. The coffee table was littered with a bottle of

Pepto, empty Popsicle sticks—orange was her favorite—
and a box of tissues. The wastepaper basket was lined in
plastic, just in case she didn't make it to the bathroom in
time. It seemed all she could keep down was Popsicles and
she had only two left. Grape and cherry.

How totally pathetic, she thought miserably while blowing
her nose. Here she was suffering from a broken heart and the
flu at the same time. Wasn't there any compassion in the
Universe? One or the other alone was bad enough. Both
together was just mean. And lest she should forget unfair-
ness, how about Marcus' phone call saying Julian McDonald
had not completely detached and if he contacts her she
should send him away? Like she needed to be told that!

He looked pretty detached to her. Yes, she'd bought the
issue of *People*, unable to resist seeing the picture of him
and Victoria Armatage together with Senator Burke. She had
been embarrassed for herself as she'd paid for the copy and
then had leafed through the pages, like some lovesick
teenager.

That's what was wrong with her.

She was lovesick.

Who knew it was an actual illness?

So how was she supposed to go to the doctor tomorrow
and ask for a cure? For lovesickness? Wrong doctor. Maybe
she should see a counselor. And why, she wondered as her
thumb again pushed down on the remote-control button, did
every channel on a late Sunday afternoon have to be broadcasting sports? Golf. Preseason repeat of football. Sports talk
show. World soccer. Didn't women count? She should get
cable, even if she rarely had the time to watch television.
Times like these demanded access to movies. If she had the
energy she'd go to the video store and pick up some tear-
jerker so she could wallow in another woman's troubles and
self-pity. Unable to gather the motivation to get dressed, she
settled for PBS and a documentary on Komoto dragons.

Fascinating creatures. Cha'right. She couldn't imagine
shape shifting into one of those! Though they did have the
ability to run quite fast. She was trying to prompt her mus-

cles into getting up from the sofa to go into the kitchen. Her mouth was dry and she wanted another Popsicle. When the doorbell rang she called out, "Go away!"

Of course they couldn't hear her, so the bell rang again and again and again.

Damn it, whoever it was must be leaning on the damn thing! It was probably D., who'd called her last night and sounded concerned she hadn't seen a doctor yet. Or it might be Alan who'd surprised her Friday afternoon in the store by opening the bathroom door and finding her on her knees before the toilet. She didn't know which of them was more embarrassed. Knowing whoever it was wasn't giving up, she dragged her sorry body up from the sofa and trudged over to the stairs.

Each step felt like her stomach was dropping and she held her hand over it to ease the feeling. She glanced at herself in the hall mirror and was shocked by her appearance. Her face was pale, almost gray, and her eyes seemed sunken and surrounded by dark circles. Her hair looked like she'd stuck her finger into an electrical socket and her lips were parched and pale. She was sure to scare whoever it was away and be left in peace.

Summoning her strength, she took a deep breath and unlocked her front door.

Nothing could have prepared her . . .

"My God, Maggie! What the hell is wrong with you?"

She blinked. It wasn't possible. Maybe she was into hallucinations from lack of solid food. "Julian?" she asked in a weak voice.

He seemed to take over, grabbing her shoulders and pulling her away from the door. "What's happened to you?" he demanded, his expression filled with concern.

"What are you doing here?"

"I was driving up from Virginia on I-95 and when I approached Philadelphia I—What difference does it make now? You're sick, aren't you?"

She kept staring at him, looking so handsome in tan pants and a white shirt rolled up to his elbows. Dear, dear Julian . . .

What was she thinking?

Her resolve strengthened as she pictured him in that photograph and her spine stiffened. "I haven't been feeling well lately. You should go. You might catch it." Okay it was a lie, for no one else in the store seemed to have any of the symptoms.

"Let's get you upstairs. You should be lying down."

"I was lying down until you sat on my doorbell."

His eyes narrowed. "I didn't sit on your doorbell. It would be impossible. I only rang it a few times."

"Many times," she insisted.

"Look, why are we arguing about a doorbell? C'mon, let's go up."

She was too weak to fight him and so she allowed his arm around her shoulders and his right hand to clasp her right arm as they took each step as though in slow motion.

It was only when they were in such close proximity that she realized how she must look to him. Pathetic.

Totally unfair, she mentally yelled to the Universe. How much more was a woman expected to endure?

"Do you ever use a phone to let a person know you are going to appear on their doorstep?"

He ignored her question. "I can see you've made a bed for yourself on the sofa. Let's get you back there," he said, leading her across the living room.

"I'll be fine," she insisted, pulling out of his arms and gathering up her used tissues from the coffee table to throw into the wastepaper basket. She sank to the soft cushions, feeling like she had just undertaken a marathon. Out of breath and exhausted.

"You're not fine. Have you seen a doctor?"

"I just caught a bug, that's all."

He sat opposite her on the edge of one of the chaise longues. "How long have you had it?"

"A while. It takes time for it to leave the system I'm told."

"And who told you that? A professional?"

"Look, Julian," she said, trying to keep her patience. "You shouldn't have come here. You should have kept driving back to New York."

"I'm not allowed to see you?"

"Not now. And not like this!" Damn, she could feel those traitorous tears gathering at her eyes again.

He smiled gently. "Now you look, no matter what took place between us, I would like to think we could be friends. Friends help each other out when they're sick, right?"

She shrugged, sniffling. She could detect pity in his voice. Pity! "I appreciate your concern, Julian," she said, straightening her shoulders even though it hurt to pull on her abdominal muscles. "I have friends. There's nothing anyone can do. I just have to wait it out."

"Maggie, stick out your tongue!"

Her mouth opened in shock. "I beg your pardon?"

"Stick out your tongue," he again ordered.

"I will not! You aren't a doctor."

"It doesn't take a doctor to see that your tongue is orange and purple. I'm going to have to insist we go to the emergency room." He stood up and put his hands on his hips, like he was some general ordering his troops.

She waved her hand in dismissal and then sank back against the cushions, dragging her feet up and pulling the throw over her legs. She was way too tired for this. "Chill out, will you? It's from Popsicles, the only thing I'm able to keep down." She pointed to the sticks on the table, the bottom half stained the color of the Popsicle.

He exhaled in relief and sat back down. "Can I get you something? Another Popsicle? A doctor's appointment? Common sense?"

She grinned weakly. "Another Popsicle would be appreciated. There're only two left." Okay so she could cave on that issue, but she would remain strong on any other.

When he rose and headed to the kitchen she ran her fingers through her hair and wiped the sleep from her eyes. How come that man had such rotten timing to catch her now twice unwashed and undressed. She pulled on the edge of her oversized T-shirt, noticing an orange stain above her right breast. Right, the bottom of the Popsicle had melted and dropped to her chest. She'd just picked it up and had popped it into her mouth.

She actually shook her head, as if to clear it. What did she care what he thought of her appearance? If anything, it would put him off. And that was what should happen, right? Still, she wished she could have put him off looking a little bit better. . . .

"Here we go," Julian announced, coming back into the room carrying a cherry Popsicle with the stick stuck through a paper towel.

Like a kid's, Maggie thought. It would have been sweet, except she couldn't afford sweet. She couldn't allow herself to weaken in his presence. "Thank you," she whispered, taking it from him. "It's the only thing that helps."

He sat back on the edge of the chaise, legs apart, elbows resting on his knees as he stared at her. "How long have you been sick?"

"About ten days now."

His head jerked higher. "Ten days! A flu doesn't last that long!"

The coolness of the Popsicle hit the roof of her mouth and a sharp pain exploded in her head. Brain freeze. She should be so lucky not to have to deal with Julian McDonald sitting there staring at her as though she hadn't any common sense. "A summer flu can last longer," she managed to say while waiting for the pain to subside, which it did a few moments later.

"You're throwing up?"

She cringed, hearing him say that. "Please. Don't even mention it."

"What other symptoms?"

She sucked on the Popsicle, careful not to let it give her another brain freeze, and slowly withdrew it from her mouth. Sighing, she answered, "Just tired. Drained, really." She wasn't going to tell him about the crying jags that had started this whole mess over a month ago. She must appear pathetic enough as it is.

"I really think you need to see a doctor, Maggie. Seriously. Have you seen yourself? You look terrible."

"Well, thank you so much. I am so glad you came to give your opinion on my appearance."

He shook his head and grinned. "You know exactly what I mean. You look terribly sick."

"Why did you come, Julian?" She might as well get on with it, before her stomach began churning again. "Why are you here?"

He laced his fingers together and then stuck out his arms as he stretched. "What if I told you I missed you?"

"Not good enough. Besides, you said you were driving back from Virginia. I was just a stop over, a road stop, to get out of the car and stretch your muscles?"

"Ouch! You know how to wound a guy."

She didn't want to be reminded of wounding, especially if she had to do it again.

"I was with a friend of yours," he said casually, picking up from the surface of the coffee table the dead petals of a flower arrangement she didn't have the motivation to throw into the trash.

"A friend of mine?" Her tired brain tried to piece it together.

"Senator Burke."

"He said he's a friend of mine?" she asked cautiously. What did that mean?

"He said he met you once. Here. In July. The night before I arrived unexpectedly for the Fourth of July weekend."

Julian wasn't fishing. He knew facts. She tried to get her head clear, for this was important. "Did he say what we discussed?"

"Me? The foundation?"

Maggie sat up straighter. "He *told* you that?" she demanded, stunned the senator had divulged her association with the foundation.

Julian suddenly clapped his hands together and Maggie jumped at the sudden noise. "Hah! I *knew* it!" He looked elated. "You work for this foundation too, don't you?"

She didn't say anything for a moment. Her heart was slamming against her rib cage. "You bluffed me?"

"I told you once I was a good negotiator. I should have told you I'm a hell of a poker player, too." He stood up and began pacing. "It all makes sense now. You heal my broken heart, open me up to a relationship again, and then Burke takes over. He hand-picks me to replace him in the Senate and begins matchmaking me with the right kind of woman whose family credentials are an asset. Perfect planning." He stopped pacing and faced her. "Only I'm turning him down. I don't want to enter politics. And I don't want to marry Victoria Armatage. Are you going to ask me why?"

"No," she muttered, terrified he would say the words.

"Because I love you."

She burst into tears. "Don't say that, Julian. Please . . ."

He crouched down before her and pulled her hands away from her face. "I told you I wasn't giving up on us, even if you had. I'm your one, Maggie, and you know it."

She pushed him away and he landed on his behind. "You're not my one. Can't you get that through your head?" She dragged herself up and raced for the bathroom.

Slamming the door behind her, she fell to her knees before the toilet. She held her forehead tightly for it felt as though it would explode from the dry heaves that were contorting her body. "Oh God, I can't bear this . . .," she whimpered, tears running down her cheeks while her nasal passages swelled up and closed off breathing. "This is too much!"

"Maggie?"

"Go away," she called back to the closed door through her tears. "Leave me in peace."

Hearing the door open, she knew she couldn't care any longer what he thought. She was too weak to care. She heard him walk behind her and then he turned on the water.

"Here," he said in a soft voice while holding out a damp washcloth.

Her hand was trembling as she took it from him and held it to her face. "Thank you. Please go, Julian . . ."

"I'm not leaving you like this. Why won't you let me call a doctor? You need something, some medication, to stop this. When is the last time you've eaten anything besides Popsicles?"

"I don't know," she moaned. "I can't keep anything else down."

"You're weak because you haven't eaten. You can't keep going on like this."

"It's just a flu . . ."

He leaned over her and flushed the toilet. Gently he helped her rise and then he slipped his arms under her despite her protests. "I'll take care of you, honey. Let's get you back to the sofa."

She had to grab his shoulders as he carried her out of the room. It was the second time in as many weeks that she had the sensation of someone cherishing her like this. The first had been a dream. This wasn't. Julian . . . he really did love her. He didn't want Virginia Armatage. He wanted her. . . . For just a moment, she gave in to it, resting her head upon his shoulder, feeling like she was absolutely precious to him.

She knew what she had to do. She just wanted this one little moment.

She deserved it.

SIXTEEN

He sat next to her hip on the sofa and stroked the hair back from her forehead. "Okay, now what have you taken? I saw the Pepto-Bismol, what else?"

She looked to the coffee table. "That's about it. Some Tylenol."

"You sound like you're congested, too."

She shook her head. "It's only when I . . . get sick. The crying doesn't help."

"I hate to see you cry," he whispered, cupping her face in his hand.

"Then stop being nice to me," she answered, closing her eyes for just a moment, not yet willing to let go of his tenderness.

"I don't want to stop," he said, bending down and kissing her cheek.

She froze. She couldn't let him continue. Pushing gently against his shoulders, she said, "You need to go, Julian."

"You are continually throwing me out, aren't you?"

"I'm not throwing you out. I'm asking you to leave me in peace. There's a difference."

He grinned. "Well, I'm going. But just to the store. You've only got one Popsicle left. Can't leave you like that, can I?"

She couldn't help chuckling. "You are a good man."

Staring into her eyes, he said, "I'm glad you still think so, Maggie. Now, what else can I get you? Crackers? Tea? A new digestive system?"

"If only you could," she moaned. "I'd appreciate the Popsicles, though." His kindness was making those damn tears reappear. "I just don't have the energy to get up and get dressed, let alone go to the store."

He squeezed her hand. "Always wanted to be my woman's hero. Who thought all it'd take was Popsicles?"

She smiled weakly. "Julian McDonald. Popsicle hero. We should get you a white hat."

"So you agree I'm one of the good guys?" His smile was teasing.

Her eyes started watering again. "Will you just go already? And I'm not your woman."

"That remains under discussion." He stood up. "I'm going. Are the keys still in the bowl downstairs?"

Not trusting her voice, she nodded.

"Okay. I'll be back as soon as I can. You'll be all right?"

Again, she simply nodded.

When he headed down the stairs, she summoned what strength remained and called out, "Orange is my favorite."

She heard him laugh.

In the silence that followed his departure, Maggie felt like her whole world was tilting at a dangerous angle, creating a space where she could free fall. She simply had to get through to him that there wasn't any future for them. Marcus was right. He hadn't detached. If anything, he was more determined than ever. Her mouth trembled when she thought of him telling her he loved her. He wanted her and she had to send him away. Her head ached with the cruelty of loving someone and doing the right thing. It could never be solved . . .

She suddenly stopped crying. If Julian had turned down Senator Burke, did that mean Julian was free to marry whomever he loves? Of course he's free. But would she be violating anything if she stayed with him? It occurred to her that if Julian didn't replace Senator Burke, then why would it matter who he married?

Right?

Filled with the first spark of hope in over a month, Maggie propelled herself off the sofa and went to the table

by the windows. Overcoming a wave of dizziness, she
opened a drawer and pulled out Gabriel Burke's card with
his private number. He said if she ever needed anything to
call. And right now she needed some answers before Julian
returned.

She picked up her phone and dialed, reminding herself to
breathe as she waited through each ring.

"Gabriel Burke."

Swallowing the lump in her throat, she said, "Hello,
Senator. This is Maggie O'Shea. I'm sorry for calling, but
you said if I ever needed anything and . . ."

"I'm very happy to hear from you, Maggie," the man
answered quickly, filling the void with ease. "How can I be
of help?"

She cleared her throat as she sat on the arm of the sofa.
"It's Julian McDonald. He stopped here on his way back
from Virginia."

"Yes, we had a very good visit. I enjoyed his company
immensely."

"Did you tell him about the foundation, about me being a
part of it?"

"We spoke at length about the foundation. He tried to
connect you with it, but I didn't confirm or deny anything."

"Then it's true he bluffed me. He knows now."

"I don't see any harm in it. He also knows I'm a part of it.
Is there anything else that I should know?"

"Well, you see . . . he said he turned down your offer and
doesn't intend to go into politics."

"He did?"

She could hear the surprise in the man's voice. "Yes. Are
you saying he didn't?"

"He didn't say one way or the other. We agreed to speak
again."

Closing her eyes, she asked the question she had to have
answered. "Senator, if Julian doesn't enter politics, if he
doesn't want to marry another, is there any reason I should
continue to reject his . . . his attention?"

Silence.

She could feel her heartbeat in her ears as she waited. She opened her eyes. "Senator?"

"Are you saying you're in love with him?" The man's voice was gentle, not recriminating.

"I'm afraid I am."

"Then if what you say if true, Julian has chosen you over becoming my successor."

It hit her like a punch to her solar plexus. "You're saying Julian can't have both. That I . . . I'm not . . ." She searched for the word, one that wouldn't feel like a knife through her heart. "I'm not suitable to be a politician's wife?"

"I would never say that. It would make things more difficult, but difficulties can be overcome."

"I understand," Maggie murmured. And she did. It was as she thought. Her pedigree, or lack of one, would only hurt Julian. The media would make a circus out of her background, even her store, and wouldn't focus on the real issues. She would be an obstacle. "Thank you, Senator."

"Maggie?"

"Yes?"

"You are a wonderful woman. Any man would be blessed to have you in his life."

"But not Julian?"

"I didn't say that. I said there would be difficulties. I wish you would have told me this last month when we spoke in your home."

Maggie remembered evading the truth when Burke had asked her outright if she loved Julian. "Would it have made any difference? You're right. Julian would be the perfect man to replace you. I'll send him away for good. He won't come back."

"You are certain this is the way you wish to proceed?"

"I'm not certain of anything, Senator, except my heart can no longer withstand this pain. I never meant to fall in love with him like this. I thought it would be like every other assignment, but it wasn't. If I needed proof that it's time to end my working relationship with the foundation, this is it. I'm no longer useful. I'm a . . . difficulty."

"I'm so sorry you feel like this," Burke answered.

Maggie could hear the genuine sympathy in the man's voice. "So am I," she said with a sniffle. "Well, I shouldn't keep you and I'm sorry for interrupting your Sunday. Thank you for listening to me."

"Shall I contact Marcus? You might need support and—"

"No," Maggie interrupted. "Do not contact Marcus Bocelli. He's the very last person I want to see."

"All right. I'll respect your wishes." He paused. "Maggie, don't hesitate to call me if you need me, for anything. I'm concerned."

"No need to be," she answered, feeling beyond weary. She slid down the sofa arm, cradling the phone at her ear. "But thank you anyway."

"May I call you in a few days?"

"Really, Senator, there's no need. I'll be fine."

"Humor an old man then."

She sighed. "All right."

"Good. I'll speak with you on Wednesday evening."

"Good-bye, Senator."

"Take care of yourself, Maggie."

She hung up the phone, knowing what she had to do. Focus on the bigger picture, not just her small piece of it. Julian would be a bright light to others, illuminating the shadows where fear resides. She may want him, but the world needed him. Never had she felt more of a connection to her namesake.

She forced herself to get up and go into the bathroom. Staring at her reflection, literally a pale shadow of her old self, she whispered, "Please give me the strength to do this, to end it once and for all time. Help me; put the right words into my mouth to make him see it has to be this way."

She turned on the water and washed her face.

Ten minutes later Julian returned to the apartment, announcing he'd found orange Popsicles, crackers, and bottles of Powerade because she had to be dehydrated. Maggie steeled her heart against softening, yet in some small place in her mind she knew she would retrieve this memory of his kindness to take out later and examine.

"Thank you for going to the store," she said, sitting up with her elbow resting upon the arm of the sofa. "That was very thoughtful."

"Thoughtful?" he asked, walking past her into the kitchen. "Somebody had to take care of you, honey. Face it. You need me, even if it's just to get you orange Popsicles."

She didn't answer him, just waited until he returned to the living room. He placed a glass filled with an orange liquid on the coffee table along with a small paper bag.

"Now you have to drink that. It's got all sorts of minerals in it that your body needs, like potassium citrate and phosphate and . . . other stuff," he added with a grin. "Go ahead. No Popsicles until it's finished."

Her hand was shaking slightly as she reached for the glass and Julian quickly picked it up and helped her, steadying her hand as she brought it to her mouth.

"There you go," he said, as though helping a child drink.

She finished half of it and then shook her head. "That's enough for now. I'll finish the rest in a few minutes."

"Okay, now I think you should nibble on some crackers. I'll go get them." He left her for the kitchen.

Maggie heard him taking out a plate and when he retuned to her, the crackers were arranged in a straight line. She took one. "We need to talk, Julian."

"I couldn't agree more," he answered, putting the plate on the coffee table and sitting down next to her. "Where do we begin? I know you're connected to this foundation Senator Burke spoke of and I'm sorry for the way I went about tricking you into admitting it. I had to know, Maggie. Everything made sense then."

"There's a much bigger picture, Julian, than you or I are aware of, even Senator Burke would admit he doesn't have a complete view of what's going on right now."

"Then tell me what you do know," he asked, shifting his body sideways and placing his knee on the cushion to face her. "Help me understand this because I'm telling you, Maggie, I'm blown away by what I've heard so far. These people, whoever they are, have been in my life

since I was a kid in high school and I'm finding all of it
hard to believe."

She closed her eyes briefly, praying for the right words.
Taking a deep breath, she let it out slowly. "Try and picture
a vast puzzle, billions of pieces spread out as far as the eyes
can see. It would seem like chaos. The only way you could
make sense of it was to have a different point of view, a
much larger point of view. You and I don't have that, can't
even conceive of it. We can only make sense out of our own
piece and maybe a few more when we manage to fit them
together. I'm a small piece of the puzzle. You're a much bigger piece. I helped you to smooth out your rough edges, your
fears if you will, so you could more easily fit your piece in
with that bigger picture. This isn't just about you or me. This
is about humanity, the planet, the continuation of humanity
upon the planet. The Chinese have a curse—may you live in
interesting times. What they didn't add was that it can also
be a blessing. These are interesting times, Julian. There's an
imbalance of energies. Everyone can feel it. Time seems to
be speeding up, even young people sense it. So many are
under stress and there are those who want to keep them that
way because it's easier to manipulate them, to fly in under
the radar of fear and hijack their independence, their free
will. It's about power. It's always about power. Now it's
about the misuse of it. That's where you come in. That's
where you can be of service."

"Politics," he stated.

She nodded. "Senator Burke is right. You would be the
perfect candidate to replace him."

"You want me to do this?" he asked in a surprised voice.

She turned her head slightly and smiled. "Yes, I want you
to do this. And I think you want to do it too. You would
make a wonderful statesman, Julian."

"I don't know, Maggie. Why give up a very profitable
career where I have my privacy, in exchange for little
money and turning my life into an open book? Every move
I make would be dissected."

"It's a big decision, I agree, but sometimes we have to

give up what we want to get what we really need. I think you need the challenge in your life. I think you would thrive in politics, especially with Gabriel Burke as your mentor. I think you would love to make a difference in people's lives beyond a charitable donation. And I think it's possible your voice could be heard clearly above the clamor of fear because you're a man of integrity. People would sense that and listen."

"Would you be there with me?"

She stared out into the space of her living room, though no object was clearly defined. "No, Julian. This is where you go on by yourself. Someone else will be by your side. Not me."

"*Why*, Maggie?" His voice sounded desperate. "You love me. I know you do, so don't deny it."

"Didn't you hear me? Julian, please believe me. There is more going on than you can perceive. You have to trust me on this. This isn't about just you and me. Besides, I would only make things more difficult for you and I won't have that. This is too important to be selfish. I don't know what you could accomplish as a Senator, but I do know you might never get the chance if I was at your side." She willed the tears away and took a deep breath. "I am not an appropriate wife for you."

"How the hell did you get that idea?" he demanded.

"Because I'm not an appropriate wife for anyone."

"Now listen, before you get any farther in this ridiculous notion, there's something I want you to do." He reached across the coffee table and picked up the small, white paper bag. "Don't get angry, okay? When I was in the drugstore, I picked up this."

He withdrew a pregnancy kit.

Her breath left her in a rush of outrage. "I am *not* pregnant! Don't you think I'd know if I was?" Those damn tears appeared and glazed her vision. "Dear God, how much more will I have to endure?" she muttered, using her knuckle to wipe away the tears.

"Listen, I wasn't going to say anything, but the last time . . .

you know you said you'd stopped taking the Pill? And, well . . . damn it, the condom was old, Maggie. I don't know how long it was in that bag and . . . and it ripped, okay? When I removed it I saw a tear, a small one, but definitely a perforation. And they say the Pill is only ninety-eight percent reliable. Add to that a ripped condom, your sickness, and what else am I to think?"

"I don't care what you think!" she nearly shouted as she pushed herself up and away from him. "You've gone too far. I am not taking a pregnancy test!"

He dropped the box onto the table. "Then I'm not leaving until you do. If you are pregnant, it would explain this mysterious *flu* that doesn't go away. And, besides, I have a right to know. Take the test. We can find out in ten minutes. It's either that or I'm taking you to the emergency room, even if I have to carry you there on my back."

She supported herself by leaning onto the chaise longue, gripping the back cushion between her fists. "You're giving me an ultimatum?"

He simply nodded and his action infuriated her. Anger swelled up inside, giving her energy she didn't think she had. She would make him leave if it was the last thing she ever did. Enough was enough. "Do you want to know why I will never marry?" she asked in a deadly low voice.

"I suppose you're going to tell me," he said, looking casual and a bit smug as though he had the upper hand.

"What's your favorite animal?"

"What?"

"You heard me correctly. What is your favorite animal?"

"What the hell does that have to do with this discussion?"

"Answer me!" She felt the blood in her body rushing through her veins, raising her adrenalin.

He shrugged. "I don't know. A lion. Yeah, I always liked lions." He actually had the audacity to grin. "King of the jungle. Great title, don't you think?"

Maggie found she had to relax her jaw to stop grinding her back teeth. "Of course you know it's the lioness who hunts and feeds the pack to keep it viable."

"But the lion protects the territory, fighting off challengers. Without him there is no pack, thus earning him the title of king. Why in the name of God are we arguing about lions? Are you losing the thread of this conversation, hon? You were going to tell me why you'll never marry, remember?"

She took a deep breath. "I'm not going to tell you anything, except to keep in mind I told you there is more to this world than you can perceive. There is an invisible force that can be harnessed. I'll show you. And speaking of losing things, try to keep it together when you see the answer for yourself." She closed her eyes, shutting out her anger, everything, the room around her, Julian, going within and envisioning in detail the bone structure, the muscles . . .

Within moments she gracefully walked out from behind the chaise and stared at him.

"*Holy shit!*" he yelled, coming to his feet and backing up toward the window, a look of sheer terror on his face. "Holy fucking shit! This isn't happening!"

She sat down and stared at him, calmly watching as he stumbled around the coffee table, hitting his knee on the corner, climbing over the other chaise longue and scrambling to the stairs. Turning her head, she watched him take the steps two at a time.

Good-bye, Julian, she thought, no longer able to sustain the transformation.

She collapsed onto the floor in her own body. Grabbing the plastic wastepaper basket, she threw up potassium citrate, phosphate, and all that other good stuff Julian had tried to get in her.

It was over.

He would never come back.

From the corner of her eye, she saw that flat rectangular box on the coffee table.

Or was it over?

She reached out and picked it up, knowing she'd soon find out.

• • •

Again she had the dream, the one where someone was caring for her, cherishing her. She felt his hand on her cheek and turned in to it, wishing it would go on forever. She didn't want to wake up, to face reality. This was so much better . . .

He stared down at her and his throat closed with emotion. He'd seen the stick in the bathroom and his heart went out to her. Sweet Maggie. He vowed she wouldn't go through it alone.

SEVENTEEN

Smiling, she inhaled deeply while looking up at the tree branches decorated in breathtaking shades of yellow and russet and aubergine. Fall had definitely arrived. The October air was crisp yet the sun bathed the Maryland countryside with its warmth, making the need for a sweater unnecessary. *What a beautiful, beautiful world*, she thought as she walked the dirt path. And what a difference a few months make. Maggie remembered the end of the summer, how absolutely miserable she had been, and now it was as if life had turned magical. The morning sickness had ended abruptly the morning after she'd found out she was pregnant. Once she had accepted the miracle growing within her, she began to thrive once again. Naps, however, seemed a part of her daily routine.

"You're positively glowing, Maggie. I'm so glad you accepted my invitation."

She turned to the man at her side and grinned. "Thanks for inviting me, Gabriel. It's certainly beautiful here in Maryland."

"Well, it took you long enough to get here. Ran out of excuses, did you?"

She couldn't suppress a giggle. "You seem to know me too well, Senator. I didn't want to impose."

"Now you would never be an imposition, Maggie," he answered as they turned toward the river. "I'm very fond of you."

"Thank you," she replied, pleased that the older man had

been persistent. This break from the city was just what she needed. She was taking more and more time off, letting her staff assume responsibility and it felt right. Her driving need to oversee everything had dwindled now that she a new focus.

Senator Burke walked next to her and sighed audibly. "I suppose I should tell you I've spoken with Julian."

Maggie nodded, feeling her stomach muscles tighten. She hadn't heard from him since that night when she'd scared the living daylights out of him. "How is he?"

"He seems all right now. That was a very cruel thing to do to him, shifting in front of him. I don't think he quite believed what he witnessed."

"I was at a loss how to make him stay away. I'm sorry if I crossed the line, but I was becoming desperate."

A few moments passed in silence as the two of them continued their leisurely walk through the woods.

"He's turned me down. He wants nothing to do with the foundation or politics."

Maggie crossed her arms over her breasts as the heaviness of guilt draped across her shoulders like a wet shawl. Wasn't that just perfect! She shape shifts before him to set him free to enter politics and he turns it down. Now that he's free, he's terrified of her. When she screwed up, she did it big-time. "I'm sorry, Senator. I know how much you wanted him to be your successor. I guess I ruined everything for everyone."

Burke shrugged. "Who knows the answer to that, my dear? Many a time in my life I thought disaster was around the corner and later learned that the disaster was just what was needed to put me in the right place at the right time. Still, it doesn't feel good in the moment, does it?"

"No, sir, it doesn't. But I'm doing so much better now."

"I know you are, Maggie. I might as well tell you, I know your secret."

She glanced at him sharply, yet he kept his attention focused on the path before them. "My secret?"

"Yes, my dear. I know you're pregnant. Is the child Julian's?"

It took her a few moments to recover. She wasn't showing, not really, and she hadn't told a soul. The knowledge of her pregnancy was hers, to be treasured and protected until she couldn't hide it any longer. "How did you know?"

The older man nodded to a rough wooden bench at the water's edge. "Let's sit for a bit, shall we? And I will tell you."

Glancing at the large men who followed them for security, Maggie sat next to the senator and then looked out to the peaceful river. "I haven't told anyone. Was it just a lucky guess?"

"I don't believe in luck and I don't think you do either."

She couldn't help smiling. "No, I don't. So how did you know?"

Senator Burke studied the water and sighed. "This talk we shall have, dear Maggie, is long overdue. I know you are carrying a child because I saw the proof of your condition in your bathroom the night you shape shifted for Julian and sent him away."

Her brows came together in confusion. Besides being embarrassed to be discussing a pregnancy kit, Maggie couldn't figure out how he saw it. "I don't understand. How . . . ?"

"I was there that night."

"There? In my apartment?" It was just too bizarre. For a moment, she questioned her sanity. She had been pretty out of it that night, but still . . .

"Remember when we first spoke on the July holiday weekend? When I told you I understood how difficult and lonely your childhood was?"

"You shape shifted into my apartment?" she asked, feeling he had intruded upon her life and she couldn't understand why.

"I was worried about you after your phone call when you admitted your love for Julian and decided to send him away. I wanted to make sure you were all right."

"Was that the first time?" Maggie asked, remembering what she had thought to be a dream.

"No, Maggie. It wasn't. I have put you to bed before, stroked your hair before."

"You were the one who . . ." How could she say he'd made her feel cherished?

He reached out and took her hand. "Please try to understand. I have watched over you for many years."

She didn't understand, not at all. "But why? Because I was a shape shifter?"

Burke shook his head. "That was only part of it. I ask for your patience and I will tell you the whole reason. I find myself in a strange position, Maggie, one I have avoided for too many years. Somehow, I knew this day would come . . ."

"Senator, I don't understand."

"I know you don't," he answered softly, gently squeezing her hand. "Let me begin. Long ago when I was starting my political career by running for a seat in the House of Representatives I had a great staff, young people who supported me, many who were students at nearby colleges. There was one woman with a great dedication to justice, a hard worker for good causes who truly believed in me and in a better future. We became lovers and she became pregnant. I wanted to marry her. We planned on marriage, but I knew I had to tell her the complete truth about myself. She deserved to know. No matter how gently I tried to explain this gift of shape shifting, she refused to believe me. So I did what you did, Maggie. I showed her."

"How did she react?"

"The same way Julian did to you. She ran away, screaming she never wanted to see me again."

"And you loved her?"

"Oh yes. I loved her passion for life, her belief in my destiny, her desire to be of service to humanity, so many things. Many of the same things Julian loves about you."

"What happened to her, to your child?" She had to ask the question, though a part of her sensed she wasn't going to like the answer.

Senator Burke turned his head and a film of tears covered his eyes. "You're the child, Maggie. It was your mother, Barbara, who couldn't accept me."

She stared at him, thinking she must be dreaming. This couldn't be true! "My mother . . . ?"

He nodded. "She left school, disappeared. It took me three years to find you both in Philadelphia. She refused to speak to me and threatened to expose me to the media if I didn't stay away. So I stayed away, but I have always watched over you, Maggie."

Maggie was shaking her head, feeling as though she'd just been punched in her temple. None of it made sense. "*You're* my father?"

Senator Burke nodded. "Please believe me when I say that you have always been under my watchful eyes. And if not, a member of the foundation kept me informed. Do you remember your neighbors, the Kilbournes? You were their baby-sitter and one summer you went to the Berkshires with them to mind their children. Do you remember?"

Dumbfounded, she could only nod.

"The Donatellas where you had your first job at an ice-cream store?"

Again she nodded, thinking back on those families that had tried to include her, to make her feel as though she wasn't so alone. "They were all members of the foundation?"

He nodded. "Two of your teachers in college, and then there was Marcus. You were his assignment and became his student. It was time for you to acknowledge your gift and put it to good use."

"But what about you?" she demanded, pulling her hand away as the reality began to sink in. "You married and had children."

"Eventually I did." Gabriel nodded. "I married Amelia Anderson. She was a very good woman and she gave me a son. You have a half brother, Maggie. His name is Sean. Sean Michael Burke."

"I have a brother," Maggie whispered in shock. "Why didn't you tell me? Why didn't someone tell me I wasn't alone? Do you have any idea how lonely my childhood was, how angry my mother was? She blamed me for interrupting law school and ruining her life."

"I know you were a lonely child. Try to understand the situation I was in with your mother. She wouldn't allow me to even visit you, but I tried to help out whenever I could."

Suddenly, like an old movie she had forgotten, scenes flitted across her brain. "You gave us money, didn't you? I remember my mother getting sudden windfalls. She would buy us new outfits and then bank the rest for a rainy day." Her voice hardened. "There were a lot of rainy days, Senator."

"I can understand your anger, but I had to think of the bigger picture. I was doing good work. Many times I played with the notion of acknowledging you, especially when you went away to college, but I was advised the time was not appropriate. Today, such a claim wouldn't raise many eyebrows, but then . . . it could have had disastrous results for both of us."

"The bigger picture!" Maggie found her back teeth grinding together. "You were my father and you allowed Marcus to send me on assignments?"

"You were running wild. This way your gifts were at least channeled toward good, toward assisting that bigger picture to unfold."

"Do you have any idea how the bigger picture has played with my life? I am so sick of sacrificing for the *bigger picture*!" The anger welled up within her. "I could have had a father, if it wasn't for that. I could have had a husband, if not for the damn bigger picture. It's ruined my life!"

"Now, Maggie," the senator said in a voice meant to be soothing. "You know that isn't true. You had a pretty good life, compared to millions across this planet. You never went hungry, you always had a roof over your head. You had running water and sanitation. You had an education and the opportunity to earn a very good living. You were more fortunate than most who can only dream of what many of us in this country take for granted."

"I was an outcast and you used me. You used your child to promote the bigger picture! Yes I had a roof over my head and I got an education, but what I wanted was love. I had no father and a mother who resented me, and I was cursed with this shape shifting which I now know came from you!" She wanted to shout at him, shake him into seeing what he had done to her. Incredibly, the man smiled at her. Smiled!

"You are resentful because your parents weren't perfect? Well then, you're not alone. I would bet as a child you watched television and saw what you assumed were perfect families—the Cleavers, the Bradys, the Cosbys. You thought what you were living was abnormal. You were, in truth, brainwashed."

"What I was living wasn't normal!" she muttered, resentful of his casual manner. Her whole life was being rewritten in this moment and he was acting as though it was a weather report. "If I was brainwashed, it was because I wanted a life that even resembled normal."

Sighing, he nodded. "I understand. But you do know there is no such thing as normal. What's normal for one person doesn't necessarily fit another's concept of it. Hasn't humanity been constantly adjusting to the new normal? What about a man who made his living with a horse and buggy? He had to adjust to the Industrial Age. Ask a man who made his living as an accountant, using his mind and a piece of paper, then an adding machine, and now a computer. We're always adjusting, for to stay rigid and stagnant means we will be left behind. What I'm trying to say, Maggie, is your childhood, for you, was your normal. You had to make adjustments and you created your new normal. Now you're doing it again. Thirty years ago your pregnancy might have been something to hide. The new normal is that you're free to be a single parent and glory in it. The same instrument, television, that gave you those images of a perfect family all those years ago is now giving you images that a single parent is accepted by society. So what's normal? Beaver Cleaver's idyllic life, or Maggie O'Shea's? If you think Beav's life was ideal then you being pregnant would be shameful. Society has moved on. There's no winning that game, Maggie, you know that. Judgments always muddle the issue."

"I wanted a father," she muttered, gulping down the emotion that threatened to erupt.

Senator Burke lifted his arm and stroked her shoulder. "You have a father, Maggie, if you'll accept me."

"So now I fit into the bigger picture? I can finally be told the truth?"

"I won't deny that you suffered as a child and I'm so sorry for that. However, who knows what your life might be like today had I forced the issue with your mother. Do you think you would have become the same independent woman who owns a business, who lives her life as she sees fit, who gave of herself so unselfishly to assist others to heal? Would you have been in a position to have met Julian McDonald and be carrying that child beneath your heart?"

She didn't answer as her head filled with possibilities and not all of them ending with the miracle of this unique child she carried.

"You would have been a totally different woman. Those men you helped heal might never have met their soul mates, never have fathered those children, never have been a light to others who still walk in the darkness of fear. Change one thing in your past, Maggie, and it all alters. Choices. That's really all we have. Your mother made a choice. I made one to respect hers. That child within you is the present result of all our choices. Can you look back and still judge it as terrible or unfair?"

"I don't know anymore," she murmured, staring out at the river. "I just don't know . . ."

"And there is the greatest truth. You don't know, Maggie, any more than I do. How we hate to admit that. It was Socrates who said, 'Know thyself.' Yet most of us never read the rest of the quote. He said, 'Know thyself. As for me, I know nothing.'" Leaning forward to see her better, Burke added, "The scariest truth is that, save for the moment we are breathing in, we really know nothing for sure. Any of it could change in any moment. We're like gamblers who put our money on what we believe is a sure thing only to find out the odds are always in favor of the house. The house, in our case, is the bigger picture. We will come and go. The best we can do in the interim is to play our hand with a true heart and listen to our intuition. My heart has always loved you from afar and my intuition has told me it's time to reveal the truth, to perhaps bring us closer."

She didn't know what to think and wanted to be alone. "I . . . I need time to digest all of this," she said, standing up. "I think I'll go for a walk and . . . I'll see you later, okay?"

He rose from the bench and answered, "Take all the time you need. Just remember two things. I love you and I'm sorry I couldn't say that to you before now."

Sniffling, she crossed her arms at her waist and nodded. There were no words, not yet. She walked away from the river, following the same path they had taken. She barely saw the changing colors of the leaves. They were a blur before her eyes as her mind tried to make sense of what had just happened.

Senator Burke was her father.

She had a brother. Sean.

Gabriel Burke had loved her mother.

It was so hard for her to imagine no-nonsense Barbara O'Shea as being young and wildly in love. She pictured her pretty, strong-willed, red-haired mother in her mind, wishing she was still alive to help sort this out, to get her side of it. Why was she never told the name of her father? Why did she refuse to acknowledge that something was different about her daughter? It would have made such a difference if someone would have told her the truth.

Secrets . . .

It seemed her life was composed of them. She'd been conceived in secret, born in secret, raised with secrets. And now she had her own. What was it she had told Julian about children subconsciously trying to heal their parent's wounds? She was doing the same thing as her mother, keeping the baby a secret from the father.

Maybe her mother had been afraid Gabriel might make demands, try to get custody of her. Maybe her mother thought that by not acknowledging Burke she could protect

Maggie from her father's curse of shape shifting. Was that why her mother resented her? Because she knew, even if she never would admit, Maggie had those same powers?

It happened in a timeless flash, memories flooding her mind with long-forgotten words.

As a child . . .

"But, Mommy, I really *can* be a bird. I did it!"

"Stop it! Stop it right this instant, do you understand me? You *cannot* be a bird, or anything else, except what God made you. A little girl. And God would be very displeased to know that little girl was making up stories and listening in on her mother's conversation with a neighbor. Lying is a sin, Magdalene. Didn't those nuns down at that school teach you anything about sin yet?"

"Sister Francis Joseph said I'm named after a sinner and she says she's going to call me Mary instead. But I'm not lying, Mommy. I'm not!"

"If you continue to talk like that, you will be a sinner. You must behave, do you hear me? You will *not ever* talk about this again. Not to me and never to anyone else. Sister Francis Joseph would take you to the priest and do you know what happens to little girls who lie? Their heart is blackened with sin and if they die with that black heart they go straight to hell. Do you know what hell is?"

"A bad place?"

"A very bad place. Fire burns your skin off, burns the sins right out of you. Is that what you want to happen? Do you want to burn in the fire of hell forever?"

"No, but I didn't—"

"If you ever talk about this again to anyone, that's what will happen. You'll be sent to hell. Only the devil would want you."

As a rebellious teenager . . .

"Why did you name me Magdalene?"

"I don't understand. It's your name."

"A name you gave me, mother. Why Magdalene? You're so religious with the whole confession, mass, communion thing, you must have known what naming me Magdalene would be like in a Catholic school. I want to know why."

"It was simply a name I thought of when you were born. I was . . . unmarried . . . and I thought it was appropriate at the time."

"To name me after a whore?"

"How dare you use language like that in front of me, in my home? You had better watch your step, young lady. My patience with you is running thin."

"Then tell me who is my father. I have a right to know."

"How many times are we going to have this discussion? Your father has nothing to do with us."

"Thanks to you, he doesn't! I have a right to know who he is. He could help me get out of here and—"

"You will *not* bring up this subject again, do you understand? Your father doesn't exist."

"Well, it wasn't the Immaculate Conception, was it?"

"You're pushing me, Magdalene!"

"He exists! You don't have the right to keep his name from me!"

"I am your mother and I have the right to raise you however I choose. The man is dead."

"He is not!"

"He is to me."

As a young woman . . .

"Why is it so important to you to know who your father is?"

"Because it *is*, Marcus. Whoever he is, he's part of who I am. And I have a right to know."

"Magdalene, if the time is ever right you will know. Your mother may tell you eventually. People tend to soften in their feelings as they grow older."

"Not her. She's a mean woman who's resented me my whole life."

"But she gave you a beautiful name. Not many carry it."

"Oh, c'mon, Marcus. I went to Catholic school, all right? I know who Magdalene was."

"You do? Tell me."

"She was the whore. The repentant whore, I should say."

"I will allow the use of that term just once, because of your ignorance, but don't ever repeat it again."

"What do you mean? Everybody knows it. It isn't like some religious secret. Believe me, it's right out there. I was the brunt of too many jokes not to have gotten that one right."

"Sit down and listen and, perhaps, you can learn the truth for a change."

"Another lesson. How long are you going to keep me holed up in this godforsaken depressing cabin?"

"Until you are no longer ignorant. Until you wake up from the brainwashing and indoctrination that has been done to you. Until you can listen with an open mind and can *think* for yourself."

"So . . . like maybe a month? What d'ya think, Marcus? Will I be enlightened in a month?"

"I wonder if you deserve to carry her name."

"Who? Magdalene? Gimme a break. My mother took one look at me after I was born and decided to ruin my life."

"If your life is ruined, look no further than yourself. Stop blaming your parents."

"What parents? My father is unknown. That's what it says on my birth certificate. *Unknown.* Like he didn't exist."

"He exists."

"How do you know? He could have been anyone. Maybe my mother was the victim of an alien abduction and that's why she refuses to talk about it. Maybe an alien impregnated my mother and I'm part alien. That would explain it."

"An alien would be more intelligent than you are. It would listen when one is trying to get across a lesson that may be of importance."

"Okay, we're back at the lesson I see. I wasn't very successful in diverting your attention then."

"No, you were not. And we will sit here in this godforsaken depressing cabin until you do listen."

"Then go ahead. What were you talking about this time?"

"I was beginning to tell you about your namesake."

"That's right. Magdalene. Go on."

"And you will listen?"

"To every word."

"Without interruption?"

"Promise."

"Fine. To begin with, from earliest evidence, in just about every prehistory archaeological dig, there has been discovered a statue, small, round, fertile. That statue depicted the Feminine Principle of God. The Goddess."

"Goddess. You're saying God is a woman?"

"I am saying keep your mind open and your mouth closed until I'm finished."

"Right . . ."

"Thousands of years ago, when man decided in his arrogance that God must resemble him, all references to the Goddess were obliterated and women were no longer seen as equal with men. History will reflect this, but it is important you understand this is about power. The female is powerful. She nurtures life and brings it into the world. No matter how hard those men tried to wipe the Goddess out of the minds of people, it couldn't be accomplished and never will be, for there must be balance in power. Male and female. Even in our divinity. If one principle is missing, power can corrupt quickly. Magdalene knew this. She came from the royal House of Benjamin and was a high priestess, not a whore. She was a brilliant student of the teachings. Not a whore. She was the beloved of the Beloved. Not a whore. And because of that she was envied. What better way to demean a woman seen as threatening to the male ego than to call her a whore? For over two thousand years Magdalene's name has been soiled. Don't you add to that. Unbeknownst to her, your mother actually blessed you when she gave you that name. You should be honored to carry it. We shall see if you can live up to it."

"She wasn't a sinner?"

"Sin was invented by man, Magdalene."

"I'm . . . Magdalene. Magdalene O'Shea."

"Keep that respect in your voice. Someday you will have a child and you will break the chain your mother's ancestors started. You will tell your child the truth."

Standing in the middle of the woods, she placed her hands over her abdomen and stared up beyond the tree limbs to the blue sky. "I don't know how all of this is going to turn out," she whispered, "but I promise I'll always tell you the truth. There will be no secrets between us."

"Magdalene?"

Startled, she jumped at the sound of her name and spun around.

There he was walking toward her, handsome as ever with a welcoming smile upon his face.

"I was just thinking about you," she said, staring into his eyes as he came closer.

"How did I know that?" he asked, searching her face for signs of welcome.

"You look well," she stated, "but then you always do."

"And you look . . . amazing. There is something, some spark of brilliance that radiates from you."

"I'm pregnant, Marcus." There. She said it out loud.

After the briefest expression of shock passed over his face, he held his arms open. "*Cara mia . . .*"

She welcomed his embrace.

EIGHTEEN

It just might be the last weekend he could drive with the top down, he thought, glancing at the trees that lined the road. Fall. One of his favorite seasons. Wearing a turtleneck sweater and a suede jacket with the collar turned up, Julian enjoyed the brisk air hitting his cheeks as he neared his destination. It made him feel alive, smacking him in the face and not allowing his mind to wander too far off the road. He had no idea why he'd allowed Gabriel Burke to talk him into spending the night in Maryland, except he thought a long drive alone might clear his mind and, in truth, he respected the older man. The senator had accepted his refusal to enter politics like a gentleman and had asked that they remain friends.

Despite the cool air and colorful scenery, his mind did take side trips as he again attempted to make sense out of his life. Once so normal and organized, now it was full of confusion. He'd lost not only interest in work, but also his patience. Hannah had, on more than one occasion, taken him aside and told him to go away on vacation and get a new attitude. Not even Bermuda could fix what was churning inside of him. His entire concept of normal was fuzzy, no longer sharply delineated as black and white. Life, it now seemed, was made up of gray. He found himself following the news more closely, even watching C-SPAN to listen to the debates on the floor of Congress. He was seeing how hidden in the legal jargon certain bills benefited certain industries, to the detriment of the common taxpayer or the environment. He'd already turned down Burke, so he couldn't explain his interest in politics, except knowing what he did about the foundation, about Gabriel Burke, damned if he didn't find it more interesting than the world of acquisitions.

Even his personal life had taken a sharp nosedive in the last few months. For some unexplainable reason, he found himself turning down social invitations, spending more time alone with Max, reading, listening to music and, to be honest, thinking about Maggie O'Shea.

He hadn't tried to contact her since that night in Philadelphia.

That night.

Try as he might, he couldn't get it out of his head. She must be a witch of some kind. She had to be. Until he saw what he thought he saw with his own eyes, he would have ridiculed anyone giving credence to the supernatural. Now he wasn't so sure. He'd gone over it in his head a hundred times or more and he couldn't come up with a rational explanation.

She could have used drugs to make him hallucinate, except he hadn't eaten or drunk anything that night in her apartment. He *saw* a lioness, saw Maggie turn into a lioness that calmly walked out from behind the chaise longue and sit down. He'd never forget those eyes, the same eyes of the lioness he'd thought he'd seen when they'd made love that last time. She'd done something to him, for it was as though he was cursed with her image. He looked at other women and compared them to Maggie. He listened to other women and thought Maggie's conversations had always been more interesting. She'd made him think beyond the box and now he'd give all his fortune to be back inside that box. The box was normal. Outside it was chaos, things that couldn't be explained, things that rattled his safe perceptions about life.

It was shocking enough to know there was a secret foundation, an organization of people who had been influential in his life and his rise to success, but that this same organization quietly worked behind the scenes in every aspect of humanity to create balance in the world? He had found himself looking at people, Hannah, strangers on the street, and wondering if they were operatives like Senator Burke and Maggie. To know that these people, these "light workers," walked and lived among the rest of humanity, appearing normal yet working for a common cause against fear was beyond bizarre. He'd tried to find information about the so-called foundation, but came up with nothing. He would think the whole thing had been a huge hoax, if Senator Burke wasn't involved.

He was coming to believe what he'd thought of as normal was simply an illusion. It was as if he'd been awakened sharply from a deep and peaceful sleep and was disoriented about what was reality. The dream of normal? Or Burke's world, where people were double agents, appearing normal to society yet were beyond ordinary men and women. How else could he explain what had happened?

He knew what he'd seen with his own eyes.

Maggie O'Shea was no ordinary woman.

And he wished, with all his heart, that he didn't still love her, that he could wipe her out of his mind. Yet, still, he couldn't say with honesty he was sorry he'd met her.

She'd changed his life in more ways than he thought possible. That heaviness he had carried around with him for nine years was miraculously gone. Now when he thought of Cat and Morgan he was able to miss them and be grateful for the time he'd had with them. He'd thought of them now as being close to him, watching over him, wanting him to be happy. Crazy for an intelligent man to be thinking, yet he couldn't seem to deny the feeling. It was as if he'd made peace with whatever force had taken them from his life. And he had to admit he felt lighter, as though a deep weight inside his chest had been lifted and removed.

And he had Maggie to thank for that.

God, he missed her. How many times over the last two months had he looked at the phone and then talked himself out of dialing her number? He simply couldn't be involved with . . . her, whatever she was. Yet it was like he was in withdrawal. An addict whose weekly fix of Maggie's Magic had stopped abruptly, though his mind and his body continued to crave her touch, her smile, her voice. There were no twelve-step programs to support a man who desired a woman who could somehow turn herself into a living breathing animal. This insane addiction and withdrawal had to be handled alone.

Maybe, he thought, turning onto the road that led to Burke's farm, that's why he was here in Maryland. Gabriel Burke might be able to help him understand. Because he wanted to understand. He didn't want to think he was losing his grasp on reality.

Pulling up to the hundred-fifty-year-old farmhouse, Julian noticed a large man walking toward his car. He figured it was another of Burke's bodyguards, though he had no idea why they were needed. Again, just as in the city, he wondered if they were part of that mysterious foundation. Appearing ordinary, yet anything but normal.

"Mr. McDonald?" the man asked, bending down and giving the interior of the car a once-over.

"Yes. I was invited by Senator Burke." Julian looked at the man's face, seeing his own reflection in the mirrored sunglasses. "He's expecting me."

The man nodded and waved his hand toward the driveway where several other cars were parked. "Enjoy your stay, sir."

Julian simply nodded back while taking his foot off the brake. He parked his car under an old oak tree and began putting up the top.

"Julian. Good of you to make it."

He turned his head and saw the senator walking up to him. Gabriel Burke was dressed casually in brown slacks and a cashmere sweater and he held out his hand in welcome.

"It was a nice drive. I'm glad I made it," he said, shaking the older man's hand. "How are you, Senator?"

The other man grinned. "I'm doing well. And will you please call me Gabe? I think we're friends, aren't we, Julian?"

He nodded. "Yes," he admitted.

"Hope you don't mind that I've invited a few people to join us."

Julian looked at the other cars. "Not at all," he remarked, opening the trunk and pulling out his overnight bag. Though he hoped it wasn't other members of the foundation who thought they could make him change his mind about a political career.

"Well, good. Let's get you settled and then we can catch up."

Walking next to the senator toward the house, Julian looked at the license plates of the other cars. One was from Pennsylvania and the other from New York. Pennsylvania. Immediately he thought of Maggie and banished her image from his mind. He simply had to stop thinking about her.

"You're looking well, Julian."

He smiled as they approached the front door. "It must be the sun and the wind from the drive, Gabe. It was invigorating."

He walked into the square foyer and immediately felt alert, waiting to be introduced to the other guests.

"I'll show you to your room," Gabriel said, nodding toward the long hallway on the left. "The others are still outside, most likely taking in the fall foliage."

"Sure," Julian answered, following Burke.

"Are you hungry?"

Julian walked into the bedroom, the same one he'd occupied months ago. Its quaint country style with a four-poster bed covered in a quilt and big heavy oak furniture was comforting. It was a room where a person could fit in and relax easily. "A little," Julian admitted. "I kept telling myself I'd stop at the next restaurant for a sandwich, but didn't because I thought I was making such good time."

"Then we'll put together something as soon as you're settled."

Julian simply placed his overnight bag on the floor. "I'm settled," he said with a chuckle. "Just let me wash up and I'll be right with you."

"I'll see you in the kitchen then," Gabe answered as Julian headed for the bathroom. "And, Julian . . . ?"

Stopping, he looked over to the older man at the door. "Yes?"

"Thanks for coming."

"You're welcome, Senator. Thanks for asking me."

Burke nodded and closed the wide oak-paneled door with its wrought-iron latch.

Minutes later Julian walked through the rustic farmhouse, tastefully decorated with overstuffed furniture centered around a huge stone fireplace, antique accents and scenes of rural, bucolic life depicted in paintings on the exposed stone walls. He could see why Burke wanted to retire here. It was a more down-to-earth life, devoid of pretense. A place where a man could just be himself surrounded by nature. He wondered if the senator was a man who, like himself, had worked his way up from modest beginnings to acquire wealth, prestige, and influence and at nearing the end of the struggle realized that it was the simple things in life that gave the most pleasure.

He opened the door to the kitchen and saw Burke preparing a sandwich. The older man looked up and smiled.

"Hope you like ham."

"Ham sounds fine, Senator."

"Not just any old ham, my boy. Baked Virginia ham. There is a difference."

"Yes, sir," Julian answered with a grin. He stepped up to the kitchen table, made up of long planks of wood, polished to a high gloss. Running his finger over a deep scratch, he wondered who had done that. The large table was old, maybe over a hundred years in age, yet it showed the signs of good use by generations of families. "I really do like this house, Senator," Julian remarked, pulling out a high ladder-backed chair and sitting down.

"So do I," Burke commented while placing slices of ham onto thick bread on a plate. "Actually my wife found it and I fought her on buying it until she kidnapped me and brought me here to see for myself. I think she knew something I've only recently discovered."

"And what's that?"

"That the older I get, the more I respect women. They know things we don't give proper attention to until we're old men."

Julian laughed. "Things?"

Burke nodded. "Things . . . I read somewhere that it's chemical, something to do with hormones. When the male's testosterone level drops, he finally realizes what women have known all along. The important things in life are family, relationships. If he's fortunate, he's got the time to pay attention to them. He's not ruled by his hormones any longer."

"Are you saying that men are unbalanced?" Julian asked in an amused voice. "I know that's an important issue for you . . . balance."

"I honestly don't know the answer, Julian," the senator said, placing the sandwich in front of him. He pulled open a drawer and handed Julian a square cloth napkin. "How about a beer to go with that?"

"Sounds great, thanks." Julian watched as Gabriel took a bottle of beer from the refrigerator and handed it to him. He took off the top and brought the bottle to his mouth, savoring the icy, familiar taste as it hit the back of his throat.

"Now don't get me wrong," Gabriel said before sitting down opposite Julian and tilting his own bottle of beer. "If it wasn't for testosterone we might never have invented the wheel, built bridges, put a man on the moon. But it also drives us to conquer and impose our beliefs on our fellow man, thinking we know more. It's what wars are about. Out of control, out of balance, testosterone. Do you really think women would send their sons and daughters to war, to be killed? I bet they'd find another way to resolve problems besides sacrificing their children. It's like that line from Kipling, 'If they question why we died, tell them because our fathers lied.'"

"That's pretty deep," Julian remarked, bringing his sandwich to his mouth. "Especially considering the world situation today."

Burke nodded. "President Kennedy spoke eloquently about this, saying when we seek peace it shouldn't be Pax Americana forced upon the world by our weapons of war. America is, Julian, at its core an idea, a dream. A journalist once wrote, 'Take away roads, malls, cities, even our people and our armies and the idea will still be there as pure and great as anything conceived by the human mind. It is the best, perhaps even the last, hope for this world.'"

Julian swallowed. "I can see why you devoted your life to politics, sir. That was a pretty passionate speech."

"I apologize. It wasn't my intention to make a speech."

Shaking his head, Julian said, "Don't apologize. I enjoy our talks. You're a fascinating man, Senator."

Burke laughed. "Hardly fascinating. Just getting a bit more contemplative in my old age." He paused as his mood sobered. "I'm just afraid that dream, Julian, might very well be in mortal peril."

"America?"

"The idea put forth about freedom, decency, justice, civil liberties that generations have tried to uphold for well over two hundred years. To keep an idea alive, it has to be carefully nurtured and tended. When abuses occur, when any group tries to hijack that idea and twist it to suit their needs, there have to be those who act as watchdogs, making enough noise to awaken the slumbering public to the danger." He suddenly laughed. "I guess that's what I am. An old watchdog who wants to retire to the back porch." He looked directly into Julian's eyes. "It's time for new blood. Younger blood, whose instincts are sharper."

Julian put down the sandwich half. "I gave you my answer, Senator."

"I know you did. And I accepted it. What else can I do? Certainly this position could never be filled with a reluctant candidate. It needs someone with passion . . . for the truth, for the delicate balancing of power. I'm sorry if you feel I'm pressuring you. I'm not. I already have someone else in mind."

Julian jerked his head up. "You do?" he asked with surprise.

Burke nodded. "Because a basic tenet of the foundation is respect for free will, we always have an alternative, a second choice in the wings."

"Who is it?" Julian didn't know why he suddenly felt a

tightening in his stomach, as though he'd just lost something he'd wanted. He didn't want it . . . did he?

"I can't tell you just yet. There are many things that have to be put into place first."

"I see," Julian murmured, turning his head and staring out the wide kitchen windows. In the distance he could make out the figures of two people leaving the woods and walking in the direction of the house. Must be the other house guests. It was a man and a woman, arm in arm, leisurely strolling and . . .

His eyes narrowed as he made out the flash of auburn hair.

He heard the senator sigh deeply and turned his head toward the man.

"Yes, Julian. It's Maggie. I invited her here and she has no idea you were also invited."

He didn't answer as confusing emotions wrestled for his attention. He wanted to see her. He wanted to run out of the house and be gone before she reached the door. He wanted to demand she explain herself and what she had done to him. He looked back out the window. And he damn well wanted to know who that man was and why his arm was linked through hers.

"Why, Senator? Please don't tell me you're back at matchmaking."

Burke shrugged his shoulders. "It is my belief that the match was already made. Only slight differences keep you apart."

"*Slight!*" He knew his voice sounded almost shrill. "Pardon me, Gabe, but watching a human being turn into an animal is not slight! That's beyond a major difference. A chasm separates us."

"It's called shape shifting, Julian. In certain circles it's considered quite common."

"And on what planet might that be?"

Gabriel Burke threw back his head and laughed.

Julian found nothing humorous about the situation. "I should leave before she gets here and save all of us embarrassment."

"That's your choice, of course, but I would suggest you stay. Not for matchmaking purposes, but to resolve any issues that remain between the both of you. Unless you are free of entanglements, you'll find it harder to move on. I may be assuming too much, but I take it you *are* finding it hard to move on?"

He couldn't help looking back out the window. "I suppose."

Maggie and that man were getting closer to the house, close enough that he was able to see the guy with his arm now around her shoulders was very handsome. He suddenly felt like he was in high school. There were certain guys you knew you couldn't compete with, who seemed to have been blessed by nature with extraordinary skills in sports or movie star looks you could never hope to possess. He didn't know if that tall dark-haired man could even throw a ball, but he certainly had cornered the market in the looks department. And it appeared Maggie was appreciating them as she laughed out loud and tilted her head to rest on the man's chest in an affectionate display.

His back teeth were clenched and the muscles in his body were tense.

"Calm down, Julian. That is Marcus Bocelli, an old friend of mine and of Maggie's. He's known her since she was a young woman."

Trying to keep the anger out of his voice, he answered, "They seem to be old friends all right. Very friendly." And they were. Even though plate glass separated them, Julian could sense the intimacy between them. Somehow, he knew they were lovers.

"So that is Maggie's new assignment?" he asked, knowing he was fishing for details. Any details.

Gabriel tried not to grin. "Actually, Julian, Maggie was Marcus' assignment many years ago. He was her mentor. She was his student."

He knew it! They *had* been lovers. It was obvious in their body language. Unable to handle that fact, he pushed his chair away from the table. "I'm going to leave," he announced while rising. "It's best."

"For whom?" Burke asked.

Julian clutched the back of his chair. "For all concerned. She doesn't need me here and I certainly don't need to witness their reunion."

"I don't think you really know what Maggie needs right now, but if you would take the advice of an old man who has developed a deep affection for you, you will remain here and find out the truth for yourself about Maggie's needs."

"I don't understand," he muttered, desperate to get away before they opened the back door and came into the kitchen. "And I don't have the time right now to listen."

"If you leave," Burke said in a surprisingly strong and authoritative voice, "it might very well be the biggest mistake in your life. I don't say this lightly. There are things you need to know, Julian, and the only way to find out about them is to summon your courage and stay right where you are."

It was too late anyway. Maggie and Bocelli were right outside the kitchen door. He could hear her voice and he knew if he turned and ran she would see him. He'd already run away from her once and he didn't intend to repeat that now. It would be beyond embarrassing.

"Stand and meet your fate with your shoulders back and your chin high, son. And relax, for heaven's sake," Gabe added. "You're not facing the third armored division. It's simply a woman who loves you deeply."

His head jerked toward Burke, who only nodded his reassurance.

Maggie loved him? Well, he knew she'd loved him once, but she still loved him? Even after he'd run away from her? Even though he hadn't called her or sent her—

All thought stopped as the door opened.

She was smiling and looking positively radiant, until she saw him standing by the refrigerator. She stopped short, a look of terror on her face, and Bocelli walked right into her. She stumbled and three men at once reached forward to steady her. Burke from his chair, Bocelli from behind, and he found himself stepping forward and holding her arm.

"Hi," he said in a breathless voice while looking into her eyes as she straightened.

"Julian." She simply said his name, then looked to Burke for an answer to her silent question.

"I invited him, Maggie. Please don't be upset with me. I thought the two of you could meet on neutral territory and resolve any issues that remain between you."

She seemed to pull herself together as she looked at him and said, "It's good to see you again, Julian. Forgive me, this is Marcus Bocelli, an . . . old friend of mine."

He hated her hesitation because it spoke volumes. Old friend! Why didn't she just say it truthfully? He was an old lover of hers. Straightening, he extended his hand. "How do you do, Mr. Bocelli?"

The man shook his hand. "It is indeed a pleasure to meet you, Mr. McDonald. I had no idea you would be joining us this weekend."

If possible, the guy was even better looking close up. Tension seemed to seize his shoulder muscles and he may have tightened his grip on the other man's hand. He forced himself to release it, rather than embarrass himself with a macho display of hand strength. "Actually, I had no idea there would be other guests. And as I'm just passing through I won't be staying long."

"You know you're welcome to stay as long as you want, Julian," Burke threw out.

He tried not to glare at his host. "Thank you, Gabe, but I really should be getting back. I have a long drive facing me."

"Do stay," Marcus said, passing by Maggie and making his way to the uncovered ham still on the counter. "The more the merrier, as the saying goes," he remarked, slicing off a thick piece of meat. "You really should take in the woods while you're here. It seems like Mother Nature has gifted us with an exquisite painting in autumnal shades. Don't you think, *cara mia*?"

Maggie looked uncomfortable by the situation. "It's very beautiful."

Cara mia! Oh, give me a break, Julian thought, watching

the two of them as the man offered Maggie a piece of ham that she declined. What a perfect prop for the overly dramatic Italian. His continental charm was sickening. How could Maggie put up with him?

"Maggie, why don't you show Julian before he leaves?" Burke suggested. "Surely he has enough time for a short walk."

"I . . . well, I guess I could," she answered, obviously embarrassed by the overt suggestion. She looked at Julian. "Would you like to go for a walk?"

He shrugged, hating that this was being played out in front of Burke and a stranger. "Sure. Okay. I guess I could." Damn if he wasn't sounding like an insecure teenager again.

"Here, take this," Bocelli said, handing a ham sandwich wrapped in a napkin to Maggie. "You must eat, *cara mia*. You don't want to get light-headed again."

Maggie took the sandwich and then shot the Italian a warning glance. "Thank you, Marcus."

Julian walked to the door and opened it for her, eager to be away from the others. As she brushed past him, he inhaled the scent of her perfume and he knew for the rest of his life he would always associate Chanel's Chance with Maggie O'Shea. Light. Feminine. Mysterious. He never realized how mysterious until recently.

They walked side by side along the stone path that led to the woods and then to the river. Neither one of them spoke and Julian was beginning to feel nervous. Knowing someone had to break the silence, he said, "It appears we've both been set up by the senator."

She simply nodded.

Glancing at her, he couldn't help but feel that something had changed in Maggie. She looked . . . radiant. That was the only way to describe it, as though there was an aura of light around her. Everything sparkled in the sun, her hair, her skin and, before she'd seen him in the kitchen, her eyes. There was definitely something different. Had that Italian stallion produced this glow? Was she falling back in love with him?

"I want to apologize, Julian," she murmured, clutching

the sandwich between her hands. "It was unfair of me to have frightened you the way I did. I would never hurt you. That wasn't my intent."

He sighed deeply. "What *was* that, Maggie? Gabe called it shape shifting, but I'm finding it hard to believe anyone has that capability. I mean, I know what I saw. I just can't believe I saw it."

She grinned slightly. "You saw it, Julian. You can believe that. I've been able to do it since I was a child. Do you remember that peregrine falcon you saw in your office?"

His mouth dropped open. "You?"

She shrugged. "Not exactly, not in that moment. I used the falcon to get into your apartment. Then I shifted into Max. That's how I knew he was having joint problems."

Julian stared ahead of him, yet kept shaking his head in disbelief. "You broke into my apartment? Why?"

"Because you hadn't contacted me after the charity ball. I wanted to put my business card in a visible place to nudge you. I'm sorry about that, too. Makes me sound so calculating and manipulative. Please try to remember it was for a good cause."

"I was your assignment."

She nodded. "That's what I used to do, use any means to further the assignment."

"Used to do?"

"Yes, I've officially retired." She hesitated, before adding, "The last one broke my heart."

He stopped walking and stared at her back. She soon turned around to him. "I broke your heart, Maggie?"

She shook her head. "Not you, Julian. I didn't expect to fall in love with you."

"But you said you loved all of your . . . assignments." He hated that word, so impersonal when deep emotions are involved.

"I did love them, unconditionally. I didn't fall in love with them. I was able to let them go easily, happily, knowing they were meant for someone else."

"So what was different?"

She turned around and resumed walking. Catching up to her slow pace, he asked again, "What was different, Maggie?"

"You were," she whispered, and he could see tears were forming in her eyes. "It wasn't supposed to happen."

"But it did," he said in a rough voice, fighting the urge to take her into his arms.

Nodding, she added, "I broke all the rules with you, Julian, so I had to try and fix it. But you wouldn't accept anything I said. So I had to show you to make you go away, to let you see why I couldn't marry you or anyone else."

He let his breath out slowly, deliberately. "How often do you do it? Shape shift."

"Not often. Only when necessary."

"You did it when we were making love, didn't you?"

She clenched her eyes shut, as though cringing. "You saw that?"

"I thought I was hallucinating or it was lack of blood in my brain."

"I'm sorry if I frightened you. Spontaneous shifting is rare. I suppose I lost self-control for a few moments."

"So you can be any animal you want?" Surprisingly, he was interested in this phenomenon.

"Just about. It has more to do with a strong, vivid imagination and the ability to rearrange particles of energy. It's easy enough to do, but difficult to explain."

"Easy?" he asked in disbelief.

"Easy for me because I was born with the ability and learned how to use it without the complication of understanding the physics involved. I inherited it through my father."

"But you said you didn't know who your father was."

"I didn't. Not then. Look, do you mind if we sit down for a few minutes?"

There was an old-fashioned wooden swing to the left. It was the kind with opposite benches where the momentum of the people kept it going back and forth. "Sure, let's sit."

She stepped onto the wooden floor and sat down on a bench. He sat opposite her, realizing he hadn't been on a swing like this since he was a young child. He watched as Maggie uncovered the ham sandwich.

"Do you want half?" she asked, offering it to him.

He shook his head. "I already had some. It's very good."

"Have some more then. I'll never finish all this."

He took the half and bit into it. They began swinging very slowly, just a tiny movement as though neither wanted to take the lead. Julian looked to the woods about fifty feet away and saw the rich colors of the leaves. In a flash he retrieved a lost memory of being on a swing just like this, sitting next to his mother, cuddled against her hip and resting his head on the side of her breast as she read to him. He couldn't have been more than three years old. He found himself smiling, glad he had a good memory of her.

"We're very polite with each other now, aren't we?"

Looking at Maggie, he saw the sadness in her eyes. "Polite," he repeated. "Yes. It seems awkward now."

She nodded. "I'm sorry for that, too. I find myself sorry about a lot of things lately."

"Like what?"

"Like you turning down Gabriel and the foundation. I thought by scaring you away from me I was freeing you to follow your destiny. How arrogant of me, believing I knew what was best for you. I can't imagine what you think of me."

"Quite honestly, Maggie, I'm not sure what to think about you." He looked down at the remains of the sandwich in his hands. "For a while there, I thought maybe you were a witch and had put some magical spell on me. I'm not a man who believes in . . . in the supernatural. That kind of stuff belongs to kooks, the fringe of rational society."

She alleviated the tension by bursting into a giggle, one that made him smile. "Welcome to the fringe."

"I'm serious, Maggie."

"I know you are. That's what's so funny."

She bit into her sandwich and Julian watched her eyes sparkle with merriment. If possible, she was even more beautiful to him in that moment.

"Witches are misunderstood," she finally said. "Even though I see nothing wrong with being one, I'm not. Witches follow an ancient tradition called Wicca, based in nature, and the primary rule is to do no harm. Considering the mess I've made of everything, I guess I wouldn't even make a good witch."

Despite her words, she looked so adorable, sitting on the swing, eating her half of a sandwich, the sun making her almost shimmer with life. He felt the stirring inside of him. It was as if there was an invisible thread between them that hadn't been broken and it was beginning to shrink, drawing him in again. To stop it, he cleared his throat and tried to keep his voice light. "So tell me about the Italian, Mr. Bocelli."

"Marcus? What would you like to know?"

He didn't know where to begin. It wasn't as though he could demand to know if she looked so . . . so radiant because she was sleeping with him. "How long have you known him?" That question seemed innocent enough.

"Let's see . . . fourteen years now."

"Burke says he was your teacher."

"That's right. What else did Gabriel tell you?"

"Not much else. I take it he's part of the foundation?"

She nodded. "Yes."

Obviously, she wasn't giving away anything and he'd have to dig deeper. "Since you only recently met the senator, you must have been working for Bocelli."

"I was working for the foundation, but I did get my assignments from Marcus."

"So he gave me to you?"

Again, she nodded.

He wasn't sure if he should thank the man or strangle him. "Then he must report to the senator."

"I don't really know, but you're probably right."

"Were you lovers?" It popped right out of his mouth before he could censor it.

She jerked her head up and her eyes narrowed. "Does it make a difference?"

"It does to me," he answered, keeping her steady gaze.

"Yes. We were lovers."

"What about now?"

"I suppose you feel you have the right to ask that question, Julian, because of how I've treated you."

He shrugged his shoulders and found himself pushing harder on the floor to make the swing move faster. "Just curiosity."

"Then I won't repeat the cliché about cats."

"No, please don't. I never was a cat person, no matter the breed or size. Dogs are more to my liking." He tried to keep his words from sounding sarcastic, but could tell by her expression he hadn't succeeded.

She exhaled heavily as she held on to a wooden side post to balance herself with the movement of the swing. "No. We aren't lovers now."

He looked away to the line of trees, losing his momentum on the swing. Why did he feel a surge of relief wash over him? He shouldn't care. He shouldn't. . . . But, damn it all, he did. The thought of Maggie in that man's arms nearly nauseated him. He didn't know what else to say to her. Everything he wanted to know would only shorten that thread even more, bringing him more closely to her, and he knew it would never work.

Looking back at her, he smiled. "Well, I'm glad you kicked that flu. You look wonderful." It was the truth.

She smiled sweetly. "Thank you, Julian. And thank you for taking care of me. I really appreciated that."

"It's okay. I'm glad you're better . . . you know, there's something about you. Different."

"Different?"

He nodded. "I can't put my finger on it. You seem happy. Happier."

"Of course if you're comparing me to the last time you saw me, I should hope I look and act different."

"You still looked pretty good," he conceded. "Especially with an orange Popsicle in your mouth."

He watched a film of tears cover her eyes as she smiled

sadly and he had to look away. He wanted to take her hand and pull her over onto his bench, ask her if they could start all over again. And he knew it was madness. "Here comes the senator and the Italian stallion."

She sniffled and laughed. "Don't be mean. You don't even know him."

"You're right, I don't. But I do know his kind. Charming, great looking. A gift to woman."

"Ah, yeah . . . that's Marcus all right. But he's also intelligent, compassionate, and—"

"Don't defend him," Julian interrupted. "Please."

"If I didn't know better, I'd think you were jealous."

"Think what you want. You always have anyway."

"Jealousy is about possession and control and—"

He held his hand up to stop her. "I know. I've heard it already, Maggie. You won't be possessed or controlled. You made that point very clear, right before you turned into a huge cat. Take my word for it, I got the message."

"Julian, when I did that, shape shifted, it was because I thought I was freeing you."

"Well, you've done that, haven't you? Mission accomplished. Assignment finished. You get a gold star, Maggie. Go to the head of the class. I'm a free man."

"You're still angry," she whispered.

"Damn right I am!" he whispered back, not wanting the two men approaching to overhear him. "I loved you! I would have done anything for you and you lied to me, you manipulated me, and you made a fool out of me!"

She looked down to her lap. "I'm so sorry. You'll never know how sorry I am. I was only trying to help you and—"

"Help me?" he interrupted again. "You're incredible! How does it help me if I can't stop thinking about you? It's like you put this curse on me and I want you to take it off!"

"Children, children, play nicely," Gabriel Burke called out as he and Marcus walked up to the swing. Marcus stood with his hands in his pants pockets, trying not to look interested.

Julian was furious with all of them. With the Italian for sleeping with Maggie, with Gabriel Burke for setting it all in motion, and with Maggie for ruining something precious. He stood up and left the swing. "I'm done playing," he announced. "I have a long drive back to New York."

The senator looked disappointed. "Did you two resolve anything at all?"

Julian was about to tell him that he'd resolved not to have anything to do with any of them when his attention was caught by a tiny red light on Gabe's sweater that was wavering but centered over his heart. A laser. The light was from a . . .

Without thought, he reacted on some instinct that made him push the old man to the ground just as a muffled crackle came from the line of trees behind him.

"Julian! *What* are you doing?" Maggie shouted as Bocelli pulled him off the senator. Everyone froze as they watched a dark red stain rapidly spreading over the senator's cream cashmere sweater.

"Dear God, he's been shot!" Bocelli muttered, falling to his knees.

Maggie knelt down, cradling Gabriel's head. The senator's eyes were open and he was staring into Maggie's. "You know what you have to do. Tell him . . ."

"Don't," she pleaded as tears fell down her cheeks. "Don't you dare leave me now! Hang on." She lifted her head and yelled to the security men who were running toward them, "*Somebody get an ambulance!*"

She then pulled on Julian's hand until he was kneeling over Gabriel's head. "Stay with him. Don't leave him," she commanded and then stood up and said, "Marcus!"

Julian watched as the two of them seemed to communicate without words and then . . . he'd never be able to retell the story accurately . . . but then he saw with his own eyes Maggie transform herself into a cat . . . a *big*, sleek black cat . . . while the Italian stallion became some kind of hawk. He watched in amazement as the two of them took off toward the line of trees . . . the hawk using its huge wingspan to lift it above the trees as the jaguar raced into the woods.

He and the senator were surrounded by three men with guns drawn as a fourth tended to the wounded man. A part of his brain was sending out messages that none of it could be happening. Things like this just don't happen! Another part of him was worried that Maggie would be hurt. He felt light-headed, dizzy, as though his whole world had just been thrown into a foreign axis and he hadn't yet found his balance.

"I told you," Gabriel muttered through clattering teeth.

Julian looked down at him. He was pale and starting to shake with shock as the man who was at the driveway ripped off his shirt and began applying pressure to the wound. "Tell me what, Gabe?" he asked, extending his hand and holding on to the old man's to offer strength.

"I told you . . . it . . . was commonplace."

Julian closed his eyes and prayed to whatever force was running this crazy planet to save the old man and keep the woman he loved safe from harm.

NINETEEN

Maggie was shaking as a terrible fear seemed to take hold of her body and no matter how hard she tried to calm down, she still couldn't stop the trembling. She and Marcus had just arrived at the hospital and were told that Senator Burke was in surgery.

"Sean has been called. He'll get here as quickly as he can," Marcus said, sitting down next to her and putting his arm around her shoulders.

Her brother. Her half brother. She would meet him today under the worst possible circumstance.

"It's going to be all right, Magdalene. We must believe that. You know how powerful your thoughts are. We must see without a shadow of a doubt Gabriel recovering and back at work. No other images can be allowed."

She simply nodded as Marcus rubbed her arm, as though to bring warmth into it. She wasn't cold. She just couldn't stop trembling.

"You were magnificent, *cara mia*," he whispered. "The way you took down that sniper."

Her body involuntarily shuddered again, thinking of cornering the terrified assassin, her powerful jaw at his neck, sensing his pulse driving blood through his arteries and knowing instinctively it would be so easy to sink her teeth into him, tear at his flesh, and finish him off. And she wasn't sure she wouldn't have done just that if Marcus had not come soaring down, shifting a few feet off the ground back into himself to pull her off. Marcus had rendered the man unconscious with a swift kick to the temple and they only had to wait a few minutes for the security guards to take over.

"Why?" she asked, staring out at the sterile hospital room where everyone seemed to be busily going about their duties admitting patients. She marveled that they acted as though it was like any other day. For her, it was anything but ordinary. She had found her father. The Universe wouldn't be so cruel as to take him away.

"I don't know why," Marcus murmured. "I just know Gabriel had been cautious for the last six months. Ever since he'd gone up against the special interest groups he had been receiving anonymous threats. Recently they had become more serious."

"Is that why he wanted to retire?" If she kept talking she wouldn't allow her mind to be pulled into fearful thoughts, into what was happening to her father in this moment, or inmto the fact that she had no rights in the situation. She couldn't demand information as his only next of kin present. No one would believe her and she didn't want to cause a scene.

"I think that's part of it. But, truthfully, Gabriel no longer was enjoying his role in the Senate. I do think it would only be a partial retirement, for I don't believe he could stay away from politics completely."

"He would mentor his successor," she murmured, thinking about Julian and wondering where he was. He wouldn't leave Gabriel alone. He must be here somewhere in the hospital.

"Do you want me to get you a cup of coffee?"

She shook her head, noticing the blood stain on the cuff of her blouse. Her father's blood. "No. I want to know what's going on. You don't think it was his heart, do you? I mean Julian reacted quickly and shoved him, so maybe it was only his shoulder?"

"Yes. I think McDonald may have saved Gabriel's life." He paused. "I can see why you fell in love with him, *cara mia*, but you must know it will never work."

"I don't want to discuss that now, Marcus. I have enough to worry about without you telling me . . ." Her words trailed off as Marcus pulled away from her and stood up. He was staring at a man with sandy-colored hair, dressed in a navy sweater and khaki pants.

"Sean! Over here!" Marcus called out as he closed the distance between them.

"Marcus, how's my father? Have you heard anything more?"

"He's in surgery right now and we're not sure . . ." Marcus stopped speaking as Sean looked past his shoulder and stared in her direction.

"Maggie? Maggie O'Shea?"

She rose to her feet and nodded to the man who looked so much like their father.

Sean Burke opened his arms. "Dad told me about you a few weeks ago. He did tell you, didn't he? I mean, before . . ."

Yes," she breathed in relief as she came into his waiting arms. Clutching the younger man's sweater she added, "He told me I have a half brother."

"Not just a brother, a sister-in-law and a nephew, Conor." Sean pulled back and looked into her eyes. "It's one hell of a way to meet, isn't it?"

She found herself smiling sadly into his blue eyes. "It sure as hell is."

"You're prettier in person than your pictures."

"Pictures?"

"Yeah, Dad had them. He's kept a photo album of you, didn't you know? Ever since you were little."

Tears flooded her eyes. "I didn't know."

"Look, we'll have lots of time to catch up on the last thirty years. Let's go find dad and see what's happening."

She simply nodded, as Sean put his arm around her shoulder and led her to the admitting desk. "Excuse me, our father was admitted a short time ago. We think he's in emergency surgery and want to know where to wait for some word."

"Patient's name?" the overworked admitting nurse asked without looking up from her desk littered with forms.

"Senator Gabriel Burke."

She looked up. "Oh . . . *Senator* Burke. No one told me he was a senator."

"Where is he?"

"Now you just go through those double doors and walk down the corridor until you see . . . ."

Maggie wasn't listening. Sean Burke was holding her hand. Like a real brother. She had a sister-in-law and a nephew. She was someone's sister and someone's aunt. A family. She was part of a real family. She felt a surge of joy wash through her and in that moment she sensed her father was going to be all right. Whatever happened after this, she knew this day had altered her life. It would never again be the same.

"C'mon, Maggie," Sean urged, pulling her toward the double doors. "You too, Marcus. Dad would want you there."

"What's your wife's name?" Maggie asked, trying to keep up with him.

"Virginia. We all call her Ginny," Sean said, looking for his markers to follow the directions given to him. "And she can't wait to meet you. She said she's thrilled to have another female to balance out the males on my side of the family. Here. We turn here."

Maggie tried to take it all in as she was pulled through another set of double doors.

And there he was, bolting to his feet as soon as he saw her.

"Maggie, where *were* you? I was so worried!"

She could read the tension in his face, the rigidity of his facial muscles. "We were right outside, waiting for Sean."

Julian stared at the man who was still holding her hand.

"Julian, this is Sean Burke, Gabriel's son and . . . my brother."

Julian looked from her face to Sean's and then back again. "Your brother?"

"It's a long story," Sean interjected, extending his hand. "What's the word on my dad?"

Julian tried to pull himself together as he shook hands. "He's . . . ah . . . in surgery right now." He looked back at Maggie. "Your *brother*?"

She nodded. "I know. It's all very confusing. What did they tell you about the wound?"

"They said it hit a bone in his shoulder and they have to go in and clean out any fragments while they remove the bullet. It's been about thirty or forty minutes since he went in but the doctors seemed hopeful."

"Good." Sean let his breath out in a rush and sat down. He looked as though he'd been keeping himself together until that very moment.

Marcus sat next to him and when Sean leaned forward, resting his elbows on his knees, Marcus gripped his shoulder in support. "He's going to be fine. He'll probably use his recuperation to make more of those bug lures for his fishing. You know how many hours he spends doing that?"

Sean laughed and hung his head. "Hey, I grew up listening to the virtues of fly fishing. You should have seen my father's face when he finally got it through his head I'm all thumbs when it comes to the intricacies of a Black Ghost or a Royal Coachman or a Mickey Finn."

"Listen, Maggie, can I talk to you?" Julian asked, touching her arm.

"Of course."

"In private," he whispered, obviously not wanting to offend the others.

She looked at Marcus and Sean who were telling stories about Gabriel's passion for fly fishing and how he tried to turn everyone on to it, and no one was exempt. Man, woman, and child had to endure his lectures on his favorite pastime.

"Let's go into that room over there." She pointed to a side room. The door was open and she could see a sofa and chairs.

Julian nodded.

"Would you excuse us for a few minutes?" she asked the others. "We'll be right in that room."

Julian waited for her to lead the way. When they were inside, he quietly closed the door.

"What is it?" she demanded. "Is Gabriel worse than you said? You didn't want to alarm the others and—"

He grabbed her shoulders to stop her. "Maggie, I told all

of you the truth about the senator. The doctors seemed hopeful."

"You saved his life, Julian. If it wasn't for you, he might have died right there on the ground."

He shook his head. "That's not what I want to talk about."

"Then what is it? What else is wrong?"

Julian walked away from her and began pacing back and forth, running his fingers through his hair. "What's wrong?" he asked the wall in an incredulous voice. "I'll tell you what's wrong! I witnessed a friend being shot and the woman I love turning into a *jaguar*!" He turned his head and looked at her. "Is that enough? 'Cause I'm tellin' you, Maggie, this kind of shit just doesn't happen in my life. Or anybody else's life that I've ever known!"

She felt tears come back into her eyes as her throat tightened and began to burn with emotion. He said he loved her.

"Oh, and let's not forget this same woman just introduced me to a brother which means her father is Senator Gabriel Burke! It just gets better and better!"

"You still love me?"

He stopped his rant and stared at her. "Of course I still love you. I just don't know what you are!"

She took a step closer. "I'm a shape shifter."

His head titled from side to side. "Great! I'm in love with a shape shifter! See what I mean about this day?"

She tried not to laugh. "I know exactly what you mean. It's been pretty astounding all around. I just found out today that Gabriel is my father."

Julian's eyes widened. "Any more surprises? On the way to the hospital Gabe kept saying *make sure she tells you*. What does that mean? That you're his daughter?"

She lifted her shoulders and kind of cringed. "I don't think that was it."

"Then what?" He held his hands up, as though defenseless. "Hit me with your best shot. If I've been able to stay upright after everything I've seen today I'm pretty sure whatever it is isn't going to take me down."

She proceeded delicately. "Well, you see you were right and I was wrong."

That stopped him. "Normally I would be extremely pleased to hear that, except with you I have no idea what it means."

She took a deep breath and began what she hoped wouldn't end with a rejection. "It means that you were right when you said you were my one."

He stared at her, studying her face, and she didn't know if she could take the silence when it felt like her future was in the balance.

"Go on. I take it there's more."

"There's more," she admitted. The *more* is what scared her.

He nodded. "I'm learning there's always more with you."

"Okay," she said, feeling her heart beating against her rib cage. She rolled her fingers into fists, digging her nails into her palms. "I also learned that you were right when you said I . . ."

"You what?"

She silently prayed for the right words. "Remember when you brought me the Popsicles? Remember I said you were my hero?"

He only nodded, not giving away any emotion.

"Well, remember when you bought that pregnancy kit?"

He didn't react and she had to swallow down saliva to continue speaking.

"You were right, Julian. I'm going to have a baby."

Nothing.

"Julian?"

Nothing. He looked like he had turned to stone!

"Julian, say something!"

"Ach . . ." His mouth was open, yet nothing intelligible was coming out.

And then Maggie understood that old saying about all the stuffing going out of a person in shock, as Julian fell into a sitting position on the sofa with his arms hanging down by his legs. She slowly came to sit next to him and gently patted his shoulder. "I know it's a shock. Imagine my surprise when I took the test and then—"

"When?" he asked in a hoarse voice. He began shaking his head. "No. No. Not that time when you . . . you turned into a lion?" Poor man sounded as though he just couldn't take any more revelations.

Again, she cringed as she nodded. "I'm afraid so."

"Then this means . . . how does a person know these things . . . does it mean the baby is going to be a . . . shape shifter?"

"I would say there's a pretty good chance of it," she admitted, wishing she could spare him.

He fell back against the sofa cushions. Staring up at the ceiling he muttered, "My child is going to be a *shape shifter!*"

She tried to suppress a nervous laugh and compose her face into a serious expression. "See, I've had time to get used to the idea of it all. After everything that's happened today I understand your shock."

He looked at her and his face suddenly alighted with animation, and not exactly the friendly kind. "You did it again today! You shape shifted into a damn jaguar and went after that shooter! What the hell were you thinking? You could have endangered yourself and the baby!"

Okay, he was definitely not immobilized by shock any longer as he sat up straighter and glared at her.

"I'm fine. *We're* just fine." she answered in her defense. Then she realized the risk she had taken and her shoulders slumped. "I didn't think. I saw Gabriel lying there and the blood spreading over his sweater and, see, I just found out today that he's my father and I kinda lost it, I guess. I was furious. Actually, the man was so stunned to see a jaguar in the woods of Maryland that it was fairly easy to take him down."

"*Take him down?*"

"Well, yes. I had him by the throat when Marcus took over."

"What the hell *are* you? You look like a normal woman.

You talk like a normal woman, but you're really some shape-shifting super-agent! You are *not* normal!"

"But I love you," she whispered. "And I so wanted normal, Julian. I tried. I really did."

He grabbed her shoulder and turned her sideways to face him. "You are never, *ever*, to do that again! Do you understand me?"

She looked into his eyes and her heart melted. "I promise," she began meekly, "not to shape shift while I am pregnant. I can't promise forever, though. What if something happened and I had to save the baby after she crawled out the window onto the roof? All kinds of emergencies could pop up."

"The baby is not going to crawl out of a window," he stated patiently. "I'll have a grate put up to keep her in." He paused for a moment and then he transformed . . . the tension left his expression and he slowly began to smile. "A baby," he whispered, as though the image was finally taking shape in his mind. "How do you know it's a girl? I mean is it some kind of supernatural instinct or something?"

She smiled back as her own muscles finally began to relax. "I just feel it. Ordinary female instinct."

He ran his hands through his hair, as though trying to activate neuron connections to make sense of it all. "Oh, honey, there is nothing ordinary about you."

She shrugged, trying to keep from crying with relief. "I guess you're right. After all my struggling, I've come full circle. I'm not normal and I never will be. Our baby may not be normal either. I have to accept it and just be what I am." She searched his eyes as he turned his head. "Can you accept it?"

"Do I have a choice?"

"Of course. We always have a choice. Free will."

She saw the surrender in his eyes.

"Well, you're certainly not boring, Maggie O'Shea. I will say that for you."

"Am I still your one, Julian?"

She watched the moisture enter his eyes and his mouth

tightened in an attempt to ward off the display of emotion. "Yes, Maggie, you are still my one. And I've missed you," he muttered, pulling her into his arms and burying his face in her hair. "You'll never know how much."

She clung to him, inhaling his scent, closing her eyes as her heart filled with gratitude. He loved her. He wanted her. He wanted the baby.

He leaned back against the sofa cushion, taking her with him and enclosing her within the circle of his arms. She felt him kissing the top of her head.

"So it's settled. You retire from . . . this foundation, and we raise our child in peace."

She snuggled in closer to his chest, wrapping her arm around his waist. "Well, I have already retired from taking assignments . . ."

"And? I feel there's an *and* or a *but* coming."

"Not really, it's just that I am committed to what the foundation stands for. My father is . . . well, he's very involved and . . . you might as well know everything now."

"I'm afraid to ask what."

"I inherited my ability from him."

He didn't say anything for a few moments.

"Don't tell me, Maggie."

"No, really, Julian, Gabriel is also a—"

"I don't want to hear any more," he interrupted in a weak voice. "Have pity on an ordinary human being."

"Okay." She tightened her arm around him in protection as she looked up to his face. "The brain can only assimilate so much in one day."

He laughed. "No kidding! In the span of a few hours everything I've believed has been turned upside down. Life is never going to be the same."

"Is that so bad?" she asked, searching his face for signs of regret.

He looked deeply into her eyes and grinned. "You came into my life like an angel disguised as a whirling dervish, sweeping away all my illusions. You took me into places I never believed existed. Life with you, Maggie, is not going to be boring."

"And that's a good thing, right?"

Holding her face between his hands, he nodded.

"And you're okay with everything now? You're not—"

"Shh, no more talking," he interrupted, right before his lips came down on hers taking away her words, her thoughts, and any idea of regrets.

"I just can't believe I'm here for your wedding!"

Maggie turned from the mirror and grinned at D., who was peeking out of the window to once again take in the gorgeous Bermuda scenery. "I know. It's hard for me to believe too. My wedding . . ." She shook her head in wonder. "Everything's happening so fast."

D. looked back at her. "I also can't believe I'm privy to one of the biggest stories around and I can't do an exclusive."

"You promised," Maggie warned. "No press and that includes you. It was a circus in the hospital."

"Well, you're news, sweetie. When I saw Senator Burke in that wheelchair giving a press conference and you standing beside him, I almost fell off my chair."

Maggie smoothed the cream silk of her simple slip dress over the slight bump at her abdomen and closed her eyes, recollecting how Gabriel had called a news conference to discuss the attempt on his life and to publicly acknowledge her as his daughter. The fireworks of camera flashes in her face, the madness of questions being shouted had unnerved her. "I've had enough of the press for a while, D. You're here as my guest at a private wedding."

"I know, I know," D. moaned. "But you'd better get used to it if Julian is going to throw his hat into the political ring."

Sighing, Maggie looked back into the mirror. The candidate's wife? How would she ever pull it off? So much had happened so quickly and now in less than a half hour she would become the wife of Julian McDonald.

"Scared?"

Maggie shook her head.

"Nervous?"

"Not about marrying Julian," she answered, looking down at the ring on her finger. A round two-carat diamond stood up from the eternity band of tiny diamonds that circled her finger. It was the most beautiful ring she'd ever seen and it had been totally unexpected when Julian had slipped it on her finger the morning of the news conference. He'd said he wanted her to face the world as his future wife. It was only later when she'd questioned him that she had found out the ring had been delivered overnight from New York by special messenger.

"So what's wrong then?"

Maggie smiled sadly. "I wish my mother was here. I wish she knew she didn't have to be so frightened for so many years of her life. It all turned out well."

D. stroked her arm in sympathy. "Maybe she knows?"

"I hope she does."

There was a slight knock on the door. Maggie glanced at D. and said, "Julian can't see me. I know we're in the master bedroom, but if he's forgotten anything tell him you'll get it."

D. held up her hand as she walked toward the door. "Calm down, will you? I didn't know you were so superstitious. Leave the men to me. I'll handle all prospective grooms and . . ."

Maggie watched as she opened the door a few inches and looked out.

"My, my, Mr. Bocelli. You have a visitor, my dear," she called out over her shoulder.

D. opened the door to allow Marcus entrance into the bedroom.

"Would you mind, Deborah, giving me a few minutes with the bride?"

D. looked from Marcus to Maggie and then back to Marcus. "Not at all, Mr. Bocelli." She walked up to the bed and picked up her matching clutch bag. Kissing Maggie's cheek, she whispered, "I'll see you out there. And put in a good word for me here, will you?"

Maggie grinned. "Thanks, D."

Marcus held out his hand to D. "Please, Deborah, call me Marcus. And, since neither of us is with a companion today, I would be honored if you'd join me."

D. nearly swooned. "Certainly."

It was the first time Maggie had ever seen the woman at a loss for words. When she closed the bedroom door behind her, Maggie said, "You are shameless, Marcus. Positively shameless."

Looking quite handsome in his impeccably styled suit, he grinned as he came up to her. "It's part of my charm, *cara mia*. I have no shame."

She laughed. "That's true." Her expression became more serious. "Don't hurt her. Let her know right off there's no chance for anything permanent."

"Who knows, Magdalene, I may take a page from your book and think of settling down."

There was a prolonged moment of silence when it seemed the room was filled with their shared past.

"You're really going to do this. Marry him."

"Yes. I am."

"And you believe it can work?"

"I have to believe that, Marcus."

"You think you will find a normal life with a normal man?"

She chuckled. "No. Not normal. But we will make a life together and work to keep the love strong. We have no expectations."

"None?"

"Not really. Not of each other. I don't expect Julian to be anything except himself. He can't make me happy or fulfill me or any of those things I thought marriage was about. All he has to do is be himself. That's good enough for me."

Marcus looked deeply into her eyes. "And what about him? Surely he must expect certain things of you?"

"He's accepted me. All of me, Marcus. Even the shape shifting."

"So it seems love has finally conquered you, *cara mia*. Something I could never do."

She touched his arm as tears came into her eyes. "You were my teacher, my friend and, once, my lover. You know, of all the things you taught me, the most important was that love, real love, isn't about possession." Her fingers moved to his finely sculpted cheekbone. "I'm not your student any longer, Marcus. I must move on and claim my own life, but know this . . . I'll always love you. That's unconditional. You're part of my soul family."

He turned his head and kissed her fingers. Holding her hand, he blinked away the moisture at his eyes and said, "The student has become the teacher. Be happy, Magdalene. You deserve it."

She nodded as she tried not to cry and ruin her makeup.

When he left she sat down on the edge of the bed and took a deep, steadying breath. Everything was done. It was time. Julian had flown in family and friends and they were all waiting for her out at the thatched hut that had been decorated with white gardenias and jasmine.

"Are you ready?"

She looked up and smiled. "Come in, Elizabeth."

The older woman was dressed in a light blue suit and she wore an extraordinary hat that had flowers and feathers at the crown. She handed Maggie a bouquet of white tulips with a cream satin ribbon wrapped around the stems. "It's time now, child. The senator is waiting for you."

Nodding, Maggie stood up and looked at herself in the mirror. Her own hat, dyed to match her dress, was wide and of the finest straw with fresh jasmine sewn in this morning all around the crown.

Elizabeth came up behind her and squeezed her shoulders. "You are a beautiful bride. Surely the Universe was smiling down on Mr. McDonald when he met you."

She touched Elizabeth's sturdy hand on her shoulder. "I think it was the other way around. I'm the blessed one."

"So you both are blessed. Now let us begin this ceremony before all the food spoils," the woman declared as she steered Maggie out of the room. "Though why you wouldn't let me prepare the wedding feast I do not know."

"You are a guest, Elizabeth. Family. You will be waited upon today."

"And speaking of family . . . here is your father. Now, doesn't he look fit and quite handsome?"

Maggie looked down the hallway and saw Gabriel waiting for her with a wide smile upon his face. She couldn't help smiling back. He did look handsome, dressed in a gray suit and wearing a matching silk sling for his left arm.

"You are stunning, Maggie!" He leaned in below her hat and kissed her cheek.

"Oh, Maggie, you're so pretty," Amy, one of Julian's nieces, squealed. Her younger ten-year-old sister, Lori, agreed.

"Thanks, girls. And you both look beautiful." They were dressed in tea-length white cotton dresses with white sandals and white satin ribbons holding back their blonde curls. "Are you ready?"

Elizabeth came forward. "Come now. Get in line. And you, my little man, are you prepared for your very important duty?"

Seven-year-old Conor nodded to the older woman while holding out for inspection the small pillow with the wedding rings attached.

"You're doing such a great job, Conor," Maggie whispered down to the boy.

"That's my grandson," Gabriel declared. "The Burke men know how to stand up and be of service when required, right, boy?"

Conor turned around and winked back at his grandfather.

Maggie looked at Elizabeth and nodded, who in turn looked out of the wide-open doorway and nodded to the musicians. Pachelbel's "Canon in D" began with its hauntingly beautiful strains and Amy and Lori walked outside and started their march down an improvised aisle of fragile hibiscus petals.

"This is one of the proudest moments of my life. Thank you, Maggie."

She turned her head to her father and smiled. "Thank you, Dad. I have a family now."

And she did, she thought, as she and Gabriel walked outside to the courtyard, following Conor, past the pool, down the steps. They were gathered there. Her new family of relatives and friends. Beautiful, funny Ginny, her sister-in-law. Hannah and her husband, Abe. Bill and Allie Myers. Alastair and Elizabeth. Mark, Kelly, everyone from Soul Provisions, and Alan, who now would be managing the store for her. She smiled into each face, grateful for their presence. Deborah was standing next to Marcus and wiping her eyes with a handkerchief.

And then she looked beyond them, to the improvised chapel of flowers.

There he was.

Her beloved.

Her eyes filled with tears of joy. Standing with his hands clasped together in front of him, he was dressed in a navy blazer and white slacks like a typical Bermudan. A small white tulip was attached to his lapel. And he was beaming at her as she closed the distance between them. They each had picked a member of the other's family to stand as witnesses. Sean was his best man and Emma, Cat's sister, was her matron of honor.

She smiled at each of them and then looked at Julian.

"Who presents this woman in marriage?" the minister asked in his lyrical island accent.

"I do. Her father. I proudly present my daughter, Magdalene."

Gabriel placed her hand into Julian's outstretched one and Maggie stood next to the man she loved.

"You look exquisite," Julian whispered, his eyes nearly devouring her since they hadn't seen much of each other in the last week of wedding preparations.

Maggie stared into his eyes and whispered back, "So do you, my love. Are you ready for this?"

"I am so ready for you, woman, that I might just throw you over my shoulder and take you—"

The minister cleared his throat.

Two hours later, Julian held Maggie's hand and raised his voice to the wedding party. "Maggie and I want to thank all of you for being here and sharing in this wonderful day. I recently read an old Chinese saying that when two souls who are meant for each other are born they are connected with an invisible thread, and over time that thread shortens until they are joined together in marriage." He raised their hands and kissed the back of Maggie's. "That happened today. So I am asking that you remain as long as you wish and continue celebrating, but I am taking my wife away from the festivities."

Moans were heard amid the laughter from the men.

He turned to Maggie and waved his hand toward the sea. "Madam, your boat awaits."

"My boat?" she asked, turning around and seeing two men waiting at the shoreline next to a speed boat. In the distance was the Stardancer, anchored in deep water. Julian must have arranged for the captain to bring the boat during the party. "The speed boat is mine?" she asked.

"No, hon. That's the tender that will take you to your boat."

Astonished, she simply nodded.

"She can't leave yet!" Lori yelled, waving her hand. "She didn't throw her bouquet."

"Throw your bouquet, dear," Julian said, smiling politely at his young niece as he took the flowers from her hand.

Maggie giggled as she took the tulips from him. "Are you just a little impatient?"

"Ah . . . yeah!" he answered with a laugh. "Will you just throw it?"

She turned around. She looked back to the crowd once and then turned around again. Closing her eyes, she made a wish and then lifted her arm. Quickly turning, she saw D. scoop up the bouquet before any other female could lay claim.

Maggie applauded with everyone else while Julian muttered, "Why didn't you just hand it to her?"

Before she could answer, he grabbed her wrist and led her toward the beach. Everyone was cheering and yelling good luck and Bon Voyage. The men at the tender were in white shirts and navy shorts and helped her into the small boat. Julian got in next to her and wrapped her in his arms as the wedding party came down to the beach and waved them off.

It only took a few minutes and Maggie marveled at the glorious sunset, a perfect backdrop for the boat which, as they got closer, was much bigger than she'd thought. "I didn't know it was so big," she said, staring at the clean lines of the white hull. "Everything's happened so quickly and we've been so busy, this is the first time I've seen it."

Julian leaned down and whispered in her ear, "Then look closely, my love. She has a new owner and a new name."

As the tender came up to the swimming platform, Maggie's mouth opened in shock.

Neatly printed in a fine script was the name . . .

LADY MAGDALENE

"Oh, Julian . . ."

"Now don't get all emotional on me yet. I still have one more wedding present. It's onboard."

She took off her heels and was helped by staff onto the swimming platform.

"Welcome aboard, madam," each one said.

She thanked them and climbed the stairs to the first deck. Julian didn't give her a chance to admire the interior of the boat, which was decorated with beautiful fabrics and fine teak furniture.

"You can inspect every detail tomorrow," he promised, leading her to the forward master bedroom cabin. "I want you to myself."

She grinned, trying to take in everything, but wanting him as much as he desired her she gladly followed.

He opened the door and the room was lit with so many white candles in glass lanterns that Maggie gasped, taking in the king-size bed strewn with rose petals. "Oh, Julian, it's so beautiful."

He closed the door behind her and pulled her into his arms.

"Do you have *any* idea how much I want you?" he murmured, staring into her eyes with such love that her heart filled with renewed emotion.

Smiling through her tears, she nodded. "I think so."

"Then you will know how much effort it is for me to do this . . ." And he left her to walk over to the coffee table in front of the sofa. He picked up a box and handed it to her. "Open it, Maggie. This is your real present."

She tore off the pretty white bow and wrapping paper and opened the box. Inside was a book. She looked up at Julian, who was staring at her every move.

"Go ahead. Look at it."

She picked up the hardcover and read the title.

Resurfacing by James Hennessy.

James Hennessy?

"Look at the back."

She turned it over and felt a frizzle of electricity rush through her body. "Oh dear God . . ."

He pulled her to him and turned her while wrapping his arms around her waist. "He never died, Maggie. I talked to Gabriel and Marcus. They never told you he died. You just assumed he did. And I found him. He never became a poet. He's a doctor of clinical psychology, specializing in depression."

"He's alive," she whispered in shock as she leaned her back against Julian's chest. She stared at the picture of James Hennessy, older, calmer, and so much wiser than the troubled boy whom she thought she had driven to suicide. "Why didn't they tell me?" she demanded, feeling anger start to build.

"Calm down. They didn't know you carried that guilt. Marcus told me the two of you were in a cabin, isolated. You never heard the news. Marcus just assumed you found out later."

"Well, I didn't," she answered, determined not to allow

this to ruin her honeymoon. What did she care now? She wouldn't take back the last fourteen years or her service to the foundation. Without them, she might never have met her husband.

"Now you're free," he murmured above her ear and her muscles once more relaxed. His hands were spread over her belly, gently stroking where their child was growing. "This is where we start, Maggie O'Shea McDonald. Right here. Both of us, free of the past. This, right now, is our new beginning."

And it was.

EPILOGUE

Maggie opened the front door to their New York brown-stone and was greeted by Max. Scratching his head, she asked, "So how are they doing? Anything I should know about?" She dropped her briefcase and purse onto the hall table and hung her coat on the brass tree by the door. "Where are they? Still in front of the Christmas tree?"

She was glad to be home, after traveling to Philadelphia to make her monthly visit to Soul Provisions. After a year and a half away from the daily grind of managing the store, Maggie felt good about her decision. The store had record seasonal sales and she'd just given the staff a hefty Christmas bonus. At least that was one area of her life where things were running smoothly.

"Maggie! Is that you?"

"Coming," she called out in answer to Julian's high-pitched question. She looked in the hall mirror and fluffed out her hair just before the door to the living room opened and her husband's expression warned her to expect trouble.

"Could you please inform your father and Elizabeth that it is socially permissible to use a door? I feel like Doctor Doolittle in here!"

"What's wrong?" she asked with a laugh, coming to the doorway and looking into the living room.

There in front of the Christmas tree sat eight-month-old Ana, giggling at the squirrel and red cardinal who were playing with her.

"They came in through the fireplace," Julian said,

wrapping his arm around her shoulders as Max began barking. "How can I run a campaign when I have *this* to contend with?"

"Max!" Maggie pulled on the dog's collar. "Calm down. It's family."

"Family?" Julian asked with a laugh. "It's like *National Lampoon* in here!"

Since he'd announced his candidacy in November, Julian had been balancing politics and family. She saw his point.

Maggie shook her head. "I knew when Dad said he'd wanted to retire, he intended to spend more time with us. I just didn't think he meant as a rodent."

"This isn't funny, Maggie. Ever since I announced, the press is digging for any dirt they can come up with. Imagine what they'd make of this."

"Oh, c'mon, Julian. Do you really think they'd believe it? Besides, it's Christmas. People make exceptions during the holiday. Can't you make one now?"

"What about Ana? It's like you're all encouraging her."

Maggie stretched and kissed her husband's cheek. "Sweetie, you can't fight it. Ana will be who she is. And if that includes shape shifting, then we'll have to deal with it."

"Now look at that!" Julian exclaimed as the squirrel ran into the Christmas tree and was peeking out of the branches at Ana, who was delighted with this new game.

"Okay, that's it," Maggie announced, letting go of Max and coming into the room. "Dad, get out of my tree. You're going to topple the whole thing. And you, Elizabeth, I can't believe you're going along with this," she said to the small red bird who flew to the top of the tree when Max reentered the room. "I thought you had more sense."

The squirrel came out of the tree and transformed into Senator Gabriel Burke and the red cardinal metamorphosed in a tall, stately Bermudan woman.

Ana was giggling and clapping her hands with excitement. Maggie picked up her daughter and stared at the two adults, who looked dejected that their playtime was over. "I should send you all to your rooms," Maggie announced.

"For goodness sake, Maggie, it's Christmas. We were only having fun with the child," her father declared, holding out his arms to Ana, who immediately leaned forward to go into them.

Releasing Ana to her grandfather, Maggie said, "Don't get her overexcited."

Elizabeth patted Maggie's shoulder as she passed her. "Don't you get overexcited, child. I'm going to find Alastair and then prepare for dinner. Calm your husband down with some Christmas cheer." Elizabeth gave her employer a pointed look as she passed him. "Come along, Senator," she called out from the hallway, "I'll show you and little Ana how to make rum swizzles. Lord knows it's cold enough in this country."

As Gabriel, Ana, and Elizabeth left the room, Julian called after them, "And none of that . . . that shifting stuff anymore!" He turned around to his wife. "Whose idea was it to have all of them for two weeks?"

"Yours," she answered, coming into his arms. "You wanted a big family Christmas. Well, hon, this is it."

He tightened his arms around her and kissed the top of her head. "How did it go in Philly?"

"Fine," she murmured, snuggling closer. "How did it go in Albany?"

"Okay, but I think Delacorte's got something up his sleeve. He was very chummy with the reps from the Teamsters. I could feel it, you know, some kind of under-the-table compromise. I just wish I knew what it was, so I wouldn't be surprised."

She hesitated. "I could find out," she offered, picturing in her mind getting close to her husband's opponent in the coming senatorial primary race.

"Oh, no you don't," Julian commanded. "If I win this thing, I win it honestly. No spying. No shape shifting. You promised."

She'd only really promised while she was pregnant with Ana and that technically ended eight months ago. Maggie grinned as she lifted her head and offered her lips for a kiss.

"Right?" he demanded. "You did promise."

"Mmm . . . kiss me, Mac. I would never do anything to jeopardize your campaign," she murmured, already picturing how easily she could find out the answer and put his mind at rest. A fly? No, it was winter. A spider then, coming in from the cold, huddling near a baseboard, unseen, but listening . . . If there was anything shady going down, she would find out and protect the man she loved.

"Promise?"

Hugging him, Maggie knew it was impossible for Julian to see her fingers crossed behind his back.

An Excerpt from . . .

HUNTER'S MOON

by C. T. ADAMS
and CATHY CLAMP

I'm an assassin.

A killer-for-hire. If you have the money, I'll do the job. I like puppies, kids and Christmas, but I don't give a shit about your story—or your problems. I'm the person you call when you want the job done right the first time with no sullying of your name. Yes, I am that good; I apprenticed in the Family.

Oh, there's one other thing I should mention. I'm also a werewolf.

Yeah, I know. Big joke. Ha. Ha. I never believed in "creatures of the night" like vampires, werewolves, or mummies. They're the stuff of schlock movies and Stephen King novels. I'm not.

I don't wear an eyepatch or have a swarthy mustache. I even have all of my teeth. I look absolutely ordinary, like I could be a lawyer, a writer, or a mechanic.

I don't look like someone that would as soon shoot you as look at you.

That's the idea.

. . . Available now from Tor Romance

An Excerpt from . . .

The Dark Lord
by Patricia Simpson

Rae fished the box from her purse and carefully opened it, setting the bottom of the box and its contents on the counter while she held the lid in her hand. The shopkeeper leaned forward, squinting at the lines of tiny writing on the parchment. Rae stared at him anxiously as he studied the parchment, and waited without taking a breath for him to speak.

"I have never seen anything like this," he remarked.

Rae leaned forward. "Can you read it?"

"I am trying! This is a strange form of Aramaic." The shopkeeper frowned, concentrating. "Water," he murmured, following the line with his finger, but not touching the parchment. "Soul. Dark. Lord. Otherworld? I am not certain of this word."

He looked up.

"Where did you find this?"

"Near the temple of Nut, at the oasis there."

He studied the writing again. "Typhon, the Devil, The Dark Lord," he whispered, and then he pushed the box toward Rae. "No!" he exclaimed. "I will read no more of this! Leave, please, at once!"

"But what does it say?" Rae asked, reaching for the bottom of the box. "What is it?"

"These are the Forbidden Tarot. Throw them into the Nile, Miss. Do not open them. Do not look at them. Throw them into the river! They are cursed!"

. . . Available now from Tor Romance